Available
from Mill

SHEIKH PROTECTOR

Julia Gardner seemed dead set against accepting his protection – for herself or her unborn child.

"Let me help," she said, interrupting his thoughts and kneeling beside him.

And because he wanted to feel her touch on his skin again, despite his better judgement, he allowed her.

Burning pain pulsed through his arms, but he said nothing as she finally dabbed away the last of the blood.

But when her work was done and she pulled away, he couldn't let her. He reached for her and pulled her against him.

Her golden-brown eyes went wide with alarm. He couldn't do this. *Forgive me, brother.* He brushed his lips over hers.

SCIONS: REVELATION

"What do you feel?" Caine demanded.

Placing his hands on the bed on either side of her, he shifted his weight very close, as if he were going to kiss her neck.

His magnetism pulled at her, but more than that she felt his heat; glorious, primal heat. "I feel how hot your skin is, even though you're not touching me."

"That's lust and desire. I want you."

His declaration made her feel light-headed.

"What does all this tell you about me? About us?" he demanded, suddenly serious.

Emma blinked. She *had* just heard him speak in her mind. She searched his gaze, sensing that whatever words she spoke next would be very important. "That you're different."

His expression hardened. *"We're* different. You and I. Tell me, damn it!"

The ferocity in his expression scared her because she thought he was going to push her away. "You're unique, and we have a connection that's undeniably mind-blowing, but...I don't know what you want from me!"

All the characters in this book have no existence outside the imagination of the author, and have no relation whatsoever to anyone bearing the same name or names. They are not even distantly inspired by any individual known or unknown to the author, and all the incidents are pure invention.

All Rights Reserved including the right of reproduction in whole or in part in any form. This edition is published by arrangement with Harlequin Enterprises II B.V./S.à.r.l. The text of this publication or any part thereof may not be reproduced or transmitted in any form or by any means, electronic or mechanical, including photocopying, recording, storage in an information retrieval system, or otherwise, without the written permission of the publisher.

This book is sold subject to the condition that it shall not, by way of trade or otherwise, be lent, resold, hired out or otherwise circulated without the prior consent of the publisher in any form of binding or cover other than that in which it is published and without a similar condition including this condition being imposed on the subsequent purchaser.

® and ™ are trademarks owned and used by the trademark owner and/or its licensee. Trademarks marked with ® are registered with the United Kingdom Patent Office and/or the Office for Harmonisation in the Internal Market and in other countries.

First published in Great Britain 2009
Harlequin Mills & Boon Limited,
Eton House, 18-24 Paradise Road, Richmond, Surrey TW9 1SR

Sheikh Protector © Dana Marton 2008
Scions: Revelation © Patrice Michelle 2008

ISBN: 978 0 263 87313 9

46-0809

Harlequin Mills & Boon policy is to use papers that are natural, renewable and recyclable products and made from wood grown in sustainable forests. The logging and manufacturing processes conform to the legal environmental regulations of the country of origin.

Printed and bound in Spain
by Litografía Rosés S.A., Barcelona

SHEIKH PROTECTOR
BY
DANA MARTON

SCIONS:
REVELATION
BY
PATRICE MICHELLE

SHEIKH PROTECTOR

BY
DANA MARTON

Dana Marton is the author of over a dozen fast-paced, action-adventure romantic suspense novels and a winner of the Daphne du Maurier Award of Excellence. She loves writing books of international intrigue, filled with dangerous plots that try her tough-as-nails heroes and the special women they fall in love with. Her books have been published in seven languages in eleven countries around the world. When not writing or reading, she loves to browse antique shops and enjoys working in her sizable flower garden where she searches for "bad" bugs with the skills of a superspy and vanquishes them with the agility of a commando soldier. Every day in her garden is a thriller. To find more information on her books, please visit www.danamarton.com. She would love to hear from her readers and can be reached via e-mail at DanaMarton@DanaMarton.com.

With many thanks to Denise Zaza, Allison Lyons, Maggie Scillia and Cindy Whitesel.

Chapter One

"Car's rigged," Karim said to the empty passenger seat next to him. His gaze darted around as he considered his options for escape, trying to determine the location of the bomb.

He wished he could see under his seat. He wished he hadn't just tossed his briefcase, which held his cell phone, to the back, now out of reach. But most of all, he wished he hadn't gotten into the damned car.

Unfortunately, he had no magic lamp and no genie to grant his three wishes.

He sat completely still, sweat beading on his forehead. The first step was to figure out the trigger. Would the charge blow if he turned the key in the ignition, or if he got out and lifted his weight off the driver's seat? Maybe the trigger was in the door. He hadn't closed it behind him yet. Or could be he had no control at all. Maybe whoever wanted him dead was watching from one of the hundred windows that overlooked the executive parking lot. Watching with the remote in hand.

"I was getting too close to the truth." He glanced up at those windows, but couldn't see much from his position and he didn't dare shift his weight.

Anger flared. If he had to die, so be it—*Insha'Allah*. But by all that was holy, he wanted to bring his twin brother's murderer to justice first.

"I'm sorry, Aziz."

If he couldn't find the killer, nobody would. His other brother, Tariq, thought that Aziz's presence at the well at the time of the explosion had been a coincidence. Tariq was predisposed to see the world as a better place than it really was—he hadn't seen as much of the dark side as Karim—and was currently too busy being crazy in love with his new wife.

Which one of them was crazier remained to be seen. Karim's thoughts turned grim. He wasn't exactly a pillar of sanity, either. He regularly talked to his dead twin brother. For the last month, from time to time, he felt Aziz's presence so strongly, he not only talked to him, but also half expected an answer.

Aziz was gone. Killed. In some regard, losing his twin was like losing half his sight two decades ago, but much, much worse. With Aziz, he had lost half of his soul. And he knew he wasn't going to find that, even if he found the killer or killers—he wasn't going to bring Aziz back. Still, he could not let the bastards go free, not even if tracking them down cost him his own life.

A bomb.

"Should have seen it coming." Except that his mind

had been on the restitutions he was making to the families of the men who'd died at the well along with his brother.

If he hadn't been so preoccupied when he'd walked out of MMPOIL's headquarters in Tihrin—Beharrain's quickly growing capital—he would have noted that the security guard wasn't at his post. He hadn't been aware of danger until he'd gotten into the car and spotted the millimeter-size chunk of blue plastic wire coating on the mat.

Another person might not have realized the significance. But people had been trying to kill him from the moment he'd been born, nearly succeeding on a number of occasions. He'd developed a keen sense for detecting death's approaching footsteps.

He glanced out at the street, at the cars passing no more than a hundred feet from him. Nobody was turning to enter the company gate where the other security guard sat in his booth, his back to Karim.

He had to do something now, while he was alone in the parking lot. He didn't want to take anyone out with him.

"Here we go." His mind sharply focused, he reached down to feel around the seat, aware that he could accidentally move a wire and set off the charge if it was there.

He felt nothing out of place as far as he could reach, but he couldn't stretch all the way. *Next item.* He leaned forward carefully, and spent precious seconds inspecting the bottom of the dashboard.

"Mr. Abdullah?" The voice was richly melodic and completely feminine, utterly out of place in the charged tension of the moment. "Excuse me, Mr. Abdullah—"

He drew his attention from what he was doing to watch, with dismay, the foreign beauty who strode toward him, full of purpose.

Since she'd spoken English, he responded in the same language. "Go back inside."

"They told me I could find you here." She flashed a nervous smile and proceeded without pause, although the blood did drain from her face as she came closer and got a better look at him. "Look, I've come a long way. You wouldn't believe the plane ride. Forget the plane. You wouldn't believe the food," she babbled on. "I know you must be busy, but—"

"Get out of here." He didn't bother with the half turn to hide his scar, but looked her full in the face. That ought to scare her off.

"Listen, I—" Her voice wavered.

"You listen." He wiped the sweat from his forehead. The air was well over a hundred degrees outside, and even warmer in the car. He had run up to his office for only a few minutes to grab some papers before he headed off to the camel races, so he hadn't bothered to pull in to the climate-controlled underground parking garage. He let loose the frustration and anger that churned inside him. "Get the hell out of here. Now."

The woman stopped, but only momentarily. Her wide brown eyes flashed with determination, and her deep auburn hair swirled around her face in the dry breeze that'd been blowing from the desert all day. Hair that flowed in soft waves well below her elbows. Her soft linen skirt fluttered around her ankles, the light color matching her modest top—clothes that accentuated her tall, slim figure. She looked as beautiful as an angel and as determined as Satan's handmaiden.

Few men would have remained standing there when he had that glare on his face and that edge in his voice. But incomprehensibly, instead of running the other way, her delicate chin came up. She was maybe four feet from him and not budging.

"All I want—"

Oh, hell. "There's a bomb—" Karim saw movement in one of the windows behind her, and acted on instinct.

He vaulted out of the car and flew across the space between them, crashing her to the hard pavement, doing his best to break her fall. He didn't stop, but rolled and rolled.

She screamed the whole time and beat on his shoulders, resisted with all the power in her slim frame, her long hair entangling them. Then the car finally blew, shaking the parking lot.

Heat.

Smoke.

Fear.

She screamed even louder, but it barely registered now over the ringing in his ears.

Head down. He kept her covered as best he could, protected her from the burning debris that flew across the air like projectile missiles. As strong and determined as she had looked a moment ago, she seemed scared and fragile as she clung to him now.

"Don't move," he said near her ear, unable to hear his

own voice, half-deaf from the explosion. "It's okay." He
made an attempt to reassure her anyway. They would
assess their injuries and face reality in a moment. For
now, he was still trying to catch his breath.

The air swirled blazing hot around them. But even
the acrid smell of smoke couldn't completely drown out
the scent of the woman in his arms: jasmine and vanilla.

In his peripheral vision, he registered security personnel running from the building.

"Ambulance. Now! Cover his position."

"Secure the grounds! Secure the grounds!"

"Are you all right, sir? Sheik?"

Karim let the woman go and nodded, the ringing in
his ears diminishing with each passing second. She
looked wide-eyed with shock, staring at the car a few
short yards from them. Her fair skin was now positively
white, to the point of being translucent, save a few
smudges of dirt.

"What happened?" She pressed a hand to her abdomen, breathing in quick gasps.

He'd probably knocked the air out of her.

After checking her over for visible injuries and not
finding any, he followed her gaze, clenching his teeth
at the sight of the twisted metal behind him. That had
been close. Too close. Aziz's death still filled his mind,
dulling his attention to other things. He had to separate
himself from the grief, had to block the memories of the
burning well—a fire a thousand times larger than what
burned in the parking lot now. He couldn't get distracted
and be taken out. He had to find who killed Aziz.

The company's private ambulance was racing through the parking lot toward them. For him.

"I'm fine. You take her." Whatever she wanted from him, he had no time to deal with her now.

He'd spoken in Arabic, but she must have understood his body language, because she began to protest.

"No, I'm fine. Really. I don't need to see a doctor." She was rattled and scared, more than a little bewildered, fighting to hide it. Her chin came up, trembling slightly and smudged with dirt from the pavement. "I can't go." She backed away a few steps. "I'm not going."

The woman showed a deep-seated aversion to do as she was told. Even if it was for her own good.

He wasn't in the mood just now to humor her. "Get in." Even his own security stilled at the growl in his voice.

"No," she said, oblivious to danger once again.

His eyes narrowed. Did she just stomp her feet or had she been flexing her knees?

He had been careful with her when he'd taken her down. She didn't look hurt. She was breathing normally now. Her clothes were barely rumpled and only slightly stained. Her hair looked the worst, tangled and with a fair amount of sand in it. The desert winds had been blowing for days, dusting the parking lot and everything else in the city.

His security force closed in a circle around them and awaited his orders. They would remove her forcefully; all he had to do was give the word. He should. He had a million things to do at the moment and no time for the distraction of a stubborn woman.

"Fine. No hospital," he said instead. "Just get in. Whoever did this could be still out here."

She paled even more, if that was possible, and stepped up into the back of the ambulance. He went after her, on second thought, not because he was scared for his life, but because if whoever was out there decided to shoot at him, the bastard might hit one of his men instead. Better to remove himself from sight.

"We can drop you off at your hotel. Please, sit." He gestured to the gurney. He remained standing, holding on to one of the restraints as the vehicle moved out. He nodded toward the lone paramedic's cell phone with a questioning look.

He handed it over immediately. "Of course, sir."

Karim's chief of security came on the line after the first ring.

"How did they get in? I want a report the second you find something," he told the man in Arabic. "I want the whole building in lockdown until everyone inside is verified. And I want a digital copy of the security tapes e-mailed to me immediately."

"Yes, sir."

He handed the phone back and focused on the foreign woman who was watching him with morbid fascination. She looked even more impossibly beautiful than his first impression had been—high cheekbones, delicate features, eyes the golden brown color of a perfectly ripe, sweet fig. Eyes that held wariness and secrets, and a certain amount of plucky determination.

Then it clicked.

Media.

A less disciplined man would have groaned. She probably wanted an interview for some foreign paper. Sheer bad luck that she had caught him at a moment like this. There'd be no way now to keep the attack out of the papers. She'd be impossible to shake off. But he had other things to do, which meant he had to get her—and the distractions she brought—out of his life as fast as possible.

"At which hotel are you staying?"

She drew a deep breath and pulled her spine straight. "I need to talk to you first. I'm looking for Aziz."

His fists clenched. He made a point to relax them. Not a reporter then. Aziz. Of course. He should have known.

Aziz had always been the lucky one between the two of them, the ladies' man, or as some Western tabloids had once called him, the Playboy Sheik. Aziz had been in his element at the high-society events of Cannes and Monaco, and had kept a party house—with Hollywood celebrity neighbors—in Miami on Star Island. He'd lived the high life and pursued a wide range of interests, had dabbled in everything from yacht racing to desert archaeology.

"And who are you?" he asked.

"Julia Gardner." She extended her hand. Some of her color had come back. Her skin was now the palest of pinks. A tangle of bead bracelets encircled her slim wrist.

He didn't move.

She pulled back immediately. "I didn't mean to offend you. Sorry. Force of habit. I have trouble re-membering all these strange rules." She snapped her full mouth shut. That lasted only a second. "Not that I think your country is strange. Just strange to me. *New*. New to me. I—"

"No offense taken."

"You look just like your brother." The words spurted from her before she pressed her full lips together once again.

His mood darkened. Maybe at one point Aziz and he had looked alike—they were identical twins. But nobody had dared compare them for a long time now, not since a childhood accident had taken the sight of Karim's right eye, leaving a hideous scar on his face. "You knew Aziz well?"

She glanced away.

So, Julia Gardner, too, had some trouble looking at his face, despite her earlier bravado. He resisted the impulse to shift into his usual half turn.

"We met when he was in Baltimore a couple of months ago," she was saying. "I haven't been able to reach him and I came here and— Look, I just want to talk to him. The man at the front desk told me I should ask you." She kept her hands clasped together tightly in her lap, but her shoulders were drawn straight and tall.

"Aziz is gone." The muscles in his jaw pulled tight. The pictures that flashed into his mind brought raw pain every time. He'd been closer to his twin brother than to anyone else in the world. The hot rage over the unfairness of Aziz's death hadn't diminished any in the month since his funeral. Nor had Karim's desire to seek revenge.

The corners of her eyes crinkled with worry, which

she tried to mask with a nonchalant smile. "When is he coming back?"

He forced air into his constricting lungs. "We had a well explosion last month."

He could see when she understood finally. Shock and pain flashed through her eyes. She stood, agitated, a hand pressed to her stomach, then opened her full, lush mouth, but no words came out. Color drained from her face all over again. She swayed.

He caught her and helped her fold to the gurney.

"She fainted, sir." The paramedic who sat in the corner, trying his best to remain invisible and give them privacy, moved forward and managed to clip a monitor on her index finger without actually touching her. Her vital signs showed on the small screen behind him.

Fainted. Karim blinked and let her go, stepped away from her. He didn't have time for this. He didn't have time for her. Period.

He would absolutely *not* allow her to sully Aziz's memory with scandal. He was fairly certain about why she was here. She wasn't the first. Others had come looking for Aziz after his international trips. They wanted to keep the party going, have access to Aziz's wealth and a shot at becoming one of oil-rich Beharrain's latest princesses.

She was too late. He watched her. Miss Gardner might not know it yet, but she was leaving on the next plane out of the country.

It seemed perversely insane that he was actually looking forward to going a few rounds with her before her stubborn nature would accept that decision.

He was ready to give her his ultimatum, but she still didn't stir.

His annoyance with her switched to concern. She did look vulnerable, her skin losing color again, all that hair tangled around her. She looked like an angel, injured after falling to earth. "What's wrong with her?"

He preferred that stubborn chin of hers thrust forward, as she faced him down, even if she were here to cause trouble.

He wouldn't let her.

"Could be from the stress or heat exhaustion. She's probably not used to our climate." The paramedic was administering an IV, again with the absolute minimum of touching. Then he drew blood into several vials. "If we went to the hospital, they could do tests as soon as we got there."

Karim rested his gaze on her face. She hadn't wanted to go to the hospital, had been pretty adamant about it. And he'd told her he wouldn't take her there. "Call ahead and have Dr. Jinan meet us at my house. You can take the blood to the hospital and call over when the results are ready."

He was about to take the troublesome angel home. He ignored the voice in his head that said he would probably live to regret his decision.

JULIA WOKE IN a strange bed in a strange and ridiculously opulent room, with a strange woman peering over her. An IV bag was attached to her arm. She panicked for a second, her gaze darting around. Her hand slid to her abdomen under the cover. No pain there. "What happened to me?"

"Hi, I'm Dr. Jinan." The woman smiled. She wore a gold-threaded, deep blue *abaya,* no veil. Her startlingly sharp eyes, which were lined with kohl, fixed on Julia. "You were near an explosion and fainted afterward."

Disjointed memories rushed her, and Julia pulled the silk cover higher on her body. The dark red fabric was as resplendent as the rest of her accommodations. "Where am I?"

"You are a guest of Sheik Karim Abdullah in his Tihrin palace. You're fine. You have a good, strong pulse. Once this IV runs out, we can remove the needle. Feeling better?"

"Thank you. Yes." She sat up to prove it. She didn't like the idea of some strange doctor examining her while she'd been unconscious. She didn't want anyone to know her secret.

"Did you have enough to eat and drink today?" the doctor asked.

Julia noticed the platter of food on a low, round table behind the woman—fresh fruits and other bite-size nourishment that looked exotically unidentifiable, but not the least bit appetizing at the moment. These days she was alternating between ravenous and nauseous, and was currently feeling the latter.

"Yes, thank you." She drew a deep breath to dispel the queasiness around her middle.

"Please do remember plenty of fluids. Our summers are mercilessly hot. I hope this little incident won't ruin your enjoyment of our beautiful country." The doctor smiled, all mothering warmth. "Looks like the IV is done. Let me take care of that." She removed the needle without causing any pain, stuck a cotton ball over the puncture wound. "Bend your elbow and hold this here for a few minutes."

She stood and began placing everything into her old-fashioned, black leather doctor's bag. "I'll be back to check on you tomorrow. Try to get as much rest as possible until then."

"Thank you, but that won't be necessary." With Aziz gone, she had no reason to stay in the country. "I will be leaving here."

Dr. Jinan gave her a smile one would give a petulant child. She was poised and self-assured, obviously a woman secure in her own power, challenging Julia's preconception of the women of Beharrain. Every rule had a few exceptions, she supposed.

Not that she had time to ponder the doctor. Karim Abdullah walked in immediately, as if he'd been waiting outside. He paused at the door and exchanged a few words with Dr. Jinan.

Julia searched their faces, unable to figure out anything. They spoke in Arabic. Did they know? They couldn't. Nobody could tell just by looking at her that she was pregnant, not even a doctor, she was pretty sure of that.

She would have told Aziz her secret. Probably. That was why she had come here. He was the father and he deserved to know, even though he had cut off communications with her. Or so she had thought. Now she knew the truth about why he hadn't returned her calls. The shock was still as fresh as it had been when she'd first heard the news.

Pain filled her chest and squeezed her lungs. Aziz was gone. It seemed impossible. She had never known anyone as filled with life and wide-open to the world, as charming.

He'd charmed a great many people; she had found that out when she ran a search on him on the Internet after he'd returned to his home, and she'd seriously considered taking him up on his invitation to visit him. The celebrity reports were full of his pictures, labeling him the Playboy Sheik. That had been a disappointment, not that he had promised her anything. The information had been enough to make her realize the brief affair for what it was: a few days of fun with an exotic stranger. She'd succeeded in putting Aziz out of her mind until those two pink lines appeared on a white plastic stick.

She took a few days to digest the news. Then called him without success. If she'd checked the Internet again, she would have found out about his death…wouldn't have come here…to his daunting brother.

A few of those news reports she'd read mentioned Aziz's twin. They had called him the Dark Sheik, without explanation, making her wonder. And now she was in the Dark Sheik's house. She looked around. *Scratch that.* The Dark Sheik's palace. God, it sounded like a gothic novel.

She had figured she would come here, would see how Aziz felt about the possibility of a baby. She wasn't going to tell him until she got a better idea of what kind of man he really was. Their time in Baltimore had been way too short. They had had some whirlwind dates and one night of passion, the day before he left. She had thought herself to be half in love with him and had been sure he felt the same. She was pretty certain now that he hadn't, but still, he was the father, and she had wanted to give it another go, if for no other reason than so she could tell her child later in life that she had tried. Her own parents had been all messed up. If she could help it, she wanted something better for her baby.

She was going to come here and see how Aziz was in his own environment. When and if she felt comfortable with it, she would have told him her news. Not a moment before that. Whatever happened, she was going to protect her baby. She was never going to let her or him go.

"Doctor Jinan tells me you are well." Karim came over once the woman left. He was not handsome, not with that scar. But he had a strong, masculine presence that drew her full attention to him. He stopped at a respectable distance from the bed, looking larger and harder than Aziz, infinitely more dangerous. Where Aziz's face had reflected humor, mischief and a sexy sort of cockiness about life, Karim's was bathed in darkness. And she didn't think all of that came from his scar.

He was wearing a fresh, crisp suit, his hair neatly combed. She felt dirty and sweaty and rumpled in comparison, but wouldn't let that stop her.

"Thank you for your hospitality, Mr. Abdullah." Grateful that nobody had undressed her, she pushed off the cover and swung her legs over the side of the bed, glancing around for her shoes. *There.* She slipped into them. "I'm sorry for all the inconvenience I caused."

With Aziz gone, she had no intention of staying here a day longer, no intention of letting Aziz's family know about the baby. Maybe it wasn't the right thing to do, but she was leery of the culture and felt none too trusting toward Aziz's twin brother. He looked as if he could—and would—take the law into his own hands if he felt the need. And he was a sheik, son of a king, as Aziz had been. He probably had a fair amount of power.

When her child was eighteen, she would reveal the truth and leave the decision up to her or him.

"Would it be possible to call a taxi?" She flashed Karim her most polite smile, refusing to be intimidated by him.

Given her social and economic background, she'd spent half her life being intimidated by the wealthy and powerful, by people in charge. But she'd had to get over that in a hurry when she had joined a nonprofit organization and had to interact daily with the elite. And over time, she'd learned that they were just like everybody else, with the same joys and fears and virtues and weaknesses.

Not that she could see Karim having a whole lot of fears or weaknesses. He had faced that car bomb down, cool as anything, and the memory of the incident was still making her heart beat faster.

"May I ask what your plans are?" He had his hands in his pockets as he rested his dark gaze on her. He might as well have been carved of solid rock, he looked that unmovable. But he was quick—she remembered him diving for her from his car. He loomed larger than life.

Exactly the kind of man she needed to avoid at all cost. She swallowed to wet her mouth.

"I'm going back to the hotel and probably flying out tonight if I can change my flight. I'm truly sorry about your brother." She was, and she needed time to deal with the sudden news. But she needed to get away from Karim Abdullah's searching gaze first.

"Perhaps you could tell me why you were looking for him?" His voice was even and low, with the sort of tone that made it clear he wasn't a man to mess with.

She'd gotten that message already.

"We were friends. I thought I'd stop by to see him. You know, long time no see. A chance to catch up. That sort of thing." She flashed him another winning smile.

He watched her as if he could see right through her, and she didn't appreciate how nervous he made her. It had nothing to do with the four-inch scar that made him look like a desert warrior despite his elegant suit. The overwhelming sense of power that emanated from him was what she was leery of.

"Thank you for your hospitality." She got to her feet and stepped around him, half expecting him to stop her.

He didn't. "Were you going to tell Aziz that you are carrying his child?"

She was halfway across the room, but the words stopped her more effectively than anything else could have. She was too scared to turn around and look at him, afraid of what he might read in her face.

"I'm not—"

"The paramedic took your blood in the ambulance. The hospital called with the results," he said in an icy tone. "You're not the first woman to come looking for him after one of his foreign escapades. I assume you're here for money?"

She winced, because that came uncomfortably close to the truth. "It's not Aziz's child," she lied. She would manage on her own somehow. She didn't want this dark sheik to have any kind of hold on her.

"My thoughts precisely, but I'd just as soon be sure. I want the case closed once and for all. I hope you won't mind a DNA test when the child is born."

She'd be long back in the U.S. by then, protected by U.S. law. They couldn't take her baby away at that point, even if they could find her, which she would make sure they couldn't.

"No, of course not." She schooled her face and chanced a look at him.

His expression remained unreadable, only his eyes darkened further, if that was possible. "Good. I hope you'll like your rooms. I'll introduce you to the staff this afternoon. You can pick your personal maid then."

The air got stuck in her lungs as she stared at him, startled. Was he completely nuts? "I'm not staying." She wanted to be very clear on that.

He paused for a moment. "That's a good strategy. Reverse psychology." He inclined his head with a small smile. "I give you this, you seem smarter than the others. But whether you prefer to stay or go has no bearing on anything. Your child might be the grandson of a king, and as such, one of the heirs to the Beharrainian throne." He watched her closely.

She felt the blood drain from her face. She'd known that Aziz was one of the king's cousins. But she knew they hadn't had a close relationship. And the king had a son. She hadn't taken succession into account. It wasn't something someone in her life and position thought much about.

"I'm sure you already considered that," he went on. "I hope you won't be disappointed to hear that a child, even if proven to be Aziz's son, would not be at the front of the line of succession. But in the line nevertheless. You must understand that I cannot allow you to leave the country until the bloodline is determined. Our very law would forbid it, except with the permission of the father. Aziz is gone. As his brother, I'm responsible for you and your baby."

If ever a sentence had the power to stop her heart, this was it. She was getting sucked in, losing control, the very thing she'd been most afraid of. She shouldn't have come here.

"This is insane. I have nothing to do with you. You can't keep me here. I'm an American citizen." She backed toward the door, relaxing marginally when he stayed where he was.

"You will find that in Beharrain, Beharrainian laws are given a priority over ideals of foreign countries thousands of miles away."

Was there a hint of threat in his steely voice?

She kept moving, but he still didn't follow. Not even when she reached the hallway and ran to the left, not knowing which way the exit was, but wanting to get away from him and the nightmare this trip was turning into.

Before long she'd reached a palatial marble foyer. The front door was open, but there were armed guards at the wrought-iron gate that led to the street.

"Excuse me," she said when they wouldn't move out of her way. Maybe they didn't speak English.

Step aside. Please, step aside. She wanted to get out before Karim decided to come after her. She didn't think he would let her go this easily. She glanced behind her, then back at the men who looked as unmovable as the seven-foot-tall brick walls that surrounded the property.

"I need to leave," she said slower and louder, knowing that was unlikely to make a difference. "Please." She pointed toward the gate. They had to know what she wanted.

"You are to leave the palace only in the company of Sheik Abdullah," one of them said after a moment, without looking at her.

So the language barrier wasn't an issue.

Her breath caught. Desperation rose inside her—desperation, fear and anger. She shouldn't have come. She had thought she would be able to keep her child safe while giving her or him the kind of large family she never had. But she understood now that wasn't possible. To keep her baby safe and with her meant that she had to escape far, far away from here. She would *never* give up control of her baby.

There had to be a way. She refused to accept that she, along with her unborn child, was a prisoner in a foreign land, held at the will of the Dark Sheik.

Chapter Two

She was fighting a losing battle. Sheik Karim Abullah's palace was better guarded than the Pentagon. But Julia wasn't the type to give up.

Since she had resigned herself to the fact that she wouldn't be able to escape on the ground level, she went up, sneaking through the night. She wasn't sure what she was hoping for, perhaps a large tree that came near one of the balconies. Trying something—anything—had to be better than sitting in her gilded prison of a room and crying her eyes out like she had done for the first half of the night.

She hated how weepy her overactive mommy hormones made her. This was not the time to give in to weakness. But she was emotionally exhausted and ravenously hungry. Hungry to the point that she was afraid her growling stomach would be heard.

She stole down the second-floor hallway, pausing in front of the first door. She pushed it open a fraction of an inch at a time and glanced around the lavishly appointed living room she discovered. Some sort of a suite. Other doors opened from here. The furniture was exquisitely made—all ornately carved wood—and was breathtaking even without her being able to make out the true colors of the luxurious fabrics in the moonlight.

Her gaze settled on a phone on a small, octagonal table. Her U.S. cell phone didn't work here and there wasn't a phone in her room. She wished she knew the number of the U.S. embassy by heart, and dialed zero, hoping to get directory assistance. Nothing happened.

She tried zero-zero, her stomach continuing to growl. No ringing on the other end. Zero-one. Just one. One-one. A disembodied voice said something in Arabic then the line went dead again. She gritted her teeth with frustration and took a banana from the fruit bowl next to the phone. An apple's crunching might give her away. She peeled it then bit in, and nearly moaned at the soft sweetness that diffused on her tongue. Heaven.

Her food tray had been removed that afternoon on her request when the smell of food had made her nauseous. She had refused dinner on principle—not the smartest thing, in hindsight.

She grabbed another banana and was stuffing it down the front of her shirt when a small noise came from behind one of the doors opposite her. She froze, nearly ran, but stopped herself. She needed to find a balcony, a way out.

She picked a door that was half-open, figuring she would make the least noise that way, and found herself in a large bedroom. The space was dominated by a sprawling bed, draped in black sheets, that didn't look slept in. A handful of papers lay tossed on the night-stand, next to a book.

Then her gaze was drawn to the source of the noise she'd heard before. A bathroom off the bedroom, lights on, the water running. She was facing a full-size, gilded mirror on the bathroom wall that was angled away from her. The picture it presented made her mouth go dry and her feet freeze to the tile floor. She swallowed the chunk of fruit in her mouth with some trouble.

Karim stood in an open shower with black mosaic tile and one of those drenching, foot-wide showerheads, water sluicing down his tanned skin. He stood with his back to her, so she had an unobstructed view of the scars that ran down his back, breaking up the otherwise perfect lines of the most incredible male body she had ever seen. He had his hands up, bracing himself on the wall, his head hanging as if deep in thought, tension evident in his corded muscles.

Shadows stretched across his back. She couldn't tell from this distance whether they were scars or some sort of tribal markings.

Another person might have looked vulnerable naked, but not the Dark Sheik. Strength radiated off him, and danger.

He reached to the side and turned off the water with one sinuous movement.

Okay, so Mr. I'm-Lord-of-All-I-Survey was sexy. Very.

She couldn't care less. She was leaving. Now.

He wrapped a black towel around his waist then

turned, his dark gaze finding hers unerringly in the mirror. He didn't show surprise. Somehow he'd known she'd be there, staring.

How humiliating.

"Is there anything you wanted from me, Julia?" His voice was low and measured, full of innuendo and contempt.

She wanted to turn and run, but his gaze wouldn't release her. When he strode closer, she backed away without looking where she was going, hoping she was backing out the door. Instead, in a few steps, her back bumped against the wall.

He was a short foot from her, looming dangerous in the semidarkness of the room, his wide shoulders outlined in the light that came from the bathroom. Drops of water glistened on his dark skin. He smelled like soap and sandalwood. He was the most erotic and intimidating sight she'd ever seen.

"Looking for a substitute sheik for your plan?" He put his right hand to the wall next to her head. His hand being higher than his shoulder, droplets of water ran backward, along his carved granite biceps.

Her heart jumped to her throat. He thought she'd come here to seduce him. She moved the other way, but that arm came down, too, and boxed her in. She didn't feel panicked as much as mesmerized. Blinked her eyes. *Snap out of it*. How dare he?

"Don't touch me." She shoved with her free hand, indignation giving her strength. She tried not to notice the hard muscles of his warm—and still wet—chest under her fingers. Her limbs were shaky. From exhaustion, no doubt. She was likely still jet-lagged, too.

He didn't budge a millimeter, but a dark eyebrow slid up his forehead. "Changed your mind? Scare you, do I?"

Maybe. Okay, more so with every passing moment. He was large and powerful and utterly overwhelming after a hellish day. She was well aware that he could kill her, and with his title and station in the country, there probably wouldn't even be a questioning.

Tears threatened to fill her eyes. She gritted her teeth and held them back. This was not the time for a hormonal moment. "Go to hell." She lifted her head and stuck her chin out. "You want to intimidate me? Congratulations, you succeeded. That's what turns people like you, isn't it? Scared women."

A muscle jumped in his face, just beneath the four-inch scar on the right side that started above the eye socket and ran straight down. And then she realized the eye didn't move along with the other one. He was blind on that side. Not that his left eye wasn't lethal enough on its own.

He took his time to look her over from her bare feet to the top of her head, returning to linger on her breasts, which had grown already during the pregnancy and were stupidly sensitive to smoldering looks from half-naked men. More misery to blame on hormones.

"The same things turn me on as any other healthy man, I suppose," he said, his voice a notch lower than before.

The space between them was insanely small. Without warning, the adrenaline that had been pumping through her already was metamorphosing into primal heat, making her fingertips tingle.

He had masculine lips, what some old-fashioned novels might have defined as cruel. Heathcliff lips. Incredibly sexy. She got a little woozy from looking at them this close.

The sharp sense of desire was insane, but perhaps understandable, considering that her body was hormonally unbalanced and out of her control.

His voice was a soft whisper when he spoke. "Why are you here, Julia? Why are you in my bedroom in the middle of the night?" He lowered his head as if wanting to carefully listen to her response.

If he came any closer, he was going to feel the banana she'd hid down the front of her shirt.

Her pulse sped, and not just from the danger of being discovered as a fruit thief. "Looking for a glass of water," she croaked out with effort. Her mouth did feel extraordinarily dry. She looked into his good eye.

His Heathcliff mouth tightened, but he didn't back away an inch. "Excuses?" He examined her. "Interesting. You're bold enough to come to me like this, yet you feel the need to come up with a pretext for seeking my bed."

Outrage quickly overcame awakening desire. Of all the conceited— "You know what I'm doing?" she asked sharply, and ducked to the right from the circle of his arms. "I was trying to get out of this stupid place. You have no right to keep me here. This is kidnapping." She darted toward the door.

If she thought the lack of sight in the right eye was a weakness, she was quickly disabused of the notion. He caught her easily.

"You will stay for as long as I see necessary," he said. "If I catch you trying to run—I've given you some freedom, Julia. Freedom that can be taken away."

What freedom? Her room? Meaning he could be keeping her closer to him? How close? His bed sprawled imposingly in her peripheral vision. She didn't want to know. Or maybe he'd meant he had some dungeons in the basement. That would be more likely. Nothing would have surprised her at this point.

Fear spiked her pulse. "I was wrong," she told him with all the contempt she felt. "You are nothing like your brother."

"And what do you know about Aziz?" His gaze slid to her abdomen. "My brother wasn't an irresponsible man."

A moment passed before she understood what he meant.

"He wasn't." And that was all she was prepared to say on the subject of birth control, which obviously was not as reliable as she'd thought.

His gaze journeyed back up, slowly, to her face.

The warning system in her brain was screaming that she should run for her life. "This baby has nothing to do with you and your family." She was desperate to escape his palace.

He didn't respond.

"You don't believe me."

More silence, just his dark gaze searching her face.

"And if I said the child *was* Aziz's? Would you believe *that?*" she said, testing him.

"No."

"So you're determined to think me a liar." Which, God help her, she was quickly becoming. But yes, she would do even that. She would lie, cheat and very possibly kill for her unborn child.

The question was, how far was Karim Abdullah willing to go for his niece or nephew?

"I'm just questioning your motives," he said.

"Is that what you call it?" She braved a sneer. "In my country this would be called kidnapping."

His masculine lips pressed into a tight line.

Her heart drummed against her rib cage. She tugged her arm. "You have to let me go."

And this time, he released her at last. "Get some sleep. I made an appointment for you for tomorrow morning. You'll get the full workup. You had a fall today. I arranged for an ultrasound."

Not one for minding his own business, was he?

Her initial instinct was to protest, but she hadn't had an ultrasound yet. Her first was scheduled for the week after her planned return to the States. She desperately wanted to see her baby. And she was no longer sure when exactly she would be back in Baltimore. Or if she could afford even the most basic medical care.

She did have that fall. And despite feeling fine, she did worry. And it wasn't as if he was going to give her a choice about going. "Fine. But don't think you're coming with me. Absolutely not."

"And I looked into testing," he said. "There's something called amniocentesis that can be done during pregnancy. They can obtain DNA and determine paternity."

She didn't know how she felt about that. The test would prove that the father was Aziz. That would bind her even tighter to Karim, an outcome she wanted to avoid at all cost. Could she refuse? What would that gain her? *Time*.

She turned from him and marched out with the half-eaten banana in her hand, calling a "Go to hell" over her shoulder on principle.

As she sped her steps, the banana under her top dislodged and fell to the floor. She picked it up, glad he didn't see her. But a glance back at his bedroom door revealed that, in fact, he had.

He'd come after her and was leaning against the door frame, watching her with a superior smirk on his face. "You may take the whole fruit bowl if you'd like."

THE RADIOLOGIST asked him no questions, one of the privileges of being sheik. Karim stared at the staticky-looking black-and-white screen, at the blurry outline of what seemed like a head and part of the abdomen. He kept his gaze studiously on the screen, ignoring the creamy expanse of skin in his peripheral vision.

He had come in with her because despite the blood test, he still half believed there might not even be a baby. Tests could be wrong. Tests could be altered for the right amount of money. She could have had it all set up at the hospital.

And if she were pregnant, he had half hoped that the ultrasound would reveal that she was lying about the child being Aziz's. The time of conception could have been wrong. Or the kid could have had stark red hair and looked obviously Irish, or whatever. What did he know? He'd never seen an ultrasound before.

But the date of conception was right on the money, during the time that Aziz had been in Baltimore. And, although the gray blob on the screen bore no resemblance to Aziz, Karim could hardly hold that against it. It barely looked human.

But here was the funny part, the thing he hadn't seen coming: the longer he looked at the kid, the more he wanted to believe the woman who lay on the hospital bed with her eyes glued to the screen and tears misting her fine eyes.

"Nice, strong heartbeat. See that?" the radiologist asked him.

And he could. The heart pulsed rapidly in the middle of the screen. The image was mesmerizing. He didn't like the softening it brought out in him.

Most likely, the woman was a money-hungry scammer.

The report he had received on her last night certainly pointed in that direction. Her family had been anything but upstanding and responsible. Her father left early on. Her mother dumped her and her siblings into the foster-care system. Julia floundered around for a while after that, then went to college on some sort of government program. Ended up with a nonprofit organization where she seemed tolerably successful.

He considered her alluring beauty, the crown of hair that to his disappointment she wore up today, that light in her eyes as she stared at the screen.

Hell, who wouldn't have fallen for that? Maybe she'd done so well because she could flirt successful businessmen into large donations. But her track record hadn't been enough. Her organization was downsizing and she was let go a month ago.

Pregnant and without any income. That had to be the definition of *desperate* for a woman.

Last night when he'd gotten the report, he'd been certain she was lying about the baby belonging to Aziz and was impatient for that DNA test. He wanted her to be gone.

Then she had come to his room, and in a moment of insanity, he just plain wanted her. He had wanted her to offer herself to him, and not only to prove him right about her character.

But now, looking at the child, the rapidly beating heart on the screen, suddenly he wanted there to be a baby from Aziz, someone left behind by his brother. He wanted the feisty, auburn-haired beauty to be true and not a conscienceless liar. He wanted her and her baby to belong to him.

Because of Aziz. He would take care of them for Aziz. There was so infuriatingly little he could do for his dead brother otherwise. Finding his killer was about it, which he would do even if he had to put his own life at risk in the process.

"Looks like you are just entering the second trimester. Everything looks well," the radiologist said. She was a petite, modest woman who wore a veil that covered most of her head and a large part of her hospital uniform. "The baby seems healthy."

"I called Dr. Jinan last night. She said something about the possibility of an amniocentesis," he said.

"That would be done sometime between week sixteen and week twenty of the pregnancy. Is there a concern about genetic problems?" The technician looked up.

"An issue with paternity," Karim growled, trying not to care that Julia flushed red with embarrassment.

"We don't normally do it for that purpose." The woman bowed her head.

"But it could provide confirmation?"

She nodded. "There are risks."

"What risks?" Julia asked.

"In a small percentage of the cases, the procedure can cause miscarriage. But if you absolutely have to—"

"No," he said at the same time as Julia, and hated the surprised look she gave him. Did it really stun her that much that he wouldn't put the baby's life at risk? "The procedure is not that necessary."

She would just have to stay around until the baby was born and they could do a no-risk DNA test. He would have to find a way to get her to agree. Despite his threats, he couldn't really hold her that long against her will, not in the current political climate. The country was trying hard to build strong diplomatic relations with the West, to prove that the place was safe for tourists and the culture prosperous and civilized. A rogue sheik kidnapping an American woman would definitely create damaging publicity.

She had come for money, he was pretty sure about that. All he needed was to figure out the price of her cooperation. They would discuss it over dinner tonight. He wasn't buying her burning need to leave, anyhow. Could be she was just being coy.

The prospect of her prolonged stay and the continued annoyance it was sure to bring should have bothered him but, oddly, it didn't. "So the child is healthy?"

"All looks as it should."

Dr. Jinan walked in and greeted them warmly, looked at the screen over the technician's head. "Everything is in order?"

"Perfect."

"Since you did have a fall, I'd recommend another day of rest. No work, no exercise, no sexual relations," Dr. Jinan was saying to Julia. "But if you continue to feel fine, you can resume all normal activity the day after tomorrow. If you have any problems, please don't hesitate to call." She gave Julia an encouraging smile.

Karim felt his shoulders relax, then tense again when his cell phone beeped. His chief of security. He turned off the ringer. He'd call the man back later. He didn't want to miss anything.

Never in a million years would he have expected to find himself in a place like this. He was resigned not to marry and have children of his own. He'd tried back in his early twenties. But he'd seen the look in the girls' eyes at the introductory meetings. The fathers were all willing. But he scared the women. And he didn't want to take a wife who would be repulsed by the sight of him, would cringe every time she looked at him for the rest of their lives.

Julia Gardner was scared of him, which didn't keep her from standing up to him, but she never once cringed.

"Can you tell if it's a boy or a girl?" The question was barely audible, her voice filled with wonder. Her face was radiant. A deep joy shone through her skin, joy that could not be faked.

He could not remember when he'd felt such unrestrained, undiminished happiness, if ever. She was about glowing with it, her beauty intensified until he could barely look away from her. Maybe a veil for her, too, wouldn't be a bad idea while she was in this country, although he didn't plan on letting her wander around without him being close behind.

"Not yet." The radiologist smiled. "Maybe in another month or so."

"Oh."

The child moved, looked like it was waving. Cute little bugger. Karim couldn't help a smile, but schooled his features back into place before Julia could notice.

If she realized that he was softening, who knew what outrageous demands she could make. If the child was Aziz's, Karim would take care of it, no question. If it wasn't… He looked at the woman who was still staring at the screen, teary-eyed. Something flipped over in his chest at the sight.

She was in a desperate situation. Had to be, to go into a far-flung scheme like this and try to pass her child off on a man who wasn't the father. He glanced at the screen again. If the DNA test came back proving Aziz had nothing to do with this, he could still see that she was able to raise the baby. Hell, he could afford it.

"Would you like some pictures?" the radiologist asked.

"I'm not sure." She glanced down. "I can't really pay for this."

"We'll take the pictures," Karim said.

"We can also make a copy of the video—"

"Send it to my palace."

She wouldn't look at him as the radiologist wiped off her flat belly, which he'd been trying to avoid taking notice of. Sure didn't look like new life was growing there. Maybe she wasn't eating enough. Something he would have to pay extra attention to.

She didn't talk to him until they were out of the examination room and going down the stairs. "Thank you. I don't have to thank you, because you kidnapped me and bullied me into this whole visit, but it was a moment, and…otherwise I would have been alone. Which probably would have been a step up from going with a kidnapper. But if I consider that you'll be my baby's uncle—"

"You're welcome." Did she always babble on when she was emotional?

She gave him a dirty look. "One more thing."

He drew up an eyebrow. Here we go. She was about to make her first demand.

"Please don't humiliate me in front of people like that again." Her words were issued softly.

Damned if he knew why he was feeling like a heartless bastard all of a sudden. His jaw muscles pulled tight. "Sorry." He didn't know which one of them was more surprised when the word was out.

"Wow, that sounded like it hurt. Was it your first time?" She grinned.

He glared back.

"You could just let me go," she said when they were in the car, the air conditioner going.

"Too cold?" he asked as he pulled into traffic.

"Are you kidding? I have a furnace inside. I could be standing on the snowfields of Siberia and be hot. Pregnant bodies produce lots of energy."

He hadn't considered that. "I can't let you go." He turned down the boulevard.

"You're a sheik. You can do anything you want."

She had an answer for everything, didn't she? Fine.

"I don't want to let you go," he said.

"Don't you ever watch international TV? Your views on life and responsibility are pretty archaic. You don't have to take care of me. I don't belong to you." As she said the last sentence, she enunciated each world deliberately.

"I don't have time for TV." He didn't bother addressing her wild notion of her not belonging to him. "I want you to write me a list of what you need. Both for you and the baby. And you need to eat more," he said just as a dark sedan cut off the car following them to get directly behind him. "I can bring a nutritionist on staff while you're with us."

He kept his attention on the sedan, his warning senses

perking up. The car was moving with too much purpose, the driver unnecessarily aggressive.

"I don't need a nutritionist. I eat healthy and I eat as much as I need. I won't be staying that long anyway."

She clearly resented his interference. And right now wasn't the time to discuss just how far he was willing to go to make sure her pregnancy went as smoothly as possible.

He looked at the rearview mirror again. "Listen, we might—" Too late, he saw the gun. He swerved. "Watch out!" He pushed her down just as the rear window exploded.

He heard the shards hit leather, but his seat and headrest protected him. A glance confirmed the same for Julia. He stepped on the gas and the car lurched around the minivan in front of them. But his attackers—two men, their faces obstructed by tribal-style headdresses—followed.

He swore under his breath. Should have brought his security along. But he didn't want anyone in his family or at the company to know about Julia Gardner and her claims yet. Didn't want to deal with the questions about him going to a women's clinic. If her story were untrue, he didn't want to unnecessarily tarnish Aziz's memory and bring his honor into question.

The car in front of him was slower than slow. For a moment, he swerved into upcoming traffic to get ahead, expecting Julia to scream at him. She didn't, but horns beeped all around them. He chanced a glance at her when he'd returned to the right side. She sat pale-faced, hanging on to her seat with a white-knuckled grip.

He snapped his attention back to the road in front of him. "We can handle them."

"We *can't* handle them. Oh, my God. Call the police!" She squeaked the last word.

"I'm a little busy." He growled under his breath, not at her, but at the men. By the time the police found them, this could be long over. Either he shook their attackers, and shook them fast, or one of their bullets would find its aim and end the chase.

He swore under his breath again. More stress was the last thing Julia needed in her condition. Not that he knew anything about her condition. But he would learn. For Aziz's child. *If*— Damn, but the uncertainty drove him crazy. He wasn't a patient man on his best day.

When they got out of here, he was going to get her to agree to stay in the country, then lock her up safely in his palace and not let her go until the baby was born. Maybe he would move to Aziz's place for the next six months. Living under the same roof with Julia might be more than he could handle. Especially if she kept sneaking into his bedroom. He was concerned about that as much as he wished for it.

"Hang on."

He was a good driver and put all his skills to use. For a moment or two, it seemed he might be able to put enough distance between his car and the assassins behind them.

Then a bicyclist, of all things, pulled in front of him, oblivious to danger. And he swerved, running the car up the cement rails of the shoulder, the right two tires leaving the ground. If they were to flip… He grabbed the steering wheel and maneuvered as best he could. He had to get the car back on the road. After an endless moment, he did manage.

"Are you all right?" He didn't dare take his eye off the road to look at Julia.

"I'm not all right. People are trying to kill me!" She sounded shaken. "What is it with everyone? Is everybody completely nuts around here? What are they thinking? Just go!"

He did, and for a moment was sure that they would make it. But the second bullet was more accurate than the first. The force of it slamming into his flesh smacked him against the steering wheel.

They were out in the open. The bullets kept coming. He had a woman and an unborn child to protect. Pain spread through him. He'd been hit. He couldn't tell how badly, and it was information he needed. All their lives depended on it.

Chapter Three

All his life he wanted to be a holy man. He had even changed his name to Mustafa, which meant *chosen*. And he indeed knew that Allah had chosen him when the only god trusted this most important task to him.

Old evil had returned into this world—old evil that offended the faith of his people and threatened their souls. He had sworn to destroy it and all who had come in contact with it, all who had been contaminated.

And the One God had been gracious and had given him followers, a tight sect of righteousness and light. They were all happy to die for the cause.

But so far, their work had been blessed and it had been Aziz Abdullah who had died. Mustafa smiled as he looked out over his garden. That first task had been done right. But they had much longer to go it seemed.

The evil objects had not been recovered. The world and his faith had not yet been saved. The idols had been passed on and contaminated yet another man: Karim Abdullah. But Karim, perhaps in his ignorance or already too tight in the grasp of the evil, did not realize that he needed to be purified.

It couldn't be helped. Mustafa stroked his beard and closed his eyes against the strengthening sun. His free hand held his cell phone. The call would come soon. Karim, the guardian of evil, would be dead.

Then, without a powerful guardian, the idols would be found. Yes. He smiled into the sun. He and his faithful followers would most certainly triumph.

"HOLD ON TO THE steering wheel," Karim said, pressing a hand to his wound, then pulling it away and looking at it, probably checking how badly he was bleeding.

Pretty badly. Then again, when it came to gunshot wounds, she wasn't sure there was such a thing as "good."

"The steering wheel," he said more urgently.

Julia stared at him. Was he crazy? Apparently, because he was letting go already, just expecting her to grab on as he pulled a gun—*a gun*—from under his suit jacket with his still-functioning right hand.

She had no idea that he'd been armed. She hadn't run around with armed men all that much before, smart girl that she'd been. Past tense, definitely. Everything that had been normal in her life had changed the second she'd set foot in Beharrain, and she was losing hope of being able to reclaim her old, sane life anytime soon.

First step was to stay alive.

She grabbed for the steering wheel as Karim twisted in his seat and returned fire.

Wow. Okay, guns were deafeningly loud when going off next to one's ear. You learned new things every day, she thought. Except all this, including how to evade armed pursuit, was stuff she didn't want to learn.

Insane. She really, really shouldn't have come here. This was another world. She didn't belong. She might not even survive it. Anger welled inside her, at her own stupidity for having come, and at the man next to her who could have let her go the night before, but hadn't. She could be back in Baltimore by now. At that moment, she hated Karim with the same fierceness that she hated the situation she was in.

"You know, if you didn't go around kidnapping people and bullying them into doing whatever you want, maybe everyone wouldn't be trying to kill you!" She might have been yelling a little. She was a smidgen on the stressed side.

He squeezed off another shot. "Everyone isn't trying to kill me. These are probably the same people who put the bomb in the car yesterday."

"That's comforting. I take it all back then," she snapped. "Could you *please* turn back to the road?"

She glanced nervously at the stick shift. As long as he kept the speed steady, they were fine. But if they had to slow for anything, she had no idea what to do with it.

Not that slowing seemed to be in his immediate plans. He was pushing the gas pedal nearly to the bottom, making maneuvering difficult to the extreme. He'd almost flipped them a few minutes ago, and she had a feeling he might succeed yet. Another experience she would have preferred to leave out if it was all the same to the gun-happy sheik next to her.

He shot another round, then—miracle of miracles—did as she asked and took back the wheel. He floored the gas and was able to gain a little more distance between them and the car that followed.

"You could drop me off here. Anywhere."

He didn't bother with a response.

They zoomed by the entrance of the boulevard that his palace was on.

"Obviously, you have some problem areas in your life." She looked behind them pointedly. The attackers were now three cars behind. "Maybe if you dealt with those, you'd have less time to meddle in the lives of others."

"I don't meddle. Stop nagging." He executed another maneuver.

"I don't nag. Where are we going?"

He frowned as if he hadn't considered that. Okay, to be fair, he'd been kept pretty busy with getting shot and all.

"They'll expect me to go back home and might head us off," he said.

"MMPOIL?" There was security at the company. She'd seen a number of guards while asking around for Aziz.

"I don't want to bring this fight to a building full of my employees. They—" he jerked his head to indicate the men who followed them "—might expect that, too. They've probably been following me long enough to know any place I could go. Wherever I go, someone might be there waiting."

Death was waiting for them all around. Not a happy thought. *Don't panic. Breathe.*

Her gaze fell on her purse in her lap, settling on the magnetic room cards visible in the front pocket. "We could go to my hotel." An idea was forming slowly in her mind. She needed to get away, and not just from the men who were shooting at them, but away from it *all.* Her brain worked furiously at one possible solution.

He seemed to be considering her suggestion, looking in the rearview mirror. "The Hilton downtown." He nodded.

So he knew where she'd been staying. Obviously, he had checked her out. What else had he found? It didn't matter. The important thing was that he was going along with her idea.

He took the next exit and was there in minutes. They had been closer than she'd thought, not knowing the city. The sparkling high-rises, all glass and steel, were testaments to modern architecture, mixed in with ancient mosques and minarets. The sight was breathtaking but foreign, and she got disoriented too easily. The day before, after careful instruction from the concierge, she'd only been able to find MMPOIL after three tries, going around in circles for over half an hour.

In hindsight, it would have been better if she hadn't found the place and Sheik Karim Abdullah at all.

"Do you have a card for the underground parking?" He cast a sideways glance at her as he pulled up to the gate.

She fished out her parking pass and handed it over to him. The gate opened. They were in. Her plan might work yet. Her number-one objective was to keep her baby safe. To achieve that, she would do whatever was necessary. And since being around Karim was the opposite of safe, what she needed was to get away from him.

Keep cool. Keep thinking. Give nothing away.

He glanced into the rearview mirror one more time before shutting off the motor and tugging off his blood-soaked jacket. His tie came next. He tried to wrap it around the wound. She got out and walked around to help him, doing her best not to look at all the blood as she pulled the silk tight.

Another scar, she thought, and was beginning to wonder just exactly what sort of life the Dark Sheik lived. She had a feeling she didn't want to know. Had Aziz been like this when he was at home? Somehow she couldn't picture it. She tied off the length of silk.

Karim didn't wince. "Thank you."

She stepped back. "It doesn't mean I forgive you. I just don't want to have to explain to my baby later why I let his uncle bleed to death." He was lucky that family was so important to her.

The corner of his mouth twitched, which annoyed her. She hadn't been trying to be funny. She meant every word she'd said.

He pulled the jacket back on, its dark fabric hiding most of the bloodstains. Not that it mattered in the end. They were lucky enough to make it to her room without running in to anyone, although the elevator ride was a tad tense on the way up.

"I'm going to wash this off so I can see the damage."

He lifted his left arm and headed for the bathroom as soon as they were inside the room and the door locked behind them.

The hotel was furnished and decorated in Middle Eastern style, rich fabrics and colors, copper tables, a multitude of pillows everywhere. The room looked as if it had been decked out with the treasures of old-time caravans. She'd been dazzled when she had arrived, but barely noticed the exotic interior now. Of course, a hotel room was never going to impress her again after having seen Karim's palace.

She sank onto her bed, which had been made since she'd left it the morning before, the starch going out of her all of a sudden. God, that car chase had been petrifying. She folded her hands over her abdomen and breathed deeply for a few seconds, gathered herself as best she could, until she felt a little better. She had not, in fact, come to harm so far, and neither had her baby. That was the most important thing.

With Karim being out of the room, even if he did leave the bathroom door open, she could almost pretend that everything was back to normal, like before she'd started out on her ill-fated trip the previous day. Except she wasn't big on pretending.

Her mother had pretended all her life and look where that got them. She'd pretended that she didn't have a drinking problem. She'd pretended that her marriage was just fine, up until the day her husband had walked away. Then she pretended that she could start over if she just got rid of her daughters, abandoning them to foster care.

You didn't face reality, your life fell apart real fast. It was a lesson Julia learned early on. She was a firm believer in confronting problems head-on. Which was why she had come to Beharrain in the first place. To face down her issues with Aziz, gain some sort of a resolution, then go home.

Instead, she'd been kidnapped by an overbearing sheik, held against her will overnight and nearly killed. *Twice*.

But Karim hadn't hurt her, had made sure she and her baby were okay. He had paid for a full checkup and an ultrasound. With video. She almost regretted that she would be leaving him before that came in. At least she had the pictures in her purse.

Time to make her move.

She pulled the nightstand door open and lifted out her travel kit, found the leaf of small, white sleeping pills. She kept them in the kit because she never slept well when traveling, but she hadn't dared take them on this trip. She didn't want to do anything that might harm the baby.

She popped a pill into her palm, then after some thought, popped a second, then a third. He was large and strong. She didn't want to make the mistake of underestimating him. She put the kit away, grabbed a glass and filled it from the bottle of bubbly mineral water on the table, then broke the tablets up, sprinkling them into the water. When she was done, she swirled the water around. The bubbles hid the rapidly dissolving chunks.

"I don't think the bullet hit anything serious. It went through muscle." Karim was coming from the bathroom.

He startled her so badly that she almost spilled his drink.

"Here. You lost blood. You should have some fluids." She handed him the glass, feeling only a twinge of guilt. None of this would really harm him. He'd have a good sleep, which would help him heal. He'd be upset when he woke and found her gone, but he would just have to get over it. "Let me tighten the bandage."

He'd used the tie again, but it looked loose, the best he could manage with one hand.

"Thank you." He drained his glass while she fiddled with the length of dark silk and held her breath.

"What are we going to do next?" It was a miracle that she wasn't trembling with nerves. As soon as he passed out, she was out of here. Her rental car was still at MMPOIL, so she would call a cab to take her to the airport. She was determined to be on the next flight out of the country. He'd taken her passport the night before, but she'd seen him put it into his wallet, which had to be in his suit jacket. She shouldn't have any trouble getting it back.

"The baby looked good," he said out of the blue. "You were satisfied with the doctors? If not, I can ask for others."

"They were fine." The medical personnel all kow-towed to them. They barely dared to look Karim in the eye. "I'm sure they'll do their best. They're all scared to death of you," she said pointedly.

"Aren't you?" He held her gaze.

"No." At least not in the physical sense. "I must be stupid," she mumbled to herself as she turned away.

"Don't say that."

"I came here." Case in point.

"You did the honorable thing. I respect that."

"Enough to let me go?" She felt another pang of guilt for drugging him.

He smiled. "No."

The moment passed.

He walked to the window and looked out, flipped open his cell phone and talked at length with someone in Arabic.

"Who was that?" she asked when he hung up and walked over to sit in the armchair by the desk.

He looked mellow. So far she'd seen him with his usual controlling expression, angry and scowling. Mellow was definitely new. Actually, it didn't look all that bad on him.

"My security." He closed his eyes for a second. "I told them to look out for anyone suspicious both at work and at home. I gave them a description of the car that followed us."

She didn't have time to ponder his looks. "Tired?"

He shrugged it off. "Tell me how you met my brother."

God, she so did not want to get into this now. But she had to do something while she waited for the drug to work. Maybe talking him to sleep wasn't such a bad idea.

"He was at a fund-raiser dinner I organized."

He nodded. "My brother lived a busy social life when abroad. Fund-raiser for what?"

"Summer camp for kids in foster care. For siblings. For the most, the system tries to place siblings together, but it can't always be done. I worked for an organization that tries to make sure that these brothers and sisters stay in touch. This way, when they get out of the system, there's a relative out there that they had contact with over the years. Sometimes the older ones can help the younger ones. We try to give them that sense of family."

She thought of her two sisters whose memory was faded and spotty. She could recall specific incidents and conversations, but the faces were becoming blurry. Finding them had been the first thing she'd tried to do when she had left foster care at eighteen. She had failed so far. Back then, records hadn't been computerized. The agency that had placed her family had been flooded out several times, many of their files destroyed.

She had managed to find her mother, but she had passed on by that time.

"You still work there?" he asked. His eyes were becoming hazy, but his gaze on her face was unwavering.

She looked away. "You lost blood. Do you want me to call an ambulance?" Suddenly she was worried that three pills might have been too much. Maybe he did need help. She could call and be gone by the time they got here. He did have that handy-dandy company ambulance at the ready, after all.

"I'll go in later and have the wound cleaned and sewn up. I want to get you someplace safe first."

Protecting her seemed to be a reflex with him. She wondered if he was like this with everyone.

"I'm safe here." They weren't going anywhere together.

He closed his eyes for another moment. "I asked for some of the security staff to come over. They should be here soon enough. Maybe I'll have them take you to Tariq's place, my other brother. His wife is American. Did Aziz tell you that?"

She shook her head. Oh, God, his security was coming?

"That's right." He looked increasingly absentminded. "Aziz hadn't met Sara." His face darkened. He leaned back in the chair. "I think I lost more blood than I thought." He pulled his gun and laid it across his lap.

"That's okay. Take a minute to rest."

She'd given him the pills ten minutes ago. They usually worked on her in about that time. And she'd given him a triple dose.

"So your organization doesn't miss you while you're here?" He didn't seem to be easily distracted.

"I'm no longer with them. They had to cut back. Some of our top corporate sponsors left. With the economic downturn, our donors haven't been able to support us like before, either. Aziz was brought by a friend of a friend." God, he probably thought that she'd just latched on to his brother for the money. "He was really interested. He thought the summer camps were a great idea. I didn't—"

"Take advantage of him?" He finished the sentence for her.

"If you're going to imply that I only slept with him to get more money…" She glared at him, knowing that her hormones made her more emotional these days, but not caring. So she was touchy lately, so what? She'd spent the last three months nauseous and tired to death, feeling as if she'd been beaten over the head.

"Did you?" he asked without emotion.

"No!"

He simply nodded. Blinked. "My brother supported a dozen charities, both Beharrainian and international."

He had to pass out before his security got here. It was her only chance. *Please, please, please,* she prayed silently, watching him for signs of fatigue without being too obvious about it.

He shook his head as if to shake himself up. "So you are currently unemployed."

She didn't bother denying it, just nodded.

"I take it you are here for money." He didn't look angry, just resigned. Yet another new look for him.

"I didn't come for money."

He arched a dark eyebrow.

"Not just that. It's not like that. I wanted to do the right thing. I wanted to tell him."

"But you would have been content going back without telling *me?*"

She should have. She should have run the moment she'd laid eyes on Karim. "I was afraid of how you would react. I didn't want anyone to assert any kind of claim over my child. I wasn't crazy about the idea of possibly getting kidnapped and held against my will." She glared at him.

His lips twitched. "Think of it as being my honored guest."

"Think of it as illegal," she retorted, wishing that he would pass out already. She was about ready to jump out of her skin.

"You could enjoy it. It could be a few months of vacation and pampering. It's not like you have anything to go back to."

Ouch. He was right, but she didn't have to like it. His assessment of her life sounded dismayingly pitiful. "You could let it go," she said. "What if I have a new boyfriend back home?"

He leaned forward, somewhat unsteady, and narrowed his dark gaze. He looked decidedly unhappy about the possibility. "Do you?"

She shook her head, didn't see any point in lying.

Her admission seemed to relax him. He leaned back into the chair again. His hands hung by his sides, his suit coat falling open. She shouldn't have any trouble getting into his inner pocket and fishing out his wallet. She would get her passport and borrow enough money so she could get to the airport. She so wasn't going to feel guilty about that. He had confiscated her purse. If she was driven to desperate measures, he had only himself to blame.

Oh, God, please, let him fall asleep. "Listen, I—" She fell silent when somebody knocked on the door. Despair surrounded her. How could they be here already?

He came to his feet, lurching forward unsteadily.

"Julia—" Then understanding flashed across his ragged face. "Julia?" This time he growled her name. The mellow phase was clearly over. He gave her a fierce scowl. Then he folded back into the chair, and finally passed out.

Oh, God. There would be hell to pay for this if they ever met again, which she would do her best to avoid.

His security was here. The scene would just have to be played out. She could stay right by the door when his men came in. With luck, they'd be focused on what was going on with their precious sheik and she would have a second or two to dart out.

The Hilton was an international hotel. There were other Americans here. She'd heard them downstairs over breakfast before she'd headed over to MMPOIL the day before. Once she reached the hallway, she would run like a champion and raise holy hell. She was prepared to scream her head off and bring all the other guests and the staff running. Even if the staff wouldn't take her side against a sheik, she was certain that her compatriots would defend her. If it was the only way to get out of this country and back home to safety, she wasn't averse to causing an international incident. She had few illusions about Sheik Karim Abdullah getting into any trouble.

She took a deep breath, ready for her escape, her hand on the lock by the time she thought to look through the peephole.

Two men stood outside, dressed in white robes and headdresses. One scanned the hallway, while the other was focusing on the door. They wore identical grim expressions. They didn't belong to Karim's security. She recognized them from earlier and the breath got stuck in her throat. It couldn't be true. This couldn't be happening.

"Karim?" Desperation made her voice high and squeaky.

She glanced back at him. His eyes floated open for

a moment before closing again. He looked formidable even slack-jawed.

She looked out the peephole again, her heart racing at double speed at the sight. The men waiting to get in were from that dark sedan that chased them, the same men who had done their best to kill Karim and her just a little while ago.

"Karim, you have to wake up." She judged the distance between her and the gun on Karim's lap, wondered if she could even figure out how to take off the safety. But before she could make up her mind, it became apparent that she wasn't going to have time to go for a weapon.

Something scraped against the card reader. She shoved her full weight against the door. That didn't seem as effective as she had hoped. She gained maybe two seconds. The security chain held the men back for another two. Before she could blink, they were already pushing their way inside.

Chapter Four

When the two men outside heaved and slammed the door open, Julia was smacked against the wall, the air leaving her lungs with a whoosh, pain exploding in her back. And she was glad that the point of impact hadn't been any lower.

She slid to the dark gray carpet that covered the floor, stunned for a moment, but pulling her hands in a protective gesture in front of her. *The baby. Don't let them harm the baby.* And it seemed, at least for the moment, that her prayer was answered, because the intruders paid scant attention to her.

One closed the door and guarded it while the other dove for Karim, shouting something in Arabic. Both men held their guns on him.

Everything was happening too fast, her mind reeling. The attack had come so unexpectedly, she couldn't catch up, couldn't think, didn't know what to do. She glanced toward the door, but she couldn't work up the nerve to tackle the guy blocking it.

At least Karim was rising to the occasion, lurching to the left, toward the bed. He squeezed off a shot but missed. His movements were definitely uncoordinated. He looked like those big game-reserve lions on the National Geographic Channel after being hit with the tranquilizer shot, ready to be tagged. Then he was on the floor, and for a moment she thought he had passed out and fallen, not realizing until he rolled under the bed that the drop had been deliberate.

Not that hiding out under there was an option. The attackers filled the mattress with lead the next second.

"No!" The word tore from Julia's throat unbidden. He was a controlling bastard, but she didn't want him harmed. Didn't want to be responsible for his death. She had given him the pills. She had immobilized him and served him up to his enemies.

He was her baby's uncle. He didn't deserve this. He was bossy and arrogant, but in some ways he was okay. Misguided as his efforts were, he did want to keep her safe. Just before the men came, he'd been talking about getting her to safety. And she had done this to him.

"No, please," she pleaded again, against the instinct to keep quiet and invisible, but the two bad guys didn't even glance at her.

The gunfire did stop, however. The guy who guarded the door stepped forward. The other moved closer to the bed and dropped to his knees in front of it, probably to check if their job was finished.

The air stopped halfway to her lungs. Karim was dead. And she would be next.

Whoever these two were, they wouldn't want to leave a witness. They just assassinated a sheik. She had no idea why and she didn't need to know right now. Their reasons were immaterial at the moment.

She had to do something. But she was frozen with fear, paralyzed by the smell of gunpowder in the air and by the sight of those guns and the assassins who held them. A terrible realization held her in place, the knowledge that there was nothing she could do to change the outcome of the situation she was in. It had been determined the moment the two thugs had busted into the room, armed against a drugged sheik and a defenseless woman.

Her hands moved protectively to her abdomen. She wanted the best for her baby, had promised the best, had sworn to provide the safety, love and family that she hadn't been given. She hated to fail even before her child was born. That was the thought that got to her more than anything, more than the possibility of Karim's death or her own. She could not face the fact that her child would never see the world.

Then something shifted inside her. To hell with the bastards. She was no defenseless woman. She was a mother. Nobody was going to hurt her baby.

She shifted and had the element of surprise on her side when she kicked at the gun in the nearest man's hand, kicked and met her aim, sending the weapon flying across the room. Almost at the same time, a gun went off, drawing her attention to the bed just in time to watch the other attacker fold to the floor, red blooming on his white caftan.

Karim rolled out from under the bed, his weapon in hand, but his movements were slow, his gaze unfocused. The remaining attacker took advantage and dove for his firearm, then fired as soon as he had it.

Karim's gaze finally caught on her for a split second before he put himself between her and the bullets. "Go!"

She didn't need to be told twice. Adrenaline pushed her to her feet. She got the door open, glancing back only to see Karim lunge after her as more gunshots exploded behind them. His momentum carried him another couple of yards before he slowed again, shook his head as if to clear his mind.

A million thoughts raced through her head in a fraction of a second, the topmost being that she was out of the room, could leave him now and he could do nothing to stop her. The guy with the gun wanted Karim. Karim would probably put up a fight, even if it would only last seconds, minutes at best. But it was time she could use. She could get away, be free.

Free. The word pounded through her head.

She would be free and Karim would be dead.

"Help! Please help!" she screamed toward the row of doors on each side.

Nobody stirred, nobody volunteered to rush to the rescue. Given the gunfire, the other guests were probably locking themselves in their rooms. Housekeeping was obviously working another floor. Not that they could have defended her against bullets with a broom.

She grabbed Karim's hand and dragged him toward the staircase. The fireproof steel door was just closing behind them when bullets pinged off the metal on the other side. She couldn't leave Karim behind. She would get him out of here, then leave him somewhere by the side of the road where he'd be safe. *Safer,* at least.

She shoved him forward then yanked on the fire hose and tied the door shut before going after Karim, who was tumbling down the stairs. She ran, grabbed his arm, and her momentum carried the both of them forward. He grunted and she did, too, along with him. He was heavy and not fully in control of his powerful body, hard to direct.

At the landing he slammed against the wall, leaving a bloodstain on the white paint. His arm was bleeding, but she didn't have time to worry about whether that was the old wound or a new one. Maybe she could put him out by a hospital, although, God help her, she had no idea where one of those would be in this city. "Go, go, go!"

The gunshots stopped outside the staircase, which meant the attacker was probably taking the elevator to cut them off. Julia raced for her life, muscles pitted against machinery.

The flight to the parking garage passed in a blur. She hadn't noticed before, but Karim had parked his car right in front of the door of the emergency exit, right where they came out of the staircase. Probably on purpose. He seemed like the type of guy who planned ahead.

He was now together enough to reach into his pocket. He opened the car with his remote, then handed her the keys.

Oh, God.

Of course, he couldn't drive in his condition. She hadn't even considered that. Which left her to handle the task. But she didn't know the city. And she was a mediocre driver at best, not equipped for armed pursuit. But she had no choice.

When he just stood there in drug-induced stupor, she dragged him toward the passenger side and shoved him in unceremoniously, slammed the door behind him before sprinting to her side. Then she remembered the stick shift. Why, oh why?

"I can only drive automatic," she yelled at him as if it was all his fault.

What were the pedals? Clutch, break, gas, if she remembered correctly. A high school boyfriend had spent some time coaching her on his pickup a million years ago, but it had turned out to be a brief relationship and she hadn't paid much attention to the driving lessons in any case, not when they were just a distraction between make-out sessions.

And make-out sessions they were, nothing more. She'd been a good girl all through high school, petrified that she'd get pregnant and would end up alone with a child. Her number-one goal had been avoiding becoming like her mother. She'd never slept with a man unless they were in a committed relationship, of which she'd had two. Then came those few irresponsible days with Aziz. And they had used protection. Not that it mattered. Fate sure had a way of laughing in her face.

She was going to have a baby.

If she stayed alive long enough.

Through some miracle, she managed to put the car in first gear. Karim had backed into his parking spot, so at least she didn't have to worry about backing out. Okay, which way? Most of the signs were in Arabic. She almost cried in relief when she spotted an old-fashioned English exit sign, a lit red box with white letters. Thank God for international hotel chains.

The first gear took her to the exit just fine. Then she stalled when trying to shift to second. She needed to start up the damn car all over again. She winced as the engine whined. She'd never driven a car this nice before, a silver BMW with more power than she was comfortable with. She really didn't want to break it. Then she thought, to hell with it, Karim's fancy car was the least of their problems.

She didn't dare look in the rearview mirror to see if the bad guy was behind them or not. She focused her full attention on the shift and clutch.

The shot Karim fired through the back window and the responding gunfire the next second tipped her off to the severity of their situation. They were sitting ducks unless she managed to get the car moving.

She got it into first gear again and moved up to the gate that opened on its own, no card required to get out. Thank God, because she had no idea where her parking pass was at this stage. She passed through and stepped on the gas, and with some grinding of the gears switched the transmission into second. They were out on the boulevard at last.

"Clutch. Shift. Now," Karim instructed.

Third gear slid into place with nothing but a small hiccup. Fourth. *Good, really good.*

Except that someone cut in front of her and she needed to slow, but knew that shifting down would make her stall all over again. She kept her foot steady on the gas pedal instead, and yanked the steering wheel to the right, going around the car in front of her, causing a minor disturbance on the road, and a flurry of beeping horns.

But the car was still moving. *Yippee.*

If her lips weren't frozen in a tight line of concentration, she might have smiled. The small burst of relief vanished soon enough.

"Where are we going?" She weaved through traffic, taking unnecessary chances just to keep a steady pace so she wouldn't have to shift.

He took a long time to answer. "Aziz's palace. Left at the next light, right, then left again." A long pause followed. "Blue." Was he still talking about the palace?

She caught a green light, thankfully, sailing through, barely slowing to make the turn. The tires squealed in protest. "Which right, the next right?"

When no response came, she risked taking her eyes off the road for a split second to glance at him. Karim slumped in his seat, completely out of it. She wasn't sure whether from the drug or blood loss. A hospital would have been great right about now, but they were clearly in a residential neighborhood.

And she had a feeling these residents were anything but ordinary. A row of palaces lined the road on each side, some traditional, some startlingly modern. She had to shift down. After some hesitation, she actually succeeded. Then she took stock of the front yards that were protected by stone walls and wrought-iron gates. There was no way she could just pull into a driveway and pretend to belong there. Especially not with the back window of Karim's BMW being blown out.

She glanced into the rearview mirror, but couldn't tell if they were being followed. She couldn't see the dark sedan anywhere, but that didn't mean the assassin hadn't commandeered another car. Assassin or assassins. She wasn't sure how badly Karim had hurt the one he'd shot. Could be they were both still out there, on their tail.

"Karim?" She reached over to shake him, couldn't be too forceful with his bad arm. "You need to wake up now."

The street she was on looked completely unfamiliar to her, all the signs on the buildings in Arabic. *Blue,* he had said. About every third house was blue.

He didn't seem to care. His head tilted to the side. For the moment, he was completely out.

She was lost in a strange place, her only possible protection injured and unconscious and there was a better than good chance that they had an assassin or two following not far behind—serious bad guys whom she was too inexperienced and frazzled to even hope to spot.

If things were going to get any worse, she didn't want to know it.

KARIM STRUGGLED to open his eyes, struggled to remember where he was. Through a slit, he caught a glimpse of Julia next to him, her hair all messed up and wild, her eyes wide as she stared at the road ahead, her face pinched in concentration.

They were in danger, but he couldn't remember why or from whom. He had to stay awake. Frustration pulsed through him, but he couldn't sustain the urgency of it. He felt like he was diving, underwater, floating in the deep. His body seemed incredibly relaxed. All was peaceful inside. He could sense turmoil outside, but felt as if it had been somehow walled off from him.

He smiled at the mermaid in the driver's seat. "You're beautiful." He slurred the words.

She barely spared him a glance. "Which house? You need to tell me which house it is."

Where were they going? He could only think that someone was after them and they must get away. But he couldn't keep focused on that for more than a second. "You shine like an angel."

"Speak English," she snapped.

Julia Gardner was an exceedingly beautiful woman. He liked her hair the most. And her eyes. Her skin glowed pink. Her lips were—

"Karim," she snapped at him again. "I need you to tell me how to get there."

Where were they heading? A long moment passed before he could remember. "Aziz."

"Right. Which one is his palace?" She sounded exceedingly impatient. Might have even growled a little.

The sound made him smile.

With effort, he turned his gaze from her and realized that they were on Aziz's street. He reached for the remote in his glove compartment, feeling darkness closing in. "Aziz," he said one more time, then sunk into oblivion.

"KARIM, WAKE UP! Wake up, dammit."

Julia took her right hand off the steering wheel, a move she could hardly afford, and shook him.

Nothing.

She grabbed the remote from his hand. What was this for? She pushed the top button. Down the road lined by modern palaces, a wrought-iron gate opened. She hoped there was a correlation between that and the remote. In any case, she had to get off the road. She had to hide.

Of course, the second she tried to shift down, she stalled the car. *Damn. Okay. Let's start over.*

First gear. Good. It got her through the gate.

She pushed buttons randomly until the gate closed and the door to a garage bay opened. Then she pulled in, gawking at the selection of sport and luxury vehicles. She closed the garage door. The lights came on automatically.

She sat motionless and listened, but could hear no car stopping in front of the house, no bullets hitting the garage door behind them. A reprieve. She leaned back in her seat and closed her eyes, wanting to stay that way forever.

But she had to get out of here, away from Karim before he came to. A glance at him confirmed that he wasn't even close to that yet.

She stepped out of the car, shaking from the chase and maybe a little with hunger. Something red caught her eye in the side mirror and she realized her clothes were bloody. From Karim. She had to find something to wear before she went out onto the street. A disguise wouldn't have been a bad idea, in any case. Just so the assassins wouldn't recognize her if they ran into each other. She needed one of those *burqas* local women wore, the black dress that made them virtually indistinguishable from each other.

A week ago she would have sworn that nothing and nobody could make her wear one of those things. Two days in this country and she was already begging to put on the veil.

Could be there was something like that in Aziz's palace. Not a *burqa,* specifically—he'd told her he wasn't married and none of his sisters lived with him— but even a black sheet would do. Karim had black sheets—the brief flashback to when she'd been in his bedroom raised her core temperature a few degrees so she pushed that particular memory away.

So she was a little attracted to him. So what? He was an attractive man. Tall and wide-shouldered. That scar of his only made him look fiercer. But he wasn't for her. For one, he was Aziz's brother. That made it all strange somehow. Plus, by tomorrow this time, she'd be home.

The only contact she planned to have with Karim was when she helped her child write letters to his uncle in a couple of years. Family was important. She was going to allow contact, she'd decided at one point. Making her daughter or son wait eighteen years for the truth didn't seem right. But she was going to take precautions. She didn't see going on vacations together in their future.

She cast a glance at him. He was sleeping, the dashboard propping up his head, in what looked like an extremely uncomfortable position. He seemed a little less intimidating in this pose. She pulled the key from the ignition and looked at the key ring. If Karim had the remote to Aziz's gate, it stood to reason that he would also have the key to Aziz's house.

She could help him in and make him comfortable. Could look at his wound and, if needed, even call for help if she found a phone book and the number for the ambulance. If she could figure out the listing in Arabic. Hopefully there was a symbol of a red cross or something along those lines next to it. In a country where illiteracy was a major problem, surely they would think of something like that.

She would find herself something to cover up with, call an ambulance and book it out of here before anyone arrived. Seemed like the perfect plan.

She walked around, dragged him out of the car and stood him upright. He wasn't completely unconscious, not so much that he was dead weight. But his movements needed firm direction and a lot of encouragement. She nudged him to the stairs, propping him against the wall while she tried the keys one by one. She hit the jackpot on the sixth try, went into some sort of an entrance room, swore at the blinking red light on the state-of-the-art security system—a flat-screen monitor built into the wall.

Of course, a palace would be secured. She was lucky she wasn't sitting neck deep in Rottweilers and security guards.

"Wake up. We need the code." She shook Karim, inhaling the pleasant, citrus smell of the palace, noting the white marble tiles under her feet. "Karim. You need to wake up. Hello."

Nothing.

The security system beeped once.

She took that as a warning and tentatively touched her hand to the screen. A window appeared with a fingerprint drawing on it. She reached for his hand and pressed his thumb against the spot. He didn't resist. Another window appeared with a blinking cursor. Probably waiting for a password.

"Wake up!" She pried his good eye open with her fingertips. Only the vacant look spoiled the gorgeous sable color. "What's the code?"

He shook his head and tried to focus on her without success. She was beginning to feel real guilty for doing this to him. Then hardened her heart. If he had listened to reason, she wouldn't have had to take things so far.

"The code." She turned him toward the screen. Him being bossy was annoying, but having him completely helpless wasn't all that fun, either.

He gathered himself and lifted his hand, punched in a series of numbers she didn't quite see as she had to hold him up. But she did see when the light switched to green.

"Thank you." She leaned him against the wall and let

him go, closing the door behind them. Mission accomplished. She was practically on her way to freedom.

A small beep sounded again. By the time she turned around, he was sitting on the floor with his back resting against the wall and his eyes closed. The security light was red once more. He had rearmed the system.

And just like that, she was trapped again.

"FAILURE WILL not be accepted. This is a holy mission. Do not come back," Mustafa yelled into the phone before remembering that his men needed encouragement as well as discipline. He switched to a more fatherly tone. "You will find them. Your path will be guided by righteousness."

So there had been setbacks. He knew he was merely being tested. He was prepared to show the strength of his faith by never giving up, never letting an unexpected problem get the better of him.

He'd lost a man. A noble sacrifice.

Every cause had martyrs. The loss would only strengthen him and his small group of true believers. They were all prepared to die for what was true and right.

You fought against the devil, you had to expect that there would be casualties. He had expected that a few men would have to be sacrificed. He was willing to give that to the cause. In truth, he was willing to give so much more.

His calling was to rid the world of evil, and he was prepared to do that, whatever the cost. But some of his followers were untrained yet, their minds not as strong as they should be. They didn't see losing one of their own as glorious as he did. They would learn. Teaching them was part of his responsibilities, a sacred duty entrusted to him.

But his enemies were multiplying, it seemed. Who was the woman? A whore no doubt. No woman of honor would spend the night at a strange man's house, nor would she take him back to her hotel room with her. If he had any doubts about whether Karim stood on the side of righteousness or darkness, that alone would have revealed the truth. Karim had been infected by evil, his actions turning immoral already. Who knew what he would do if Mustafa didn't stop him?

He felt the full weight of that responsibility. He would not lay down his burden until his task was done, his mission completed.

"Check our primary points. I will also send out the others," he told the man on the other end of the line.

His team had been following Karim around for weeks now. They knew all the places he regularly visited. He was wounded; he would want someplace familiar to hide, someplace he felt safe.

Little did he know that for a man who sided with evil, there was no safe place among righteous believers.

Chapter Five

If she left now, the alarm would go off. Julia could see it all: a foreign woman running into the street with blood on her clothes and a palace security siren blaring behind her. If they caught her, if they found Karim, a bleeding, semi-conscious sheik… She would be tossed in jail quicker than she could say, "I want to call the American embassy."

She didn't want to stay here with Karim, but she didn't cherish the thought of a Middle Eastern women's prison, either, or the chance of running into the assassin or assassins on the street. She would see to Karim's injuries then think of something, she decided, and headed off to find some water and some strips of clean linen. She called a "Stay where you are" over her shoulder, knowing it to be unnecessary.

The first thing she registered when she opened the door that lead to the rest of the palace was that the place was a complete mess. Drawers overturned, furniture pulled away from the walls, books and clothes scattered all over the place.

But even through the mess, the splendor of the palace was obvious. It had been built in a more modern style than Karim's, with a lot of straight, clean lines and a certain amount of masculine severity. Everything was the best money could buy: the marble, the crystals, the furniture and the electronics equipment that was the latest on the luxury market.

She found a bathroom, used it then washed her hands thoroughly with soap, looked for something to collect water in, but couldn't find anything. She moved on, hoping to find a first-aid kit. Then realized that the place was too enormous to search from top to bottom just now and settled for a clean white towel.

On the way back, she picked up a priceless-looking modern art vase and filled that with water in the bathroom.

Karim was still completely out, coming to only when she began removing his clothes. His jacket was bloody all over. Guilt pricked her again over drugging him.

"Sorry. It seemed like a good idea at the time."

Then again, if he hadn't tried to stop her from going home, she wouldn't have had to resort to such desperate measures. She focused on the task ahead.

"I'm going to try to figure out what your injuries are, see if any of them are life-threatening." If he could on some level comprehend what was going on, she wanted him to know that she was removing his clothes for a perfectly valid reason.

She tried not to pay too much attention to the strong column of his neck as she unbuttoned his shirt, barely gawked at his wide shoulders, tanned skin, the muscles of his chest and his arms. He was perfectly built, perfectly proportioned, his body all masculine grace and beauty. Not that she was impressed or anything.

She did her best to think of Steve, the weasel who'd broken her heart. She'd thought they'd been in a committed relationship for the past five years. She'd made it clear that all she wanted was marriage and kids, the stability and warmth of a family. And Steve had strung her along, promising all that, but always asking for just a little more time before they got started. Then he moved to L.A. and left her behind like he left his old job and old apartment. He needed to reinvent himself, he'd said.

And then along came Aziz, who treated her like a princess and charmed her so thoroughly her head was spinning. He'd promised nothing and at that point, she appreciated the honesty and, on the rebound, couldn't resist the man. She knew it had been a mistake as soon as the short fling was over. It hadn't fixed anything, hadn't made her any happier.

Then she'd found out that she was carrying his child.

She was petrified that she wouldn't be able to care for a child on her own, like her mother had been unable to care for hers. But not for a moment did she regret this baby.

"That should do it," she said when she had Karim stripped to the waist. She couldn't picture Karim wooing a woman with outrageous gestures. "I bet you're the strong, silent type."

He gave no indication of hearing her. He actually was

softly snoring. Good news, that. Seemed he was just asleep and not unconscious from blood loss.

She wet the towel and began washing him with it. A bullet wound and a couple of grazes. She did her best to scrub away the dried blood, leaving only the area of the bullet hole untouched. That was a deep wound that thankfully stopped bleeding. She didn't want to chance opening it up. He didn't need to lose any more blood. She wished she could find a phone book and figure out the number for an ambulance.

"I hope you won't get an infection this quickly. When you wake up you can call that doctor. You'll be fine."

She bandaged his wounds and left them alone.

She needed more cloth and more clean water to wash him completely clean. There was dried blood on most of his torso. When she was done with the front, she leaned him forward carefully to look at his back. And gasped at the angry scars that marred his skin, a horrific testament to his past.

She couldn't image what could have happened to him. Whatever it was, it seemed a miracle that he had survived. She cleaned off the blood, not so much of it here. Then tentatively dragged a finger over the largest scar, feeling the rough edge that ran down his skin.

She might have been overwhelmed by the dangers of the last two days, but it was clear that Karim Abdullah was no stranger to violence.

She pulled away, resolving again to get away from him at the earliest possibility. But first, she might as well make him a little more comfortable.

KARIM LET HIMSELF sink into the most pleasant dream he'd had in a long time. A woman's soft fingers were caressing his skin. Her touch was as smooth as the finest Arabian coffee and took away the pain that burned his arm.

Her voice was warm and sweet like a honeyed treat he was particularly fond of. Her scent of jasmine and vanilla invaded his senses. Her fingers ran down his chest. The dream disappeared for a while then came back again. She was touching his back now, very gently. He was aware it was a dream, even as he dreamt it. No woman would want to touch his scars, no woman would willingly look at them. But he pushed reality away and pulled the dream closer, not wanting to let go the sweet comfort of it.

The dream faded again and other images came. Pain. People dragged him over cold, hard ground. He was a child now, kidnapped and beaten when he had tried to run. The men who dragged him talked openly of killing him, of dividing the price his own stepbrother put on his head. But they decided to beat him first to pass the time and to teach him a lesson for having tried to escape. They used a camel whip to peel the skin from his back.

But that light, feminine touch brought his dreams back from the dark past. Slim fingers placed a cold cloth on his forehead and washed his face. A soft torso pressed against his midriff as the woman leaned over him.

And as sleep wore off, his body awakened. Instincts warred. A part of him warned of danger. Another part wanted to forget about everything else and take all that softness that moved around him. Jasmine and vanilla. Arousal washed over him as he woke, and a sudden awareness. On reflex, he caught the slim wrist that had been the first thing he saw, a hand rising above him. Then he rolled, pinning the woman under him.

In the next second two things registered: the pulsing pain in his arms, and that the person looking at him wide-eyed was Julia Gardner, the woman who possibly carried his brother's child. *Off-limits*.

But just now, his brain still slow from drugs and sleep, he couldn't deny that he wanted her, wanted her with a fierce need he hadn't experienced in a long time.

The room was shrouded in semidarkness. Dusk was settling outside. She hadn't turned on the light. Smart. Her intelligence had never been in question. Her stubbornness was the thing that had gotten her in trouble.

He pulled away and sat up, his mouth as dry as the *Rub Alkali,* the Empty Quarter, the deadest part of the desert. His limbs were still weaker than he would have liked, his movements not completely steady.

Memories of the hotel room and the attack flooded back. "You poisoned me." The words came out on a rasp of outrage. He cleared his throat.

Her eyes grew huge for a second, then she looked down, away from him and backed up a few more steps.

He glanced around. They were at Aziz's palace. "How did we get here?" His memory had some serious gaps when it came to the last couple of hours.

"I drove. You gave directions. Sort of."

He reached up to his arm, to the bandage. So she had

helped. Tried to kill him then changed her mind? "What have you done?"

She moved farther away. She wore a pair of men's linen pants and tunic, the soft material clinging to her figure, the straight front of the shirt stretching over her full breasts. The sight did nothing to dampen the arousal left behind by his dreams, arousal that he tried hard to ignore. Apparently, it was possible to be spitting mad at someone and want her at the same time. A damn inconvenient situation.

"I'm not going to be your prisoner." She raised her chin and looked him square in the eye at last.

"And you're prepared to kill me to get away?" He pinned her with a hard look. "Because it is my duty to protect you on my brother's behalf. A duty I will not betray."

"I didn't poison you. I was trying to put you to sleep long enough to get away from you."

"You rendered me useless before my enemies." He kept his anger in check. Barely a touch of it showed in his carefully controlled voice.

"And if the tables were turned? How would you feel if *I* kidnapped *you?*" She used typical women's logic.

But the suggestion did inspire a brief fantasy. He shook his head to clear it. He was a man. Their situation could not be compared. He didn't need protection.

He had, when he was a child, he thought then. And felt again that sense of hopelessness and desperation, the stark fear of his childhood. He hadn't had that dream in a long time. It brought back some dark memories. But it also made him understand a little why she wouldn't like the feeling of helplessness, the idea that her fate was in someone else's hands.

"You are not my prisoner. You will not come to any harm." He hoped to set her at ease. She had to accept her fate and stop trying to fight him, putting both of their lives at risk.

"You're protecting me? I was just fine before I met you. Since—" She sputtered with indignation.

"You have a sharp tongue and a strong will that is most unbecoming in a woman." He felt it his duty to point it out. But he couldn't truly mind. She was something to behold when she got all worked up. Those fine eyes of hers came alive with sparks, energy vibrated off her in waves.

"It's a miracle I'm not dead yet," she snapped and made a frustrated gesture.

Her slim hands reminded him of another part of his dreams, and made him realize that at least some of them had to be true. She had undressed him and cleaned him, bandaged his wound.

"If you want me safe, let me go," she said with some vehemence.

"Those men wanted *me*." His statement didn't negate the fact that she had been in real danger. In that parking lot with the car exploding, on the road when they'd been pursued, at the hotel. A problem he needed to solve. Without letting her go. That was nonnegotiable. "What happened has nothing to do with you. Wrong place, wrong time."

"So I would have been only collateral damage. That's a comfort." She gave him the evil eye. "You have no right to keep me here."

Really, she was pushing him too far. "You have no right to decide the fate of a prince of Beharrain. I will make sure that you are safe. I will make sure that you and the baby are well and get the best possible medical care."

She pressed her tempting lips together.

Good. Maybe she'd be quiet and stop fighting him. He needed to deal with other things. Later, after he had a chance to think over this latest attack, after he had taken the appropriate security measures to deal with the obvious step-up in the attacks against him, he would set aside some time and figure out what she would need from him to consider staying. Be it money or any other advantage, he was willing to give it.

He reached for his cell phone, but it wasn't in his pocket. It must have fallen out during the fight at the hotel. Plenty of phones in the palace. He called his head of security, filled him in on the developments, set up a meeting for the morning. They should be all right here for the night. He wanted to stay put until the drug wore off completely. His enemies didn't know he was here. If they did, they would have come after him already. No sense in giving his location away by ordering his men to his side.

When he was done with the call, he checked the bullet wound and decided not to call a doctor to the palace, either. At the moment, aside from his closest people, he didn't trust anyone. He started for Aziz's safari kit that contained every tool for every possible emergency, but stopped in his tracks when he opened the door that led from their room to the rest of the palace.

"What have you done here?" It seemed impossible a single person could cause so much damage in such short a time, but he was starting to learn that Julia Gardner was no ordinary woman.

"The place was like this when we got here," she said defensively.

He shot her a skeptical look. But as he moved farther inside, he realized she was telling the truth. Some of the heavy furniture that had been pushed away from the walls she couldn't have possibly moved alone.

"Looks like someone broke in here." He wondered how long ago. He hadn't been out to Aziz's place in a week since he'd paid off the servants, sent them away and closed the palace down.

"They took some paintings and other valuables. But they didn't find what they were looking for." He walked through the great meeting hall where low, overstuffed chairs and a modern take on the traditional oval, Arab coffee table occupied the middle of the room.

"How do you know?" She came up behind him.

"If they came for money, they could have taken a lot more things." The amber chandeliers alone were worth a fortune. "They were searching for something." He indicated all the overturned furniture. In one place, they'd even chiseled up the marble tile. "They didn't find it and got angry, caused some damage to blow off steam." He pointed at the smashed ebony chest. "Then they grabbed a couple of things so their operation wouldn't be a complete waste."

"What were they looking for?" She moved forward and scrutinized the scene. She was definitely not the type of person to quietly sit in a corner while someone else took care of any problems at hand.

He surveyed the room for a long moment. "If we can find that out, we might be able to find out who they are."

"The same people who want you dead?" She followed him as he walked through the palace, surveying the damage and looking for clues.

He couldn't not be aware of the graceful way she walked, of her feminine presence beside him.

"Most likely." He stopped and took in the stubborn look in her eyes. He had to be crazy for even considering telling her the truth. He had figured he would protect her from that. But Julia Gardner seemed dead-set against accepting any sort of protection.

He hesitated for another long moment. Glanced around one more time, just to delay. They were in the kitchen. Expensive china was scattered on the tile floor. Signs of violence were all around them. Maybe it would be better if she weren't completely ignorant of the how and why. "Take a seat."

She walked to one of the many boxes the servants had packed, and opened it.

He had a feeling she'd do the opposite of what he asked just to spite him, no matter how reasonable a request he put to her. "Suit yourself." He shrugged off his annoyance.

She pulled out some canned food and puzzled over the flowing Arabic script that must have looked like scribble writing to her. "Do you cook?"

He raised an eyebrow.

"Forget it." She mumbled something about rich people and their private chefs.

"I haven't told you everything about Aziz."

Her eyes snapped to his face. She dropped the can back into the box. He had her full attention now.

A shadow crossed his heart. "I have reason to believe that Aziz was killed. I've been working on tracking down the men responsible for his death."

Her face went white. He watched as the fight went out of her, replaced by stunned denial.

"Why would anyone want to hurt someone like Aziz?" She paled another shade.

He stepped closer and put a steadying hand under her elbow, cursing himself for being so aware of the fact that he was half-naked and her clothes hid little of her charms. Jasmine and vanilla. He tried not to breathe. He really was a better man than this, wanting blindly what wasn't his.

She had made it clear that she wanted to be as far from him as possible and was willing to risk her life to get there. The thought stung, so he pushed it away. But could not push away the awareness of how soft her skin felt in his palm.

He was relieved when she pulled away to sit.

"And now the same people want to kill you. Why?" She looked up at him, bewildered.

"You wanted to kill me," he pointed out, smiling at the irony.

"I wanted you asleep. So I could escape." She asserted her previous claims once again, and he was tempted to believe her.

"You drugged me unconscious when we had two assassins on our trail." In his book, that came pretty close to wanting him dead. "What did you think was going to happen when they caught up with us?"

If possible, she turned whiter. "I didn't realize. I—" She fell silent and braced her elbows on her knees, leaned forward to bury her face in her hands.

Her hair was undone, tumbling over her shoulders, cascading to shield her face. She looked lost and fragile just then, bringing out all his protective instincts until he reminded himself that she was more than capable of handling herself. She had rendered him helpless, something his enemies hadn't been able to do.

And yet, she hadn't left. Something to think about.

"You changed your mind. You didn't leave me to them. Why?"

She murmured something like, "I must be too stupid to live."

If anything, she was too smart for her own good, certainly for his. He watched her for a long moment before making up his mind. "You did it for honor," he said. "Because you are an honorable woman, you will do what you must. You dislike me, but you protected me. So you have to understand then why I must protect you."

"Because you dislike me?" She glanced up.

She didn't need to know just how far that was from the truth. "Because honor demands it."

"I hate the whole concept of honor. It's frustrating." She drew herself straight in the chair. "And it's stupid."

"You might hate it, but you have it."

"Well, it's damn inconvenient."

He grinned at her. She was the only woman he knew to swear. He should have been shocked. But to be honest, he liked the starch in her. He could easily see why Aziz had been captivated by her strange personality. *Aziz.*

Had she been the woman of Aziz's heart? Had Aziz planned to go back for her? He couldn't imagine any sane man not wanting to go back for her. For that matter, he couldn't imagine any sane man willing to leave a woman like Julia Gardner behind in the first place.

Perhaps he hadn't known his twin brother as well as he thought he had.

His mood turned dark as he left the kitchen and strode toward the back storage areas, not stopping until he found the safari kit, which had been riffled through, but not destroyed.

He pulled out a bottle of disinfectant and a sheet of butterfly bandages, some sterile gauze, and sat on the floor to take care of business.

"Let me help." Julia kneeled next to him.

And because he wanted to feel her touch on his skin again, despite his better judgment, he allowed her. He sat still as she unrolled the stained strip of linen and poured the disinfectant over the wound, didn't move when she gently rubbed away the dry blood. He clenched his teeth when she massaged the arm so that the disinfectant could dribble as far into the wound as possible.

Burning pain pulsed through his arm, but he said nothing as she finally dabbed away the last of the blood and put the butterfly bandages in place to hold the holes together in the front and the back.

But when her work was done, and she pulled away, he couldn't let her. He reached for her and pulled her against him.

Her gold-brown eyes went wide with alarm. He couldn't do this. He shouldn't do this. *Forgive me, brother.* He brushed his lips over hers. And as though someone had flicked a switch, he felt no more pain.

Her lips were soft and warm. He was aware of her hands coming up to his chest. More than aware that they weren't pushing him away. Nor did they caress him or pull him closer, but in his current state, her lack of resistance was the only invitation he needed.

He ran his tongue along the seam of her full lips and felt the effect straight to his toes. She'd made him feel as wired, as alive, as acutely aware of all sensations as sitting on that car bomb had. But this was so much more pleasurable.

Her mouth yielded under his pressure and he tasted her at last, feeling as if he had lived his life up to this point for that taste. The thought was too startling and too out of character for him to consider just now. So he simply stopped thinking and, going forward, only felt.

Warm. Silky. Sweet.

His.

Every part of him was clear on that. It wasn't so much a surprise discovery as a quiet recognition. And as he explored her with his tongue, he could lull himself for a while longer into going with the tide and not fighting what every cell in his body was insisting was good and right.

Heat gathered in his groin, heat and need. *Take,* a treacherous voice whispered, then demanded. And he was more than willing to listen to it.

His thumb rested against her pulse as he cradled her face in his hand, and he felt the mad rhythm. His own heart matched it. He kissed her over and over again. Pulled her closer. So close he was no longer sure where his body ended and hers began. And it wasn't close enough.

Honor. The single word popped into his consciousness, which was otherwise filled to the brim with the feel of Julia against him.

Hadn't he just preached about honor not long ago? He had to find his own and in a hurry. He stopped the kiss first, separated his lips from hers with great reluctance, then sucked in air. He let her go then stood abruptly and strode out of the damned storage room.

He had kissed her.

And he had wanted to do more. So much more, wanting it so strongly that it scared him.

He was a man of self-discipline. Surely he had more control than that. For the sake of his brother's memory.

And even beyond that, there were the laws of the

country to consider, common sense and decency. If he let things get out of control, he would be forced to marry her.

And the scary thing was, for a man who had sworn never to wed, the thought didn't seem half-unappealing.

Chapter Six

Her stomach comfortably full with whatever canned food they had shared, Julia pretended to sleep, wondering if she were fooling him at all. Her head was so full of questions, she wouldn't have been surprised if Karim could hear her thinking.

He had kissed her.

What had *that* been about? was the first and foremost question on her mind. How could Karim kiss her like that then ignore her for the rest of the evening? Maybe he always kissed like that. The thought bothered her more than she cared to admit. She didn't want to think about him kissing other women.

Aziz had never kissed her like that. Nobody had ever kissed her like that. She hadn't realized there were kisses that could still make your knees weak hours later in the night.

To say that he surprised her didn't begin to describe how she felt. He'd spent most of their time together up to that point snarling at her and giving her orders. He'd always been cool, and solid, collected. She wouldn't have guessed much could make him lose that iron control, certainly not her.

And she would not have, in a million years, guessed her own response to the man. Something really weird was going on between them. The threat of imminent death, most likely. That was the thing that sharpened all her senses. Subconsciously, they wanted to reaffirm life or something like that. Or it could be that her hormones were the culprit. She'd heard a former co-worker say once that after making her tired and pukey for the first trimester, in the second, her hormones made her incredibly horny.

Julia squeezed her eyes together. Oh, yeah. She was there. Hot and bothered. And nowhere near being able to forget the damn kiss. Give her a year or two. She really hated having no control over her body. And she had a feeling it was going to get worse before it got better.

But no matter what her body wanted, she was *not,* under any circumstances, getting involved with Karim. She was leaving. He just didn't know it yet. And she wasn't interested in getting tangled up in another relationship again. She was going to be a mother soon. She was determined to spend her life trying to be a better mom than her own was, to give all the love and attention to her child she or he needed. From now on, the baby was going to be the focus of everything she did.

She'd tried relationships and failed every single time. She wasn't willing to risk continuing that track record and messing up her baby's life. For as long as this kid needed it, she or he would have her full attention.

But that kiss was— She pushed her lips together when they tingled from the memory. She couldn't afford to think about that kiss.

Definitely not now.

But—

No but.

Maybe—

She sighed into her pillow. Okay. In eighteen years, when the kid went off to college, maybe she would look up Karim.

KARIM WOKE to a scratching noise in the middle of the night, out of a very pleasant dream of kissing Julia again. She'd leveled him without half trying. He couldn't afford to lose his head like that again.

He looked at her across the room on the divan, her hair spread across her pillow. She didn't stir. He slowly rose from his own couch. There were plenty of rooms upstairs, but he didn't want to have her in a separate room from him. Didn't trust her that much. And to share a bedroom with her didn't seem right, although they had already broken so many rules of his country. Having her in the same bedroom with him would have meant the same bed. *Don't think about it.* He didn't trust *himself* that much.

The noise came again.

He pulled his gun from under his pillow, held his breath as he listened, caught a brief shuffle that definitely didn't come from mice. Someone was in the back of the house, near the kitchen.

He stole quietly over to Julia and for a second just

watched how beautiful she looked in the swath of moonlight that illuminated her face. She breathed softly in her sleep. It was the first time he saw her relaxed since they had met.

He needed her awake, and kissing her awake was a sore temptation. But he resisted, putting a hand over her tempting mouth. Her eyes immediately popped open and filled with fear as she struggled against him. But a few seconds later, when she finally recognized him, she stilled. He leaned close to her ear, inhaled her scent of jasmine and vanilla. That scent was going to be the death of him yet.

"Go into the bathroom. Lock the door," he said, then added, "No noise."

He didn't remove his hand until she nodded.

As she crept toward the hall, he stayed where he was and snored softly at first then picked up some volume to cover her movements and the sound of the door when she turned the lock. When he knew she was safe, he eased off on the snoring and moved slowly toward the back of the house.

The moonlight that came in the windows hindered him about as much as it helped. He could see, but it also meant that he would be seen. And the furniture was all pushed around and turned over, all strangeness instead of the familiar shadows he was used to.

He kept to those strange shadows and peered ahead in the semidarkness, hoping to spot the source of the noise. Before he could make any plans, he needed to know how many intruders were in the house. And it wouldn't have hurt to know who they were and with what they were armed.

His left arm was stiff. He rolled it a few times, ignoring the pain. He had to make sure to compensate for the arm. Compensating for his right eye had become second nature over the years, not something he ever needed to think about.

He spotted the intruder as the man slipped from the kitchen, moving toward the stairs that led to the second floor. Young and thin, the guy moved without a sound, his sandals barely touching the floor. There was no other sound. And the guy's body language said he was alone. His gaze darted all over the place, expecting trouble from every direction. He wouldn't have been this jumpy if he had backup.

Karim waited until the guy reached the stairs, climbed and disappeared down the hallway above him. Only then did he sneak toward the kitchen, needing to be one hundred percent sure there was no one else to worry about. He wouldn't leave Julia behind until he confirmed this.

But the kitchen was empty, one of the back windows cut out of the frame, cleverly fooling the security system. It monitored windows being opened, the frame moving away from its place. But with the removal of the glass there had been no need to move the frame at all.

He moved faster now that he knew the intruder was alone, thanking Allah for that favor as he reached the stairs. Gun held in front of him, he took the steps carefully. He could see no one when he reached the top. The long hall had doors to the various rooms on each side, the hallway itself widening into an octagonal sitting room at the end. He had no choice but to check the rooms one by one.

He didn't find the intruder in any of them. *Another floor.* Karim headed toward the stairs again and went up and up, disappointed when he found this floor empty, too.

He nearly turned to rush back to Julia, worried that the intruder had somehow gotten by him and might be a danger to her, when he remembered the attic. His own palace was of traditional Muslim design with its flat roof and the single dome over the middle. But Aziz had some fashionable American designer work on the plans of his home, and the man had added that strange foreign roof line that contained an attic that could be, of course, no use at all in this climate, due to the unbearable heat that gathered up there.

Just past the last room, the attic door was a hidden panel that looked like a piece of carved art, a swirling image of verses from the Quran, decorated with geometric patterns. He found it slightly ajar and eased himself inside.

Heat and stale air hit him in the face, and he thanked Allah that the stairs were made of stone because wood would have dried out long ago and the creaking would have given him away. He made his way to the top.

The large space wasn't empty as he had expected. He stared with surprise at the collection of strange things. The first item he walked by was a stone statue. He couldn't make out much. Barely any light filtered up from the partially open door below. He didn't want to turn on the overhead lamps and give himself away. He couldn't see deep into the attic, but as far as he could see, the place was filled to the brim. It was like a very hot, very dry, overcrowded sauna.

Aziz apparently used his attic to store some of his finds from his amateur archaeological adventures. Odd, really. Karim had been under the impression that everything Aziz had found went into Queen Dara's museum. The country's foreign queen had an obsession for preserving the past—the first thing his countrymen had agreed with her about before she had irrevocably wormed her way into the people's hearts with her many projects.

There were crates up here. Not one of them broken, nor any of the statues disturbed. Whoever had ransacked the house below had not been in here.

But the attic did hold an intruder tonight.

Where was he?

Karim peered into the darkness and tried to breathe in the oppressive heat. He moved forward, passed another statue and realized why these never made it to any museum. Most of the statues depicted human shapes, a practice forbidden by Islam. What on earth was Aziz doing with them?

He heard noise from the back and stole forward, spotted the man's dim flashlight. He stayed hidden behind the crates and statues as he moved forward, careful not to make noise. The attic was enormous, spanning the whole width and length of the palace. A few minutes passed before Karim could make out what the guy was doing. The intruder had a sheet of paper in one hand and the flashlight in the other. He was examining the statues, looking carefully at each one before moving on.

He had both hands full and no weapon that Karim could see.

"Stop," Karim called in Arabic and aimed his gun at the man.

He turned off the flashlight at once, enveloping them in complete darkness. They were too far from the entrance for any light from there to reach them. He heard clothes swish and made a grab that way, but caught nothing but air.

He moved quickly toward the exit, knowing the man would head that way, too, not wanting to become trapped up here. He was about halfway when they bumped into each other at a fair speed. The man went down. Karim saw stars when the guy slammed right into his bullet wound, and lost his own balance, toppling forward as well.

"Who are you?"

He grabbed the man tightly, and they rolled on the floor, bumping into crates. He could have shot the guy, but he didn't want to, not unless he had no other choice. More than anything, he wanted answers.

"Who are you?" he repeated.

The only response he received was a grunt.

They rolled again and something sharp burned his side. A blade? He reached out and found that hand, immobilized it, felt the handle of a knife.

He outweighed the intruder by close to twenty pounds, but the man was wiry. And fought dirty, he realized the next second when the intruder bit his neck hard. Karim brought up his elbow sharply, hit the guy on the chin by chance and heard the man's neck snap back. Then his opponent went limp.

Karim secured the man's hands with his own before he dragged him toward the light, down the stairs.

A youth, barely over twenty. He was shaking off the injury by the time they reached the landing.

"Who sent you?"

The intruder was grubby, most of his front teeth missing, his clothes and hair unkempt. He spit at the floor by Karim's feet and lunged at him. Karim held him back, reached for a curtain pull, yanked it off the wall and tied the guy's hands.

"All right. I'll call the police. They'll know what to do with a thief."

The young man went white. Until recently, the punishment for thievery was cutting off the criminal's right hand in the marketplace. Although most of Beharrain's ancient laws were being reformed, a thief could still count on a severe caning and considerable time in prison.

"In Allah's name I beg you for mercy." The intruder fell at Karim's feet.

"When you tried to kill me, was that in Allah's name, too?" He wasn't impressed by the plea. "Who are you?"

No response.

"Who sent you?" He had a fair idea that he was a street boy turned beggar-slash-thief. How would someone like him know about Aziz's attic? He'd gone straight for it, didn't bother with the rest of the house. How did he know there was something of value up there? And what the hell was it? He hadn't grabbed any of the statues. Looked like he'd been searching for something specific.

"I meant no harm. I was to take nothing." He remained prostrate.

"What were you doing up there?"

"I was given money to find something. That is all. I swear to Allah, that is all." His forehead nearly touched the floor, the back of his shirt stained with sweat.

"Find what?"

"Just some stone. Worth nothing. Just to find them, not to take them. I swear to Allah, sheik."

The man probably had no idea who he was, and was only calling him sheik as a sign of respect. Probably would have done anything to get away. But Karim couldn't let him go.

"Why? Who wants to know what is in Sheik Aziz's attic?"

The man stayed deeply bowed before him.

Karim pulled his cell phone from his pocket, opened it and dialed.

"Abdul Nidal from the *souk*," the man said quickly, probably fearing the call would go to the police. "Just to look, he said. Just to look." And he paled when Karim didn't shut the phone.

The call was answered on the other end.

"I need you to come to Aziz's palace and pick up someone here," Karim told his chief of security.

The young man looked up, his face now completely white with fear.

Karim dragged him to his feet. He had broken in, had attacked him in the attic, would have killed him if Karim had been slower. All that for a handful of change, most likely. And he would do it again.

His chief of security would figure out who he was and hold him until they knew for sure that he'd spoken the truth. Then they'd see if the police were looking for him for anything. If so, he would be handed over to face justice. If not… Karim would think about giving him a chance and a job at one of the company's oil wells. The men who worked the wells in the middle of the desert were a tough lot. They could handle him.

Abdul Nidal. He turned the name over in his mind. It didn't ring any bells. Then again, there was no reason why it should. He hardly knew every store owner at the *souk,* the local market.

How was Abdul connected to Aziz?

There was only one way to find out.

"NOTHING." Julia kept scanning the floor.

She had followed Karim up after his security picked up the intruder. Four of his men were now stationed downstairs, guarding the house from further disturbance. They were pretty-grim looking men. Hence her preference for the attic, even though the place seriously creeped her out with its eerie statues. Despite the fact that the light was on, the scene still looked like a graveyard. And it *was* still the middle of the night.

She didn't understand why finding a scrap of paper couldn't wait until morning. Karim was convinced he'd seen some sort of a drawing in the guy's hand when he'd first spotted him, but by the time he caught the man, the intruder had been empty-handed.

Statues and crates loomed in the heat. She tried to stay near Karim, but the whole point was to search different areas of the attic so they could cover ground more quickly. Still, she hated it when he disappeared from sight.

So when had he gone from being a threat—a person she needed to get away from at any cost—to being a point of security for her? Something to think about.

She could not let a single kiss addle her brain this much. But it had been a good kiss. Great. *Beyond great.* She was so busy reliving it that she almost missed the stained piece of paper that had slid half under a crate.

"Found it," she called out, more excited about being able to go back downstairs now than about her find.

Karim was by her side in seconds, taking the crumpled sheet. A careful drawing of four primitively carved statues filled the page, complete with measurements. They were smaller than the ones up in the attic, small enough to be carried by a man, and looked like they might have been made of something different than stone. Their shapes were shaded to indicate color and shine.

Still, they weren't exactly the sort of thing that took your breath away. To her, the larger stone statues of the attic were far more impressive. "What are they?"

Karim shrugged and folded the paper carefully. "I have no idea."

"Can we leave now?" she asked, full of hope. She was exhausted after a tumultuous day. It was about three in the morning. She longed for some more sleep.

Karim watched her for a moment. "You go get some rest. I'll check the crates. I'd rather not involve even my security in this for now. Things like this—" he motioned around "—are controversial in our country's religion. I want to know if Aziz had what our intruder was looking for."

He wasn't the type to quit before he got what he wanted. She'd be smart to keep that in mind.

She drew a deep breath. If he thought she was going back down to his mean-looking guards all by herself, he was nuts. "I guess I'll stay."

He gave her a faint smile, which brought her attention to his masculine lips. And made her wonder what the chances were of repeating that kiss before she somehow broke away from him and made her way home. Probably not very high.

But he didn't walk away from her. "You were scared."

She didn't respond. Of course she was scared. She didn't normally have criminals breaking into places where she was sleeping. And thank God for that.

"I wouldn't have let him get to you." The words were firmly spoken.

She believed him. He was a tougher, harder man than she had ever met before.

And she relaxed fully, finally, realizing only now that the panic of huddling in the downstairs bathroom not knowing where Karim was or what he was doing, not knowing if some assassin was going to kick the door in and shoot her between the eyes the next second, was still there, and that it had settled into her muscles. And when she finally let the fear go, her limbs began to tremble.

She was such a wuss. He was a strong man, probably as disgusted by displays of weakness as her ex-boyfriend, Steve, had been. She tried to still her tremors as she waited for him to walk away.

Instead, he stepped closer and drew her into his arms. "It's okay."

The comfort he gave felt incredibly good. She pressed closer, against the hard muscles of his wide chest, knowing that she should be moving in the opposite direction. Her goal was to get as far away from him as possible. At the moment, she found that goal exceedingly hard to remember.

His hands came to her back to comfort her. Odd that she would feel so incredibly safe in his arms. It had no logic to it. He was not her ally by any means. He meant to keep her prisoner.

She tilted her head to look at him, brought her hands to his chest like she had earlier to push him away. Her hands stayed where they were, like earlier. She couldn't move them all of a sudden. She couldn't move anything. Not when he was dipping his head and she knew that he was going to kiss her again.

This time she braced herself for the effect and it didn't make a damn difference. He still blew her away. The soft brush of his lips against hers aroused her more than anything any other man had ever done to her.

Insane.

Impassioned.

Impossibly good.

A lot of *I*s. There was another one, one that she wasn't going near with a ten-foot pole. *In love*. If there ever was a man who could drag her down that perilous road again, it was the one who could kiss like that. But she did stupid things when she was in love. Handed over her heart and let it get stomped on. If she did another round of that, she was afraid she might not be able to piece it back together again.

No matter how Karim Abdullah made her feel, she could not fall for him. A simple matter of self-preservation. Having had the childhood she had, she was good at self-preservation, wouldn't have survived this long if she weren't.

She *would* leave. But not tonight, she thought and gave herself over to his kiss.

JULIA WOKE TO the sun shining into her eyes through the window, and looked around disoriented. She was lying on a sofa in some sort of an office, Karim working on the computer, intent on the screen.

He looked freshly showered, crisp in a clean suit. The sun glinted off his jet-black hair and outlined his wide shoulders. He radiated power even when he was doing something as mundane as sitting at a desk.

She remembered looking through crates in the middle of the night, and some more phenomenal kissing, the memory of which was enough to set her tingling all over. She must have fallen asleep when she had sat down to rest. And he must have carried her down here.

Her first thought was embarrassment, the second disappointment that she hadn't been awake for it.

"Did you find the statues?" she asked.

He glanced up. "Nothing that looked even remotely similar. But at least I know what they are." A shadow crossed his face.

She sat up and smoothed down her clothes then her hair, although the latter was hopeless.

"They were made before Islam." He pointed to the drawings they'd found in the attic. "My people, the Bedu, had a different religion back then. They worshipped idols. False gods. Today, religious extremists call this time *Jahiliah*—a time of ignorance and evil. They do whatever they can to destroy all history and evidence of these ancient religions."

"That's what the statues are, idols?" she asked. She'd never heard of any of this.

He nodded. "Statues of ancient gods. Back then, when people came to the Kaba stone, they placed their god statues there. When Muhammad came to power, his armies conquered Mecca. He purified Kabba of pagan idols, and the sacred stone became the focus of Islam."

"When you say purified, you mean?"

"Destroyed the idols."

"So to find one is rare?" She was beginning to understand why Aziz's house had been searched so thoroughly, why tonight's intruder had been here.

"Extremely."

"I'm guessing they're worth a lot."

"Their worth is indefinable, but they could be never sold or exhibited in a museum."

"Why?" That made no sense at all. Especially not the museum part. The stuff in the attic was definitely museum material.

"Religious extremists consider them the very devil."

"So those are probably the people who are looking for them, to destroy them."

"Destroy the statues and everyone who has come in contact with them, who had any role in their survival at all. People get rabid about this kind of thing. It probably seems strange to you. But here, for some people, religion is a matter of life and death. Some are willing to die or kill for it."

That took a few moments to digest. She particularly disliked the *kill* part. "How do you know all this?" He hadn't had a clue about the drawings when he'd first looked at that sheet.

"I sent a digital picture to the royal palace."

Oh. Well, the king *was* his cousin.

"Queen Dara identified the statues. What that woman doesn't know about Beharrain's past isn't worth knowing."

How strange, she thought, considering that the queen was born in the U.S. But she was glad that Karim had access to an expert. She wondered if Aziz might have consulted with the queen, as well. Then another, darker thought occurred.

"You think there is a chance whoever is after these statues killed Aziz?" She could still scarcely believe that anyone would want to kill Aziz. Aziz was fun and open and giving. If she had to place bets on who made more enemies between the twin brothers, her money would have been on the Dark Sheik, Karim.

He stood from his desk, his grave expression betraying that he had considered her question already. "I'm becoming more and more sure."

"And now they want you, why?"

"I'm handling my brother's affairs. Since they weren't able to find the statues, they are assuming they've been passed down to me."

He closed his eyes for a moment, his face turning grimmer.

"What is it?"

"You asked after Aziz at the reception at MMPOIL. You were with me in the parking lot, then in the car, then at the hotel. They might think you are involved with this."

"That's insane. I just got here."

"Aziz could have called you to appraise the statues. You could be here to take them to the U.S. Any number of things." He made a gesture of frustration.

"So now they want to get me, too? Just how powerful are these religious extremists?"

His lips flattened into a tight line. "Very."

"And they are coming to get us." Her heart beat in her throat.

"They are not going to stop until they have the statues, and they think we have them."

"But why kill Aziz? Why not capture him and try to get the location of the statues out of him?"

He thought for a second. "They probably thought they knew the location of the statues. They figured if they got Aziz out of the way, the statues would have nobody to protect them."

"But now that they realize they don't know where the statues are, why try to kill you? I mean, if they think you know the location. Wouldn't that be lost if you died? They would never find them."

"They haven't killed me yet," he said darkly. "Not in that chase and not at the hotel. Maybe they were going for capture."

"And the car bomb?" That would have been enough to finish anyone off.

"Remote control," he said pensively. "Wasn't activated until I dove from the car. They wanted to scare me, set me off balance."

"So they want to kidnap you and torture the location of the statues out of you before they kill you?" She felt faint.

His face darkened. "Not just me, I'm afraid. I'm fairly sure that at this stage, they want the both of us."

She thought for a moment. "To be honest, from where I was standing, they didn't look like they were just trying to scare you."

He shrugged. "Maybe not. Maybe they think if they take me out, it'll be easier to get one of my men to talk. I'm sorry that you got involved in this."

She was ready to run for the hills. Her first thought was that he had to let her go now, had to let her leave the country. Her life was in danger here and so was her child's, Aziz's child. She knew he wouldn't be indifferent to that.

But after a moment she realized that if some religious wacko decided to take her out, her simply crossing the border wouldn't stop him. If she'd learned anything from watching the news in the last couple of years, it was that fanatics were more than resourceful and extremely mobile. And even if she left, that would still leave Karim in danger.

She cared only because he was her baby's uncle, she told herself. She had so little family. Really, Karim and the baby were it for now, and the rest of Aziz's family, whom she hadn't met yet. And was in no hurry to do so. If they were anything like Karim, they would want her baby and wouldn't be averse to locking her up and throwing away the key to get what they wanted.

She'd spent years fantasizing what it would be like to have family, people around her that she had a connection to. And now she found some, not a connection of blood, but a connection through her child. Still, a stronger connection than she'd had to anyone in a long time. She'd met only one so far and he was already driving her crazy. And frankly, based upon this initial experience, she was a little scared of meeting the rest of them.

She planned on doing whatever was necessary, in fact, to avoid such meeting and get sucked further into the Abdullah family. Karim was all she could handle. Who was she kidding? The Dark Sheik was more than she could handle. So much more.

And yet she felt obligated to do what she could so the Abdullahs didn't meet a bad end. Family stuff was crazy, she thought, then something occurred to her and she saw a ray of hope at last. Running and hiding would only work for so long. And she didn't want to spend "so long" in this country. She still had her original goal firmly in mind, although her priorities had been reshuffled.

Objective number one: Don't let the crazies capture and kill her.

Objective number two: Get home.

She drew her lungs full of air, wishing she could draw herself full of confidence as easily. They needed a plan. *Think*.

Karim's security could get no more information out of the intruder. They were looking for the man who had supposedly paid him for the break-in. But even that guy might just be another link in the chain and not the one who'd actually put a price on Karim's head.

Okay, here it went. The single idea she'd been able to come up with to get them out of this jam. "What if you found the statues first, and tried to bargain with them?"

Chapter Seven

Karim stared at her. Not a half-bad idea. He liked that she was always thinking—except when she plotted to get away from him—and liked her intelligence. She was the kind of woman any man would be proud to call his wife. Any man who meant to marry. His life was too complicated to allow for that. He funneled his thoughts back to the problem at hand.

If they could locate the statues, they could pretend to bargain with them. He was not willing to hand them over for real. For one, whoever wanted them destroyed would kill him and Julia afterward anyway. Two, he believed in preserving history, whether it was positive or negative, whether he agreed with it or not. Everything had value in life, even one's mistakes. Bad or good, there were always things to be learned from the past.

If he had the statues, maybe he could draw his enemies out into the open with them. Draw them out, identify them, take them out. It was the only way to safety for him, for Julia and her child.

His enemies believed that Aziz had the statues. Having seen the collection in the attic, he was inclined to think that they were right. Obviously, Aziz had found a large pre-Islamic cache he had told no one about.

But someone knew. Aziz's men for one. He hadn't dug out the statues and moved them to the attic on his own. And this Abdul Nidal guy in the *souk*.

He would start with them, Karim decided, and began to plan.

JULIA PACED while Karim made some calls, hating that she didn't understand a word of what he said.

"So?" she asked when he finally put the phone down.

"Abdul Nidal is a disreputable antiquities dealer. His name has been connected to smuggling valuable artifacts out of the country in the past, but there was never enough proof to do anything about it. He is from an old, respected family with connections everywhere. Even the police are reluctant to touch him."

"So there is nothing we can do?" Disappointment tasted bitter on her tongue.

He flashed her an amused look. "I am Sheik Karim."

Then he said something to one of his men, who took off immediately. Next he sent another man away, who returned within ten or fifteen minutes, with boxes of food.

She could have hugged Karim with gratitude as she inhaled the wonderful aromas, saliva gathering in her mouth. Fresh-baked meat, couscous, seasoned rice, fruits and cheeses found their way onto plates.

His men drew back from the upstairs dining room

after setting it right, having picked up overturned chairs and taking out a broken crystal bowl. The two of them were left to eat in private.

Karim seemed preoccupied, but she wasn't sure he'd be in any better mood later, so she pushed ahead.

"I'd like to have my passport back."

"You won't need any identification. While you are here, everywhere you go I'll be with you."

"I'd like to go home. I'm not much use to you in finding the statues. You knew Aziz much better. You'd know better where he hid them. You know the country much better. I would only be in your way."

"You've been through a lot. Rest a few days. We'll talk about this and find a solution."

He didn't mean a word of that, she was sure. He was just playing for time. She hated how unreasonably stubborn he could get. "I have to go back and find another job. I have to pay my rent or they'll kick me out of my apartment and confiscate the furniture." That had been something she'd worried a lot about just a few days ago. Not so much since the threat of imminent death came into the picture. "I have a life back home and the longer I stay, the more thoroughly that will fall apart."

He looked up with an expression that said he hadn't considered that.

"Not everyone lives in their own fully staffed palace." She couldn't help the jab.

"I'll have the apartment taken care of. Just write down the details."

He would? She'd half expected him to say not to

worry about the apartment because she'd be locked up here, a prisoner for the rest of her life. His acknowledging that she would eventually return was a good thing. But he clearly thought it wouldn't happen for a while yet, which was not. "I don't want you to take care of my life."

"If I don't—" impatience made his voice harsh "—you won't have it much longer."

"I'll be safer at home." She wanted to believe that and even succeeded from time to time.

"Will you? Because religious extremists never went to the U.S. to do their dirty business there?"

And she could say nothing to that. The bones in her body seemed to go soft all of a sudden with the thought that he was right, that if these maniacs had set their sights on her, there'd be no hiding from them.

She shored up her defenses against the panic. Those men couldn't want her badly enough to follow her. She had nothing to do with the statues. He was exaggerating. He had to be. He just wanted her scared and compliant so he would get his way.

The words were on her tongue, but she bit them back. If she were to get away from him, it would be better if he thought that she agreed with him, that she'd given up. She went back to her food.

She was just about finished when one of his men came in and said something in Arabic.

"I'll be right back." He stood. "Why don't you stay here and relax for a while."

She didn't respond, only scowled after him, feeling

slightly juvenile. Not that she wanted to be involved in this any more than she already was. As she'd told him, she could be of no use whatsoever. But if he was so sure that her life was on the line, too, he could have at least told her what was going on.

She finished the last of the food on her plate then looked around, took a deep breath. Okay, so Karim had no intention of letting her go. But she had to go, had to go now before the baby was born. Because once her child was born, they would do the test and would know for sure that the baby was Aziz's. Then they would never let her go, or would force her to choose between her freedom and her baby.

An escape now, when she was barely showing, had to be easier than later on when she had twenty or thirty extra pounds on her, or with a baby that she had to hide.

The only tempting thing about staying was the high-quality medical care she would get here. From what she'd seen, sheiks and their families got the red-carpet treatment at the Tihrin hospital. She regretted that she didn't have a job and the health care she could afford from her meager savings was less than stellar. If she didn't succeed in getting work when she got back to the U.S.… She couldn't think about that now. She had to stay positive.

Even if she couldn't get a job right away, everything would be okay. She did have savings. But as a first-time mother, she spent a fair time worrying about what would happen if something went wrong.

She couldn't afford complications.

She pushed her chair back and stood, went to the door to listen. Couldn't hear anything. She opened the door a crack. Nobody seemed to be out in the hallway. She stepped out and crossed over to the end of the railing that looked out over the open space below.

Karim sat on the couch with his back to her. Still, she pulled half behind the wall to her right. She didn't want him to see her if he turned around. Two of his men were standing in front of him. The other two brought a stranger in as she watched.

Karim and his men wore dark suits. The newcomer had traditional robes on and looked decidedly nervous. He bowed to Karim, who offered him a seat, then he said something to his men and they left the room, but somehow the gesture made this seem more threatening than if they had stayed. The visitor must have thought so, too. Julia saw sunlight glint off the beads of sweat on his forehead.

He spoke in rapid Arabic, his eyes shifting to Karim then to the ground, as if he was desperately trying to explain something.

Karim said a single, hard-edged sentence.

Now the man began to protest, his expression wavering between worry and desperation, interspersed with some forced smiles.

Karim asked a question now and then. He didn't raise his voice. He made no threatening gestures. But even so, there was something in his posture, in the way he directed his focus on the man that even made Julia uneasy.

At long last, the man rose from his chair and collapsed at Karim's feet. She couldn't tell from her vantage point if his forehead actually touched Karim's shoes, but it sure looked like it from here.

Then Karim called for his men and stood as they led the visitor away.

He turned, his gaze unerringly finding hers, his face expressionless. Had he known, once again, that she had watched?

Since there was no point in trying to hide now, she stepped away from the wall and walked down the stairs. And realized as Karim walked forward and waited for her—all wide shoulders and intense looks—that medical coverage was not, in fact, the only tempting thing about remaining in Beharrain.

"Who was that?" she asked him as he reached the floor.

"Abdul Nidal. The man who sent that thief in here to look for the statues." He was all business now, all hard angles, focused on whatever plans he was assembling in his head.

"What does he know?"

Karim watched her face for a moment, as if debating whether to tell her or not. Which really galled her, but she kept quiet. Fighting him at every turn would just get his dander up.

"He was contacted by someone who received information that my brother unearthed some valuable items and was asked to locate them."

"Who asked him?"

"The contact was made anonymously, through a carrier."

Her heart sank. She wanted Karim to catch those bastards who'd killed Aziz and very nearly killed her as well. Plus, if he was busy chasing after them, she might have a better chance of getting away. Things would be much easier if both Karim and the bad guys were distracted long enough for her to get out of the country.

Even if she wouldn't be much safer from them at home than here, she would rather face any unpleasantness on her home ground with the full power of U.S. laws and law enforcement to protect her.

"He knew nothing else?" she asked.

"He seemed to think that whoever his customer was, he'd gotten his information from someone close to Aziz. He seemed to have a lot of details about the drawing."

"Do you know who it could have been?"

"Anyone who was there when Aziz made the find. Plus anyone who helped him to move those statues here. He had a regular crew he used when he went out into the desert on one of his treasure hunts." He looked off into the distance. "He was obsessed the last couple of years. First, the king found our great-grandfather's treasures that had been raided from the caravans. Then the king's brother found a whole lost palace." He shook his head. "Aziz was determined that other things were out there, waiting for him. He never lived to see our brother, Tariq, find the last king's hidden hoard of gold bars at his oasis resort in the desert."

"He did have his own find," Julia said.

"That's right." Karim looked up, his face etched with sadness. "I can't believe he didn't tell any of us."

Was that hurt in his voice? Was he close enough to his twin brother that he had expected Aziz to share everything? She had no experience in that department. The last time she had seen her siblings she'd been nine. But losing them still hurt. She couldn't imagine how much it must have hurt to lose a twin after sharing everything for the past thirty years.

"I'm going to start with Aziz's security," Karim said. "They'd been reassigned to the company." And he was dialing already to summon them.

As IT TURNED OUT, Karim and she returned to Karim's own home under heavy guard where he interrogated members of Aziz's security who'd been ordered to report there. She took a bath and ate another little snack while she waited for him to finish. And when he hadn't come to her quarters to give her an update by noon, she went looking for him on her own, finding him in his office.

He looked up from his computer, his full attention immediately focused on her. "Do you have need of anything? Is everything all right?"

And she blinked for a second, because those weren't questions she'd heard a whole lot in her life. Certainly not from her parents, and not from any of the foster families, either. She had a few trusted friends now, friends who were probably frantic not having heard from her for days. But that circle was a small one. She had trouble taking relationships from businesslike and superficial—which she had mastered with the donors at work—to a more personal level.

Odd that despite being seriously annoyed at Karim, on some level she felt comfortable with him, and that had happened with lightning speed. Perhaps because he did remind her a little of Aziz and because he was her baby's uncle, so in that way they were now related.

After all these years she had family. She couldn't help the grin that split her face.

"Is everything okay?" Karim asked her again, with a look of suspicion this time.

He hadn't seen her smile a lot, or ever, she realized. But, hey, that was his own fault. He shouldn't have kidnapped her.

She had a family member who'd kidnapped her. Someone she was ditching at the first opportunity to escape. Another thought occurred to her. Her newfound family was decidedly dysfunctional. It barely dimmed her smile. Even that sounded so wonderfully real.

"I broke the comb in my room. Sorry." She ran her fingers through her hair to indicate what a tangled mess it was. "Could I have another one? I need industrial strength."

He looked at her for a moment then opened his top drawer and rifled through it. Didn't look as if he found what he was looking for, because he moved on to the next drawer after a few seconds.

"Try this." He held up a shiny object before bringing it over. A pick comb, but not like any she'd seen before. The handle was thick and sturdy, decorated with what looked like turquoise, the whole thing as large as Karim's hand.

She couldn't resist taking it. "It's beautiful. Is it... um...gold?" The piece was obviously handmade, with stunning workmanship.

"I helped the Bedu women of my tribe once with the wool trade. Some of them gave their jewelry, had it melted and remade into this as a thank-you gift."

She tried not to think how much the comb was probably worth, or that it really belonged in a museum. She stuck it into her hair and tried to work the knots out. He probably wouldn't want her to remove the thing from his sight.

He walked back to his desk. "I have the name of the man who most likely betrayed Aziz by selling his secrets. When asked specifically, a couple of security guys remembered that one of the oil well workers who also went on digs with Aziz bragged about coming into money soon, an inheritance from an uncle. They didn't think anything of it at the time. I just checked into it." His attention was on his computer screen again.

"And?" The comb worked amazingly well.

"His uncles are alive and well." His face turned dark.

"So he's likely the one then. Track him down and question him."

"His name was Jusuf. He died at the same well explosion as Aziz."

She sank into a chair while she took that in. A couple of minutes passed before she gathered her thoughts. "Do you think that was on purpose? To get rid of any possible links to the man he worked for?"

Karim leaned back in his chair. "I was sitting here

considering the same thing. Aziz had no business at the well that morning. He could have been asked to go there by his enemies for some made-up reason. He must have gotten suspicious, because he called Tariq and wanted to tell him something but not over the phone. Tariq nearly went out there, but then the chopper broke down."

His face turned darker yet, and Julia remembered that Tariq was his other brother. His only living brother now. If not for the faulty chopper, he could have lost both of his brothers on the same day. The thought of that squeezed her heart, brought back the memory of losing her sisters, suddenly without warning, never to see them again.

"Jusuf, the worker we are suspecting, was reassigned to work at the same well at the last second that morning."

"Do you know who blew up the well?"

"A madman who wanted to take over leading the tribe. A half brother, actually. Long story," he said. "But he is dead now."

The hard glint in his good eye said he might have had something to do with it. Julia chilled from the cold expression on his face.

"Everyone thought Aziz's death was an accident. Collateral damage. But I—"

"Whoever wanted Aziz dead could have known about the well being set up and made sure Aziz and Jusuf were there at the right time," she said.

"That would be my best guess. I already put my men on investigating any possible connections."

She closed her eyes for a minute as she ran all that information through her head. That had to be it. They had to be on the right track. She went back to combing and yanked a strand to make it cooperate.

He stood and walked over, held out his hand. "Let me help."

She only hesitated for a second. When it came to her hair, she could use all the help she could get.

She wasn't prepared for how intimate it would feel as he sank the comb into her unruly mane and worked through the knots one slow stroke at a time. The temperature was definitely rising in the room. Odd that she had never felt like this with her hairdresser. Karim affected her in many unexpected ways.

She needed something to distract herself. Talk.

"So, do many Bedu women have hair like this?" She turned to indicate the sturdy comb, pitying them.

His intense expression softened, and a smile came to hover over his lips as he considered her question. "These kinds of combs are used to comb wool. Not this one. Wooden ones. This was a ceremonial gift."

"Wool, as in sheep?" She made a face.

"Sheep, goat and camel. What's wrong with that?"

"I always knew my hair was bad, but I didn't think I was in the sheep, goat and camel category. It's kind of embarrassing."

He laughed. And she couldn't help staring. It was the first time he had allowed more than a hint of a smile. The sound was warm and deep, resonating in her chest. He stopped too quickly, as if he had surprised even himself.

"Any idea where the statues might be? Could they have

been at the well?" She asked the first question that popped into her mind, to dispel the intimacy of the moment.

"Not likely. We've been rebuilding that. The whole area has been worked over. If anything was there, it would have been found by now."

"Do you know the last place Aziz searched for treasure?"

He made a snortlike sound. "It's not like he had a method. More like he fancied himself the Arabian Indiana Jones. Always searching old scrolls, and taking his findings to Dara and—" He froze midsentence.

"What is it?"

"The week before he died, he was up at the royal palace for dinner. We were supposed to go over some company business that night and I was angry at him for cancelling at the last second. What if—" He was dialing already, and spoke in Arabic first, before he switched to English, his face softening. Clearly he was fond of the person on the other end of the line.

"How are you and the children? I trust all is well with the family." He paused. Listened. "And my cousin?" He listened again.

"Yes. Thank you. Nothing serious. I meant to ask you about that dinner with Aziz before he died. Had he mentioned any new finds?" He paused. "Are you sure?" He shook his head. "Any idea in what area he's been digging?" He listened for the answer. "Thank you…soon…yes."

"So?" she asked impatiently as soon as he hung up.

"Aziz spent some time at our grandfather's cave that

the king and the queen discovered not that long ago."
He didn't seem as excited as she would have expected.
If anything, he seemed troubled. "But that cave had
been completely explored. All the treasure from the
cave, which is in the middle of the desert, had been
removed to the National Museum in the capital city,
Tihrin. And there had never been any statues in there in
the first place. The artifacts gained from there were
much newer."

"Maybe Aziz didn't find the statues there. But
maybe he hid the god statues in that place." She was
thinking out loud.

"Maybe. But it wouldn't make any sense. It's not as
if the cave is hidden anymore. The entrance has been
widened and built out. It's a tourist destination for the
locals. Young people go out on trips to see it. I don't see
any way to hide anything there. But I'll go and check it
in any case. I will leave you protected." He handed the
comb back to her. "You're done. I'll be glad to help
anytime." Banked fire glowed in his gaze.

She felt her temperature rise. She held the comb out,
back to him.

"It's yours." He pushed her hand back gently, lingering for a brief moment with his long fingers on her hand.

"I can't. It's too—"

"It's yours. Now you should rest."

What was it with all the rest, anyway? She'd rested
all morning. She was entering that grace period of pregnancy when the nausea and endless fatigue of the first
trimester had left her, but the bulk and all the aches and

pains of the third trimester were still in the distant future. She felt completely well and energized. She didn't need rest. She needed to go home, something she would see to as soon as Karim left the palace. Except he had her passport. She glanced at his suit jacket.

There didn't seem to be a way to get to that. She had only one other option: going to the American embassy and requesting a new one and their help along with it. Her plane ticket was for a week from now. She didn't want to linger in this country that long. But she was sure they could assist her with that, too.

She felt a brief pang of guilt for deserting Karim in the middle of this mess. But she had nothing to do with it. She had gotten dragged into all this, quite against her will. Her first duty was to her baby. Everything else came second to keeping her baby safe.

"What if whoever is after you is watching your palace?" She didn't want him getting hurt.

"I'll have some delivery made. I'll be leaving in the delivery guy's clothes and car."

Sounded like a plan. "Good luck. I think I *will* rest." She walked to the door. When she turned, Karim's gaze was on her, a speculative look on his face.

She pressed a hand to her abdomen.

The look instantly switched to concern. "I'll have the doctor check on you again. I'll make sure she'll stop in every day while I'm gone."

She took a last long look at him. The thought that she would miss him sounded too crazy to consider. She walked out before she could feel even more guilty about deceiving him and did or said something stupid that would betray her plans.

She hurried down the hallway and didn't slow any when she'd gotten inside her rooms, which were a mess. Karim had a carload of clothes delivered for her, and she hadn't gotten around to picking a personal maid yet and hadn't had a chance to sort everything and find a place for it all to be put away. At this stage, it was something she didn't need to worry about.

She had plenty of other things to occupy her mind, thank you very much.

To get to the embassy, she had to first get out of the palace. Which would be impossible on her own. But Karim was leaving. And his men wouldn't be searching his car. He was going on an expedition, which likely meant he'd be taking lots of equipment if he meant to be digging. The perfect opportunity for one small woman to hide among them. She'd leave at the first red light they stopped for.

She put the comb on the desk in the corner. She couldn't take that, she thought with some regret. Never in her life had she owned something so beautiful. It was too valuable a gift. And it would only remind her of Karim.

She pushed him from her thoughts and braided her hair to keep it out of the way, looked around at her new belongings and chose comfortable slacks and shoes. At the last moment she then grabbed a black, nondescript *abaya*. She should be able to make her way safely to the embassy in that.

She was about to put it on when someone knocked

on her door. She shoved the *abaya* back into the pile. "Come in."

The door opened to reveal Karim.

"The staff is instructed to take care of you. Anything you want, you need only to request it," he said.

And she nearly asked if that included her freedom.

Looked like he'd read her intention in her eyes. "You'll be safe inside the gates."

She shrugged. Let him believe that she'd given up.

He moved closer, stopped a few inches from her, his gaze burning into hers. The air grew thick between them, got stuck in her lungs. His good eye searched her face. She could smell the scent of his sandalwood soap, could feel the heat of his body. He was close, too close, too intense, too easily reading her mind.

"Don't."

"Don't what?" She played the innocent.

"I don't want you to get hurt. Don't try to leave while I'm gone."

"I won't." And she wasn't lying. She would be leaving *with* him.

He shifted, as if ready to walk away, but stayed where he was, holding her gaze.

Heat gathered between them. His gaze dropped to her lips. The heat dropped to the V of her thighs.

She desperately wanted him to kiss her, knowing it would be the last time. She would be gone by the time he returned from his trip to the desert. She swayed forward a little. He stayed where he was. How disappointing.

"This thing—" he started to say.

"It's not a good idea," she finished.

Not that either of them moved back an inch.

"I don't seem to be able to help myself," he admitted as he lowered his head at last.

She knew how he felt.

But in the next second, she forgot all she knew, the only thing real being the feel of his lips against hers. He was gentle, incredibly gentle as he always had been. But soon a fiercer undertone crept between them, and the heat increased, and he didn't cajole anymore. He took.

She could feel the whole of his need in that kiss, and it shook her, because it said he wanted to take more, wanted to take it all. And in that moment, she was willing to give it, mindlessly losing herself to him.

Then the kiss changed again, to that of possession and branding. He was claiming her. She didn't have it in her to protest.

She was struggling to find any control at all by the time he finished with her, hell, struggling just to stay upright. But before she could even catch her breath, he was leaning low again, and she braced herself for the next assault on her senses.

But when his lips reached dangerously close, instead of claiming her again, they parted to issue a warning.

"There is no place you could run where I wouldn't find you."

Chapter Eight

The plan had been great and it could have worked. The delivery truck had canvas flaps for sides, easy to get in and out of. And since the truck bed sat low to the ground, it wouldn't have been difficult to jump off once the vehicle stopped at a red light. Julia had gotten into the very last crate, a large one right next to the tailgate. It held ropes and a pickax. The only mistake she'd made was not realizing how much equipment Karim meant to take. At the last minute, he'd put a box on her crate. Then a box on top of that. Enough weight so she couldn't push it aside.

Luckily, her crate had plenty of cracks in it so she could breathe. But the pickax dug into her side. Her limbs were going numb. They'd been traveling for hours, and she was thirsty and hungry. She could have brought food and water—there'd been plenty of it in her room—but as she had planned on parting company with Karim within minutes of him driving through the palace gate, she hadn't. She had to go to the bathroom so badly her eyes were crossing.

The space was too uncomfortable to sleep, too small to move. She hadn't cared back when she'd gotten in, just considered herself lucky that there was enough room for her. She hadn't known that she would be spending hours in there. Now she cursed her rash decision.

She'd been rash because she'd been desperate. She'd been desperate because of Karim. The way his kisses made her feel notwithstanding, he'd been nothing but trouble since she'd set eyes on the man. And how dare he kiss her, anyway? She had plenty of time and felt plenty miserable to have worked herself up to a good, righteous anger. To hell with Karim, she thought just as the car stopped.

Kind of lurched to a stop, actually, rattling her in the crate. Had they arrived or was something wrong? Desert bandits came to mind. The receptionist at the Hilton had warned her about them, after giving her some flyers at check-in that listed all the fun activities one could do in Tihrin, including guided desert tours. Apparently, there'd been recent attacks. Which hadn't bothered her much at the time, as she hadn't intended to do any sight-seeing, especially not in the desert. Her plan had been simple: get in, see Aziz, get out.

The door on the truck's cab slammed shut.

She listened for voices as she grabbed for the handle of the pickax.

"WHAT ARE YOU doing here?" Karim growled as Julia awkwardly climbed out of one of the crates with a pickax in her hand.

She moved slowly. Her legs had probably fallen asleep. She looked a little peaked all around, her full lips parched. "Fighting for my freedom," she said, looking very much like a woman on the edge.

Did hormones do that? Make pregnant women utterly unreasonable? He hoped so. Didn't want to think that she would be like this *all* the time. She could be the mother of his nephew, after all. But, by Allah, she was a lot of trouble, more perhaps than she was worth. And for a moment, he couldn't understand what Aziz could have possibly seen in her.

Then she raised the pickax and her eyes flashed their golden-brown depths, her amazing hair having come undone from its braid, flitting in the breeze. And he had to admit that even as unreasonable and disobedient as she was, she was magnificent.

"Relax." He took the ax from her.

"When we stopped, I thought maybe the bad guys caught up with us. Or you ran into bandits."

So the ax hadn't been for him. Good to know.

"I saw tracks in the sand. This is the last place where Aziz had been digging. We're in the middle of the desert. People come out now and then to see the cave, but not that often. The tracks could be meaningful, maybe. I didn't want to run them over. I want to look at them and see if I can figure out anything." Now, however, he was considering turning around and taking her back home before he did any investigating out here at the cave at all.

Except, she looked as if she could use a break. The

long drive back was more than she should be subjected to right away. He swore under his breath then carefully swooped her into his arms and carried her into the cave, into shade, keeping his eyes on the tracks that looked a few days old on closer inspection. Two cars, a handful of men. No sign of anything having been dragged out of the cave.

She wouldn't put her arms around his neck, but she leaned against his chest to balance her weight. She felt light in his arms, too light, making him wonder once again if she was eating enough.

"How are you feeling?"

She lifted her head and flashed him a scathing look.

Apparently, she felt good enough to fight him every step of the way. She thought she fought for her freedom. He bit back an annoyed remark. Then paused. If their situations were reversed... A crazy thought. He was a man, a sheik. He did not need anyone's protection, while she was obviously in desperate need of it.

He could have put her down as soon as they were in the cave, but he walked to the back with her, not wanting to let go. She felt fragile pressed up against him, bringing out protective instincts. Her full breasts were plastered against his chest, bringing out another response altogether. He wanted to kiss her again, wanted more, but the scowl on her beautiful face warned him that this might not be the best time.

He placed her gently on a large, flat rock. "I'll bring you some food and water."

She was looking around with a disappointed frown. "This is Aziz's cave?"

"The antechamber, so to speak." He brought a bottle of water from the cooler his cook had packed, and handed it to her.

She drank deeply, then looked around again. "Where is your security? I thought you would bring at least two guys. Two could have fit in the truck's cab."

"One man came in the delivery truck, so the least suspicious thing to do was to have one man leave in it. If I jammed the cab with security personnel, whoever is watching the palace would have known something was not right. And I wanted to leave as many men behind to protect you as I possibly could," he said with some exasperation.

His response seemed to give her pause, but she recovered pretty quickly. "Are you sure your enemies won't figure out that you left the palace if they don't see you move around for a while?"

"I put the word out that I'm recovering from a gunshot wound."

She fidgeted. Bit her lip. Shuffled her feet on the ground. "I have to go to the bathroom."

"You can go behind the rock that tops off the cave." He had driven around it to make sure the area was empty on all sides. They were alone. "Don't spend too much time out in the sun," he added, then turned from her and walked outside to unload the truck.

She seemed to be all right. They were already here. A preliminary search through the lower chamber of the cave shouldn't take more than an hour or two. At least he would know what he faced when he came back later. He might need more tools. It only made sense that he looked around while she rested. Time was not to be wasted. The sooner he got to the end of the mystery of the idols, the sooner she would truly be safe.

He brought in the crate she'd been hiding in, moving awkwardly due it its sheer size, appreciating that the temperature was twenty degrees cooler inside the cave. He glanced around the cavern, which had been expanded to accommodate visitors. He'd never found this part of the cave particularly impressive. He was on the third crate when she joined him, carrying a canvas bag.

"I don't want you to lift anything heavy."

She rolled her eyes. "It's bread and dried food."

He took the bag from her nevertheless.

She walked away from him, looking at the sheer stone walls, the path to the corner and the hole that led to an underground chamber of the cave, a sole rope dangling there for support.

"I'm guessing that's where we are going."

Did the thought scare her? Good. "You should have seen the place before it was remodeled. King Saeed, who discovered the cave, said the way down was a rabbit hole carved in the rock. You squeezed through dark passages that led to small enclosures barely large enough to sit up in. There you had to find the opening of the next tunnel, excavate it and move forward."

She looked suitably impressed.

"Anyway, I'm going down there. You're staying up

here." He headed out for the last crate that held equipment he figured he would need even for a quick look around.

"And if somebody comes?" She stared down the hole, into the darkness, her shoulders tense.

He slowed and considered. Somebody *could* stop by. Even if they weren't the people who wanted them dead, there could come a party of young men, the kind who sometimes drove deep into the desert for drunken parties their fathers wouldn't allow at home since alcohol was illegal in Beharrain, as in most Muslim countries. She would be up here alone—

He had made plans for her. Left her under guard. Safe. Of all the insane things she could have done— Frustration made him stop what he was doing and turn around. "Why are you here?"

"You have my passport," she said evenly, as if she were being completely reasonable.

Stubborn. She was exceedingly stubborn, that was what she was. He had made a mistake by not taking that into consideration, by assuming that she would heed his words at least to a degree, because she was a woman and his sole intention was to protect her, and not the least because he was a sheik and everybody else heeded his words. Damn.

"I'm a little scared staying up here alone." She looked away.

And he could tell that it cost her to admit that.

"Don't worry about it. I'll stay right here until you rest, then I'll take you back home. I can come back here later."

"Tomorrow?"

He nodded. By the time he got back to his palace, the day would be pretty much over.

"It would cost you the whole day," she said, sounding dismayed.

He shrugged. It couldn't be helped.

She looked down into the darkness again. "I could go down there with you. I'm not completely helpless, you know."

Far from it. She'd outsmarted him and had gotten out of his closely guarded palace without anyone catching her. "I don't think it's advisable in your condition."

"I don't have a condition." She scowled. "I'm not sick. I'm pregnant." She had stubborn written all over her face.

"Can you climb rope?" He indicated the hole against his better judgment. In truth, if she got tired, he could carry her down on his back. She weighed nothing.

"Can you act insufferably imperious?" She drew herself straight in response to his challenge.

She was funny.

He was not.

He'd had few light moments in his life, was aware that he'd grown up to be a harsh man, hadn't questioned it much. Until now.

Aziz had liked to joke. Strange how the same childhood experiences could form two very different men. Aziz sought to make up for his bleak past with jamming as much adventure and excitement as possible into his life. Karim couldn't forget. He coped with the past by being involved in the law-making process in what little time his corporate job at MMPOIL left him. As sheik, he had input into the judicial reforms, and he took advantage of that to make sure that what his stepbrother had done to his family and his country, could never happen again. His only entertainment was the occasional trip to the camel races.

He wondered what Julia would think of that. She'd find his life unbearably boring, no doubt. She was stubborn and feisty, but by Allah, with all that wild hair and that determination in her eyes, she was a sight to behold. He couldn't help the smile that tugged up the corner of his lips. And she smiled back in response and visibly relaxed, and something passed between them, a moment, a sort of understanding.

He realized that until now he'd been too angry at her for stowing away to see that she'd been scared. Of the desert? Of him? She'd be smart to be cautious on both counts. But she had no cause to be scared of him. Allah only knew what nonsense her head had been filled with, growing up in the West.

"All I wish for is your safety." Maybe if he said it enough times, it would reach her at some point.

She gave no indication that she believed him, but at least she didn't fight his declaration, either. "Let's go," she said.

"I'll go first." He lifted a sack that had been filled to the brim with essentials and clipped it to his belt. "It's about fifty feet down. If you need to stop and rest at any time, let me know."

He found the hole in the rock for the safety line and put in a pin and attached a second rope. Then he sat on the edge of the hole and grabbed the original rope that was fastened to a steel stud someone else had driven into the rock. He shifted his weight onto the rope carefully. It was a sturdy piece and held. When he was a couple of feet down, he turned his flashlight on and let it hang down his belt, pointing to the cave floor below, then called up to her to follow.

He watched as she came over, moving gracefully, and caught up with him in no time.

"Everything okay?"

"Perfectly fine," she said.

When they got halfway down and she hadn't called for rest yet, he stopped on his own. "You can put your feet on my shoulders and take your weight off your arms."

"I don't have to. I'm okay."

"Humor me."

"You already have that bag hanging on you."

"I can handle it."

"So why can't you believe that I can handle it?"

Stubborn. He could be that, too. "The sooner you take a break, the sooner we can move on."

She murmured something he couldn't catch, but she did move down, and her slim feet came to rest on his shoulders for a few seconds.

"Okay. I'm good now," she said too soon.

He made her rest another minute before he continued downward.

The underground cavern they landed in was ten times larger than the one above. The sounds of running water came from the back, and a small pool came to view as they moved forward on the uneven floor. This was the attraction that drew visitors.

"Wow." She was staring wide-eyed at the area his flashlight illuminated.

He'd had the same reaction the one time he had come down here. It seemed amazing that all this should be hidden under the arid desert above.

"According to Queen Dara, Aziz spent a whole week here not long before his death." He panned the area with his flashlight.

"What did he do?"

Exactly. What did Aziz do in a bare cave for a week? Aziz had never been the introspective, meditative type. He lived for excitement. What excitement could he have possibly found here that held his attention for a full seven days?

Karim had a fair idea. "I think he might have found another passage. When Saeed came across our grand-father's hidden treasure down here, it was such a surprise that nobody looked much beyond it. What they carted off to the National Museum was staggering. It wouldn't have occurred to anyone to look for more."

"Why would it occur to Aziz then?" She cocked her head.

Good question. "He was always studying ancient scrolls. Could be he found some information in those." No way to tell. He'd spent a couple of hours looking for some of his scrolls while he and Julia had stayed at Aziz's palace, but had found nothing. Whoever had ransacked the palace had taken those, along with who knew what else.

"So we look for another passage." Julia was already walking toward the rock wall.

"You can check around the perimeter and see if you find something. If you do, do not go anywhere. Watch out for large crevices in the cave floor so you don't fall in. Here." He tossed her the flashlight and she caught it.

"And you?"

"I'll get the rest of our equipment down here."

KARIM'S INITIAL estimate of one to two hours for a quick scan turned out to be optimistic. The cavern was larger than he had remembered. They searched late into the evening, with him persevering in getting Julia to take regular breaks, since she refused to leave until they examined every inch of the cave wall. He'd even set up ropes to check higher up all around. They'd found nothing.

"This is it." He rappelled back down to her. "I don't know where else it could be."

She was standing at the water's edge. "Mind if I take a dip before we go back? The ride will take hours yet. I can't believe how hot and sweaty I am."

The images that flickered through his mind froze his hands to the harness for a second.

"Trust me, you would not want to sit close to me for the next couple of hours."

Just because she was an intelligent woman, didn't mean she couldn't be at times utterly wrong. He would have liked to be as close to her as possible. Closer.

"Go ahead." He carried the harness to the area of the

cave where a wall of boulders blocked the pool from view, and considered the trip back to occupy his mind. A couple of hours in the car. And she looked exhausted already. He'd been telling her to rest, but here he was, planning to drag her all over creation for hours yet.

He made up his mind and went to the crate he had lowered earlier because it contained most of his pulleys. As luck would have it, he had wrapped his equipment in his sleeping bag along with a couple of blankets. He had planned to spend a night or two here before he'd known that she would be joining him. They could stay a single night, he supposed, and start on their return journey in the morning, refreshed.

He was blocking thoughts of Julia naked in the water so vehemently, that he hadn't heard her come up behind him and was startled when she asked, "Do you have a towel I could use?"

She hadn't even undressed yet.

He could get her there. In seconds. About three would be enough. Instead, he drew a slow breath, removed a towel from the crate and handed it to her. "Here."

"Thanks."

He shouldn't have turned to watch her walk away, but he found himself leaning against the crate. She took his flashlight with her, the swinging light outlining her silhouette. She wore her slacks and tunic, her shapeless *abaya* discarded at the top of the cave. She wouldn't have been able to climb the rope in that.

He couldn't look away until she disappeared behind the boulders. Then he pulled over one of the dozen cave lights he had strategically placed on the floor, and began to set up the few supplies he had. Since he'd planned on spending only a couple of nights—alone—he had brought little.

He was done and sitting on their bedding by the time he heard water splashing at the back of the cave. He clenched his jaw, his hands going still on the food bag. He drew a deep breath, looked up in the direction of the ceiling he couldn't see. The lights he had weren't powerful enough to light the whole cavern all at once. They'd been working in sections. "Take your time. We'll stay the night. You need your rest. It's too hot out there for another long ride," he called out to her.

She didn't respond. Probably didn't like being told what to do, yet again. He couldn't afford to worry about that. His first priority was to protect her and her child.

He closed his eyes and tried to picture Aziz in this cave, what he had found and how he had found it. Images of Julia Gardner naked in the water kept breaking in. She was beautiful, strong, honorable, smart. He wanted her, there was no denying that. He wanted her and was jealous of Aziz that he had found her, that she had fallen in love with him, that she was carrying his child.

"Karim?" Her voice reached him from a distance.

He opened his eyes, and for an insane moment held his breath that she might ask him to join her in the pool. The hope of it alone was enough to make his body harden. "Yes?"

"I think I found something."

SHE WAS OUT OF the water by the time he reached her, and partially dressed. Her tunic came to midthigh. She hadn't put on her slacks yet. He tried not to stare at her shapely limbs and failed.

"What is it?" He dragged his gaze upward at last.

"Look." She squatted and pointed at the rock with her flashlight where a hole had been drilled about the width of a finger.

He squatted next to her to examine it, looked around and soon found another.

"Do you think it's marking something? What do you think it means?" she asked.

He knew exactly what it meant. His mind was moving a mile a minute. "There was a hook for a rope here, and a backup rope." He peered into the water then stood to shed his shirt, shoes and socks, leaving only his pants. He slipped in.

"There's an undertow there," she warned when he had resurfaced. "That's why I grabbed on to the edge and my finger slid into the hole."

He stood right in the undertow and felt the wall of the pool with his hand. Solid rock. Then he extended his right foot forward and felt a crevice. He dipped under, and found a tunnel that started on the pool's floor and was about three feet wide and tall. He couldn't get to the end of it, the flow of water working against him, carrying him out. He gave up after another moment and broke the surface for air.

"I think I found an underwater passage. That's how this pool is fed. The water is coming from there."

"Did you bring scuba equipment?" She glanced up. He still had crates on the truck he hadn't removed.

"Everything but."

"You can come back another time."

He wasn't going to turn around without giving this a serious try. He pulled himself out of the pool and brought over two ropes plus a helmet with a waterproof light attached to it. He fastened that on first, then set the ropes up and secured himself before slipping back into the water. "Hang on to this." He handed her the end of one of the ropes. "One tug, I'm okay. Two tugs, pull me back."

"I don't think—"

"This could lead someplace."

"Maybe Aziz had proper gear."

"But the people who hid those statues hundreds of years ago didn't. If they could get through so can I."

"Hundreds of years ago, the cave could have been dry. Don't things in the earth shift over time?"

She was right. But still, he had to try. "I'll come back." And with that, he took a deep breath and went under.

He could see much better with the light on. The tunnel was slightly smaller than he'd previously judged, but as far as he could tell, he wouldn't have to worry about getting stuck. He kicked away with all his strength, swam against the current, pushing against the tunnel wall with his feet.

He pushed again, got jerked back and realized his rope had gotten caught on something. He had to turn around to free it, losing a few feet as the current pushed him back. Using all his strength, he kicked away.

Nothing but water and rock for as far as he could see.

Had Aziz been here? Were those screw marks by the pool his? Other possible explanations came to mind now. Maybe after they'd emptied the cave of treasures, the archaeologists had dredged the pool. He hadn't followed the proceedings closely, knew most of what he did from the media.

He wondered if he'd been in a full minute yet. Time had stopped as soon as he'd entered the tunnel. It seemed he'd been here long, too long already. But that couldn't be. It didn't seem he'd gotten all that far. He pushed forward again.

Rock and water. *Push.*

His lungs began to burn. He spotted some sort of obstruction ahead. He would just go that far and see if that was the end of the tunnel, if it narrowed down so much that passage was impossible. That way, they would at least know this was a dead end.

He held his breath and moved forward until jagged rocks protruding from the bottom blocked his way. Only one way to figure out if he could get through. He pushed through them carefully. The space was impossibly small now, his air all but gone. He shoved his body forward. He would give this a good try then yank on the rope and between the water pushing him out and Julia pulling, he should be back in the pool in no time.

Unless Julia had taken her passport from his wallet, climbed up the rope and was even now driving the van away from here. He shut the uneasy thought down.

Some of the rocks were loose, he realized, and tried to

roll one out of the way with little success. Had Aziz blasted in this section so that nobody could come back here?

He twisted and his rope got caught again. No, not the rope, he realized after a moment as protruding rocks scraped his side. He'd gone too far.

And now he was stuck.

Chapter Nine

Without having a watch, it was hard to tell how long he'd been underwater, but it sure seemed like a long time. Julia glanced toward her sandals at the other end of the pool, her wristwatch on top of them. She considered running over there and grabbing it, but she didn't dare let go of the rope in case Karim signaled that he needed her help.

Her best guess was that more than two minutes had passed since he'd submerged. Had to be more than that. She tugged on the rope tentatively. It gave. Too easily. And she knew without a doubt that there was nothing on the other end.

Maybe the rope had gotten tangled and Karim had to cut himself free. She tried the security rope. That one didn't give at all, stuck. She yanked as hard as she could. All she got were rope burns on her palm.

"Karim!" she called, knowing he couldn't hear her, getting panicky now. "Karim!" She yanked frantically at the rope.

He was overbearing and bossy and very difficult to deal with. There'd been a time when she would have been happy to be rid of him, but now she wanted him back. His stubbornness aside, he was a good man, he really was. He was honorable, he cared for others, he stood on the right side.

Dozens of images flashed through her mind. Some had to do with the way he had protected her from the assassins, others with the way he had kissed her. She let go of the rope and slipped into the water as she was, not wanting to waste time taking off her clothes. "Hang in there," she said to the water.

She couldn't give up without trying to get him out.

THE FIRST THING he heard over the ringing in his ears when he broke surface was Julia yelling, "Where have you been?"

The first thing he registered was relief that she was still there. He grabbed on to the side of the pool and gulped air, trying to catch his breath.

"What happened to your ropes?" She was in the water with her clothes on.

Had she jumped in to pull him back?

"Had to cut one when it got tangled." He helped her out then dragged himself up on the rock next to her, still breathing hard. "The other one I tied out as a lead line."

She stared at him, her face awash in the remnants of fear then relief. She cared whether he lived or died. That came as a surprise. He would have thought the only thing she cared about was getting away from him.

She had tried to save him. The wet clothes plastered to her tempting body were a testimony to that. And it hit him suddenly what could have happened to her, venturing into that passage without a rope, without anyone watching out for her.

If he had gotten out of the water on the other side, if he had tarried instead of coming straight back… She could have gotten stuck. She could have…

He stood to shake off the gut-wrenching feeling that came from that thought. And when she stood, too, still visibly shaken, he couldn't help taking her into his arms.

He could feel the rapid beating of her heart against his chest, and he held her until it slowed, a moment passing between them, an understanding of what they could have lost. He *hated* the thought that he could have lost her just now. How easily he could have lost her a number of times since she had walked into his life.

"Lead line to where?" she asked after a while as she pulled away, curiosity having replaced fear in her eyes. Trust her not to overlook a thing.

The tension in his shoulders eased and he grinned. Because what he had found was so unbelievable he couldn't help himself. "Another cavern."

"Are the idols there?"

And now that the tension of what could have happened leaked out of the moment, he registered nipples protruding under her wet top, and got momentarily distracted. Of course, the helmet light was still on, spotlighting whatever he turned his head toward. He reached up and turned it off. "The place is too big. I need more lamps."

"I'm coming, too."

Again, hard to focus with those perfect breasts not two feet from him. Deep breath. "No."

"You might need help."

He needed a lot of things right now. None of which she would willingly give, he was betting. "I won't."

"You lost your rope."

"I had backup."

He considered telling her to take her clothes off before she caught a cold. But the air in the cave was a comfortable temperature. And truth be told, Julia Gardner without clothes was more than he could handle.

She was glaring at him, pursing eminently kissable lips. "My baby's father died for whatever is in that cavern. I'm coming."

He drew another long breath, sobered by her mention of Aziz. "Were you in love with my brother?" Suddenly, it was important to know.

"No. I—" She closed her eyes for a second.

He nodded, feeling immeasurably lighter, then feeling guilty about it. "I won't be long." With some luck.

"I can come after you anyway. You can't keep me here." She flashed him a *so there* look.

Technically, he could. He could tie her up, worst came to worst. But he didn't want to. Truth was, he had an idea that something extraordinary waited on the other side of the passage. And he wanted to share that with her.

He didn't dare closely examine that piece of insanity.

"Fine." He would have liked to argue further that it wasn't safe, that she should be careful in her condition.

But her condition hadn't slowed her down so far and, Allah knew, just mentioning that word to her was dangerous enough. The tunnel wasn't too bad now that he had cleared the obstruction. They should be able to get over to the other end relatively fast with the help of the lead line he'd left.

His gaze dipped to her breasts again. Damn, that was it. He looked up with effort. "Get packing," he said.

"THERE ARE VISITORS at the cave."

Mustafa paged through a religious newspaper as one of his men reported over the phone. He had his followers patrol all of Aziz Abdullah's latest digs. They had searched them thoroughly, finding nothing. But he hadn't given up yet. He had a strong, holy purpose and it gave him strength to see the task through, no matter how difficult it was becoming nor how long his mission stretched out.

"Who is it?"

"I don't know. I can only see the truck. Should I go in?"

"No." Mustafa dropped the paper and rubbed his burning eyes. "What kind of truck?"

"Delivery. White and yellow."

His fingers tightened on the phone. The only vehicle that had left Karim Abdullah's palace in the past twenty-four hours had been a white-and-yellow delivery truck.

"It's him." His pulse quickened at the knowledge of how close he was to his prey now. Karim was out in the middle of the desert. Possibly alone. Only a single driver had been reported leaving with the truck, although he couldn't be sure that some of his men hadn't hidden in the back. Still, the number of guards he could have taken was limited.

"I could go in and find him," his man offered.

"Wait outside. Report if anything changes. I'll be there as fast as I can."

He couldn't trust his man to take care of Karim. Karim was a true warrior, a worthy adversary. Mustafa stood. He would bring backup. And he couldn't trust his man with the idols, if they were in there with Karim. Those idols had corrupted two eminent sheiks already. Who knew what power they had over lesser men?

Only he should be the one to handle them. Allah had chosen him for that glorious task.

JULIA'S CHIN was hitting her chest as Karim lit the last lamp and the full magnificence of the new cavern was finally revealed. The water that fed the pond she'd bathed in did, indeed, come from here. An underground stream broke the rock high above her, creating a stunning waterfall before collecting into the larger pool at her feet that was connected to the pool in the cavern they'd come from.

Next to the fall, black rock rose up as far as they could see, its dark color a contrast to the rest of the cave. As Karim directed a lamp at it, the stone sparkled.

"Some kind of granite," he said.

But her attention was focused on the niches carved out of the granite, four perfect indentations, six inches wide and about a foot tall, overlooking the pool. Each niche held a carved and painted figure she couldn't quite make out from the distance. They were situated so they would be at the focus of attention, everything leading toward them, even the odd undulations of the rocks, the cracks in the ground and on the cave wall.

But as Karim raised the light and panned it, she realized that those cracks and other shadows were not random, nor were they natural. Man-made patterns decorated nearly every square foot of the cavern. And as she looked down at her feet, she realized that the lines she stood on, too, were part of some bigger whole. As she walked forward, following it with the lamp on her helmet, she realized she was moving through a garden.

Pictures depicting plants of all shapes and sizes covered the floor, some with familiar leaf motifs, others she'd never seen. Animals hid in the grass and behind bushes. Trees towered on the side with exotic birds sitting among the braches. All of that faced the four niches. And all, from the smallest parrot to the largest tree, seemed to have this awed feel to it, as if they were in the process of worshipping.

The closer she got to the granite, the thicker the air felt, heavier. She stopped, feeling like an intruder at an ancient, secret ceremony. She felt a distinct sense of being pushed back and down, to the ground. "What is this place?" She couldn't raise her voice above a whisper.

Karim stood completely still, in that warrior readiness state of his she'd seen before. "A pagan temple."

She could believe it.

"And that?" She motioned toward the granite rock

with the four carved images that appeared to have some human features. They looked similar at first glance, but upon closer inspection, she could tell that two were definitely male and two female. They had large, round eyes painted in white that took up most of their faces.

"I'm guessing those would be the idols. See that?" He pointed up to a circular hole in the wall above the four figures, at an empty niche she hadn't noticed before as it was well above eye level.

"What do you think was there?" The drawing from the thief who'd broken into Aziz's palace only depicted the four idols.

"I don't know, but look." He went to the back of the cave.

She moved over to him.

"The patterns seem to come in stripes." He pointed to the ground and the cave walls. "Connected to the niches like sun rays." He walked forward several feet.

She examined each picture they walked over, and the farther they went, the more she understood what he meant. There were definitely several themes here. The first section was the darkest and scariest. She hadn't come back this far before and now noticed that the "forest" she had stood in had disappeared. The shadows were deeper, the rocks more jagged. The drawings resembled weapons and twisted limbs and torsos, faces distorted in pain, bones, in places piles of them.

She moved closer to Karim and stuck to him. "What do you think it means? Could be a warning to anyone who violates this place." Kind of like Indiana Jones and the Temple of Doom, she thought and shivered when she remembered that the last person who'd been here before them, Aziz, was now dead.

"I don't think so." Karim turned toward the darkly glittering granite. "It's all connected to that first niche, to that god statue that's in there. I'm guessing he might have been the god of war or something like that."

Could be. She moved out of the "war zone" as quickly as possible.

The next swatch of images seemed like an ancient city, a jumble of mud brick dwellings. She felt easier treading among those, until she noticed a large dark circle to her right. Karim caught her gasp and moved that way immediately.

"Charred rock. Something has been burned here."

"You think Aziz—"

"My brother might have been only an amateur archaeologist, but he would have known not to violate a find. He would not have camped here and lit a bonfire." He squatted and ran his finger over the dust and ashes. "This is much older. Not just the ashes of one fire but many."

They moved on to the next section, but the geometrical patterns of this she could not begin to recognize. She looked at Karim. He simply shrugged.

The last section, belonging to a goddess, encompassed the waterfall and the pool, leaving little room for drawings. But, although the available surface was much smaller, the ancient artist or artists had been determined to overcome that handicap; not a rock was left un-adorned here. This was the magical forest she'd seen when she'd first looked around. The picture was teeming with life.

"The Garden of Eden?" she asked.

"You could say that." He moved forward. "I'm guessing this quadrant belonged to some goddess of fertility."

That explained the appearance of human forms as they neared the pool, always in pairs, always touching.

He stopped at the edge of the water. "This could be where they performed fertility rituals."

And the way he looked at her suddenly sucked the air out of her lungs. Thinking about Karim and fertility rituals at the same time, and looking at the suggestive images all around them, was scrambling her brain big-time.

"Um. Okay." She stepped back too quickly and almost slid into the water.

Karim steadied her elbow. And kept his hand there.

"So I guess we can go back then." She slipped away from him, hoping that if she moved beyond his reach, maybe her brain cells would return to work.

"I think we should sleep here." He watched her.

"Here?" Her voice positively squeaked.

He pointed at the pool. "Water." Then toward the area where the charred circle was. "Fire."

"Earth. Air," she finished for him. "The four elements."

His first response was a smile. "Feel that?"

"What?"

"The air. There is fresh air here. A flow of air. Which means there might be a small opening to the outside. It's dark out there right now, so we can't see anything. Tomorrow morning when the sun comes up, we could see where the air comes from."

"And?"

"If air can come in, maybe sunshine can, too. Maybe it will illuminate some portion of these drawings that will give us a clue to the round item that is missing. I want to be here at first light. I want to see where sunshine falls when the sun is highest in the sky. I'd like to see what the last rays illuminate in the evening."

"We can't sleep here," she protested weakly.

"I have some waterproof bags. I'll bring our sleeping bags and some food over. You pick a spot."

She so didn't want to. But she looked around anyway. Definitely not the *valley of death,* she thought as she looked toward the quadrant that belonged to the god of war. The drawings of the city would have been fine, save that large charred circle. She didn't want to think what those pagan priests might have burned in their sacrificial fires. She felt uneasy about the geometric patterns of the third quadrant since she didn't understand them. They looked positively psychedelic. Which left her with the quadrant of fertility and love.

And Karim.

"Listen—" she began to say, but he was slipping into the water already.

She didn't dare move from the spot until he came

back ten minutes later. He pushed himself out of the water next to her then pulled a large bag after him.

The first thing he pulled out of the bag was his wallet. He took her passport out and handed it to her without a word.

She didn't understand why he was doing it, or why now, but wasn't about to question him. She took it without a word.

He held her gaze for a long moment. "Let's settle in for the night," he said.

"What do you think the missing item is?"

He shook his head. "Something of religious significance. Beyond that, I don't have a clue. Could be a chunk of meteorite. A ball of gold. An uniquely sized gem." He considered. "But probably not. I can't image a gem the size of a basketball."

"You think, whatever it was, Aziz took it?"

"We have to consider it likely."

"How do you think the bad guys knew what those idols look like?"

"Aziz probably made the drawing. He probably showed it to someone he shouldn't have."

She was only too aware even without the reminder that the idols peering at them in the semidarkness of the cave had been the death of Aziz. "And if we find the fifth component?"

"We'll take it with us, along with the others."

A gust of cold air ribboned through the cave as Karim spoke. Julia wrapped her arms around herself, feeling the chill of her wet clothes for the first time. And she shivered.

THE PLACE UNSETTLED him and mesmerized him at the same time. The same could be said about the woman sleeping next to him.

Karim watched her face in the light of the sole lamp they'd left burning. She had asked that they didn't turn off all the lights, and he was fine with that.

She whimpered in her sleep. What she'd been through since she'd met him—a car explosion, a car chase, being shot at—would probably give her night-mares for years to come. He sincerely regretted that. He wanted nothing more than to keep her safe, her and her baby.

She whimpered again, but while he debated whether to wake her from the dream or not, she opened her eyes on her own and after a moment they focused on him.

"Bad dreams?" He willed himself not to move closer. He'd nodded off, too, when they first turned in, and had seen his own share of dark images of a fight to the death, blood and destruction.

"I dreamed about the city."

"Baltimore?" It came as no surprise that she would be homesick.

But she shook her head. "The city drawn on the cave floor. I was running through the streets and people were chasing me."

"Who?"

"I couldn't tell. Dark figures. But I knew if they caught me, they would kill me." Her voice weakened on the last words.

He did move closer then, but stopped short of taking her into his arms. "I would never let that happen."

She still seemed shaken, and leaned toward him, looked up into his face. "Want to hear something strange? I had one of those robe dresses on."

"An *abaya?*"

"Kind of, but it was a lot fancier. Kind of sheer." She looked embarrassed as she said that. "And there were other people around, not a lot, but enough. I ran through some kind of a market. They were all looking at me."

He reached to her face to smooth the hair out of her eyes, intending only to skim her cheek if that. But she reached up and held his palm to her skin.

"Karim—"

Her eyes were dark and large in the dim light, her face the most beautiful thing he'd ever seen. He wanted her, had wanted her from the first second he laid eyes on her. For a moment yet, he fought the overpowering pull. Then he gave up the fight and kissed her.

Her mouth was warm and soft. A brief brushing of his lips over hers wasn't enough, just as skimming her cheek with his fingers hadn't been enough. And in that moment when she opened for him, he knew with clarity that nothing would ever be enough but having her fully, forever. She would have to be his wife and her child his own.

He put all that into the kiss, hoping she felt it, too, hoping she wouldn't put up too hard a fight while he tried to convince her.

She tasted like honey-cured figs, of which he'd had

copious amounts in his childhood. Now, like then, he couldn't get enough.

A deep fog of pleasure saturated his mind as he explored her mouth with his tongue, as he ran his fingers down her back, over her slender curves. His hand strayed to her abdomen, hesitantly, unsure how she would feel about that. But once again, she reached for him and held his palm over the life that was growing inside.

Something shifted behind his breastbone, and outside him, too, maybe. The air did seem to change in the cavern, hazier, thicker, as if some sort of an enchantment had descended over the pool and the flat plateau next to it where they had set up their sleeping bags.

He could almost swear he could smell the flowers drawn on the rock, and could hear the chirping of birds over the sounds of the waterfall that seemed quieter than earlier. An illusion, no doubt, because at the moment Julia was filling all his senses.

Their clothes seemed to fall away without much effort. There was not an awkward moment, not a doubt in him, just the sure knowledge that this was it, she was it, this was right.

When he moved over her, she parted her lean thighs with a smile, sighed in contentment as he tasted every inch of her skin. Time lost meaning. He spent a couple of years with her enlarged breasts that seemed extra sensitive.

Then out of all that easy pleasure a sense of urgency began to grow, and her body opened for him, accepted all of him, surrounded him with tight heat. They moved together to the sound of the water, swallowing each others' moans.

When her body contracted around him, he felt more than just his control shatter. They floated away on twin tides of bliss and satisfaction to a place from which he never wanted to return.

THEIR PASSIONATE lovemaking had been, in many ways, like a dream. Julia was still under its effects the next day, could barely believe it had been real as she was waited for a ray of light to penetrate the cavern's darkness.

The lights were off, so as to more easily spot the arriving sunlight. They talked. About the statues and old religions, about everything but what had happened in the night. And she was grateful for the darkness that made it impossible for Karim to see her face.

They had made love. And something between them had changed.

She wasn't going to ignore that. Ignoring never made any problems go away. But she needed some time to gather her thoughts. She was about to address the issue when Karim announced that the daylight was pretty much gone outside. And since there had been no light coming in, that meant that there were no cracks in the rock above them, no ancient, hidden signal to show them any new clues. They should be going back.

"Back, back? To Tihrin?" Relief flooded her. The cavern seemed different today. Colder. Darker. Somehow ominous. She'd gotten the distinct feeling that they had outstayed their welcome. When Karim slid into the pool, she didn't waste any time following him.

"It's more comfortable driving at night. The air is much cooler." He grabbed on to her hand and ducked under.

She followed him.

The way back was a lot easier than their way in, the current pushing them forward. She was breaking surface in less than a minute.

She got out and walked toward their equipment, intended to help him pack, but he stayed in the pool. "Are you bringing the idols over?"

"Just our things." He paused for a moment. "I think we should leave the idols here."

And strangely, some of the tension she'd been struggling with all day suddenly lifted. "Good idea." She felt that without a doubt. Now that she'd seen the idols, she didn't think they should bargain with them. They would have to come up with a new plan.

"Take a break. I'll be back in a minute." Karim slipped under the water.

She put her pants back on and borrowed a dry shirt from his bag then began picking up his tools, thinking about the strange night and strange day they had spent here. She could see their truck in the moonlight, parked in front of the cave's mouth exactly where they had left it.

She wasn't about to try and lift any of the larger crates, but she figured she could take small things over— a coil of rope, a couple of lamps. But when she put her hand on the truck's door handle, it wouldn't give.

Karim would be here in a minute.

But then a hand grabbed her shoulder from behind, and someone spoke harsh words near her ear she didn't understand, in a voice that was definitely not Karim's.

Chapter Ten

They dragged her aside, out of sight of the cave's opening, and Julia could see the beat-up Jeeps now, two of them, filled with enough dents and scratches to make her think they'd seen their share of desert battles.

"Julia?" Karim was calling for her from the cave.

The hand that stunk like tobacco tightened around her mouth, half covering her nose, too, making it difficult to breathe. She struggled only briefly before she felt something cold at her temple and gave up.

"Listen, I think—" Karim fell silent when he came into view. He went completely still, taking in the situation.

She had a pretty good idea what he saw. Her with a gun to her head and who knew how many men behind her. They hadn't allowed her to turn around.

The man who held her spoke in rapid Arabic. Karim didn't respond, but his face was getting darker with every passing second.

Since her captor still wouldn't let her mouth go, she couldn't say anything. She tried to communicate with her eyes. *Do something. Don't mind the gun. Don't let them take us.*

And for a moment, she saw Karim's muscles bunch, his powerful body shifting smoothly into a warrior's stance. More guns were cocked behind her. Her captor pressed the barrel of his gun to her skin so hard it hurt. People shouted.

Karim still hadn't said a word. But she could tell when he made his decision, a shadow shifting across his good eye. She did her best to groan out a *No!* as he lifted his arms to the side in a sign of surrender.

Two men came from behind her, carefully, rifles aimed at his heart. One strode behind him and shoved the rifle into the middle of his back, hard. Karim swayed, but two more slams were needed before the guy could send him to the ground, to his knees.

The other guy took Karim's car keys, and moved to his truck with two other men to search through it. They had probably already searched the cave. Ransacking the truck took them only a few minutes. When they came back, angry that they hadn't found what they were looking for, they wrestled Karim's hands behind his back and tied them.

Another strode into her view, an older man, his gray beard reaching to his paunchy abdomen. His robe was made of a finer material than the others', stark black, his bearing measured, despite the fact that his face was red with rage. He directed most of it at Karim and barked questions at him, one after the other, angered even further when Karim wouldn't respond.

At last, the man gave up and stepped toward Karim, fingered his wet hair and shouted something. Two guys ran up from behind her and disappeared into the cave.

At the same time, the men who held her thrust her forward, shoved her into the back of one of the cars. And she could finally see all the men, dressed in traditional robes and a full headdress, leaving nothing but their eyes showing.

Her hands, which had been simply twisted behind her, were getting tied now. Tight enough for the rope to scratch off some skin.

Shouts came from the cave, Arabic words she didn't understand. Then all the men ran in there, save two that stayed to guard them, their rifles aimed to shoot. Karim remained silent, and she followed his example. Twenty minutes passed and her arms began to ache from the un-natural angle the ropes twisted them into.

She couldn't take her eyes off the cave, waiting for the men to return, growing more and more uneasy when they didn't. Another twenty minutes passed. She became certain now that the men had found Karim's ropes and followed them to the pagan sanctuary on the other side of the underwater passage.

When the first man came out of the cavern with wet clothes, her heart sank. Then came the next and the next, the old man walking out last, cradling two idols in each arm like a mother cradling two sets of twins. But instead of love, hate burned in the man's eyes.

One of his men ran to him with a brown sack and he transferred the statues, his gaze scathing when he looked at Julia and Karim. Then he gave a brief order to his men and got into the first car. Karim was dragged over and shoved into the backseat.

"Whatever happens, I'm going to find you," he called back, and that earned him a smack with a rifle in the back of the head.

The car she was in followed the first. That was good. They were going somewhere together. But she had few illusions, knew they were in the hands of murderers.

She spent the first half hour of the ride in sheer panic, and it wore her out fast. She had to get a grip. Maybe she could distract herself by taking stock of the situation.

They'd been captured. But they hadn't been hurt. Yet.

Maybe the old man had a special plan. That didn't bode well for them. Or maybe the people who captured them wanted information on the fifth idol and thought Karim and she knew about it. She blanched at the thought of what they would be willing to do to get it.

She had nothing but the clothes on her back, no weapons. She could only guess the same about Karim. Her hair, too, was still damp from the pool, her braid unraveled. The water dripping from it had soaked her shirt. But the air was hot enough to dry it in another few minutes. And none too soon. She didn't miss the way the men were eyeing her top as it clung to her breasts.

The thin material didn't leave much to the imagination. Probably the reason they hadn't bothered to search her. It would have been great luck if she'd had anything, even a paring knife, but unfortunately she had nothing.

Which meant if she were to get her hands on a

weapon it had to come from someplace else. Like her captors. She spent the rest of the trip surreptitiously observing them.

Three men were in the truck with her. Three with Karim, plus the leader with the idols. Another man drove the delivery truck behind them. They were all armed as far as she could tell, with AK-47s and knives. She didn't think she was ready to handle a rifle just yet, but if the chance presented itself to get her hands on a knife, she would take it.

The drive seemed to last hours. The sun was getting high on the sky, the heat nearly unbearable even with the breeze moving through the doorless Jeep. She felt faint, her lips parched, sand gritting between her teeth by the time she spotted a town on the horizon.

Hope rose in her suddenly, strong and fierce. They were going into civilization. She'd been afraid that they'd be taken to the middle of the desert and summarily executed. But in a town, people would see them. Someone would recognize the sheik. Someone would help. She tried to swallow, to wet her mouth, getting ready to scream her head off as soon as they got within hearing distance of anyone.

Which happened later than she'd expected. The town had been farther than it seemed, the flat, homogeneous sand throwing off her sense of distance.

First she could make out the buildings in greater detail. They must have been approaching on the slum side. The houses were made of mud, in places nothing more than a fraying piece of carpet serving as a roof.

Poverty and a general lack of caring was stamped over everything she saw.

Then the people finally came into view. She leaned forward, caught sight of the unfriendly faces, the hard glares. Ninety percent seemed to be men, only a handful of cowed women here and there in frayed *abayas* who kept their heads down, not daring to meet anyone's eyes.

She had a bad feeling here, something that made her keep her mouth shut. Everyone they passed was armed to the point of overdoing it, ammunition belts hanging off them like garlands from Christmas trees.

The men in the Jeep with her tensed, too, and made sure their own weapons were displayed and their fingers on the trigger. They drove through narrow, winding streets where sewage ran openly, the stench unbearable. The few children she saw looked around either with vacant eyes or scared expressions, most of them with scars over their small bodies.

The heat and the smell were nearly too much to bear. If her hands weren't tied behind her back, her palms would have been over her mouth. As it was, she tried to breathe as shallow as she could.

They drove through a busy market and for a few minutes she lost sight of the other car. Then she breathed a sigh of relief when their Jeep came to a halt in front of a large, disheveled building, and she spotted the other vehicle already there. Empty.

"Out." One of the men shoved her roughly, and she tumbled to the sand.

"Please. You don't have to hurt me. I'll go." She was

afraid of what they would do to her, afraid not only for herself but for her baby.

The man shoved her again, this time through the doorway, then up the stairs, shoved hard even though she had sped her steps. She was pushed down a long hallway, then into a tiny, dingy room with bars over the glassless window. Then the door slammed shut behind her, and she could hear the lock sliding into place.

She waited for Karim. When a few minutes passed and they didn't bring him, she went to the window and looked out over the busy market. A few stands sold food. Most of them openly displayed weapons and what looked like used electronics. Stolen merchandise most likely.

Another ten minutes passed before she was willing to consider that Karim might not be coming. They had been separated. And she had no idea where he was, what they were doing to him. She didn't even know for sure that he was still alive.

THE REST OF THE DAY passed frustratingly slow for Julia, nothing happening but an old woman bringing her water. She had begged for help, to be told where Karim was, for food. The woman looked right through her with the vacant stare of a drug addict. She wasn't impressed by the plight of a foreigner. She looked like she would sell her own daughter for another hit—probably already had.

And she had nothing beyond the water jar, nothing Julia could have taken from her and used as a weapon. But at least she had some water, which she drank greedily, and one piece of new information. There was a guard in front of her door. She heard someone lock the woman in with her, then unlock the door again when the woman knocked to signal that she was ready to leave.

When the sun went down, two men came in, bringing an oil lamp with them. The one with the gray beard she already knew; he had put on a strange headpiece, looking like a leader of some religion. The other looked like all the other men she'd seen as they'd driven through town, a bandit through and through, but better dressed than most.

The old man watched her with naked hate in his small black eyes. The other one measured her up with some interest. She drew back, all the way to the wall, unsure which one to be more afraid of.

The old one spoke first, harshly, spit flying from his mouth, and made one decisive hand signal she couldn't interpret. The other one kept examining her thoughtfully.

The old man spoke again. The bandit responded this time. Rage contorted the old man's face, his full attention on his buddy now, as he protested. Seemed like they were in some sort of a disagreement about what to do with her.

Which suited her just fine. Any delay gave Karim more time to find her.

The old man was nearly shouting now, the other speaking more reasonably as if trying to convince and appease him. Finally, he pulled some money from his pocket, and the man of religion instantly mellowed. He was still shooting Julia hateful glances, but at least he was no longer yelling. He did say something, though.

The other guy looked her over one more time, then asked her one word. "Virgin?"

His accent was so thick she could barely understand. Then when she did, she was too shocked to answer.

"No lie. Will exam."

Over her dead body, she thought, knowing full well that could easily be arranged. She shook her head.

The man nodded. "No need exam." Then turned back to the other man and gave him another single bill, which made the old guy scowl and start arguing again.

She felt faint with hunger and with the realization that she was most likely witnessing her own sale. She had few illusions what for.

"I'm pregnant," she said without meaning to, the horror of the moment pushing the words out.

The man buying her merely shrugged. "Men no mind. If do, we fix."

All the blood ran out of her face, her hands cradling her abdomen, the barely there bump. *We fix.*

Oh, God.

She was, for the first time in her life, scared wordless. She could not utter a single syllable, not to beg, not to protest.

The men barely glanced at her when they left, the old man's gaze still holding hate, the other one's now glinting with satisfaction.

She sunk to the dirty floor when the door closed behind them.

She had come to Beharrain full of hope to find her child's father. But she had already lost Aziz without knowing it. And now she was about to lose everything else: her freedom, possibly her child, her life. Karim.

She wasn't sure when he'd begun to matter, but all of a sudden she knew that he did, more perhaps than any other man had mattered in her life.

Her arms wrapped around her abdomen, she stayed where she was and choked back her tears.

Soon the old woman came again, this time with a chunk of what looked like leg of lamb and some flat-bread. And a dress. Julia ignored the latter but threw herself on the food as soon as the woman left. When she sucked the bone clean, she drank the last of her water. She'd been dehydrated all day, but now that she'd finished off a whole jar of water, she really, really had to go.

She knocked on the door. They had to let her out. No response. Knocked again. Banged. Nothing. The guard had probably been ordered to ignore her. Oh, great.

The room was dark now, the only faint light coming from the waning moon, what little the small window let in. The only things in there with her were the water jar, the lamb bone in the corner and the dress. Clearly, only one of those was suitable for her purposes. She did the deed, praying that she would be able to get out of here tonight, because she had a feeling that would still be the same jar they'd be using for her water tomorrow and she didn't think the drugged-out old crone was going to bother with rinsing it.

Getting out. Tonight. Fed and relieved, she could actually focus on escaping. She was exhausted, but there was nothing like the threat of being sold into prostitution to give a woman a little extra boost.

She moved to the bars and shook them. Since the bricks they'd been embedded in were mud, they wiggled a little, but not nearly enough. She needed a tool. She glanced at the water jar again. Nope. Not going there. Then her gaze settled on the lamb bone. She grabbed it up, ran her fingers over the knobby ends. Not exactly the best tool for digging through sun-hardened mud. She'd have better luck with her fingernails, which were growing strong and long from the prenatal vitamins. She needed something sharp.

Running her fingers over the metal bars gave her an idea. They were old and rough, almost like a metal file. She pressed the bone against one and dragged it along the abrasive surface a couple of times, felt again. Better. Ten minutes of work left her with one end of the bone as sharp as a knife. She scraped her new tool against the mud brick and some flakes of clay dropped to the ground. She smiled.

Then stepped away quickly and hid the bone behind her back when she heard her door being unlocked again.

KARIM LOOKED AT his torturers through the miniuscule slit in his swollen good eye. One more hit there and he'd be completely blind, a deep fear that had plagued him all through childhood.

"Who else knows about the idols?" the old man in the black robe asked again. "What do they mean?"

"Where is the woman?" he asked through bleeding, swollen lips.

They'd been through this script a couple of times. Next came the beating. The play did not improve with repetition.

Predictably, the man on his left slammed the butt of his rifle into Karim's face again. This time it hit his jaw, with nearly enough force to shatter the bone.

As it was, Karim felt his skin split. "I'll tell you everything I know in exchange for the woman." His words slurred through his swollen lips. He had no information to give. Mustafa—he'd learned the name the hard way—knew more than he did, had the fifth item in his possession already. It sat on a low table along with the four idols, a webbed globe of gold, enclosing an ancient human skull.

"I'll tell you everything," Karim said again. For the last fifteen minutes he had stayed alive by pretending that he had information that was crucial to the idols. "For Julia."

"There's no more woman!" the old man shouted, his eyes bulging with fury, the veins standing out at his temples.

Karim saw red, too, and not just from the blood that dripped down his forehead and into his eye. What the hell did he mean, there was no more woman? What in hell had they done to her?

He'd been biding his time, waiting for them to think he'd been beaten enough, waiting for them to let down their guard. One man leaving would have been enough. Or one man taking his damned rifle off him. Then he would move. That was the plan.

There's no more woman.

He rose from his knees with an enraged roar. To hell with the plan.

He caught the guy off guard, and managed to bowl him over. They crushed to the floor in a bone-jarring slam. He couldn't get to the gun at once, had to break the man's neck first. He didn't hesitate.

Nor did the others. Bullets flew at him from every direction. He caught sight of Mustafa from the corner of his eye as the man slipped out of the room; the rest of them were coming straight for him.

JULIA DROPPED her makeshift tool to the floor and stepped on it to cover it up. Whatever they did to her, she was not moving from that spot. But it was only the old woman who came in, with a lamp and a scowl on her face.

She pointed at the clothes she'd brought earlier and yelled at Julia. Apparently, she should have gotten changed.

She didn't want to think of the details of what might happen tonight. Couldn't afford to get bogged down in the sheer terror of that or it would paralyze her and she wouldn't have the strength to do what she needed to do to escape.

The old woman yelled at her.

The dress was in the other corner of the room. She couldn't move there without revealing the sharpened bone, which she was not willing to give up. She shrugged.

The woman hustled over, picked up the dress and tossed it at Julia.

The material was sheer, the golden silk ribbon around the hem and split neckline a little worn, but the fabric was clean. Still, it was such a ridiculous outfit that she held it away in distaste. Just the right thing to do to push the crone over the edge, it seemed, as the next second the woman was coming over, hooking a gnarled finger into the neckline of her tunic and ripping it all the way to the hem.

"Hey!"

The woman glared at her with all sorts of threats in her previously vacant eyes. She was in obvious need of a hit and was going to be as grouchy as she pleased until she got it.

Fine. Julia shook out the dress. If it would make the woman leave, she would put it on. She pulled the dress over her head. *Oh.* It was a lot more sheer than she had thought, leaving little to the imagination. Her bra showed clear through.

The woman clucked her tongue.

Julia wanted her to be gone so she could get back to her work. She could put on her other clothes later. She unhooked her bra and let it drop, crossing her arms in front of her to cover herself.

"Good enough?" she asked when the old crone still didn't look happy.

The woman glared at her slacks.

Oh, for heavens' sake. Julia lifted her left leg first, stepped out then let the material pool around her right foot, so when she stepped out of that side, the woman wouldn't see her secret lamb bone weapon.

And it still wasn't enough. What else did the hag want?

She made it clear when she stepped closer and reached under Julia's dress.

"Stop!" She held her hands out and put as much threat onto her face and into her voice as she could. She assumed the fighting stance she'd seen Karim do. She was *not* giving up her panties.

And the old crone must have understood that this here was the end of the line, because she grabbed the rest of Julia's clothes from the floor with a quick swoop, then disappeared from the room. Since she took her lamp with her, Julia was plunged into darkness again.

One deep breath was all she allowed herself, one second to gather her strength and determination, then another so her eyes could get used to the darkness again. When she could see a little better, she grabbed her tool and went back to work on the mud bricks.

An eternity passed before she got one end of one bar free. Maybe it would have been better to hold her sharp tool to the old woman's throat and hold her hostage, try to gain her release that way. Except she wasn't sure just what the old woman's value might be to her employer. Could be considerably less than the money the guy had just paid for Julia. Which meant, there could hardly be a trade.

She went to work on the next bar, scraping dried mud as quickly and quietly as possible. When she was done, she rattled the whole thing again. It didn't give much more than before. And her fingers were bleeding in three different places where she'd scraped them.

Once, she nearly cut into her own arm when the sharpened bone slipped. But she couldn't afford to slow down. Even at the frantic pace she worked, she wasn't going to scrape her way out, she was beginning to realize, not even if she had the whole night, which she seriously doubted.

They had fed and watered her, dressed her. She had a fair idea what was coming next.

Where was Karim? He had promised not to let anything happen to her as long as he lived. He hadn't come to see her all day. She tried not to dwell much on the thought that chances were good he was already dead.

He couldn't be. She needed to talk to him. They needed to discuss what had happened at the cave. She had to tell him how she felt about him. She had to get out. She had to call for help. She had to do something to save him.

Something scraped against the lock behind her. Were they coming for her already? Her heartbeat sped as the damn lock scraped again.

Here we go.

She faced the door and hid the sharp bone behind her back. The window was still impassable. She had two choices—fight now and be most likely killed, or go on and let them do whatever they wanted to do to her, in the hopes that later, a few days or weeks from now she might be able to escape and at least save her child. Unless they did something to her in the meanwhile that could cause her to lose her baby. *Oh, God. Please, not that. Anything but that.*

She was saved from having to make a choice when Karim burst into the room the next second.

One fleeting moment of hope was all she was allowed. Then she saw the army of bandits behind him.

Chapter Eleven

Karim slammed the door and turned the key he'd wrested from the guard, knowing it would give them only minutes of safety at best.

"Did they hurt you?" His heart thumped as he took her in, noticing the sheer dress. Black rage filled him. They had her dressed for— He didn't want to think that he might already be too late.

He focused on the fact that there were no visible signs of injury on her. Looked like they spared her the torture. And he knew why, and fury swirled out of control inside him.

She was staring at him in horror. "What happened to you?"

And he realized he probably looked like something that had come through the meat grinder. "Nothing serious." He handed her the bag of idols he'd managed to grab, then pushed her behind him and faced the door, holding the rifle, knowing he was dangerously low on ammunition.

Most of the men who'd tortured him were dead, but there were plenty of others in the building to take their place, and their leader in the black robe, Mustafa, was still alive and still wanted his head on a pike.

There were people outside, systematically trying to break down the door. He checked the rifle.

"How many bullets?" she asked from behind him.

"Six."

She put a slim hand on his shoulder. "I want you to save one for me," she said with gut-wrenching courage.

He turned around and saw that she was serious. More than anything, he wanted to draw her into his arms and promise her that everything was going to be fine. But he could make no promise beyond the one he had made before, that no harm would come to her as long as he was alive. Which might not be a long time, judging by how the door was creaking and splintering.

"When I run out, I'll get another weapon," he said.

"I have this." She extended a makeshift bone knife.

He looked at it then at her in surprise. "Good. Use it."

"I was trying for the window but didn't get far."

He moved to examine the bars for the first time. He hadn't paid much attention to them since he'd checked the ones in his own cell before his torture began and they were solid. But here he could see that she'd put serious effort into weakening them.

He handed her his weapon. "Hold this and stand by the door." Then he grabbed the bars and went to work on them.

Movement. There was definite give. He put all his

strength to wiggling the iron rods out of place, chunks of dried clay getting dislodged. He gave it a good shove. Then another. And the first bar came away in his hands. Then the next and the next.

When the hole was large enough to fit his head through, he looked out. There were shacks below, sharpened poles holding up frayed carpets with people settling in for the night underneath. They couldn't jump without risking being skewered by those poles. He looked up. The distance to the roof wasn't too bad.

"Come on." He pulled back into the room and took the rifle from Julia, hooked it over his shoulder and gave her a boost. "We're going up."

He didn't have to explain. She was already scrambling for the roof. He went after her just as the door broke into planks behind them.

"Go, go, go!" He pushed her to the flat clay tiles, grabbed her hand then ran with her. But they ran out of roof too fast, a six-foot gap between their building and the next. "Can you make the jump?"

"You bet." She pushed away without slowing down, which was the exact right thing to do.

He stumbled when they landed, too focused on keeping her with him. She didn't. This time, she was the one to tug him after her.

The first bullet coming from behind made them both duck. Then a whole buzz of them followed, and they jumped to a lower roof where they would be temporarily out of sight. They were at the edge of the market that was still not entirely deserted. A couple of people still strolled among the weapon stalls; others drank with their friends or played games of chance with goat-bone dice.

"What is this place?"

"Yanadar. Town of thieves and murderers." He growled the words as he considered the maze of stalls for a moment before slipping to the ground from the low roof and heading for it, Julia close behind. On the rooftops they had no cover. The maze of the market was what they needed.

A couple of the men loitering around piles of weapons looked up and reached for their guns. But the rifle in Karim's hand and the look in his nearly swollen-shut eye must have communicated his intent clearly, because not one chose to get involved in his business.

They ducked between stalls, ran through a couple, but their pursuers were close behind them, shooting at them at regular intervals. He knew he couldn't keep up the pace forever. They were not going to be able to outrun these men on foot, not when those bastards knew every path of the market by heart and he was half-lost already.

Then Julia tugged him to the right suddenly, and he knocked over an oil lamp as he adjusted course. He ran on without slowing to apologize.

"This way." Urgency rang clear in her voice.

It wasn't as if he had a better idea. She zigzagged through stalls, and he followed her without hesitation.

"What are we looking for?" he asked at the next turn.

She didn't respond for a while, and when she did, it

was with visible reluctance. "This is the market from my dream. There was a car this way."

And before he could even finish thinking how crazy that was, they came upon a beat-up pickup truck with two goats in the back. The driver's-side door was open, the key in the ignition. No owner in sight.

He didn't hesitate but pushed Julia into the car and over to the passenger side, hopped in behind her and took off before even closing the door.

"Which way out?" Maybe her dream had shown her that, too.

But she shook her head, hanging on to the dashboard for dear life as he flew over the potholes in the road. The trouble with the market was that it consisted of a hodge-podge of buildings, makeshift stalls mixed in with mud homes people clearly lived in, and the occasional large, multistory abode that must have belonged to the more successful thieves.

After a few minutes, he got the distinct feeling that he was driving around in circles. Then his choices became limited as he noticed light in the rearview mirror and realized that a part of the market was on fire, stalls going up in blaze. He drove in the opposite direction.

He reached the edge of the desert within minutes and stepped on the gas, following the makeshift road, having no idea where it led. Away from the fire and the men with guns was good enough for him.

For a while it looked like things were working, that they had successfully left their pursuers behind. Then dark spots dotted the sand behind them, and he realized that they were still being followed. Four vehicles, faster than his ancient pickup, were closing the distance.

When they got close enough, he could see that they were all jam-packed with armed men, at least two dozen of them.

He was outnumbered, outgunned and outsped.

He put all that from his mind and pressed the gas pedal to the floor. He knew what would happen when the men got within shooting range. They were out in the middle of the desert without cover. And those guys probably had fifty bullets to every one he had.

He took Julia's hand, sharing his attention between her and the barely visible road. "I'm sorry I dragged you into this. I should have let you go that first day."

She simply squeezed his fingers.

He would have felt better if she screamed at him.

"We don't have long, do we?" Her gold-brown eyes were filled not with fear, but with acceptance.

He couldn't say the word.

"I'm glad I met you," she said.

"I wanted you from the moment I first saw you. I told you that I kept you close to protect you, but deep down, I kept you for myself. I was selfish, and—"

"Last night at the cave was the best night of my life."

That shut him up for a few moments. He didn't deserve her.

"If things were different, I would have asked you to stay. Of your own free will. For me."

Her fine eyes misted a little. "If things were different, I would have."

Joy mixed with pain inside his chest until it felt like bursting, then anger at not being able to do anything about this.

He checked the rearview mirror and for a moment thought they had gained some ground, then realized that the reason he couldn't see the enemy's cars as good as before wasn't because they were farther back, but because the sky was darkening behind them.

"Roll up your window," he told Julia, and did the same.

"What is it?"

"Sandstorm." He wished he could give more gas, but the pickup was going at maximum speed already.

The storm was upon them in minutes, fast as a tornado and just as violent. He stopped the pickup and hung on to Julia while the wind rocked the car as if it were a toy. The sound of tons of sand hurling through the air was unbearably loud. They could see nothing beyond the windshield, had no idea how much sand had piled on top of them, whether they had been buried alive.

"The goats?" Julia attempted to go for the door.

He held her back. "They're animals. They have good instincts." Not that a severe sandstorm had never decimated a herd, but for the most, the animals were better equipped for inclement weather than humans.

He pulled her over to his side, into his arms. He didn't know how long they had, but every minute was a gift. The storm that stopped them would also stop their enemies, of that he was sure.

"I wish it would last forever." She snuggled against his chest.

The pain that still raked his body from Mustafa's torture disappeared as soon as they touched, but a new one was now building behind his breastbone. He was supposed to be able to protect the woman he loved. He pressed a kiss to her forehead, then to her lips when she lifted her head.

Her lips parted, and he tasted her, and felt the full grief of knowing he would be tasting her for the last time. Her breasts pressed against his chest. He locked his arms around her, not wanting to let her go, not ever.

They broke apart only for a moment, only to refill their lungs with air before coming together again. She pressed kisses along his right eyebrow. When he closed his eyes, she kissed his eyelid, then trailed her lips down his scar.

"I want to kiss all your scars," she said.

Not long ago, he would have been happy if a woman could just look at his scars without flinching. But those scars no longer mattered. The darkness of the past no longer bound him. And he knew without doubt that, somehow, Julia had done that to him.

"Forget the scars. I have no feeling in them anyway."

"Where should I kiss you then?" she teased.

"Anywhere you'd like," he said. "But I was hoping we weren't done yet with the lips." He could have kissed those lips of hers forever.

"Make love to me," she whispered into his ear a while later.

That, he could hear even over the storm that sounded like it was never going to stop. And when she reached down to pull her dress over her head, he helped her.

He slid over to the passenger side and she straddled him, her glorious breasts in line with his lips. He drank from them as if drinking life itself, and in a way, he was. She was his life, for as long as he had her.

Each caress, each kiss gained special meaning, was a bittersweet greeting and saying goodbye at the same time. His heart was filled to the brim with love he felt for her, with need that he had never felt for any other woman.

She set his body on fire, and he shoved off his clothes, wanting more than anything to be skin to skin. She lifted up, and he grabbed her hips, sheathed himself inside her tight heat, felt like he'd reached heaven and wanted to stay there forever.

They took it slow. The storm showed no signs of abating, and they both knew that this was all they were ever going to have. Their hearts melted together along with their bodies. He could feel all the darkness that had weighed his life down drift away. There was nothing and no one but Julia.

When the pressure built to the point of being beyond his control, his movements sped on their own, and Julia matched them, her head thrown back, her hair spilling down the sweet arch of her naked back, her breasts thrust upward. And they went over the edge together, then held on to each other for an eternity, until he could hear the storm quiet.

When the wind died altogether, he kissed her one last time, then put his clothes back on and gave his door a good shove. A few more were needed before it gave. He got out and looked for their pursuers. He couldn't see as far as before; there were still trillions of small particles of sand in the air, dimming the sun, making visibility worse. But he could see the men who'd followed them from the lawless bandit town of Yanadar.

They were down to three cars. One had been completely buried in the sand. And when he looked more carefully, he realized another one was at least half-buried. They would have trouble getting that out in a hurry.

He checked on the goats. They were shaking sand off their fur, looking nervous but unharmed. He walked up front and cleared off the windshield, pushing several buckets worth of sand off with his bare hands. Then he got back behind the wheel and gave thanks to Allah when the motor turned over on the first try.

The sandstorm completely covered what little road there had been, so he set out blindly. He couldn't even navigate by the stars as he couldn't see them. But they were definitely in better shape than they had been half an hour ago, he confirmed as he looked into his rearview mirror and saw that only two vehicles followed, overflowing with men, Mustafa in the passenger seat of the first car. Everyone from the buried cars had piled into and onto the remaining ones, adding considerable weight and slowing them down. The good news was that now they were matched for speed with Karim. The bad news was that they still outnumbered him a dozen to one.

It would all come down to who had more gas in the tank. He felt the first touch of optimism when he noted that his was three-quarters full. Then a pang of dismay when the first fat raindrop hit the windshield.

"Rain?" Julia sounded as surprised as he felt.

It wasn't the season for rain. The windstorm must have blown some clouds in from someplace far away. "It does rain, even in the desert. Just not a lot."

Another fat drop followed the first. And within minutes, they were in the middle of a downpour.

He headed toward the tall dunes to his right, not wanting to get caught in a low-lying area. An hour passed before he reached them, navigating by his headlights. The visibility in the dark night with the rain coming down like that was about the same as it had been in the sandstorm. When he reached the top, he shut off the truck. They were going to have to wait this out, too.

"Water," Julia said in a weird voice.

"Yes. Lots of it." He turned toward her and drank in her beauty, wondering how long the rain might last, ready to pull her into his arms again.

"The market was on fire," she said, apparently focused on something else entirely.

He shrugged. "I kicked over an oil lamp."

"The sandstorm. It's wind. Air."

He couldn't really focus on the sandstorm. His mind was filled to the brim with images of what they had done while waiting it out.

"Fire. Air. And now water." Gingerly, she held up the sack that hid the god statues. "Do you think—"

"Coincidence," he said, despite the unease that sent a small shiver down his spine.

"What would earth be? Quicksand?"

"Don't say that." He looked through the windshield, feeling decidedly uncomfortable now.

They waited out the rain in tense silence, each contemplating the impossible. They didn't have to wait too long. When the sky cleared and the stars came out, the rain having washed all the sand out of the air, he got out once again to survey the damage.

He could see nothing where the two cars had been, half a mile behind him in the low passage. Not the top of a car, not a radio antenna, not a single man. But some of the sand dunes on the other side were gone, the landscape rearranged. And suddenly he knew what had happened. Too much rain had come down all at once, the sand unable to absorb it that quickly. The wet sand had run like a mudslide, had buried the two vehicles and all the men inside them.

Not all. He swore as gnarled hands grabbed onto his ankles and yanked him off balance. Mustafa rolled from under the pickup. He must have crawled up to them in the storm unseen.

A curved dagger sliced the air in the direction of Karim's throat. He jerked out of the way. He understood now that Mustafa would never stop until he was dead. In Mustafa's mind, Karim was connected to evil just as Aziz had been, because of the idols.

"You have offended the One God. You must die." Mustafa got to his feet at the same time as Karim. He was between him and the truck, the rifle on the front seat.

Mustafa hadn't brought his. Could be the sand had jammed it when they'd gotten caught in the sandstorm.

Karim could see from the corner of his eye Julia lifting the weapon. He didn't dare to fully look at her, wanted Mustafa to forget all about her and focus on him. He feinted to the left, then lunged forward on the right side, caught the man in the middle and they went down.

Down, down, down. All the way to the bottom of the dune where muddy sand pulled at them. The side of the dune could still cave in and bury the both of them as it had buried Mustafa's last two cars.

He grabbed the man's right wrist, but the old man's zealous hate doubled his strength. Karim got on the bottom somehow as they rolled, the tip of the dagger less than an inch from his good eye.

Careful now.

He rolled Mustafa and they broke apart, then stood again.

Karim could feel every one of his broken ribs, every knife wound they had inflicted on him during his torture. He hadn't had food or water in nearly twenty-four hours. He was unarmed against a fanatic whose sole purpose in life was to kill him.

To the ball of pain that was his body, death might have been a relief.

Except that Julia was waiting for him on top of the dune. Doing more than waiting.

The next second, a bullet slammed into the sand between him and Mustafa. Karim stepped back. Would have been good to know just how good a shot she was.

It didn't matter at the end. Mustafa looked up at her, and the momentary distraction was enough to take the man down. This time, when they rolled, luck seemed to desert the old bastard as his dagger pierced through his clothes and skin, straight into his heart.

When Karim got back to the truck and took the rifle from a trembling Julia, he had her sit back in the cab while he checked around the tires and made sure the soil was stable. He had brushed off what Julia had said about fire, air, water and earth, but he couldn't shake his sense of unease. He'd seen quicksand up close and personal before, and he didn't care for seeing it again.

Looked like they'd run out of human enemies. He didn't want to have to face more of nature's peril on this trip. They'd had plenty enough adventures already.

He got back in and drove slowly, in the direction where the sand looked the most stable. He didn't dare breathe easily until he reached the edge of where rain had fallen and he was back on dry sand again, then on a rocky plateau he recognized. They had somehow gotten back to the area that hid his grandfather's cave.

In a few minutes, when the distinct shape of the rock above the cave came into view, Julia figured out where they were, too.

"Why did we come here? Shouldn't we ride straight to Tihrin?"

"We are putting the statues back," he said.

She offered no objections.

In five minutes they were at the cave, in another fifteen down at the pool in the first cavern.

"I'd like to go with you," she said.

And this time, he didn't argue.

They made it through the underwater passage without trouble—his rope was still stretched in place—and entered the second cavern. They were in complete darkness, had to go by feel.

"Stay right behind me," he said, and felt Julia's slim hand on his back. "The granite was straight ahead."

He walked that way until he hit the cave wall, groped around until he found the first niche. The rest was easier after that. He wasn't sure if he put the right statue in the right place and wasn't too concerned about it. He wanted to be out of there.

"Okay, now the skull." He reached up but couldn't feel the hole the last artifact belonged in. And the granite was a sheer vertical wall, no purchase for his feet anywhere to climb. "I'm going to have to lift you up."

She moved closer immediately. "What do you think the skull is about?" She'd already examined it up in the first cave.

"The skull of a tribal ancestor. Could be of some mythical hero." He handed her the golden piece, a shiver running down his back as the skull rattled inside, then lifted her up.

"I got it. It's in there," she said after a moment. "You can put me down."

He did so gently, passing up the opportunity to pause and hold her in his arms.

The first time they had come here, the cavern was a place of wonder. He had felt comfortable spending the night. Now the air pressed down on him, goose bumps rose on his skin and his only thought was to get out of there as fast as possible.

They stumbled toward the sound of the waterfall and that led them back to the pool. He slipped in first, caught Julia as she came after him, groped around for the rope.

"I got it," she said next to him and held his hand as they submerged.

They went back as quickly as they could. The journey home was always easier.

They didn't hang around in the first cavern, but went up the rope.

"I will talk to the queen and make sure she has the cave locked up and off-limits," he said.

Julia simply nodded thoughtfully. She didn't speak until they were in the car and he was pulling away from the cave.

"How do you know which way to go?"

He understood her question. The sandstorm and the rain had done a good job of obliterating the road. But he had the knowledge of his Bedu ancestors, the knowledge of the desert. "I can navigate by the stars."

They were about half a mile from the cave when the earth began to shake. And they watched in the light of the full moon, stunned, as dunes rose up and others sank, the landscape undulating before them like waves on the sea. He'd been through earthquakes, but never one in the desert.

He grabbed on to her when their car lifted, moving gently up, then down as the earth shifted beneath them. The whole thing lasted less than two minutes, leaving them both more shaken than the sandstorm and the rain put together.

"Are you all right?"

She didn't respond. Instead she was staring over his shoulder.

He turned, reaching for his gun at the same time. But it wasn't their enemies miraculously catching up with them again. It seemed they had been stopped for good, stopped forever, had stayed where they'd been, buried in the sand.

He blinked when he realized at last what Julia was looking at. The giant rock that had marked the cave was gone. Nothing but flat desert as far as the eye could see. He could hear Julia swallow behind him.

"I think that was the earth part," she said.

Epilogue

Five years later

Julia took another handful of postcards from the maid just as Karim strode through the door. As always, he took her breath away. And when he opened his arms to her, she walked into them.

He kissed her thoroughly, then bent to kiss her belly. "How is my little princess doing in there?"

"Impatient to come out. These are for you." Each summer, they received dozens of postcards from the Sibling Link Camp. Karim had donated Aziz's Star Island home to the charity. They, of course, immediately offered Julia her job back, but her hands were busy at the moment with other kid-related projects. She was, however, thinking about setting up a similar program here in Beharrain, had already talked about it to Queen Dara, who had pledged her support.

"How was your day?" She smoothed a dark lock of hair into place on his forehead.

"Good. And it's about to get better." He grinned and kissed her again. "I got an e-mail from the P.I. He traced your sisters to Texas. Looks like they were adopted together."

Her throat tightened. He had hired a top-rated agency to conduct the search for her lost sisters, no expenses spared. He had promised godmothers for their daughter. And when Karim promised something, he delivered.

"Thank you." She smiled at him, her heart filling with love and hope.

A smile hovered over his lips. "How grateful are you?"

She swatted his hand. "I'm too huge to be *that* grateful."

He gave her a tragic look that made her laugh. She kissed him. "I suppose I should show some gratitude." She nibbled his lips. That distracted them for a while.

"Almost forgot. Tariq is ready to show off his twin girls. We are invited tomorrow for dinner," he said when they reluctantly pulled apart.

"I can't wait to see them." The timing all worked out perfectly, her sister-in-law delivering just weeks before Julia was due. Their girls could grow up together. A cramp nudged her in the back. "I wish this kid was out already and *they* were coming to visit *us*," she said as her son, little Aziz, flew across the room and lunged himself at Karim.

"Are we going to the camel races, Dad? Are we leaving right now? I'm ready." He was a bundle of energy, deep dark eyes and dark hair, always ready for adventure. He was a happy child, always a smile on his face, secure in the knowledge that his parents, the rest of his large family and the tribe adored him.

"After lunch."

"I already had lunch. Mom let me have it early. I couldn't wait."

Karim crooked an eyebrow and put on his sheik face. "All your vegetables?"

"All." Aziz's face twisted with distaste.

"Your mom and I have to eat, too."

"You could have *maraq* at the races. You always say they make the best *maraq*."

"Maybe it will rain." Karim was teasing him now.

"Dad, it won't rain."

"What if we have a sandstorm? It's the season for it."

"We are not going to have a sandstorm," Aziz announced, full of confidence. And if he said it, they could believe it. He seemed to have a strange connection to inclement weather. "We could get some sweets after the *maraq*."

Julia smiled at her son, always a wheeler and dealer. She answered Karim's questioning look with a nod.

And her son caught that, of course, and lunged himself at her next. "Thank you, Mom!"

She kissed the top of his head before rubbing the dull ache in her back.

She had been organizing the new nursery all day—not that she couldn't ask the staff to do it. But arranging her daughter's things gave her so much pleasure. She'd rearranged the baby books on the shelves a dozen times, along with the stuffed animals at the foot of the crib; she'd looked at then refolded pink onesies and layette sets. The nursery was large and bright, one of the most beautiful rooms in the palace.

Her new home was a far cry from her cramped apartment in Baltimore. She didn't miss her old life—she was surrounded by love and family here. But she did miss her ache-and-pain-free body. Even a sheik's physician couldn't make that side of pregnancy disappear. She rubber her back again.

Karim immediately looked concerned, reaching for her arm. "Are you going to make it? We could stay home."

She smiled at the gentle way he touched her, at the love that shone in his gaze, her breath catching at the answering love in her heart. "Are you kidding me? She's her father's daughter. She would never interrupt a camel race."

And her smile widened as her firstborn whooped at hearing that.

* * * * *

Don't miss Dana Marton's next fast-paced story of romantic suspense, Tall, Dark and Lethal, *coming in October 2009 only from Mills & Boon® Intrigue!*

SCIONS: REVELATION

BY
PATRICE MICHELLE

MILLS & BOON

Patrice Michelle worked as a financial analyst before giving up her financial calculator for a keyboard and never looking back. Thanks to an open-minded family who taught her that life isn't as black and white as we're conditioned to believe, she pens her novels with the belief that various shades of grey are a lot more interesting. She's a natural with a point-and-shoot camera, likes to fiddle with graphic design and, to the relief of her family, strums her guitar before an audience of one.

Visit Patrice's website at www.patricemichelle.net to learn about her upcoming books, read excerpts and join her newsletter.

To my family, thank you for always believing in me!

Acknowledgements

To my amazing agent Deidre Knight for believing in my writing and finding a home for my books, to my editor Ann Leslie Tuttle for her astute editorial input and endless drive to make the story better, and to Charles Griemsman – the go-to guy for pretty much everything. I can't thank you enough for all that you do!
Thank you to my brainstorming partner-in-crime Rhyannon Byrd for always being there!

Prologue

No one will ever look at me the same again. Caine Grennard's hand shook as he lifted it toward the mansion's main door. Clenching his fist, he focused to calm his rage before he turned the knob. As he entered, the Lupreda sitting in the living room and standing in the hall turned and stared. Every single member in the wolf pack was there now. Only a few had witnessed his fight with Brian.

It had been a great battle—painful and bloody, but satisfying to kick the jerkoff's ass and finally put him in his place. Brian, the surly, ready-to-mutiny Lupreda, wouldn't dare disparage Landon as Alpha Wolf again, at least not in Caine's presence. Yet all the satisfaction Caine had when the fight was over disappeared the moment he realized he couldn't shift back from his dominant werewolf form, known as Musk form among the Lupreda, to human.

Was the pack waiting to see if Caine had gone full zerker—
to see if he was permanently stuck between man and wolf, like
the other three Lupreda in the past?

He saw it in their eyes: the worry, the condemnation. Brian
had the nerve to smirk. Caine wanted to kick his ass all over
again. When Caine's gaze locked with Landon Rourke's, the
Alpha's stoic expression told him nothing. Resentment burned
in Caine's stomach.

Landon uncrossed his arms and pushed his tall, broad form
away from the thick column separating the living room and
the foyer. "Everybody, out!"

The Lupreda scattered, moving so fast that Caine saw only
blurs zooming past. A pair of folded jeans landed with a
thump on the floor in front of him.

He looked up and caught a glimpse of Kaitlyn's red hair
through the rails in the catwalk overhead before she disappeared. Landon's half human–half Lupreda mate was one of
a kind. Only she would anticipate the turmoil and self-doubt
that had festered within him while he'd paced in the woods
for two agonizing hours, waiting for his body to finally shift
back to human form. Kaitlyn intuitively sensed something as
simple as a pair of jeans would help him feel more human as
he faced the pack's leader.

Caine quickly pulled on the jeans and buttoned the fly. As
soon as he met Landon's steady gaze, the Alpha tossed something in the air toward him. Catching the metal, Caine curled
his fingers into a fist around it. The chain felt both hot and
cool against his palm.

"Put it on," Landon said in a hard tone.

Caine tensed and glanced at the silver chain in his hand.
He'd been there, done that. All the Lupreda had experienced

having a thick silver collar locked around their necks to keep them from shifting to wolf form until the Sanguinas vampires were ready to hunt them as prey. Ever since the vampires got sick from humans' poisoned blood over twenty-five years ago, and they'd retreated from their land into exile, Caine had relished his freedom. He swore he'd never let anyone put silver around his neck again. He sure as hell wasn't doing it willingly, even if he was at risk of going zerker.

Clenching his hand around the chain once more, Caine met Landon's steady stare. "No."

Landon's green gaze narrowed. "I won't have you going zerker. You'll wear it if you want to stay here."

If Caine couldn't shift to Musk form on the fly, he couldn't protect his pack. He'd be nothing to his brethren. Useless to his Alpha, the man who'd mentored him all his life. Why didn't Landon see that?

Caine shook his head and flexed his jaw. For as long as he could remember, his faith in Landon as the pack's true Alpha had never wavered—even while Landon had lived away from the pack for eighteen years—yet now that Landon had recently become Alpha, he was the one who would force Caine to leave.

"I guess the decision's made for me." Turning, Caine slipped the chain around the neck of the carved wolf statue sitting on its haunches by the door and walked out of the Lupreda's mansion—the only home and family he'd ever known.

Chapter 1

Why would an alluring smell make me feel so free? Emma Gray wondered as she waved good-night to her boss before pushing the café's door open. Her pulse raced and every nerve in her system worked overtime. She hurried across the street, heading toward the nightclub Squeeze. Despite her social hang-ups, she was finally going into that nightclub. Come hell or high water.

She stepped up on the curb and inhaled, trying to recapture the glorious smell's deep earthy notes, the essence that brought her out here in the first place. She knew if she could conjure it, the scent would help solidify her resolve and calm her stomach that felt like a snake had taken up residence inside, coiling tighter and tighter.

Nothing but car exhaust, lingering hints of rain and alley trash filled her nostrils. Damn.

She'd always had a keen sense of smell, something Jared, her boss at Jared's Java and Pastries café, often relied on. "You think these eggs are still good?" he'd ask as he held the carton under her nose, to which she could accurately predict, "You've got two days before you have to chuck 'em." Jared thought her talent was "wicked uncanny." Emma thought her "gift" was just plain weird.

Until yesterday.

She was cleaning up coffee cups left by some of the patrons, whose lingering musky smell on them made her body tingle all over. She smiled and she didn't know why. But she just felt…exhilarated, like she was flying down from the highest hill on a roller coaster—buckled in and safe, but completely free.

Then, tonight at work, she'd caught the scent again and her heart nearly jumped out of her chest, she'd been so excited. This time the smell had been very fresh—as if the person or persons had just been there. She'd lifted her gaze from gathering the cups in the dirty-dish container in time to see a tall, dark-headed guy leave the café and accompany an auburn-haired man to the popular Manhattan nightclub across the street.

Now, here she was, an hour later, her throat closing as she stood at the end of the long line of people waiting to get inside the nightclub. In the two years she'd worked at the café, there'd been many nights that she'd stared out the big display window at Squeeze's black double doors, wondering what it was like with music blaring and patrons packed inside like sardines. But curiosity wasn't enough to overcome her social ineptitude. She wasn't a sexy siren. Just a normal, average-looking woman, who'd rather talk about the latest marketing strategies being used in businesses today than prove how well she could hold her liquor or how fast she could tie a cherry stem with her tongue. Yep, she'd crash and burn the moment she opened her mouth.

If it weren't for that earthy, musky aroma that had imprinted itself on her psyche since yesterday, she wouldn't be standing here. But she had to at least put a face with the appealing, soul-wrenching scent. Maybe then she could let it go.

Techno music thumped and the crowd inched their way through the frigid, damp air, waiting to be let in. As she waited, Emma noted the distinct difference in her own attire: jeans, bulky sweater and black wool pea coat, compared to the other young women her age. Sporting big earrings, spiked heels and heavy makeup, the girls wore clubbing clothes of tight pants, miniskirts and cropped tops underneath their winter coats.

While they giggled and flirted with the guy manning the door, Emma's insides churned. *These girls have mastered the art. I could never compete.* With each step closer to the entrance, Emma's body tensed to the point she thought she might pass out. *Breathe. They're people, just like you. Well, except for the I-suck-at-flirting-and-idle-chitchat part.*

"You don't look twenty-one," the burly guy at the door said after he'd checked Emma's driver's license to make sure she was legal.

"I *am* twenty-one, but it doesn't really matter. I'll only be in there for a few minutes." She'd always been told she looked young, but was it because she didn't have on any makeup or was it because she wasn't wearing three-inch heels? She was sure her five-foot-six height made her appear much shorter and younger than the girls he normally let in. Even if half those girls were probably three years younger and sporting fake IDs.

"You still have to be twenty-one to be allowed in." Frosty plumes expelled from his nose, reminding her of a dragon.

Emma followed his frown to her feet. Her boots had mud spatters all over them from her jaunt through the woods this morning, looking for Casper. She instantly regretted not changing her shoes before she went to work. Meeting his gaze, her smile turned sheepish. "I'm going for the grunge look."

The streetlight shone on the man's bald head as he scanned her clothes. Crossing his arms, disdain laced his tone. "We have a dress code for a reason."

Emma stiffened and outraged, embarrassed heat shot up her cheeks. She didn't need to be reminded her pea coat had threadbare elbows and a frayed collar or that her jeans were so old and worn they were *naturally* faded. "Are you saying I'm not good enough to enter this club?"

She *had* to get into the club so she could at least see the guy with the innerving scent, even if she didn't speak to him. Maybe his face would ring a bell or something. There were no guarantees he'd come to the café again just because he'd been there two days in a row. Plus, working up the nerve to enter the club was a big deal for her. Seeking out this guy was a perfect excuse for her to finally get a peek inside Squeeze without feeling like she was there on a social basis.

A snotty look crossed the bouncer's thick jowls. "That's exactly what I'm—" At that moment, a thin guy burst through the club's double doors, took a couple of steps and hurled on the sidewalk. Baldy turned to him and growled, "Hey, go puke somewhere else, moron."

When he walked over to send the guy on his way, Emma's heart rate ramped. She didn't have the flirtatious skills the girls in front of her had used to make him wave them in with a lopsided, dopey smile. Instead, she'd challenged the guy. *Way to go, Emma.* Better take the opportunity to quickly slip inside the club while he was occupied.

Inside, the nightclub was so dark, the neon manga murals painted on the walls on either side of the entryway glowed vividly. When the closed door opened with a swift jerk behind her, Emma's pulse jumped. She pulled her pageboy hat low on her head and ducked past a tall guy, moving farther into the room.

It didn't take much effort to be sucked into the crowd; the nightclub was that packed. It was like she'd entered another world, full of drinking, dancing and erotic decadence. Emma was enraptured and invigorated by the laughter, talking, partying and *life* going on around her. And the smells. There were so many: thick, sickly smelling perfume, heavy musk-based cologne, strong deodorant soap aromas laced with sweat…all were mixed in with alcohol's distinct sharp scent.

Hanging above the DJ on the other side of the club, glittery gold cages held half-naked girls sliding up and down poles. The sunken dance floor three feet below the main floor was so crowded that she couldn't tell where one person began and the other ended. The partiers were one big mass of arms, legs, bobbing heads and gyrating bodies, moving to the beat of the music.

Fog floated through the room in a heavy haze, carrying with it images of excitement, aggression and…lust. She saw it in the way the people moved, the way they touched. Especially one group of three, who were dancing on the fringes of the dance floor.

A tall, broad-shouldered man with pitch-black hair danced in front of a woman with short dark hair, while her blond girlfriend plastered herself to his backside. When the blonde raked her nails down his cotton T-shirt and then along his denim-covered thighs as she leaned close and bit his shoulder blade, Emma's stomach tightened. The man laughed and turned to say something in the blond woman's ear. Emma could tell by the way the woman's eyes narrowed into pleased slits that his comment was very suggestive.

She felt like a voyeur watching the three of them, their bodies moving in tandem to the suggestive beat of the music, but Emma couldn't look away. She was totally mesmerized by the sight. The man held the brunette's waist with a gentle touch that surprised her. When he ran his lips along the woman's throat, Emma found herself tilting her head as if he were kissing her.

Her pulse thrummed and her palms turned sweaty. Sudden heat spread through her body, making her dizzy. Seeking a distraction, she unbuttoned her thick jacket and gazed around the room, looking for the auburn-haired man. He'd be easier to spot in a crowd than the dark-headed guy. When she returned her gaze to the threesome on the floor once more, the man lifted his head and stared right at her.

Embarrassed to be caught staring, Emma quickly turned and made her way through the crowd toward the bar. Maybe the two men were having a drink. Frat boy and sorority girl were making out on the stool to her left. She ignored them and leaned across the bar to scan the patrons sitting on either end.

The bartender's military-style buzz cut shifted forward with his raised eyebrows. "What'll you have?"

Emma nodded. "I'll have a dark beer." More than once she'd shared a beer or two with her aunt. Mary might be in her mid-sixties, but she could hold her own against any sailor out there.

"Come on, baby. You don't need a drink," a woman said beside Emma, drawing her out of her musings.

Glancing to her right, Emma froze. The man from the dance floor had walked up to the bar. But it wasn't his face that shocked her. It was his smell…that intriguing musky scent she'd come looking for. The blonde stroked his waist and hips, dancing in place behind him, while the brunette hung on his right arm.

Emma stared at his profile as he raised his hand to get the bartender's attention. Nothing about him looked familiar. She knew she'd never met him in her life, yet his scent evoked something strong within her. Appearing to be in his early thirties, he wasn't pretty-boy handsome. From his nose, to his square jaw, to black eyebrows over dark eyes, his looks were a bit harsh but intriguing.

He turned and whispered something to the brunette beside him. The blonde slid her hand along his backside, then wrapped her arm around his waist and tugged him against her. "You have to dance with me next," she said, rubbing her body on his.

Emma smirked. *You mean he wasn't already?*

"Here's your beer." The bartender interrupted her observation, setting Emma's drink on the wood bar top, then he turned to the man on her right. "What'll it be?"

The dark-haired man glanced at Emma's imported beer. "I'll have what she's having."

The bartender walked away before she could hand him her money. Emma thrummed her fingers on the bar top and waited for him to return. She refused to look at the guy beside her. Had she imagined *him* walking inside the club with a red-headed guy? Or maybe the other guy had girls climbing all over him somewhere else in the club.

Apparently, the brunette didn't like that the man she hung on had glanced Emma's way. Emma felt the female's avid stare as the woman moved to stand in front of him, while the blonde literally crawled all over his back. The bartender returned with another beer and the man handed him a large bill. "That's for hers, too," he said, nodding to Emma.

He had an engaging smile and smelled like sin incarnate, but Emma wasn't flattered. Handing the bartender her money, she swept her gaze over the two ladies hanging on the man and said, "No thanks. I think they've got all your sides covered," before she walked away.

Caine stared after the petite woman who'd just slammed him. He was taken aback but amused by her comment. The brunette kissed his jaw and said in a husky voice, "We'll be right back."

The blonde backed away with her friend and waved. "Bathroom break."

As he watched the women walk off, he realized he hadn't learned their names yet, but his mind was on the woman who'd turned down his offer to pay for her beer. She had the most arresting eyes. They were so light brown that the color appeared almost yellow. What was her name? He scanned the crowd, looking for her pageboy hat among the crush of people. She'd disappeared.

Laird walked up and ran a hand through his short auburn hair. "Better learn to tie a knot. That bathroom line is long." Frowning, he glanced around the bar area. "How the hell did you manage to lose *two* women while I was gone?"

"Talent," Caine grunted, then took a drink of his beer.

"Now I know why you weren't answering your cell."

Caine immediately tensed at Landon's terse tone behind him. He swiveled and met the Alpha's steady stare. Out of the corner of his eye, he saw Kaitlyn, Landon's mate, ordering drinks at the other end of the bar. "Why are you looking for me? Wasn't kicking me out of the pack enough for you?"

Landon's face turned to stone and he crossed his arms over his wide chest. "Leaving was your choice."

Resentment churned in Caine's stomach. Ninety days of loneliness and feeling completely alienated from his own kind fueled his bitter tone. "You didn't give me an option."

Kaitlyn walked up carrying two mugs of Guinness. At the same time, the song ended and the multicolored spotlights around the dance floor were doused, sending the bar into momentary darkness. She gasped and stared at Caine. "Do you see it?" she addressed Landon.

A new song started up and the colorful lights sprang back to life, reflecting off Landon's tense jaw. "I do." Grabbing the drinks from her hands, he set them on the bar. "Let's go."

Laird's attention pinged between Landon, Caine and Kaitlyn. "Am I missing something?"

Caine shrugged and took another swig of his beer. "I'm as clueless as you."

"More than you realize." Landon's cold tone spoke volumes. "Leave immediately and meet me at my office."

Caine stiffened, ready to refuse.

The Alpha got right in his face. "As far as I'm concerned, you're still a member of my pack and my responsibility. Get your ass moving, *wolf.*"

After Landon and Kaitlyn walked off toward the entrance, Laird said, "Where'd the ladies go? Did you find out their names?"

Caine shook his head. "They went to the bathroom. If the lines are like you say, they'll be a while." He set down his beer, wishing he'd gotten the hat girl's name. "Come on. Let's get out of here."

When they left the club and the heavy doors shut behind them, Caine caught a glimpse of the girl in the hat walking up the road and his pulse raced. "Get the car and meet me around the block," he called to Laird, then took off in her direction.

As he headed her way, she pulled her gloves out of her pockets and shrugged into them. Caine briefly stopped to grab the paper she'd dropped. In a matter of seconds, he was just a few feet behind her. "Hey, Hat Girl! Wait up."

She gasped and jumped, coming to a halt. "You scared the crap out of me. Don't sneak up on people like that."

"You dropped this." Caine walked up and handed her the napkin before sliding his hands into his jeans pockets. "You shouldn't be walking the streets by yourself at night. Let me walk you to wherever you're going."

"Thanks." She shoved the napkin in her pocket. "Don't you have other women to attend to?" she said before she continued walking toward a parking deck up ahead.

Caine chuckled and fell into step beside her. "Things aren't always what they seem."

She raised an eyebrow. "So I imagined those two women trying to become your second skin?"

Touché. "And yet I'm here, talking to you," he said in a husky tone.

She shrugged, unimpressed. "Everyone likes a challenge."

She was a good six inches shorter than him, but with her thick jacket and her hair tucked up under a black pageboy hat, he couldn't tell much else about her physically. No earrings swung from her ears or lipstick coated her lips. High cheekbones made her oval face more interesting than beautiful, but she had something about her…something elusive, and damn he liked her snap. "Is that what you would be? A good challenge?"

Her yellow gaze slanted briefly. "I would be the *ultimate* challenge."

No smug smile, no pretense at all. Just the determined set of her jaw and the way she walked—graceful and self-assured. She exuded the kind of self-confidence some people work all their lives to acquire but never really accomplish, yet she was so young. He'd guess a little over twenty.

They'd reached the entrance to the parking deck and she stopped. "I can take it from here. Thanks."

Caine was stunned to be summarily dismissed. Women, especially those younger than him, were usually drawn in by his smile alone. He searched her face, looking for some kind of clue to her underlying strategy. No artifice reflected in her intriguing eyes. "Will you at least tell me your name?"

She smiled and his groin hardened and his chest cinched tight in a deep primal response to her natural beauty.

"Hat Girl will do. Good night."

She turned to walk away, but Caine caught her gloved hand. Drawing her fingers to his lips, he said, "I'm glad I met you, Hat Girl."

A car horn blew and Caine jerked his gaze to the road behind him. Laird leaned out the car window. "Come on, Caine. Landon's waiting."

Small fingers folded around his, drawing his attention. Her lips were tilted in amusement, a delicate dark eyebrow elevated. "Things aren't always what they seem?"

Caine grinned. "Exactly."

Pulling her hand from his, she backed away. "It was nice to meet you, Caine. Your friend is waiting."

"I'd like to see you again."

Her low laugh made his heart beat faster.

"I'll be around."

Caine didn't like her evasive answer. He realized he'd been so caught up in trying to learn more about her that he hadn't taken the time to catch her scent. He'd be able to track her that way. Something close to panic gripped him at the thought she'd disappear and he'd never see her again. "At least tell me your name or give me your number."

"I've got to go. I have a long drive ahead of me."

"You don't live in the city then?"

She shook her head.

The horn blew again and Caine barked toward the car, "I'm coming, Laird."

When he turned back, she was gone.

"I have to deal with Landon for taking our time getting there. You don't," Laird grumbled as Caine climbed into the passenger side.

Caine shut the door harder than necessary. "He'll get over it."

Laird drove down the road. "Stubborn lone wolf."

Caine shrugged off the conflicting emotions that squeezed his chest at Laird's flippant comment. He never really understood what Landon went through while he'd lived away from the pack on the fringes of Lupreda land for as long as he did…until now. "It doesn't matter. I'm out of the pack anyway."

"It took you two hours to shift back, Caine!" Laird growled and steered the car onto a side street.

The past few months of solitude in the city, while working double shifts to pay for rent and food, had given Caine plenty of time to think about those two long hours in the woods. Going zerker was not going to happen to him.

"It's not the same without you. Landon's Second should be with the pack. You *can't* enjoy delivering packages."

Laird's comment jerked Caine out of his musings. "Second?"

"Damn straight." Laird pulled his car into a space on the street in front of Landon's New York City office. Cutting the engine, he drilled Caine with a steadfast stare. "Everyone knows it. It was only a matter of time before Landon made an official announcement."

It was true he'd assumed the role of Second the moment Landon took over as Alpha, but Caine thought Laird would take over once he left. Roman was too laid-back to assume Second responsibilities. All Caine had ever wanted, all he'd ever trained for, was to be Alpha one day. With the threat of turning zerker a very real possibility for him now, he wouldn't be allowed to enter the annual Alpha run.

Laird grabbed his arm when he started to get out of the car. "Just put the damned necklace on."

Caine's ingrained loyalty burned within him. Even though Landon had forced him to leave, he still respected Landon more than any wolf, even more than Garius, the head Omega and oldest retired Alpha. "It might've been over twenty-five years ago, but I can still feel the weight of the vampires' damned silver collar around my neck. I refuse to be shackled again."

"You can take the chain off with each full moon and run with us as a wolf. Your family wants you to return."

Family. The concept both fascinated and frustrated Caine. Unlike Caine and Landon and the wolves before them who were created in a lab by the vampires, Laird's generation were the first werewolves born into the pack. Caine's friend knew what it felt like to have siblings and parents. Laird had both pack and *family* ties. Now that the pack thought he was close to going zerker, Caine felt they'd turned their back on him. What was that human saying, "Blood is thicker than water"? Laird's parents would never walk away from him, zerker or not.

Caine shook off the sense of isolation that had consumed his thoughts while he'd been living away from the pack and climbed out of the car. As he walked up the sidewalk beside Laird, he knew the Lupreda were worried about him. Living among humans was his only option. Humans didn't rile his need to call forth his Musk form for dominance like his fellow pack mates did, like Brian had. They were a safe, if not somewhat boring, race…all except for one, apparently. Hat Girl.

With the zerker issue breathing down his neck, he felt as if he was losing touch with what little humanity ran through his veins. Maybe that's why the human appealed to him. She represented something that was slipping away from him as fast as sand through his fingers.

"Caine. You with me, bud?"

Caine blinked when he realized he was staring unseeingly in front of him. Landon Rourke Private Investigations came into focus in bold black letters on the door a couple feet away. He smirked. Landon was going to have to change that now that Kaitlyn had left her job as NYPD police detective to join his agency. Tapping on the door, he walked in when Landon called for them to enter.

"'Bout damn time." Landon scowled and leaned against his desk which was currently turned on its side.

"Shit!" Laird stared at the shambles before them.

Caine's gaze jerked to Landon. "What happened?"

"I think it's obvious," Landon said in a dry tone.

Caine walked around the ransacked room. Sniffing the air, he stepped over filing cabinets with drawers wide open. Paperwork was everywhere. Nothing. Not a glimmer of a scent. Knowing Landon's sense of smell wasn't as strong as the rest of the wolves in the pack, Caine frowned. "I'm assuming you asked us here to help you scent, but I don't detect any lingering smells."

Laird lifted a turned-over chair. Inhaling near the wood, he shook his head before he set it upright on the floor. "Me neither."

Landon stood. "That's not why I asked you here."

Kaitlyn walked into the office from the back entrance, carrying a small hard case. Opening it, she removed a strange-looking flashlight with a green shield in front of it. Handing Caine and Laird each a pair of orange-colored safety-style glasses, she said, "I borrowed this equipment from a friend's office at the lab."

"You borrowed?" Caine grinned and slipped on the glasses.

"It'll be back where he left it before work resumes tomorrow morning." She tucked strands of her shoulder-length red hair behind her ear and walked over to the light switch.

"You *know* we can see in the dark, Kaitlyn." Laird chuckled, then put on his glasses.

She flipped off the light switch. "Just humor me. I'm hoping this will work."

Laird lifted his hands in the air. "See. No difference. Everything looks the same."

Kaitlyn turned on her flashlight and swept it past them to the room in general. "What about now?"

Caine froze as the special flashlight scanned the room. He saw defined sparkling handprints all over the place—on the desk, the filing cabinets, on the paperwork and file folders, even on the chair Laird had just checked.

Kaitlyn was showing Laird and him what she and Landon had the ability to see without this special equipment. "Damn it to hell!" Caine ground out, then glanced at Laird when Kaitlyn turned the flashlight on him.

Sparkling handprints covered his friend's face, his chest, his arms, his hips, even his crotch. "Son of a bitch!" Laird hissed. "Those two girls crawling all over us like a couple of cats were—"

"Panthers," Caine finished with a snarl, his gaze snapping to Landon's. Now he knew why Landon was so furious when the lights went down in the club.

"I don't think the panthers have a clue that Kaitlyn and I can see the trail they're leaving behind," Landon said.

"Either that or the Velius don't give a damn." Caine walked over and flipped the light switch back on.

"Velius or panthers. No matter what name we call them, it's like they're taunting us." Laird snorted.

"Well, one thing's for sure…" Katilyn retrieved the glasses from Caine and Laird. "You two need to stay away from the club until we can figure out a way for you to detect them."

Frustration and anger boiled deep in Caine's chest. The club was his only connection to the woman he'd met. He didn't know her name. He didn't know her scent. "The women don't know that we know they're panthers. If Laird and I go back tomorrow night, we could follow the two of them and find out where their pride is located."

Landon shook his head. "They know I killed one of their own while trying to protect Kaitlyn's mom. But they must think we have something more on them or they wouldn't have tossed my office looking for it. If Kaitlyn and I go back to the club, we'll tip our hand. If you and Laird go back…" Landon paused and ran a hand through his short, light brown hair. "You can't see or smell them, Caine. What if the two women weren't the only panthers there? You could try to follow them and get ambushed."

Laird snorted. "We can take out a bunch of cats."

Kaitlyn put the flashlight and the glasses back in their case, then faced Laird and Caine. "I'll go with you two to the club tomorrow night."

"Hell no, you won't!" Landon growled.

Kaitlyn sighed. "My hybrid status makes it impossible for them to smell me. I'll wear a wig and glasses or something to make me look different. My heavy coat should mute your mark's scent, but you'll have to stay away from me once I take a shower."

Landon moved to stand in front of her. "I said no, Kaitie. I can't be there to protect you. End of discussion."

Kaitlyn glanced at Laird and Caine. "I'd like to talk to my mate alone. Caine, I'll call you tomorrow."

As he and Laird headed out the door, one thing Caine knew for certain…no matter the outcome of Kaitlyn and Landon's discussion, he was going back to Squeeze tomorrow night. The club was his only connection to the young human with the intriguing light brown eyes. He didn't plan to give her up.

Chapter 2

An electric current slid up her arm from the point their fingers touched, making Emma's stomach tumble. Caine was holding her bare hand. No glove separated them this time. He stood in front of her, and the dark smile on his face made him look both sinful and sexy as hell.

"I'll be around." She tried to walk away, but he didn't let go.

Instead, he spread his fingers wide and threaded them with hers, locking their hands together. "I don't want you to go." He glanced at their hands. "And I don't think you want to either."

The warmth from his palm seeped into her skin, warming her chilled fingers. She followed his line of sight. Her fingers dug into the back of his hand, clasping tight.

Emma jerked her gaze to his. "I—"

"Dance with me, Emma." Using his hold, he pulled her

close. When her chest aligned with his, he wrapped his arm around her waist and locked her against him.

The rough rasp in his voice ignited her body. She loved the way her name sounded coming from him. Much better than Hat Girl. Her nerves played havoc with her mind. He wanted to dance? She glanced at the rows of cars flanking either side of them. "We're in a parking deck—"

"Listen and you'll hear the music." He leaned close, his lips a breath away from hers.

As his hand slid up her back under her coat and sweater, the searing heat from his palm branded her bare skin, and she began to hear the steady thump of a seductive beat in her head—deep music with erotic undertones, meant to seduce the senses, to lull her mind and insecurities.

Emma realized she was dreaming. Even though she was a little sad that this arousing scenario was in her subconscious, the knowledge freed her from worry that she'd make a fool of herself by saying something stupid. This "dream Caine" was a figment of her imagination. She could be uninhibited and he would respond as if she'd said and done all the right things.

Wrapping her arms around his neck, she pressed her body close to his muscular chest and whispered in his ear, "You take the lead and I'll follow."

Caine's dark eyes blazed. "Things aren't always what they seem, Emma."

The low register of his voice made something fundamental twist deep inside her. His hard body pressed against her, combined with his invigorating smell, caused her pulse to whoosh in her ears. Her heart beat faster and the sound grew louder until all she heard was a blaring *whaaah, whaaah,*

whaaah. She stiffened in his arms. The pace felt off. The
steady noise was harsh and jarring.

Emma jerked awake to the annoying sound of her alarm
clock. Five in the morning. Ugh. She'd set the alarm so she
could go in search of Casper before her aunt woke. The older
woman would be frantic if she knew he'd gotten out again.
The dang cat had slipped through Emma's legs when she'd
opened the door last night after she'd returned from the club.
Hitting the off button, her heart thrummed as she lay back on
her bed and squeezed her eyes shut, hoping to recover the
dream. But the wisps of the surreal fantasy slipped away.

Her dream about Caine made her realize how attracted
she'd been to him. She hadn't admitted it to herself last night.
Rolling over, she punched her pillow when she considered the
fact she hadn't given him her name. Most likely, he thought
she was being coy and evasive, giving him the "challenge" he
thought her to be. Ha! The truth was, she didn't know what
to say to someone like Caine—a man obviously assured in his
seductive skills with women. Pushing him away was the best
defense mechanism she could come up with at the time.
Socially adept, she was not.

Growing up home-schooled and living in the boonies over
an hour from the city pretty much guaranteed she grew up
smart but not very skilled when it came to making friends. She
didn't give Caine her name on purpose. That way, she could
imagine all kinds of sexy scenarios between herself and this
mysterious guy with his evocative smell, so long as she didn't
have any embarrassing "real-life" moments with him to get
in the way.

Emma sighed as she stood up and dragged on a pair of
jeans and a sweater. Staring out the frosted window into the

dark early-morning sky, she grabbed her coat. A few minutes later, Emma tugged the coat tight around her to ward off the frigid air and entered the dense woods surrounding their home, calling out in a low voice, "Casper!"

Once she'd reached the stream a half mile from their home, she peered up and down the babbling flow of partially frozen water. Casper considered this area his personal hunting ground. She had no qualms leaving him out here on his own, but her aunt had other ideas, to the point the older woman had even put a lock on his cat door to keep him inside at night.

Emma was freezing her butt off and ready to get back home to a cup of hot cider. "Casp—" she started to call again when a small bundle of pitch-black fur darted across the embankment twenty feet upstream. She stepped forward to take off after him, at the same time a few drops of ice-cold rain hit her nose. Smiling in satisfaction, she turned to head back home. Casper might like his freedom, but he hated being wet even more. He'd be meowing at their back door soon enough.

With each step Emma took back toward her house, something didn't feel right. The air felt heavy and thick as if an ominous hush had fallen over the woods surrounding their small stone house—waiting for her to return. The tiny hairs on the back of her neck stood up as she neared her home. Heart thumping, she picked up her pace and broke into the clearing to see steady rain sliding in quiet rivulets down the high-pitched roof over the front porch. Still, she couldn't shake the feeling…

She came to a halt when she saw fresh, deep tire marks in the gravel driveway, as if a big truck had come and gone. Her pulse thundered in her ears at the sight of the front door standing wide open. Icy fingers of fear for her aunt traced down her back. Her boots made heavy thumps across the wooden front porch as she ran inside screaming, "Aunt Mary!"

The house appeared empty, eerily quiet. She raced toward her aunt's bedroom and her voice echoed in the hall as she gave another shrill cry for her aunt to respond. Emma's stomach knotted with each step she took. The lamp lay broken on the floor beside her aunt's bed—the only indication of trouble, other than the open front door. Emma rubbed her neck and glanced around the bedroom.

Her aunt's purse was still on the dresser untouched. So was her jewelry box. They hadn't been robbed. Feeling as if her safety and privacy had been completely ripped from her, Emma crept back down the hall toward the front of the house, trying not to panic for her aunt. Their car was still in the driveway, so unless her aunt had walked out, she didn't leave on her own. Where had her aunt gone? Completely perplexed, she pulled the front door closed.

As soon as she shut the door, a piece of paper fluttered to the floor. Emma's heart seized and she stared at the bold, black letters scrawled across the white surface. *Want to talk to you. Go to the club again tonight. Be there at ten. No police.*

To the club again? The note had to be for her. *No police?* Did that mean the person had taken her aunt to make sure she would comply? Emma bit her lip and swallowed a sob. Even though she was alone in her house, she felt as if every move she made was being scrutinized, like she were a fish floundering around in a fishbowl.

Running down the hall to her bedroom, she grabbed her purse, her cell and keys, then headed back to the front of the house. She couldn't stay here another moment. Her home had been invaded and being an hour away from the city felt—for the first time in her life—too secluded.

Casper's angry meow drew her attention and Emma grabbed a towel and unlocked his cat door at the bottom of the back door. He tried to dart past her, but she was too fast, grabbing the cat up and drying him off with brisk strokes. The cat yowled his displeasure and scratched her to be free. The moment his feet hit the floor, he made a beeline down the hall for her aunt's dirty-clothes basket—his bed every night.

Emma considered taking the cat with her, but Casper was as undomesticated as they came. He was used to the wide-open wooded spaces, not a crowded city full of concrete. Her aunt wouldn't forgive her if he got run over. Sighing, she filled Casper's bowls with enough food and water to last a few days and made sure the cat door was in the unlocked position so he could come and go as he pleased.

When she started back through the kitchen, her gaze landed on her aunt's plastic pillbox. Emma had filled the seven days of the week full of meds for her aunt yesterday. Renewed panic ramped inside her as she slipped her aunt's medicine box into her purse. Mary needed her pills or she ran the risk of a heart attack.

Closing the front door, Emma locked it, then quickly bolted for her car. Suddenly, the dense woods appeared sinister, surrounding the area around her house in a shroud of damp darkness. Emma's heart hammered out of control. Every sound seemed to echo in her head: the gravel under her boots, her erratic breathing, even the crows in the trees above squawking incessantly.

Once she'd pulled her car onto the interstate that led to the city, the rain began to come down harder. Emma gripped the steering wheel tight and sobbed in worry for her aunt. Her first natural instinct was to call the police, but she couldn't jeopardize her aunt's life. *No police.* What if the kidnappers got angry and hurt her aunt?

Why did they want to meet me at the club? Who was doing this? She'd only talked to one person last night. Then again, Caine had really wanted to know her name or her number. At the time, she'd assumed she'd just intrigued him with her evasive responses. Dear God, had he followed her home? Could Caine be the one doing this? Had she somehow unwittingly brought some psycho-stalker to her home? She began to shake all over.

Where could she go for a place to think? Whom could she trust? Right now her boss, Jared, was the closest Emma had to a friend. He'd always been understanding about her situation with her aunt's medical needs and endless doctor appointments. She tried to call Jared's cell, but her cell's coverage was spotty this far from town.

An hour later, as Emma parked her car behind Jared's Java Café—space was surprisingly available in the wee hours of the morning—it started sleeting. Rain and sleet coated her hair and coat by the time she climbed the metal stairs that led to Jared's apartment above the store and banged hard on the door.

Bleary-eyed and bare-chested, his short blond hair in bedhead disarray, Jared yanked open the door with a baseball bat in hand. "What the fu—" He lowered the bat to his side. "Emma?"

She stood there, shivering and incoherent. "Ja—Jared. I need a place to stay for a bit." Her legs barely held her upright.

The bat clattered to the floor and he caught her before she collapsed. "Emma!"

When he lifted her in his arms and kicked the door closed behind him, Emma began to shake all over. She was soaked through. Her breathing came in erratic pants and her teeth chattered. "So c-c-cold."

A half hour later, Emma emerged from Jared's bathroom, steam rolling out behind her. Tucked in a thick terry towel, her wet hair hanging around her shoulders, she turned down the hall and entered the kitchen.

Jared raised a blond eyebrow right before he poured her a mug of coffee. He'd shaven and pulled on jeans and a sweater while she'd taken a shower. When she sat down at the small two-seater table, he set the coffee in front of her. "Want cream?"

She nodded mutely.

Grabbing the milk from the fridge, he pushed the carton toward her and sat down in the chair across from her. "Start from the beginning."

Seeing him like this, outside of a boss-employee situation, he appeared so much closer to her age, even though he'd just turned thirty last month. Emma glanced down at the coffee mug tucked between her hands. "I—um, it's complicated." If she told him everything, he'd insist she call the police. She couldn't put her aunt in harm's way. What she needed was a safe place to stay and think.

"What happened? Did you argue with your aunt or something?"

She met his concerned, deep blue gaze and wished she didn't have to lie. "Yes, I brought up moving to the city. She refused to budge. We had a huge blowout."

He glanced at the streaks of dawn just showing through window and his eyebrows shot up. "This early in the morning?"

Unable to meet his steady stare, she quickly made up the

rest of the story as she poured milk into her coffee. "I was supposed to start my classwork early and get it e-mailed off to my professor before I had to take my aunt to her doctor's appointment later this morning, but I couldn't sleep. I tried to talk to my aunt about possibly moving closer and that's when the fighting started." Glancing up at him, her voice trembled. "I just needed to get away for a bit. Can I stay here?"

"Don't you have to take your aunt to the doctor in a few hours?"

His question twisted a knife of worry deep in her gut. Her aunt was a tough cookie. Not much scared the woman. *Please let her heart be able handle all that's happened to her,* Emma silently prayed. *And whoever took her better not have harmed a single gray hair on her head!* "My aunt called a friend to take her so I could come into work on time."

When he didn't answer right away, she grimaced. "At least I won't be late for work today."

Jared smiled. "There is that." Standing, he walked over and picked up his phone from the counter. "I can't have you serving customers in a towel. My clothes dryer's on the fritz. I'll call my little sister to bring you some girl stuff. She's about your size. Until then, I've got something you can borrow."

Relief lifted some of the weight off her chest. "Thanks, Jared."

He looked up from dialing. "Your shift starts in a few hours. You can use my bed to catch up on some sleep."

She cast a gaze over her shoulder to the living room. "I'll crash on your couch if that's okay."

Once Jared hung up with his sister, he walked into his bedroom and then came out and placed a stack of clothes in her arms. "Here's something to wear until my sister gets here."

Emma waited until Jared was in the shower before she

quickly changed into his clothes and then lay down on the couch. She didn't think she could sleep, her head was so jumbled up with worry for her aunt, but she forced herself to close her eyes and lay very still even as her mind raced.

A half hour later, Jared passed by the couch and lifted his coat off the rack by the door. "I'm leaving." His hair was back to its normal finger-combed blond waves and he smelled like soap. "My sister should be by later with some stuff for you." He shook his head at his jeans bunched loosely around her hips. "If she doesn't make it in time, we'll just have to declare it sloppy casual Friday." Chuckling, Jared turned and opened the door. "See you downstairs later."

"Thanks, Jared." Emma's eyelids felt so heavy, she lay back on the couch and closed her eyes. As thoughts about her aunt filled her mind, her entire body sank deeper into the cushions, and she suddenly realized why she felt so tired. She hadn't taken her vitamin last night or the night before because she'd run out. Sometimes it really sucked living with a vitamin deficiency.

Her aunt would kill her if she knew Emma forgot to tell her she needed a refill on her pills. She'd lost count of the number of times Mary had pointed a finger at her, pale blue eyes squinting in her wrinkled round face. "I don't want to lose you like I did your mom. It's not something you grow out of. It's in your genes, Emma Marie Gray. Don't skip a single day."

Closing her eyes against the tears that threatened, Emma prayed she got to hear those stern words from her aunt again. As the hours crept by, she grew more and more tense. A light knock on the door jarred Emma from her worried thoughts.

"Hey, it's Jared's sister, Tanya. I brought you some stuff," a muffled female voice called through the front door.

When Emma jumped up to answer the door, she almost fell over. Dizziness ensued and her ears rang. Shaking her head to clear it, she quickly pulled open the door. A woman with spiky, short blond hair blew her slant-cut bangs out of her eyes and handed Emma a black duffel bag. "Here ya go. I hope I picked some things that'll work for you."

As soon as Emma took the bag, Tanya turned and headed back down the stairs, waving to her. "I have to take off or I won't make it to work on time."

Knife-sharp frigid air gusted against the door, slicing through Emma's lungs as she called after Tanya, "Thank you so much." Shivering, she cast her gaze upward. The rain had stopped, but the sky was heavy with bumpy white clouds. Snow was coming. Emma closed the door and glanced at the kitchen wall clock. She had a half hour to get dressed and make it downstairs before her shift started.

Once she'd changed into Tanya's pink retro Go-Gos T-shirt and a pair of dark jeans that fit a little too snug compared to how she normally preferred her clothes, Emma glanced at her long, black, bed-head hair and immediately searched through the duffel bag for a rubber band. After looking through makeup, shampoo and other girly stuff, she remembered Tanya had short hair and gave up her search in an effort to "finger-comb" her hair into some kind of order.

Damn, she had all the pep of a slug. She needed to get her vitamin prescription refilled. Pronto. Grabbing her cell phone from her coat pocket, she found the phone book in a kitchen drawer, looked up the pharmacy then quickly dialed the number.

"MedCare pharmacy," a woman said in a cheery tone.

"Hi, this is Emma Gray. I'm calling to refill my vitamin prescription."

Keys tapped in the background. "I'm sorry, but I don't have a prescription listed for an Emma Gray."

"It's probably under my aunt's name. Try Mary Gray."

"I'm sorry, but I can't give out that information, since you aren't Mary Gray. I can tell you that we have never filled a prescription here for vitamins under the name Emma Gray."

Completely bewildered, Emma hung up the phone. Had her aunt filled her prescription at another pharmacy? She doubted it. Mary was a creature of habit in the highest order. When she found a pharmacy she liked—any store, for that matter—she stuck with it, even though she'd moved away from the city. Plus, Emma had always driven her there and waited in the car while Mary got the prescription filled.

Pulling her vitamin bottle out of her purse, she held it under the kitchen light to see if maybe she'd dialed the wrong number. No, the number on the label was the number she'd called and the label was in her name, not her aunt's. Emma squinted when she noticed what looked like writing underneath the label.

Once she peeled the white printed label back, she was surprised to see a phone number handwritten on the back of the label. Her hands shook as she dialed the phone number. The phone rang and rang. She was about to hang up when a recording came on.

"Leave a message." A man's raspy voice came across the line. At the beep, Emma spoke quickly. "Hi. My name is Emma Gray. I found your number written on my bottle of prescription vitamins. I believe my aunt, Mary Gray, might have purchased them from your pharmacy. Can you please return my call?" Emma gave her cell phone number and then hung up. She was about to put her cell phone back in her pocket when she realized she'd left her charger at home. Turning the phone off to save the battery, Emma slipped it back into her coat pocket and mentally reminded herself to check her voice mail as soon as she got off work.

Sliding the empty pill bottle into her coat's inside pocket, Emma slid her arms into the jacket and grimaced that it was still slightly damp. As she started to head out the door, she saw Jared's red baseball cap on the rack. Grabbing the hat, she tucked her rumpled hair underneath it before she ran down the stairs. Jared would never let her live it down if she were late this time.

While Emma went through the day's paces of ringing up customer's bills, making lattes, heating up bagels, muffins and other pastries, her mind turned over question after question.

Why did someone go to such lengths just to talk to her? Was her aunt okay? And what was up with her vitamin prescription? Why had her aunt led her to believe she'd gotten them at MedCare Pharmacy? A thought suddenly occurred that shocked Emma; she knew they were strapped for money with her taking classes, but good grief…was her aunt buying prescriptions off the black market? Is that what all this was about? Emma didn't know what was and what wasn't the truth at this point. All she knew was, that damned empty pill bottle sat in her jacket pocket, weighing as heavily on her mind as her aunt's safety.

She might be upset at her situation, her mind completely on edge, but as the day wore on, she began to feel better and more alert than she had in a long time. The coffee smelled stronger, the pastry aromas sweeter. Her energy level had shot up, too. Then again, the heightened sensations were probably due to the three espresso shots she'd had earlier. She

was so wound up that she felt as if she was perched on a pre-
cipice, waiting for something to happen.

The indescribable sense of awareness stayed with her all
day, prickling her skin, sharpening her senses with each
passing hour. Emma was so tuned in to her surroundings that
she found it hard to filter out the normal conversational "white
noise" going on around her.

A couple more people entered the shop and their voices
carried to her finely tuned ear while she wiped crumbs off a
table with a wet cloth.

"You don't need coffee."

"But I *like* coffee."

"Wuss."

The first voice sounded familiar. Emma's head snapped
up and her gaze zeroed in on the two guys who were heading
to the counter. The auburn-haired man was wearing only a
T-shirt and jeans. No gloves, no scarf or hat, just a T-shirt…
in twenty-degree weather? The nut. He probably *did* need
coffee.

As she stared at them in surprise, Caine's eyes locked with
hers. Pulling his hands out of his black leather coat's pockets,
he paused and smiled. Heat shot everywhere throughout her
body at once. Her primal response, mixed with fear and anger,
welled up inside her, bubbling hot and building steam. She
blinked several times to focus her jumbled, conflicting
emotions to one—anger. Emma turned away, her stomach
twisting in knots. She scrubbed the table with the cloth, trying
to decide what to do.

"Hey, Hat Girl," Caine said in a low voice, tapping the bill
of her cap. Emma slowly lifted her head and stared at him.
His friend was at the counter ordering.

She narrowed her gaze. "Why are you here? I thought I was supposed to meet you at the club tonight."

"Huh? Laird wanted a coffee and I remembered the café logo on the napkin I handed back to you last night. I came by hoping this was a place you frequented—"

Setting the cloth down, she stepped into his personal space and hissed, "Where is my *aunt?*"

A look of confusion crossed his face. "Your aunt? What are you talking about?"

"Emma, I need your key. The drawer's jammed again," Scott called from behind the register. He was trying to ring up Caine's friend's order.

"Coming," she responded. She was so tense that she thought she might lose it any second. Her attention snapped back to Caine. "Why did you take her? Answer me!"

His big hands surrounded her fists in a firm hold and his brow creased in a deep furrow. "I don't know what you're talking about. What's going on?"

Emma sucked in her breath at the tingling, near burning sensation where his hands covered hers. She jerked away and backed up a step.

Caine frowned. Glancing at his palms, he rubbed his fingers across them and mumbled, "That was…intense."

Emma's physical reaction to his touch frightened her. She honestly felt like she was going to jump right out of her skin. Electric didn't begin to describe the sensation. More like shocking. Caine had seemed taken aback by her question, like he didn't have a clue what she was talking about. "You didn't follow me home, did you?"

He fisted his hands and his black eyebrows slashed downward. Jaw flexing, he said in a suddenly serious tone, "No."

Cool wind rushed in, heralding a group of talkative business-men into the café. Emma glanced at the side counter. The milks and stirrers needed to be replenished. Coffee drinkers got cranky when their condiments weren't readily available. She would normally ask Scott to do it, but he was busy with a crowd at the register and John was in the back unloading supplies.

"I have to go," she said, even as a sense of relief released some of the tension from her chest—at least as far as Caine was concerned. She was glad he wasn't the bad person her mind had begun to think he might be, but…who else saw her at the club last night? She didn't *know* anyone in town. Shaking her head, she blew out an unsteady breath and said, "My apologies for what I said. I was mistaken," then grabbed the cloth and headed to the supply closet.

Emma stood in the back of the supply closet, trying to reach the stirrers on the top shelf when Caine leaned over her shoulder and lifted the white box down for her.

The instant his hard chest pressed against her back, his body heat made her skin prickle all over. Emma quickly stepped away and turned to face him. "Um…thanks."

Before she could walk off, Caine clasped her shoulders, his expression intense. "Emma. Talk to me. Tell me what's wrong. Maybe I can help you."

His hazel eyes were interesting, an intriguing mix of forest green and brown. The colors seemed to meld and pulse in intensity as he talked. Hearing her name in his deep baritone sounded more intimate and personal than Hat Girl, way more personal than her dream. It sent a delicious thrill zipping along her spine. The warmth and comfort of his hands soaked through her T-shirt, even as the cotton barrier buffered the electric effect that had happened earlier. Something about the look on his face and his firm grip felt dangerous and exciting…and strangely trustworthy, while his inviting smell made her want to tell him everything, to trust him completely.

It would be so easy to ask him to be there in the background at the club tonight, if nothing else but for support, but she didn't know who, among the faces of strangers at the club, would be watching. What if they did have her aunt, and Caine's presence by her side angered the people who took Mary? Emma couldn't take the risk with her aunt's life.

Regretful, she shrugged out of his hold. "I'm fine, Caine. I have to go."

He didn't say anything as he followed her out of the room. She felt his heavy gaze track her every movement while she refilled the stirrers at the condiments counter, felt the heat of his intense stare trace her every step when she moved behind the main counter to replenish the skim and whole milk thermoses.

Jared's hand landed on her shoulder, making her jump. Concern laced his tone. "Hey, you okay? You seem to be in some kind of a daze."

She glanced over her shoulder to see Caine sitting at a table near the far window. His friend was drinking a mug of coffee and talking to him, but Caine hadn't taken his eyes off her.

"Have you talked to your aunt yet?" Jared continued, drawing her attention. "I really think you should stick to your guns about moving closer to town if that's what you want to do."

Emma tried her best to smile at him, although it probably came across more like a grimace. "I'll…" She swallowed the hard knot in her throat. What if she never got to speak to her aunt again? Unshed tears burned her eyes. "I'll do that."

He tugged on her cap's bill. "You've got a free pass tonight, roomie, but tomorrow you're going to have to talk to her."

Her smile wobbled. "Thanks, Jared."

"Sure thing." An encouraging smile tilted his lips and he swept his gaze over her Go-Gos T-shirt and jeans. "I'm glad my sister made it by."

"Please thank her again for me."

He nodded. "Why don't you go ahead and take off. We have it covered."

"Really? I still have another forty minutes on my shift."

He laughed. "Take the generosity while it's being offered, Emma."

"Yeah, it happens like…never to me." Scott's curly black hair fell into his eyes. He'd glanced at them over his shoulder after ringing up another customer.

Emma nibbled her bottom lip. "I guess I could try to catch up on my sleep." *And check my voice mail to see if that other pharmacist called back.*

"That couch is hard as a rock. Use my bed. You'll sleep bet—"

Something shattered on the hard floor. Caine's auburn-haired friend lifted his hands and called across the room, "Sorry, the mug slipped."

"Scott…" Emma started to ask him to take care of it.

"I know, I know." Scott grabbed a white towel. He paused as he came around the counter. "Dude, it's in the middle of the room. What'd you do? Throw it?"

Emma had been avoiding Caine's gaze, but at that moment their gazes locked for a split second and her stomach dropped. Sitting sideways in his seat, he'd leaned forward slightly with his fist clenched on the table. He looked intense and on edge—like he was about to launch across the room.

When she turned to leave, Emma decided to exit through the back way. She had a feeling Caine had no intention of giving up on trying to talk to her. Any other time, she'd have been thrilled to have the sexy man's undivided and intense attention, but tonight she couldn't afford to screw up.

Chapter 3

"Give me your damned cell, Laird," Caine snarled under his breath.

Laird shook his head and leaned back in his seat to pull his cell from his pocket. As he handed it across to Caine, he said, "That human's got you some kind of eff'd up, bro."

Caine snatched the phone and quickly punched in Kaitlyn's cell number. Thrumming his fingers on the table, he waited for her to pick up. When voice mail came on, he clenched his jaw and ticked off the seconds before he was able to leave a message.

"It's Caine. We haven't heard back from you. I have something important I have to do at the club tonight. It's a gut call. I'm going."

When he closed the phone and slid it across the table to his pack mate, Laird nodded to the guy who'd just finished cleaning up the broken mug, then frowned at Caine, saying in a low voice, "I really wanted to finish that coffee."

Caine shrugged. "You were being a prick."

Laird smirked. "I smell the blond guy's interest in the girl, too."

When Caine narrowed his gaze, Laird sighed. "I've always trusted your instincts, but going back there without being able to see or smell the Velius will be risky. I know your going to the club tonight has something to do with the woman you were just blatantly eavesdropping on." He glanced toward Emma as she disappeared into the kitchen. "I'll admit, she smells…" He paused, like he was trying to think of the right word to describe her scent.

"Earthy and primal," Caine added, his tone full of gravel.

Laird snapped his fingers and his eyes lit up. "That's it! She smells like the woods."

Caine shook his head and his heart thumped hard. "It's more like she took a long walk in a misty forest. She's all woman, but the scent of rain-soaked leaves and earth clings to her."

When he was close to Emma in the supply closet, Caine made sure to scent her. As soon as he'd inhaled, his predatory hunting senses kicked in. In the small room, her strong scent had made his fingers itch to capture her like prey, leaving her nowhere else to turn. Caine shook off the strange, aggressive emotion that rushed full force to his brain. A human was no competition for him, and yet she'd said she would be his ultimate challenge. One thing was true, she aroused him on many levels.

Instead, he focused on the protective instincts that had sent him in the closet after her in the first place. She'd seemed both angry and fearful when she'd asked why he was at the café when he was supposed to meet her at the club. And what was this about her aunt? He wanted to know who had frightened or threatened her.

"Emma was the woman I was talking to outside the parking garage last night. I met her at the club."

Laird shrugged. "You know where she works now. Talk to her here."

Caine shook his head. "I have to go to the club tonight. I think she might be in some kind of trouble."

"You'd put yourself out there like a lamb for slaughter because of some human woman?" Laird's eyes closed to near slits.

Caine slammed his fist on the table. "Shut up and listen."

Once Caine relayed the strange conversation he'd had with Emma, he finished with, "She was told to go there tonight." He jerked his head toward the counter. "She's staying with that guy, which makes me think she doesn't have any family to turn to. I could tell by her heart rate that she lied to him about why she's staying with him. I don't want Emma going to that club alone."

Laird rubbed the back of his neck. "Damn, I hope Kaitlyn calls us. Do you know when Emma planned on going?"

"No. She just alluded to having to meet the person at the club tonight when she thought I was 'him' and something about her aunt being taken."

Laird jerked his gaze back toward the kitchen door. "Why don't you just ask her?"

Caine ground his teeth. "I tried. She wouldn't tell me."

"No wonder this woman is so appealing to you." Laird's grin was smug. "If you can't charm her, you'd see her as a challenge."

It was a helluva lot more than that, Caine thought, rubbing his fingers across his palm again.

Laird stood and Caine said in a dark tone, "Where are you going?"

"You didn't plan to camp here all day, did you?"

"I was going to try and talk to her when she got off work."

Laird raised an eyebrow. "Let's find out when that'll be."

Before Caine could tell him to mind his own damned business, that she'd be leaving soon, Laird got up and walked over to the counter to speak to the guy who'd cleaned up his coffee mug earlier. "Sorry about the mess, man. When does this café close?"

"We close at eight."

Laird leaned forward, his tone conspiratorial. "My buddy wants to ask Emma out. Any idea when she gets off work?"

"She's already left for the evening," Jared answered as he walked out of the kitchen wiping his hands on a towel. Cutting his distrustful gaze toward Caine, the café owner continued, "Do either of you two plan to order anything else?"

Annoyed with Laird, Caine bit back the fierce growl that rumbled in his chest when the blond man's tone turned challenging. The guy had no idea Caine could smell his testosterone level spiking. Did Emma know how her boss felt about her?

Determined to find her, Caine stood up from the table and said in a cold tone, "Let's go, Laird."

The second they walked outside, Caine concentrated and inhaled. He caught Emma's scent instantly. She was close. Laird followed him around the side of the building. "You scented her?"

Caine nodded and paced around the small beat-up car in the parking lot beside the café. "Her scent is on this vehicle.

It might be hers." Approaching the stairs that led to a second level above the store, his focus zeroed in on the door at the top of the stairs. "She's up there. Must be his apartment."

"You can't go up there, bang on the door and demand that she tell you everything. You'll scare the shit out of her."

Caine clenched his fists in frustration. Laird was right. "Let's go back to my apartment for now. We'll just have to be at the club the moment it opens."

"It would be helpful if Kaitlyn could be here tonight," Laird said as they stood outside Squeeze an hour later. Sleet had been pouring down on them for a good ten minutes.

"I called Roman to help even the odds." Caine jammed his hands into his coat pockets, then swept his gaze over Laird. "The least you could've done was wear a coat and pretend you're affected by the weather like the rest of the humans. You look like a freak wearing nothing but a thin shirt in twenty-degree weather. Your hair is turning to a block of ice."

Laird laughed and plumes of frost floated in front of him. Brushing the sleet out of his hair, he glanced at the long line ahead of them. "You'd think the weather would've deterred some people from coming tonight."

Caine snorted. "When it's the first big snow of the year, humans go a little nuts. Think about how it affects our pack."

"I'm here, boyeeees!" Roman slid across the icy edges of the sidewalk and came to a stop next to them. He flipped his shoulder-length blond hair away from his face, his grin wider than usual and full of mischief. "Let's par-tay!"

Of all the Lupreda, Roman was the most "at home" in the ice and snow. Whereas Laird approached his role of financial planner and investor of the Lupreda's entire portfolio with calculated shrewdness, Roman contributed financially by entering and winning snowboarding competitions. "I get paid to play" was his motto. The first snow of the year always revved him up. "Case in point," Caine said in a dry tone with a pointed look at Roman.

Laird grinned his agreement and rocked back on his heels. "Have you seen Emma yet?"

Caine shook his head and focused on Roman. "I've brought you up to speed with what we know. Got any questions?"

Roman's expression turned serious. "No. I'm good."

Caine cut his gaze to Laird. "Do you have your phone on vibrate in case Kaitlyn calls us back?"

"Yes. You grab yours before we left?" Laird asked.

Caine nodded. "Since I called Kaitlyn on your cell, I want to make sure we don't miss her call."

"Hello, my two favorite dancing partners!" The blonde from last night walked up and wrapped her arms around Laird's waist from behind. "And who's this?" she said with interest, tilting her head and eyeing Roman appreciatively.

"What happened to you last night?" the brunette whispered in Caine's ear while hooking her arm in his.

As Laird started to introduce Roman, Caine waited to see his friend maneuver his way around the fact he didn't know either of the girls' names.

Roman took care of it for them in typical "Roman" style. "Hello, ladies. I'm Roman. It's nice to meet you." He bent over each of their hands and planted kisses on one and then the other.

When the blonde said something about three men being better than two, Caine learned their names were Veronica and Mandy. Although, in this dangerous game of wolf verses panther, he highly doubted those were the girls' real names.

Caine's cell phone began to vibrate in his front pocket and the brunette rubbed her thigh against his. "Hmm, I'll have to use my cell and call you a lot tonight."

His lips tilted in a devilish smile. "Hold that thought." Pulling his cell phone from his pocket, Caine tensed when he saw Landon was calling. If he answered, the women would be able to hear Landon's voice. He couldn't take a chance in case the panthers' hearing was just as keen as werewolves. He hung up on Landon's call and quickly typed a text message— *Catya later! At the club. Now*—then sent it.

Laird's eyebrows lifted. "Who was that?"

Caine slid his cell back into his pocket. "My roommate. I told him I was here and I'd catch up with him later." Wrapping his arm around the brunette's shoulders, he hoped Landon got his coded message.

From the moment Emma walked into the club, men made a beeline to her. To bolster her confidence, she'd taken the time to at least comb through her hair, dab on some lip gloss and change into another outfit Jared's sister had provided.

Emma tensed at every offer to dance or for a drink, wondering which man was the bastard who'd written the note and kidnapped her aunt. After the tenth time she had to turn down someone, she regretted not asking Jared to come. At least with a man by her side, the other guys might've left her alone. But while she and Jared ate dinner together at his apartment earlier, he'd told her that Caine had asked about her after she'd left the café and how much it had really bothered him. He went on to tell her that he wanted to get to know her better outside of work and not as her boss.

With the way Jared's feelings seemed to be changing toward her, Emma didn't want to give him a reason to think she'd return them. She thought of Jared as a wonderful friend, nothing more. Because she couldn't tell him why she was going to the club, asking him to come along would definitely send out a mixed signal. Not to mention, his constant presence by her side could put her aunt in danger.

Emma had helped clean up after dinner, then she'd checked her voice mail once more for a reply from that number she'd called about her vitamins. Nothing. While Jared took a shower, she'd jotted a quick note saying she'd be back and left. And here she was, standing inside Squeeze an hour earlier than her designated time, being hit on left and right. She had absolutely no interest in getting to know any of these men, nor did she care if they found her boring. How ironic, considering her worries while she'd waited in line outside just last night.

Snowflakes melted in her hair as she moved her slim cell phone to her jeans' front pocket and then shoved her gloves into her inside coat pocket. Every sound vibrated within her, knocking her heart, thrumming along her jangled nerves. The people danced frenetically, their movements expressive and reckless, their touches more aggressive than the night before. The scents were stronger, too, almost like the smells themselves had been heightened by the snowstorm swirling outside. The way the wind howled as she walked over from Jared's apartment promised blizzard conditions within the hour. She didn't care. She wanted answers and for her aunt to return home safe.

Emma scanned the crowd and, once again, as if he were emitting some kind of invisible pheromone only she could zero in on, her gaze instantly locked on Caine. He was with the same blonde and brunette from last night, but this time he wasn't alone. His tall, auburn-haired friend danced on one side of the blonde, while another man with longish blond hair danced on the other side of the brunette. They made a train of male, female, male, female, male gyrating to the music.

She set her jaw. Caine might've been asking about her earlier, but it didn't take him long to find a replacement. Turning, she walked away, weaving her way through the intimate, two-seater round café tables around the dance floor. She'd climbed the three stairs and was almost to the bar area when someone grabbed her arm.

"Emma!"

She didn't look at Caine, but pulled from his hold and kept walking.

"Things aren't always—" Caine began, following behind her.

"What they seem?" She faced him with a raised eyebrow, then shrugged. "It doesn't matter. I didn't come here looking for you."

As she started to walk away once more, he gripped her elbow. "The only reason I came tonight was because I thought you might be in some kind of trouble."

"You have an interesting way of keeping yourself busy," she said in a dry tone. Even though her heart tripped at the thought he seemed sincere in his desire to help her, she needed to do this alone. Shaking her head, she continued with a sigh. "I'm fine, Caine. Thanks for your concern."

Caine's hand slid down her elbow until his fingers locked with hers. She shivered at the electric heat that swept through her. The intensity was so…conflicted, almost as if her body wanted to shove him away, yet at the same time felt drawn to his touch. Like magnets with the same ends facing each other—pushing away, while a strong pull remained along the fringes, demanding that the attractive ends finally find each other and slam together.

Lifting their locked hands between them, he used his hold to pull her closer. "I know you feel what happens when we touch, Emma. I can't explain it either, but I want you to trust me. Come dance with me."

The man towered over her. Emma tried to pull free, but he didn't budge. She should be intimidated by his forceful stare, yet she wasn't. She should be angry that he was just dancing with another woman—other *women*—but she didn't care. Instead, the moment he stepped close and his primal scent invaded her senses, a strong urge to move as close to him as she possibly could rocked through her. It was irrational. She couldn't explain the attraction or the desire to know why her nerves tingled and sparked under her skin whenever he touched her. But it was there. Intensely strong.

And he wasn't letting go.

She glanced around them to see if anyone was watching. Everyone seemed engrossed in their own activities. Caine's fingers tightened around hers as if he thought she might take flight.

"One dance," she said, *and then I can walk away*. Caine released her hand so she could shrug out of her coat, but the moment she set her jacket on a chair near the bar, he grabbed her hand once more and tugged. He pulled her to the other side of the dance floor and moved to dance along the edges of the crowd, but she shook her head and led him deep into the throng, until they were in the center with everyone dancing around them. It was darkest in the middle and less likely anyone would see her with someone there. The bright colored lights swept the crowd in psychedelic patterns, yet the spot where they stood was the one area the lights didn't shine.

They stood facing each other and the song segued into a slower one. The music thumped and the heavy seductive rhythm poured right into her soul as Caine held her gaze. Wrapping his arm around her waist, he pulled her close. When they began to move to the slow beat, he released her hand and cupped the side of her face. Emma closed her eyes and gasped when the tingling sizzle leapt from her skin to his. Or was it his to hers? She couldn't tell which. Maybe both.

Caine slid his hand into her hair and his jaw brushed her temple when he spoke close to her ear. "Your hair is sparkling all over."

"It's the snow." Emma placed her hands on his dark green button-down shirt, then sucked in her breath at the sensation of his solid chest underneath her fingers. He was hard as a rock and his musky smell was so sinfully decadent she couldn't stop inhaling.

As they continued to slowly move to the music's erotic rhythm, his thumb tilted her chin upward and his dark gaze searched hers. "Your eyes sparkle, too, like they're reflecting golden light. They're mesmerizing."

Embarrassed heat shot up her cheeks. She considered her looks passable and her smile nice, but no one had ever acted as if he was totally enthralled by her. Jared had shown interest, yet the hungry way Caine's gaze searched the planes of her face—like he wanted to taste every part of her—was downright impossible to resist. Damn, he was good.

"How many times have you said that to a woman?" She

stared at his defined jaw and tried to wrestle control over her scattered emotions. She felt so safe with him, wanted to trust him—that he really *could* help her.

Caine's jaw muscle jumped at the same time he slid his hand underneath her hair. The moment his hot palm cupped the back of her neck, Emma instantly froze in place. Her heart hammered and her breathing turned shallow. Like an animal playing dead in front of a threatening predator, she just stopped moving. She couldn't control the impulse or explain it. It was instinctual and frightening all at once.

"I've never said that to anyone. It was sincere, Emma. I want you to trust me."

When she didn't say anything, his voice lowered. "Look at me."

"Why can't I move?" she whispered. Her gaze snapped to his and her pulse rushed in her ears.

"Maybe because you don't want to," he said as his lips hovered a mere inch from hers. His fingers pressed at the small of her back and his penetrating gaze bored into hers. "Don't you want to know if the fire sparks everywhere we touch?"

The intimate suggestion made her stomach tumble. She fell into his compelling gaze and heard herself say, "Yes."

He moved his hand into her hair and his sexy smile sent her pulse whooshing at a faster rate. "Then kiss m—"

Surprising herself, Emma tilted her head and lifted on her toes to press her lips against his. When their lips met, the conflicting emotions twisting her stomach fled. The heat between them tingled and zapped, frying her mind and her body with visceral lightning-flash intensity.

Every sound around them stripped away; the press of people disappeared. All she heard was their own breathing and the thump of their hearts. She moaned when Caine yanked her against him to press his lips harder against hers.

As he slid his tongue into her mouth, the sensual glide set her skin on fire. He tested her with a steady slow rhythm, his kiss deep and thorough as he explored, tasting her...demanding a matched response. She was so caught up and surprised by how deeply his kiss affected her that her knees actually wobbled. Emma dug her fingers into his shoulders to keep herself upright. His flavor was as irresistible as his earthy primal scent, full of heat and lusty promise.

Her body quaked from the desire she tasted on his tongue and the possessive way he slanted his lips over hers. Emma instinctively locked her hips against his and twined her arms around his neck, her kiss just as aggressive. The vibration of his groan against her mouth felt primitive, passionate...and right. Maybe it was the music, maybe it was his smell or his electric touch. All she knew was, as inexperienced as she was with men, she couldn't get close enough to this one. Her trust in him was inexplicably absolute.

Caine's chest rumbled against hers and his hands slid down her waist. When he gripped her rear in an assertive hold, then pressed his thigh hard against her sex, Emma shivered at the erotic sensations scattering through her. Her body hummed, pulsing with jolts of heat everywhere at once, like she was on some kind of hormonal high. She kissed his jaw and tried to catch her breath. "Closer."

As soon as she spoke, something vibrated against her inner thigh. Emma tensed, then gave a nervous laugh when she realized it was probably his cell phone.

"Sorry, I have to get this." Caine pulled the phone out of his pocket.

After he read the text message, he glanced around the room and tucked the phone back into his pocket. Emma noted his high-alert expression. "What's wrong?"

Caine's mouth set in a firm line and he seemed genuinely torn before he grabbed her hand, his hold tight. "I need to take care of something, but I want you to stay close."

Emma glanced at her watch. She had a half hour before she was supposed to meet with the person who'd left her that note. It was probably best if she did so alone. She pulled out of his hold. "Go do what you need to do." Pointing to the bar area where she'd left her coat, she continued. "I'll be over there." *In an open area where I'll be seen by myself.*

Caine's expression hardened. "I want to help you, Emma. Come with me."

She started to argue when he cursed under his breath and reached into his pocket again, pulling out his cell phone. As he read the text message, she began to back away. "I'll be fine. Just right over there."

He frowned. "Don't move from that spot. I want you to trust me enough to let me help you."

She nodded and turned away. Strangely, now that his smell wasn't seducing her senses, she still believed he wanted to help, even though she didn't think there was anything he could do for her. When she walked up the stairs to a higher spot near the crowded bar, Emma looked around the club for Caine.

He was already on the far side of the room near the entrance, talking to another blond woman. Every few moments, he'd glance Emma's way. Her insides turned to mush. Whatever they were talking about, he couldn't be paying too much attention to the blonde if he kept staring at her.

The song ended and a large group of people from the dance

floor headed for the bar. The mass jostled her, pushing her out of the way as they each vied for the bartender's attention. A sudden painful prick along her hip made Emma gasp in shocked surprise. She tried to turn, but someone spoke next to her ear, preventing her from seeing his face.

"We've been looking for you," a man said in a calm voice. As he spoke, her vision began to blur. When her legs began to collapse underneath her, an arm wrapped around her waist. "Don't fight it. Come along."

"Nooooo," she slurred, barely able to speak, let alone try to fight him off. Whatever he'd injected her with was very powerful and fast-acting. Her ability to resist had completely disappeared.

"That's a good girl," was the last thing Emma heard before she lost consciousness.

Chapter 4

Caine glanced up in time to see Emma stumble and a man with a salt-and-pepper beard and spiky hair hold her upright. When the man turned her around and started escorting her limp form toward the back exit, Caine instantly grabbed Kaitlyn's hand and moved through the crowd as fast as he could. "Emma!" he called, but his voice was drowned out by a sudden loud alarm reverberating through the club.

Someone had pulled the fire alarm.

Pandemonium erupted and people rushed toward the main entrance, creating a wall of people between Caine and the exit where the man had just taken Emma. Across the room, Laird called Caine's name over the screams. Caine saw the two female panthers heading toward the front door. He motioned for Laird and Roman to block their path, but the ladies were quickly swallowed up by the mob.

Landon stood at the entrance of the club, his expression grim and intense as he began to shove his way through the crowd. The moment his Alpha reached them, Caine released his tight hold on Kaitlyn, and a deep snarl unfurled from his throat as he leapt over the crowd toward the exit. He didn't give a damn who saw his inhuman jump. All he cared about was saving Emma. When he landed with a heavy thud near the back exit, he knocked a man in a black shirt back against the wall.

"Watch it!" the man yelled over the alarm.

The main lights came on at that moment, highlighting the man's stark features. He scowled as he pushed himself off the wall. When he started to turn toward the back exit, Caine stepped in front of him and thumbed toward the main entrance. "Go out the other door."

The guy stared at the crowd of people squeezing out the front door, then glared at him before he stalked away. Caine grunted his annoyance at the interruption. He didn't need any witnesses when he shredded the bastard to bits for attempting to kidnap Emma.

The heavy metal door slammed against the building's brick wall as Caine burst through it. His wereclaws were already extended, ready to inflict painful damage. Only an empty alley and a Dumpster greeted him. A howl of fury erupted from his throat as swirls of snow drifted quietly to the ground. He clenched his fists and welcomed the pain his claws inflicted on his palms before they retracted.

A couple seconds later, Landon and Kaitlyn appeared behind him, flanked by Laird and Roman. "Care to tell me what that was all about?" Landon said, peering past the glow of the single floodlight above the door into the dark alley.

"A human woman was just kidnapped," Caine gritted out

before he stepped into the darkness and began looking for tire tracks, clues, anything that would help him find her kidnappers.

"Emma? Who took her?" Laird's brow creased with a frown as he brushed past Landon and Kaitlyn.

"A man with a graying beard and spiky hair." Caine kicked at the offending snow that had begun to cover the tire tracks. In a matter of minutes, he'd lose the scent altogether. Ignoring the cold flakes landing in his hair, he glanced up at Laird, his stomach knotting with guilt. "I saw him drag her toward this exit. I couldn't get to her in time."

"Everyone spread out and scent the entire area," Landon commanded in a hard tone. He walked up to Caine and put a hand on his shoulder. "We'll find her."

Caine's jaw tensed and he gave Landon a curt nod before he turned back to the task of cataloging the scents around him. Emma was scared tonight. He's seen the fear in her eyes and heard the frustration in her voice. Whom had she come to the club to meet?

After several minutes, Laird and Roman approached Caine. "We only detect one fresh, distinct scent," Laird said as he inhaled the frigid air. "There's a human male's scent and Emma's earthy one."

Landon snorted and Kaitlyn put her hand on her mate's arm. "What is it?"

"The scents are all muddled." He rubbed his neck and shook his head. "I can't put my finger on it. Something smells 'off.'" He looked at Caine. "You got them all?"

Why did Emma's scent smell so distinct and different from the human male's to him? Caine wondered, even as he nodded to Landon. "I would recognize the man's scent again if I smelled him." *Whereas I could pick Emma out of a crowd of five hundred people in two seconds flat.* The fire alarm had stopped a few minutes before and he saw red lights flashing around the corner of the building. The fire trucks had finally arrived. Caine turned away to head back inside the club. The moment he walked over the threshold, he saw one of the bartenders lifting Emma's jacket from the chair where she'd left it.

"I'll take that," Caine called out, approaching the man.

The guy eyed the coat, then frowned. "It looks a bit small for you."

Caine's gut tightened. Emma's coat might help him find her. "It's my girlfriend's. She sent me back inside to get it once the alarm stopped."

The dark-headed bartender nodded and handed him the jacket. "That's one less thing to go into lost and found."

Caine gripped the coat tight at the same time Laird and the others walked back inside. "That hers?" Laird asked while Caine felt inside the pocket and pulled out a plastic box with the days of the week marked on the outside and loads of pills in the separate compartments.

He nodded and frowned at the meds, then shoved the box back into her pocket and felt around once more. When his fingers brushed against a set of keys, he pulled them out and held them in front of him. "These might help me find out where she lives."

Ten minutes later, Laird stood watch while Caine shoved Emma's car key in her car's passenger-side door. The crowd had dispersed and the fire trucks had driven off, leaving the street strangely quiet, while the heavy snow continued to coat their hair and clothes.

"How is this going to help you find her house again?" Laird asked over his shoulder.

"Registration," Caine said. Pulling the glove box open, he rifled through the paperwork inside, then held the paper aloft. "Bingo."

A light came on above them, and a guy walked of out the apartment above the café, carrying a trash bag. "Hey!" he yelled down into the parking lot. It was the guy from the café, the owner. "That's not your car."

Caine and Laird took off the moment he went back inside, threatening to call the police.

"Damn, Caine, your woman lives in the boonies, doesn't she?" Roman commented from the backseat after Laird pulled down the long gravel driveway, then cut the engine in front of a small house ensconced deep in the forest near the Greenwood Lake area.

"Apparently she likes her privacy," Caine mused while Landon and Kaitlyn drove up behind them in Landon's truck.

Kaitlyn hopped out and was walking toward the house before Landon had shut off the engine. She'd removed her blond wig, and had pulled her red hair up in a clip. Caine tensed when she quickly withdrew her gun from the holder at her waist and motioned for Landon, her expression suddenly concerned.

Caine and Landon reached her side at the same time. "Do you see it?" Kaitlyn whispered, pointing toward the dark house.

Landon's body stiffened. "Velius," he said in a clipped tone. Stepping in front of Kaitlyn, he approached the house with a guarded stance. When he was within twenty feet, he called over his shoulder, "The house is empty. I don't sense any heartbeats."

Why were the panthers at Emma's house? Caine's chest constricted as he entered the house behind Kaitlyn and Landon, Roman and Laird following in his wake.

The moment they stepped inside, Kaitlyn gave a low whistle. "There are handprints everywhere, like they searched every nook and cranny."

Landon snorted. "They were a lot neater here than at my office." He gestured to Caine, Laird and Roman. "See what scents you can pick up, if any. Right now I only smell one human. A woman."

Roman sniffed the air and walked into the living room, then stepped briefly down the hall before coming back. "I smell one human, as well, and residual earthy scents." He tilted his head to the side. "The human's scent is laced with several man-made chemicals."

Kaitlyn came out of the kitchen holding a few medicine bottles. "You're smelling her meds." She glanced at the name on the labels. "According to these, her name is Mary Gray and she has a heart condition among other things."

That explained the jam-packed pillbox in Emma's pocket. Must be her aunt's, Caine thought. He walked down the hall to peer into the two bedrooms. One room appeared to be someone else's and the second definitely had to be Emma's with an old desktop computer and a stack of schoolbooks. He definitely picked up two scents. Why didn't they smell Emma's like he did? "This doesn't make any sense." His chest tensed as he stood in the doorway to Emma's room.

"Whoa!" Kaitlyn brushed past him and walked into Emma's room. "This room explodes with handprints." She moved to the bathroom and Caine heard her opening cabinets and pulling back the shower curtain. Something wary settled in his stomach when Kaitlyn came back out and she looked at her mate standing behind Caine.

"She's a panther."

"You're wrong!" Caine snarled even as his inner wolf acknowledged the fact Emma had smelled distinctly unique from any human he'd come across.

"*That's* what I smelled in the alley. That faint scent I couldn't place," Landon said in a low tone. "It has been a long time since I've smelled a Velius and her scent was so faint I thought I'd imagined it."

Caine felt as if someone had slammed a hot poker deep inside his chest. He suppressed the sense of betrayal that threatened within him. A panther? "There's some explanation," he said in a curt tone.

"It's all right here," Landon said as he moved to stand beside his mate in the bedroom.

Caine wanted to explore Emma's room, to see what kind of books she liked to read, what she was studying, to check out her taste in music. He didn't want to have to look at her room like this…as if she were a criminal to be analyzed. Kaitlyn approached him and put her hand on his arm. "I'm sorry, Caine, but I just checked out her most private toiletries to be sure before I said anything. They were covered in her sparkling handprints." She gestured toward the room. "Her keyboard, her books, her pillow and sheets, her hairbrush, her toothbrush. Everything carries these sparkles. No other room in the house has this much residue."

"But we smelled her earthy scent," Laird started to say, when Caine cut him off by speaking in his head. *Don't say anything.*

"You scented her?" Landon's stare was shrewd.

Caine knew what that question meant. Landon would want them to hunt her. "Neither of us thought to. She was human."

"Who happened to smell of the earth?" Landon challenged. *Why aren't you telling him?* Laird spoke to Caine in his mind.

Caine's mental reply was terse, not meant to be argued with. *Something's not right. I need to do some digging.* "We were unaware of the Velius' existence until recently when you killed that one to protect Kaitlyn's mom." He paused and glanced at Laird and Roman before he returned his attention to Landon. "Since the Velius were created and set free before our time, we didn't know that's what they smelled like."

"Now you do," Landon said. "Though I'm partially to blame for not cluing all of you in on their scent markers. It hadn't occurred to me to do so, because all the panthers we've run across have masked their scent. Hers was so faint and slightly different than I remembered that I almost missed it."

Emma's not part of this, Caine wanted to yell, even though he couldn't deny her smell or the electric shock that happened between them whenever they touched. It was something he definitely couldn't explain. He'd never experienced that before with anyone, human or Lupreda. "Fill us in on what we need to know about these panthers."

Landon rolled his head from shoulder to shoulder before he spoke. "They can't shift without a specialized injection straight into their system, and they can only stay in their panther form until the injection wears off. Usually after a couple of hours. They're powerful beasts and would be more-than-worthy adversaries, but the Lupreda who created them to hunt for prey wanted to ensure equal footing. The Velius' black coats radiate iridescence and their eyes give off a glow in the absence of light, taking away the panthers' best hunting advantage in the dark—the element of surprise."

While they were in the club earlier, Emma's hair had sparkled and her eyes had flashed in the dim light, attracting him like a jacked-up wolf on his first full-mooned run of the month. Caine's heart sank. There was no denying that she was Velius. *Why wasn't she masking her scent?* He *had* scented Emma, but he wanted to find her first, to give her a chance to explain what she was and why she was pretending to be human.

"Is there anything else we should know?" Caine's tone held a sharp edge. Frustration warred within him. He wanted to believe she was special. He wanted answers, damn it!

"They don't heal as quickly as we do." Landon's features turned to stone and his body tensed. "Maybe this whole thing is some kind of setup. A cat-and-mouse game the Velius are playing with the Lupreda. Panthers are known for their ambush hunting style."

Caine didn't like Landon assuming Emma had played them. She was truly upset at the café and the club. He tensed and started to challenge Landon when Kaitlyn brushed past them both. "Let's check out the rest of the house. Maybe we'll find more answers."

Caine moved to follow Landon and Roman down the hall when Laird spoke to him mentally once more. *You know I trust you, but holding back could put our pack in jeopardy.*

Pausing, Caine narrowed his gaze on Laird. *Spoken like Landon's* true *Second,* he said before he turned away.

Laird's hand landed hard on his shoulder, stopping him. *I'll heed your judgment on this one. You have twenty-four hours to find her on your own.*

Caine didn't speak nor did he look Laird's way. The respect his pack mate paid him was enough. He grunted his appreciation and Laird's hand fell away.

When Caine and Laird walked into the other bedroom, Kaitlyn held up several clear packets full of hundreds of white pills. A couple empty brown medicine bottles and a stack of pretyped labels were in her other hand. It appeared she'd pulled them from a box she'd set on the bed.

She glanced at the writing on the labels. "It says these are prescription vitamins for Emma Gray, but I'll bet you money this is how the panthers are masking their scent." Setting the packets on the bed, she took a pill out of one of the sleeves and handed it to Landon. "Want to pulverize this so I can see if my theory is true?"

Landon crushed the pill between his fingers, then murmured, "Son of a bitch," as he spread it across his open palm.

Kaitlyn nodded. "That's what I thought. The meds might be suppressing their scent, but they're also causing them to leave behind the sparkling handprint residue. At least we have one answer." She met Caine's gaze. "There was only one area of this room that had the iridescent handprints." She paused and pointed to the bottom nightstand drawer. "The person had this box with the medicine hidden under stacks of magazines and newspapers. I think the human woman must've been giving them to Emma." She frowned for a second. "Humans are helping the panthers?"

"Members of the mafia were working with them in the pulser gun-running case a few months ago," Landon reminded her with a shrug.

She shook her head. "This feels different to me. This is a home. There aren't any stolen pulser guns here, nothing malicious or illegal that I can see."

Landon scowled. "The damned pills give them too much stealthy power."

Caine shook his head. He needed answers and Emma was the only one who could give them to him.

Roman walked into the room holding a piece of paper. "This was on the floor behind the front door."

Caine read the note and ground his teeth. Crushing the paper into a tight ball, he tossed it to Landon. "She told me her aunt had been taken. We need to find her. Not only did they kidnap her aunt, but they've taken her, as well."

Landon read the note, then narrowed his gaze on Caine. "This could be an elaborate trap. The Velius' actions so far have been conniving and deadly. We need to proceed with caution."

"She's guilty until proven innocent. Is that it?" Caine's jaw felt like metal that had been heated then cooled too quickly. He was ready to snap.

"Have you forgotten the three zerkers they tortured and killed? I will not lose any more wolves, Caine." Alpha fury vibrated off Landon as he clenched his hand into a fist.

"I'm not volunteering anyone but me," Caine shot back, his neck hairs bristling.

"Nothing is open at this hour," Kaitlyn cut in with a calm tone. "Why don't we start with the pharmacy listed on these labels first thing in the morning." She turned to Caine with a meaningful look. "Maybe we can find out who's supplying the panthers this medicine and backtrack to other connections from there."

Caine gave her a curt nod, then left the room.

When Laird pulled up outside Caine's apartment over an hour later, he spoke in a low tone after Caine slid out of the car. "Twenty-four hours is all I can promise."

"Understood." Caine grabbed Emma's coat and shut the door behind him. Worry for her cramped his stomach as he climbed the stairs to his apartment three at a time. After he'd let himself in the door, he settled on the sofa and inhaled her coat's collar. Fresh soap and shampoo scents coated the material, but her earthy, forestlike smell still lingered faintly. It wasn't enough to scent her, though. He was relieved he'd already set her unique markers to memory earlier.

Unfortunately the snow still falling steadily outside confused his senses, making it impossible to try and find her right now. Not to mention New York was wall-to-wall people and buildings. He could search for a couple weeks before he found her...and that was if her captors kept her in one place. But he would find her. He just hoped like hell he wasn't too late to help her. If he was, no one involved would be breathing when he left the place. He clenched his fists tightly around Emma's coat.

Caine heard a cracking sound and his fingers eased up on the thick material. Sliding his hand into the inside coat pocket, he pulled out a pair of gloves and what used to be a pill bottle before he'd crushed it. As he tossed the gloves to the couch, a couple of the bottle's hard plastic pieces fell away from the label. Caine frowned when he saw black writing on the backside of the paper. Thumbing back the label, he memorized the phone number and stood, pulling his cell phone out of his pocket.

Punching in a number and an extension he'd seen Landon use before for the police precinct, he waited until a woman answered, then said, "Hi, Sandra. This is Caine Grennard. I'm working with Landon Rourke and Kaitlyn McKinney on a case and I'm wondering if you could do me a favor. I need to have a phone number traced. Can you do that for me?"

"I'm not supposed to but...because Landon helped out my little brother, I help him whenever I can. What's the number?"

Caine rattled off the number and waited for her to punch it in. "Hmm, there seems to be a block on it, but I might be able to get past it if you can get them to answer it and stay on, even for a few seconds."

"I *love* today's technology," Caine said with a feral smile. "Wait a few seconds for me to call from my cell and then lock on to the number."

"She's coming around. I sense her consciousness. Go ahead and take her blood quickly," a woman said.

The smell of rubbing alcohol preceded a small, sharp pain at the crook of her arm. Emma winced. Her body felt as if someone had laid a heavy lead cape across it. She was so tired. She tried to open her eyes, but they only rolled in her head. She caught a glimpse of a spotlight above her before her eyelids closed against the stark brightness.

There was something she was supposed to remember. What was it? She struggled to organize her fuzzy thoughts. Something important. Someone could get hurt. Her aunt! Emma moaned and flailed her arms, knocking the spotlight out of her eyes. "The pills," she groaned.

"I know you haven't taken your pills," the same woman replied.

"No," Emma croaked. "My aunt's pills. In my jacket. Take them to her!"

"She must be talking about Margaret," a man said. He moved closer. "Is Margaret sick?"

Emma picked up on the urgent concern in his voice. "Where have you taken my aunt? She needs her medicine."

"It'll be okay," the woman said in a calm tone, then her voice turned harsh, accusatory. "You gave her too much."

Emma wasn't sure if the woman was speaking to her or the man. "Needs her meds," Emma mumbled, her words slurring.

"Go test her blood. Once her head is clear, I'll give her a shot instead of a pill for expediency."

"Not me!" Emma insisted. She didn't need the pills. Her aunt did. The man seemed to know she was talking about Mary, even though he'd called her Margaret. The woman didn't. Why was everything fuzzy and blurred when she tried to see them? Why wouldn't her eyes cooperate? God, her head felt like it was going to explode right off her body. The horrific throbbing seemed as if her head was bouncing on the hard surface she was laying on.

Emma smelled the man's fear spike when he'd asked about Margaret's health. How could she smell his fear? She didn't know how, but the sharpness was undeniable. Yet she sensed nothing, not a trace of a scent, from the woman. It was as if she didn't exist, like a ghost with a voice.

Straps came around her wrists, making Emma's heart rate soar. The woman spoke again. "I wouldn't want you to fall. He gave you too much. 'Wanted to get you out quickly,'" she said, mimicking the man's raspy voice. Leaning closer, she continued. "It's going to take you a while to come out of it. You rest for a bit. I'll be back once we have the test results. We want to make sure you're healthy."

"My aunt!" Emma thrashed and her throat burned with the need to scream. Her voice croaked. Tears of frustration rolled down her temples, wetting her hair. In the back of her mind, she wondered why they wanted her blood, but her aunt was her first priority. "You have me. Let my aunt go."

Cool fingers lightly brushed across her forehead. The touch was so faint that Emma wondered about ghosts once more. "Rest. We'll take care of everything."

A door opened and closed. *They were taking care of Mary.* Relief washed over Emma, but after a few minutes alone in the quiet room, her paranoia rekindled and grew. She lifted her head and blinked to try and see her surroundings. White walls and metallic silvery shadows—reminding her of hospital-style medical cabinets—was all she could make out. The room felt sterile and cool, like an exam or operating room.

They wanted to make sure she was healthy? The thought made her heart hammer against her chest. Were they going to experiment on her? *Did they kidnap me for my organs?* Oh, God. She'd heard stories about such things but thought they were just urban legends. Jerking against the straps around her wrists, she tried to pull free, but her arms where held down too tightly.

Her pulse whooshed in her ears and she blinked several times to try and focus. Nausea rose from her belly, settling in the back of her throat. Her head swam from the burning sensation and she had to lay her head on the table once more to regain her equilibrium and settle her stomach.

She'd taken several deep breaths to calm herself when she heard a light tapping noise to her left. Emma turned toward the sound and saw a shadow outlined by what looked like a window.

Panting in fear, she opened her mouth to scream when a male voice spoke quickly in her mind. *Don't scream. I'm here to get you out.*

The voice sounded so familiar. Someone she trusted. The scream in her mind gave way to quiet mewling in her throat and she blinked again to try and force her eyes to work. It sounded like a window was being jimmied, then lifted, and a few seconds later the man was closer. Had he come inside? But she'd heard his voice clearly a second ago when he was outside. She blinked to clear her confused mind, but his image remained blurred and hazy. When she squinted, desperately trying to see, dizziness ensued once more.

All she could do was close her eyes and nod. What man did she trust? She racked her brain and could only come up with the name Jared. She knew him somehow. She'd gone to him when she was worried about her aunt. *I trust Jared.*

A couple seconds later, he was leaning over her and a gloved hand touched her face. "Emma! Can you hear me?"

She felt a jerk around her wrist and her arm was free, then her other arm was freed from its restraint, as well. She bit back a cry of shock when he lifted her in his arms. He was soaking wet and freezing cold. "Did you take a shower?" she whispered.

The storm and wet clothes make it hard to smell me, he replied. As soon as he set her on the floor, her legs refused to work. She would've collapsed if he hadn't had a good hold on her arm. *I'm going to have to lift you through the window. Think you can help me? Just nod if you think you can.*

Frowning, she bobbed her head in agreement. She realized why he'd sounded like he was inside the room before. He was speaking in her mind, but *why* did she hear his voice in her head? Focusing, she gritted her teeth and forced her wobbly legs to hold her upright. The next thing she knew, he'd lifted her and turned her facedown toward the ground as he slid her legs out the window first. Something crunched along her hip as he slid her across the windowsill. She winced at the pinching sensation.

Hold on to the ledge, then I'll grab your hands and lower you to the ground. Understand? he said in a commanding tone.

Emma nodded, even though the world around her was spinning on its axis. Upside down was suddenly right side up. Her body was dry yet shivering with cold. She was so confused, but strangely she trusted him to keep her safe. His big hands cinched tightly around her wrists and then she hung suspended in the air. "I'm flying," she whispered in awe as she glanced toward the fluffy white cloud below and kicked her feet in glee.

You're flyin', all right, he mumbled. *Focus! I'm going to let you go. The snow should buffer some of your fall, but be ready to roll so you don't break a leg. Got it?*

And then Emma was set free to fly. Her flight of freedom was over way too quickly and she landed on her side with a heavy thump. When her right hip began to throb, Emma remembered vaguely she was supposed to roll. "That hurt," she moaned as he landed on booted feet beside her.

She was scooped up in his arms once more. "I told you to roll," he chided in a low, concerned tone.

Emma realized it was snowing as a burst of frigid air and heavy snowflakes blew against them. The snow was coming down hard, and the whiteout, combined with her blurred vision, made it impossible to see his features. She wrapped her arms tight around his cold coat and settled her face against his cold collar. He smelled wonderful—how could he say wet clothes dulled his smell?—and his body radiated warmth underneath his coat. She inhaled and rubbed her nose along his shirt. "Thank you for rescuing me, Jared."

His grip around her tightened and his brisk steps stopped for a second. Then the wind whistled around them as if they were moving at a rapid speed—like they were gliding. Emma's breath caught against the bitter cold air. By the time he stopped and set her feet on the ground next to a truck, her teeth were chattering and her body shivered uncontrollably.

She blinked and tilted her head when the passenger door's handle came off in his hand. Damn, it was colder out here than she realized for the handle to break like that. She didn't realize freezing-cold metal crumpled so easily, either, she thought when he tossed the mangled handle to the ground. Above the whistle of the wind, someone was yelling off in the distance. He jerked open the door and she stepped up on the runner, then flopped into the seat. *When did Jared get a truck? He normally drove a beat-up Jetta.* Emma's muddled mind pondered as the driver-side door opened and he climbed inside.

Before she could ask about his new truck, he pushed her to a seated position and quickly snapped the seat belt around her. A second later, after he'd messed with some wires under the dashboard, the engine roared to life. That's odd. Where was his key?

The moment he jammed on the gas pedal and they began to move, the window on the driver side burst. Emma screamed as glass flew everywhere and a man's dark head came through the window. He snarled and grabbed at her rescuer, throwing haphazard punches as the truck swerved in the snow.

Emma panted and leaned to grip the steering wheel while the two men grappled with each other. She had no idea where the truck was heading. All she could think to do was hold the wheel straight and pray they didn't slam into a wall.

Jared howled his fury and drove his fist into the man's face, and then, in a swift move that left her reeling in shock, he twisted the man's head. The sickening snap gave way to complete silence right before he pushed the intruder out of the window.

Lights flashed behind them as her rescuer took hold of the steering wheel and said in a gruff tone, "They're coming. Hold on tight. They're closing the gates on us."

Pulse racing, Emma had barely gotten the words "What gates?" out when they slammed into something. Sparks flew and metal ground against metal right before a piece of chain-link fence bounced against the windshield, cracking the glass right down the middle.

As they sped down the street, the snow made it near impossible to see more than a few feet in front of them, or even if they were on the right side of the street. Then Emma saw the blinking yellow caution sign that warned of something in the middle of the road—construction maybe? She jerked her gaze his way. "Do you see it?"

"I do." He jammed harder on the gas and kept the truck straight ahead and on a collision course.

When they were within two seconds of hitting it, she panted erratically and screamed, "Turn!" At the last second, he jerked the truck to the right and she breathed a sigh of relief, quickly glancing behind them. The SUV chasing them didn't have time to react. The vehicle hit the cement median and flew through the air. Landing on its side in a metallic crunch and shattered glass, it skidded across the snow-covered road.

Five minutes later, they pulled up beside another truck. Once he'd carried her around and set her inside the cab of the second truck, locking the seat belt around her, he said in a gruff tone, "They're not going to stop that easily. Another vehicle wasn't far behind that one."

Right before he turned the key to start the engine, he lifted something from the seat between them and wrapped it around her shoulders. "Here's your coat. It's going to take a while for my truck to get warm."

As the vehicle lurched forward, Emma realized through all the chaos she missed hearing his deep voice in her head. And now that he'd spoken to her directly a couple times, his voice sounded different than she remembered. Her mind was starting to clear a little, even if her vision was still moving in and out.

All she could make out was shadows in the cab and white everywhere she looked outside the truck windows. She was amazed she even saw the yellow marker in the road. Apparently blinking warning lights and self-preservation were powerful motivators. She turned toward his shadow to see he was holding his hand up to his ear.

"I have Emma. If you want the Velius, here's their address." He rattled off an address, then paused before he spoke again in a harsh tone. "She's all drugged up and can barely say her own name, Landon. I've got someone coming on my tail. I'll shake them and then I'm taking her somewhere safe until she can detox."

The phone snapped closed at the same time she heard the ring tone shut down sequence that indicated he'd turned off the cell phone. Her rescuer had spoken long enough for her to realize… "You're not Jared," she whispered in a shaky voice.

He didn't say a word. Instead he set the phone on the seat, pulled off his glove and reached over toward her. Emma swallowed a small scream and tried to cringe away as he slid his fingers under her hair and curled his fingers around the back of her neck. She gasped when his touch locked her still in her seat. Warm heat and an inviting smell enveloped her as an electric sensation spread all the way to her belly and beyond.

Emma gripped his wrist and her heart jerked as her body recognized what her impaired sight and muddled mind couldn't. Tears streaked hot trails down her cold cheeks. "I know you, but…but my mind is all confused." She shook her head in frustration.

"It's nice to be *kind of* remembered," he said before he pulled his hand away.

They turned onto a highway and the vehicle fishtailed on the slick surface, making her stomach roil. Emma closed her eyes and put her hand over her mouth. Her stomach heaved again. "You have to stop," she moaned.

"Emma, we need to get you out of here. They're not far behind."

The urgency in his voice went right over her head when her mouth began to water. She was going to puke. "Stop the truck now!"

Quickly jerking the vehicle to the side of the road, he slammed on the brakes. Emma managed to unbuckle and get the door open just in time. She leaned out and tossed everything in her stomach onto the stark white snow until only dry heaves racked her body. Vaguely, she realized that he was holding her hair back from her face when he said near her ear, "Are you okay?"

Emma moaned and nodded. Taking the bottle of water he offered, she swished the water around in her mouth, then spit once more into the snow. Straightening, she set the container inside the door holder before she closed the door. Snow coated her hair once more, making her shiver all over. The truck began to move again and she closed her eyes, trying not to think about her stomach. When her head lolled from one shoulder to the other in exhaustion, she felt a tug on her shoulder and a strong hand pushed her head down toward his lap. "Lay down, Emma. We've got a hell of a drive ahead of us in this snow."

"Going home," she mumbled with a heavy sigh as she put her coat on his wet thigh and laid her head down on top of it. The sensation of the vents blowing warm heat over her and the swishing of the windshield wipers lulled her tired body.

He gave a strange, almost sad-sounding laugh as his knuckles ran along her cheek and jawbone. "As bitterly ironic as that statement is, yes, we're going home."

Chapter 5

Emma awoke when the truck rolled to a stop. Her head felt as if someone had stuffed it full of sawdust. She sat up and stared out at the white world outside the truck. Gusts of snow buffeted the vehicle and through the haze of white she saw the outline of trees in the darkness around them.

"We'll have to walk from here."

A deep voice drew her attention. Her vision had cleared enough for her to see him. Pitch-black hair and eyebrows brought out the emerald green in his hazel eyes. With the snow reflecting the partial moon's light through the windows as if it were almost daylight, the effect defined his cheekbones, while the overnight beard coating his jaw hollowed his features in sharp, vivid clarity.

Caine. She remembered his name now. He was more primal and hauntingly attractive than the dim nightclub light had given him credit for. God, whatever drug those kidnappers had used to knock her out earlier really had sent her mind off to la-la land for her to have had such a hard time remembering him.

"Caine."

"You remember." He touched her cheek, and the tingle from his touch was surprisingly warm, considering she could already see plumes of frost from their breath as the truck's cab quickly cooled down.

He literally sucked the air from her lungs when he looked at her the way he did—like he would've done anything, touched her everywhere and then some, to make her remember him. Her smile wobbled. "Just bits and pieces." But her peace suddenly evaporated as her past worries came back to her full force. "My aunt! Did you see an older lady in that place where they kept me?"

Caine frowned. "No, I didn't." He cupped her jaw, his expression intense. "You were my priority. I've sent friends back to the building, though, and if your aunt is there, they will get her to safety."

Emma vaguely remembered a phone call he'd made earlier. "Can you call and see if they found her?"

Caine shook his head and released her to slide his cell phone into his jacket pocket. His coat appeared to have mostly dried. "I tried to check my messages earlier, but the storm has apparently knocked out the cell tower's reception."

"Wait! I have my cell." Emma dug into her front pocket and pulled out her cell phone. It fell apart the moment it was free of her jeans. "Damn." She tossed the ruined cell to the floor and frowned at him, feeling utterly useless. *Please let Aunt Mary be okay.*

When a strong gust of wind whistled around the truck, rocking the vehicle with its ferocity, Emma glanced out the window and shivered. "Where are we?" She racked her brain, trying to remember. "Did I give you directions to my house?"

"Your home isn't safe. I went there after you were taken from the club. I found—" He paused and his jaw flexed. "We have to get you to a safe place."

What was he about to say? Emma grabbed his hand. "Is something wrong with my house? Did it burn down or something?" Caine clasped her hand, locking his fingers with hers. The electric buzz between them seemed even stronger now.

Heavy thumps of snow thudded on the roof and hood of the truck, falling from the trees above them. "No. Your house is fine." Squeezing her hand, he continued. "We need to get out of my truck before more snow falls and blocks the doors. Come on."

She held fast to his hand before he could pull away. "Why are you helping me?"

His expression hardened briefly. "That's a good question…" He glanced down at their clasped hands, then ran his thumb across her palm. The spark and sizzle that followed his finger's wake made her breath catch. The sensation was seductively erotic. His gaze snapped to hers, piercing sharp. "We'll talk later."

When he pulled away, his expression had turned guarded once more. "What's wrong?" she asked.

Caine opened the door and climbed out. Facing her, he held his hand out for her, his tone curt. "I'll expect full honesty, Emma. Safety first, answers later."

Emma shrugged into her coat. As she buttoned it, she wondered what in the world Caine was talking about. He appeared displeased about something. Was he upset she didn't tell him why she was at the club? She had no idea she was going to be kidnapped, for Pete's sake! "Yes, of course," she said as she started to put her hand in his.

Instead of grabbing her hand, he shoved his glove on her left hand, then motioned for her right. Emma scooted forward and while she waited for him to put the other glove on her, she watched the falling snow coat his black hair, turning it salt and pepper.

Now that she was fully gloved, he'd let go of one hand and she expected him to let go of the other. Instead, he leaned down a bit and jerked her forward.

Emma let out a slight yelp when she found herself lying facedown across his shoulder. "What are you doing?" Her voice was muffled against his thigh-length black coat.

He shut the door and locked the vehicle, then jammed the keys into his front pocket. Shifting her body a bit on his shoulder, he said, "I can get you there much faster if I carry you."

"I seriously doubt that." Emma snorted and reached up to tuck her coat tighter around her hips to keep out the snow. "I might be several inches shorter than you, but my legs work just fine." A heavy hand came down on her butt. "Ow! What was that for?"

Caine glanced her way and slid on a pair of sunglasses. "I suggest you cover your eyes. The snow's going to sting them otherwise."

The snow was coming down in fat, soft flakes. A gust of wind made it blow softly into her face. "I think I'll survive."

"Ready?" Caine grabbed hold of her butt underneath her coat.

Despite the cold, her face burned at his possessive, intimate hold. "Hey!" She stiffened and smacked his thigh. "Paws off!"

Caine grunted. "When I grab your butt for real, Emma, you'll know it." As if for effect, his fingers spread wide across her rear and he caressed her butt cheek, before he gave it a firm, "this is all mine" squeeze.

Despite her flaming cheeks, Emma's breasts tingled and her stomach clenched in response. "Caine!"

He laughed. "Time to go."

Before she could say a word, they were flying through the woods. *Damn, he can run fast. Maybe he's an athlete,* Emma thought, then realized with swift shock that she knew nothing about this man, other than the fact he'd rescued her and her brain refused to work whenever he was near. Then again, circumstances being what they were, they'd started off in the strangest of situations. She couldn't explain why she trusted him, but she did. Implicitly.

During Caine's rapid uphill trek, snow fell on them twice from the heavily laden trees above, and now her coat and the back of her pants were soaked. She began to shiver all over. Her teeth chattered and her lips had probably changed to a lovely shade of "popsicle" blue. The wind had really picked up as he ran. She was frozen to the point of numbness. "How much longer? I'm so tired."

Caine's grip tightened around her. He never broke his stride as he ordered in a sharp tone, "Stay awake, Emma. We're almost there."

A few minutes later, when her eyes had begun to droop once more, Caine's fast pace slowed. Then he stopped and set her down on her feet.

Emma was shivering so hard, she could barely keep her eyes open. Caine's warm fingers touched her cheeks. Tilting her chin up, his gaze searched her face and his tone turned rough with concern. "Hey, stay with me. We'll be inside in a second."

They were standing on the porch of a cabin-style house. The roof above gave them some relief from the gusting wind and blowing snow, while Caine's intoxicating smell melted her stomach and his tingling touch encouraged her frozen skin back to life.

Without a second thought, Emma pressed his hot hands to her face, then turned her mouth toward one of his palms. Kissing the warm surface, she closed her eyes and relished in his glorious heat. "Wh-why aren't your ha-hands freezing? I want *your* metabolism."

A low growl rumbled from his throat before the hand she was kissing slid into her hair. His fingers pressed against the back of her neck and he cupped her jaw in a possessive hold, his thumb turning her face upward.

Emma's breath caught when Caine leaned close. An invisible electric current hummed between them, its magnetic pull irresistibly strong. Up close, she realized with giddy delight that Caine's bottom lip was fuller than the top—the man had such kissable lips. That sexy mouth was less than an inch away from hers and she was so ready to feel their sizzle once more. Her gaze locked with his fierce hazel one, and her stomach sucked inward as she waited for him to close the small distance between them; to warm her from head to toe.

Caine's fingers flexed a couple times against the base of her skull before he took a step back. "Let's go inside and get warmed up."

The gruff edge in his voice confused her. A second ago he'd been about to kiss her. She'd swear he was. Wrapping her arms around her shivering body, she followed him into the cabin.

After Caine shut the door behind them, Emma stamped her feet to keep warm. She didn't think it was possible, but the house was even colder than outside. Caine turned on a couple of electric lanterns he'd pulled from under a cabinet in the kitchen, then walked over and handed her one. As he set the other lantern on the kitchen counter, she held hers up to see the rest of the cabin.

To her immediate left was a sofa, chairs and a huge polished tree stump that doubled for a coffee table. There were two doors to each side of the main room, which she assumed led to bedrooms and probably a bathroom. A kitchenette took up the nearest corner to her right and a bed took up the far right corner of the main room. Emma's gaze locked with longing on the stone fireplace in the far left corner. Her entire body shivered, rocking the lantern she held up. "Pl-please tell me you have wood out back somewhere." Billows of frosty breath floated in front of her, making her even more aware of the depth of the chill in the house.

"This house depends solely on heat from the fireplace." Caine blew on his hands and rubbed them together, mumbling, "Even my body temperature is dropping from the prolonged exposure."

Emma shook her head when he walked over to stand near her. It was the first she'd seen him react to the cold. *Sheesh, did the guy think he was immune?*

He glanced at her, his gaze serious. "Someone followed us for a while. It may have been them. I'm pretty sure I lost them in the storm, but I don't want to take a chance. Once the snow stops falling, the smoke from a fire could alert them to our location. There's a space heater that will provide a small amount of heat for us."

Emma realized she didn't even know where their *location* was. She shivered uncontrollably. "Wh-where are we?"

"We're in the Shawangunk Mountains." Caine's jaw tensed. "I have a feeling the people who took you won't give up looking for you so easily."

Emma's throat closed and she blinked several times to keep tears from surfacing. "I'm so scared, Caine. They took my aunt and—" her voice began to quiver "—I don't know what they want from me."

Caine put his hands on her shoulders and frowned. "You didn't know the people who took you?"

Emma shook her head in frantic jerks. "No! I have no idea who they were or why they took a sample of my blood. Maybe they wanted to check my blood type and see if I was compatible so they could steal a kidney or something." Her eyes widened. "Your friend, the man you sent to that address…he won't call the police, will he? They took my aunt and told me 'no police.'"

Caine began to unbutton her coat with rapid movements. "No, he won't call the police."

A blast of cold air hit Emma in the chest the moment he opened her coat, and she tried to step away. "What are you doing? I'm freezing!"

He held firm to her coat, his dark gaze snapping to hers. "Your clothes are as wet as mine. The first thing we need to do is get out of them."

She smacked at his hands when he tried to push her jacket off her shoulders. "The first thing we need is heat before any of these clothes come off my body."

His lips thinned but he turned away from her and walked over to open a door in the kitchen area. When he came back carrying a small heater no bigger than a shoe box, she snorted in disbelief. "Th-that's it?"

Caine set the heater on the floor near a twin-size bed, plugged it in, then turned it on. As he walked away toward one of the bedrooms, he called over his shoulder, "Set the lantern down and finish getting undressed."

Emma stared transfixed at the single bed he'd set the heater beside. "Where are you going to sleep?" she called after him. Approaching the bed, she set the lantern on the nightstand next to it.

Caine reappeared with a stack of blankets in his arms. Setting them on the end of the bed, he stepped in front of her, his expression serious. "*We're* sleeping in this bed. Your metabolism apparently can't hold heat, so I'm your best shot at getting warm and staying that way."

"There must be other beds," Emma started to say when he slid his hand under her hair and cupped the back of her neck. The blast of heat emanating from his palm and fingers sent glorious shivers down her spine. It wasn't as hot as she remembered, but damn the man had an effective way of making his point.

His smile held a touch of arrogance as he traced his thumb along her neck, leaving steamy lightning trails behind. "Take off your clothes, Emma."

Heat shot up her cheeks at the idea of undressing in front of him. "Can I have one of those blankets, please?"

Caine released her and grabbed a blanket. His dark eyebrow elevated when he handed her the navy thermal cover. "Better?"

Emma quickly nodded and gripped the thick blanket. "You, uh…are going to turn around, right?"

Chuckling, Caine moved to the end of the bed and turned away, stripping out of his jacket. When he lifted his shirt over his head, revealing rippling muscles along his back, Emma swallowed a gulp. His hands shifted to his jeans and paused. "I don't hear you making any progress."

Emma swiftly turned around and kicked off her shoes, then took a deep breath before she began to peel off her own wet clothes. Holding the blanket around her became an impossible task, especially with her fingers refusing to work in the cold air. Abandoning the blanket, she unbuttoned and began to shrug out of the tight wet jeans. Grunting in frustration, she had to wiggle and tug in a weird dance of hopping feet and chattering teeth before she finally freed her legs from the soggy material.

"That was *interesting*."

Caine's amused tone jerked her to attention. Emma had all but forgotten about him in her effort to be free of the suffocating frigid jeans. Standing there in her bra, underwear and socks, she quickly grabbed the blanket from the floor and wrapped it around her shoulders. Facing him, she narrowed her gaze. "That wasn't meant for your entertainment."

He approached, his expression serious. Emma noticed that he'd tied a blanket low on his hips, leaving his gorgeous upper body on full display. Broad shoulders gave way to a narrow waist, but it was the trail of dark hair that started at his sculpted abs and disappeared past the blanket's edge that drew her gaze. God, he was built.

Taut stomach muscles flexed as he grabbed up her clothes from the floor and then held out his hand. "All of them."

Emma frowned, but moved to stand in front of the space heater while she peeled off the rest. The moment Caine walked away with their clothes, she called after him, "My aunt's meds are in the coat pocket." Shaking the last bit of snow out of her damp hair, she wrapped the blanket tight around her body before diving under the thin quilt and sheet on the twin bed.

Even wrapped in the thermal blanket and underneath the quilt and sheet, she shook as much as the house did with the howling wind battering its walls from all sides. A door slammed and a dryer started up a few seconds before Caine stepped back into the main room and set her aunt's medicine container on the kitchen table.

She watched him through slitted eyes and chattering teeth as he covered the twin bed with five layers of blankets. The extra blankets didn't really warm her, but the heavy weight made her eyelids slowly close. *I could just fall asleep and the cold wouldn't bother me anymore.*

It didn't even faze her when the bed dipped. *Caine was getting in. That's nice.* Her mind floated on a different plane, meandering down a path of cool darkness, seeking the sleep her body seemed to need.

"Emma, no!"

Caine's sharp tone made her eyelids flutter, but they wouldn't open. His hand touched her shoulder and she shrugged it away, murmuring, "Just let me sleep."

"Son of a bitch!" When he began to tug hard on the blanket she'd wrapped around herself, Emma's heart jerked and this time her eyes flew open. She gripped the blanket. "What are you doing? Let go!"

Caine didn't even look at her. His expression held fierce determination as he continued to unwrap her body. "Your body temperature has dropped too much. You must get warm quickly."

She flinched at the anger in his voice. Caine's gaze locked

with hers and his jaw muscle began to jump. "You know I can provide the warmth your body needs, Emma."

He was right. Closing her eyes, she slowly nodded and let him unwrap the thermal blanket completely from her body. When warm hands clasped her waist and her back was yanked fully against a warm, hard chest, Emma couldn't help the sigh of pleasure that escaped her lips.

Pulling the covers back over them, Caine spooned her entire body with his, from the top of her shoulders to the back of her thighs. He even entwined his muscular legs with hers, sliding his warm feet along her lower calves and feet.

For several minutes Emma just shivered from the contrast in his body temperature and hers before she began to glory in the warmth that enveloped her. Caine leaned close and breathed hard against her neck. She tensed until she realized he was using his breath to warm her. Only then did she relax against him.

Caine felt the difference instantly when Emma's body fully yielded. He'd been scared when he came into the room to find her already dozing. The moment he touched her and her body temperature was so low, fear drove him. He didn't give a damn if she'd refused to give him permission. He'd have ripped the blanket off her anyway and dealt with her affronted anger later. She wasn't going to die on him.

In the short time he'd known her, Emma had become someone special, someone he wished hadn't turned out to be a panther. She claimed not to know who kidnapped her, and instinctively he believed she was telling the truth, but what other secrets did she hide? She'd yet to admit she was something other than human. And why did the other panthers kidnap her and take her blood? The man who'd shoved his way through the truck window was too strong to be human. He had to be panther.

Tons of questions flooded his mind as he wrapped his arms around Emma and tucked one hand underneath her armpit, then slid his other hand between her legs—the two areas he'd been trained in search and rescue to warm first to prevent hypothermia. When Emma didn't question what he was doing and her eyelids began to droop, Caine's chest tightened. He needed to keep her awake, at least until her body temperature was back to normal. "I saw schoolbooks at your house. Do you go to NYU? That's a heck of a commute for you from Greenwood Lake."

Emma gave a tired laugh. "No, I have to take care of my aunt. She's gotten to the point where she can't drive as well as she used to. I didn't like to have to cut her off, but I finally insisted on driving her to various doctor appointments, running errands for her and such. I'm too busy to be a full-time student. I'm in a part-time satellite program with the community college."

That's a lot of responsibility for someone so young. Caine stared at her with respect. "What's wrong with your aunt?"

Emma sighed. "Age and I guess a family predisposition for ailments. My mom died young. I don't remember her at all. My aunt has a heart condition." Her body tensed. "God, I hope she's all right."

Caine regretted reminding her about her aunt's predicament. "If she was there, Landon will take care of her, Emma. Don't worry."

They lay there for a good twenty minutes before he saw a bit of color start to return to her cheeks. After what she'd told him, Caine understood why Emma had seemed mature and confident for her age. Taking care of an elderly aunt, she'd had to grow up fairly quickly. Once again, he realized just how much he appreciated the past support of his pack. Sadness knotted his throat now that he'd pretty much cut himself off from the Lupreda and faced life alone.

The skin along Emma's thigh was soft under his fingers and her earthy smell was driving his wolf nuts, making him want to howl. Caine couldn't resist. He leaned close and inhaled deeply before he let his breath flow over her neck and down her back to warm her. Fierce pride welled within him to feel her skin warming under his touch. "What are you studying?"

"Marketing. Having some college training under my belt should help me get a better-paying job. Instead of using my aunt's savings for school, I can contribute to her retirement. I hope to switch to the university at some point if I can convince my aunt to move closer to town."

He could tell she was still worrying about her aunt. "As soon as this storm subsides, my cell's reception should return and I'll give Landon a call." Sensing her anxiety, Caine released his tight hold on her body and sat up and leaned on his elbow to press his lips to her bare shoulder. "I'll find out for you. I promise."

"Thanks." Sighing, she arched her spine, then clasped the covers to her chest and rolled onto her back to meet his gaze in the dim light. "What about you? You've risked your life to save mine and I hardly know you. What do you do when you're not saving girls who've been kidnapped?"

I was Second in my Lupreda wolf pack. "I used to be a tour guide for the Shawangunk Mountains, and on the side, I led search-and-rescue teams if a hiker got lost. Now that I'm in town, I deliver packages among other small jobs here and there."

She let out a surprised laugh. "All that hiking must be what kept you fit. I assumed you were a professional athlete or trainer or something. You ran through the snow as if it wasn't in your way. I know *I* couldn't have kept up with you."

I know that's not true, my little panther. "It's time for the truth, Emma." Caine's voice turned serious as he slid his knuckles down her cheek. Now that her skin wasn't frozen, the tingling started the moment his fingers touched hers.

Emma gasped and pressed her face closer to his hand, surprising the hell out of him that she seemed to crave the humming sensations between them. "I've told you everything already. While I was out in the woods looking for our cat, Casper, early this morning, someone took my aunt. The note they left behind at my house told me to come back to the club tonight and to not call the police. That's why I had initially thought the note was from you, because I'd never been to Squeeze before last night, and you were the only person I'd spoken to while I was there."

"What else?"

Her eyes widened. "There *is* nothing else. You seem to want an answer I can't give you. I told you I don't know who they were, why they kidnapped me or why they wanted a sample of my blood."

Why did they take a sample of her blood? Caine wondered while he trailed his fingers down her throat.

He wanted to shake her for not telling him everything, yet at the same time he ached to explore every part of her. From her beautiful dark head to her frozen toes, he wanted to run his hands all over her skin, to warm her everywhere until she writhed and moaned and spread her legs, pleading for him to touch her in every intimate, sweet place on her body.

He'd revel in her moist heat and in the intimate act of sliding his fingers deep inside her, of pleasing her and stroking her body to orgasm. His groin heated and his erection hardened instantly as the fantasy played in his head. Nothing would be more erotically satisfying than revving Emma up and hearing her beg him to take her, to claim her body and soul—nothing more…than the act itself.

As the spark of electricity charged higher between them, he felt her swallow beneath his fingers and his entire body tensed in need. The more they physically connected, the more sensitized his skin became, making the electric sensations between them highly arousing. Caressing Emma had quickly turned into an addiction. As easily as breathing, it had become a necessity to touch her, to feel their connection every chance he got.

"And this electricity between us?" he said in gruff voice. "Why do you think we're like two live wires when we touch?" He waited for her to speak, hoping she trusted him enough to tell him the truth.

Emma tensed and lowered her gaze, then rolled onto her side away from him, whispering, "I don't know."

Why had she turned away? He'd heard the uncertainty in her voice. Caine instinctively reached out to comfort her, but caught himself and fisted his hand above her hip. He couldn't believe just how much he'd grown to care for this woman in such a short time—a woman whose DNA alone should give him reason not to trust her.

When he'd scented her at the café, an involuntary predatory awareness splintered through his mind and senses, quickly followed by an intuitive need to dominate. But her scent, combined with their unique physical connection, had ignited his predatory awareness of her, shifting his natural domination instincts to a strong physical need to stake his claim and protect. Every time he looked at Emma, Caine felt savagely territorial over her, to the point that…if it came down to it, he'd go up against his own brethren in order to keep her from harm.

Anger weighed heavily on his chest that she'd burrowed so deep under his skin, twisting his mind and disrupting his steadfast loyalties. He clenched his jaw so hard his teeth hurt. Why was she pretending to be human? Did she not smell his musk? Scent how much he wanted her? He was supposed to be her deadly enemy, yet the way she'd looked at him earlier, her beautiful golden eyes reflecting vulnerability and trust, made his chest burn like hot coals had been raked across it. Why wouldn't she trust him enough to tell him the truth?

When Emma's shoulders began to shake again, Caine realized he'd pulled his warmth away from her too soon. He quickly gathered her chilled frame against his chest and wrapped his arms tight around her. "Rest now. I'll keep you warm."

Emma's slight frame began to relax in his arms and when her body temperature leveled off, she murmured, "Thank you," right before her breathing finally evened out in sleep.

The lantern closest to them finally flickered, then died, dousing their area in darkness. Caine brushed his lips lightly against her temple and thought about the kiss they'd shared on the dance floor that evening. Her avid participation had been damned convincing. But the fact she'd turned away from him just now made him wonder…had his chance meeting with Emma in the club the night before really been a random encounter? She'd have nothing to gain by using him. He was no longer with the pack. Then again, maybe she didn't know that.

Caine's gut tightened at the distrustful thoughts that slammed through his mind. He'd wanted Emma to tell him what she was on her own without him confronting her and forcing her hand. He'd proven he would protect her, but that apparently hadn't been enough to convince her to tell him everything and admit who and what she really was.

The fact remained, she was Velius. Even now, her black hair reflected the truth. Spread across the white pillow, her hair sparkled as if covered with flecks of iridescent glitter. Caine's mind warred with his heart.

She whispered his name in her sleep and his grip on her tightened as his gaze shifted to the log walls around them. The cabin had been assigned to the zerkers before their deaths a few months ago. It would become his permanent home the day he discovered he could no longer shift back from Musk to human form. As he stared, the logged surface appeared to slowly move inward, closing in on him.

Caine closed his eyes against an inevitable future and focused on Emma. Inhaling her earthy scent, he hoped she'd been sincere about her fear of the panthers who'd kidnapped her. In the brewing conflict between the Velius and Lupreda, he had to know for certain that Emma's loyalties weren't firmly ensconced with the panthers—that she hadn't played a part in the Velius' torturous murders of the three Lupreda zerkers in an effort to start a war between the vampires and the werewolves.

When she woke up, he would get the answers he needed. One way or the other.

Chapter 6

Something smelled strong and delicious. Food. And it smelled like chicken. Emma inhaled deeply and the sensation of steam touching her nose made her eyes fly open. Her gaze swept the muscles along Caine's shoulders and his bare chest as he pulled the oversized coffee cup away from her face and sat down on the bed bedside her.

"Your stomach kept growling while you slept. This is the best I could come up with."

When she quickly checked to see that he'd pulled on a pair of jeans, his lips quirked upward in the dim light. "Disappointed? Here, take this. It should stave off the hunger pains until I can go out and hunt for something to eat." He glanced back toward the main window where streaks of light shone through the crack in the closed curtains. "It stopped snowing a little over an hour ago."

The room was still cold, but nowhere near as frigid as it was earlier. Emma sat up and held the covers around her chest with one hand, while she took the mug with the other. "Thank you." Her words came out in a low, husky rasp, and she instantly put the warm mug to her lips. When she leaned forward to take a sip, her hair fell in her face.

Before she could blow it out of the way, Caine reached over and tucked the errant strands behind her left ear. His fingers lingered on her skin for a couple of seconds and she shivered at the humming sensation arcing between them. Lowering his hand, he watched her take another swallow. His gaze held a mix of desire and avid interest, making the steaming chicken broth the most provocative meal she'd ever had.

While Emma was busy gulping down the broth, she had an excuse to remain silent, which meant she wouldn't possibly make an embarrassing faux pas and ruin the charged moment between them like she had before she'd fallen asleep.

When Caine ran his fingers down her throat earlier, sending sparks ricocheting throughout her body, and then asked why she thought there was such an electric charge between them, she'd frozen up. She'd wanted to say something worldly and sexy, but she didn't have a clue how to go about that.

And the truth was, she honestly didn't know what was going on between them. Only that the amazing pull felt seductive and irresistible. Whenever he cupped his hand around her neck, electricity vibrated between them, but it was more than that. She literally couldn't move. It was both scary and incredibly erotic that he had that kind of power over her, because instinctively, even though he came across as an intense, dominant man, she knew he'd never use his control to hurt her.

Now that she wasn't shivering uncontrollably and her loud

stomach had calmed to a random low gurgle, her confidence was bolstered. Setting the cup on the nightstand, Emma bit her lower lip.

Caine cupped her cheek and turned her face toward him. "What's wrong? Are you feeling okay?"

Emma sighed into his palm, then met his concerned gaze. "I've never been very good at small talk or making friends. I wouldn't have gone to the club on my own the other night, but there was just something about your smell when you came into the café that day that I couldn't let go. It felt familiar and comforting."

Caine's eyebrows shot up. "*My* smell seemed comforting to you?"

She nodded and her cheeks heated with embarrassment. "I know it sounds crazy, but I just wanted to get a glimpse of your face—to see if I'd met you somewhere before. I planned to run in, assuage my curiosity and leave. And then you were there, standing beside me wearing 'women' as a second set of clothes and offering to buy me a drink."

Caine chuckled as he ran his thumb along her lip in a gentle caress. "I saw you watching me on the dance floor." He moved his fingers in slow reverence along her skin, as if he couldn't resist touching her. "But when you refused my offer to buy your beer and then slammed me all in one shot, I had to get to know you better."

Emma shook her head. "I wasn't trying to play hard to get." Shrugging, she continued. "I always speak my mind. It's a character flaw, but there you have it."

Caine moved closer until his thigh brushed against hers. Sliding his fingers into her hair, he locked gazes with her. "Honesty is very important in a relationship."

Pulse racing, Emma's eyes widened and she gripped the covers against her chest. "We have a relationshi—"

Caine's warm mouth covered hers, cutting off her question. She laughed at the sizzling pop that zinged between them, but Caine nipped at her bottom lip and Emma gasped in excitement, opening her mouth to his intense kiss. A low growl rumbled in his chest as he traced his tongue alongside hers. Her insides melted at the sexy, primal sound. Emma teased him with slow swipes of her tongue before she pressed quick kisses against the corner of his mouth and along his jawline.

"You're everything I want," he murmured at the same time big warm hands cupped her face. When he tilted her head and slanted his lips across hers in a harder, deeper kiss, the intensity sent shocking heat splintering through her system. Her entire body lit on fire, the flames singeing every intimate place at once.

Emma groaned when her sex began to throb deep inside her in a near-painful physical ache. Holding the covers against her chest, she used her other hand to clutch him closer, inhaling his fresh outdoors scent. Primal and musky, and full of sensual promise, his smell surrounded her in a blanket of arousing seduction.

"Your smell is… I can't describe how good you smell to me. It makes me feel so free." Emma's heart thumped and her breasts tingled in response to his strong essence inundating her senses. Sliding her fingers into his thick dark hair, she was shocked to hear herself moan as she pulled him closer.

"I have a pretty good idea," Caine grated out and pressed hot, electric kisses across her jaw. Easing back, he met her gaze. "What do you smell?"

Emma couldn't believe how much his aggressive smell

called to her inner temptress, melting away her insecurities and inhibitions. She might not have much sexual experience, but when it came this man, pure instinctual desire drove her actions beyond her own conscious thoughts or understanding. Closing her eyes briefly, she inhaled. "You smell musky and exotic, masculine and…unique. I could pick you out of a crowd by your scent alone."

His fingers traced her jaw. "The musk you smell is heightened interest, Emma." He leaned close and pushed her hair out of the way to press a kiss behind her ear. "Tell me what you hear," he whispered.

Her breathing turned erratic and her heart ramped up at the things he was making her feel. She closed her eyes once more and listened. The rapid whoosh, whoosh, whoosh of her pulse rushed in her head. She heard his heart beating steady with a slow upward tick. Jerking back, she met his gaze with wide eyes. "You have a powerful heartbeat. I can hear it rising."

He touched her chin, his smile darkly feral. "That's excitement." Placing his hands on the bed on either side of her, he shifted his weight very close as if he were going to kiss her neck. "What do you feel?" He moved his chin to within an inch of her shoulder, then slid it along her collarbone. Not touching but close enough that they'd connect if she moved forward the slightest bit.

His magnetism pulled at her, but more than that, she felt his heat. Glorious, primal heat ran along her skin, warming it. "I feel how hot your skin is, even though you're not touching me," she said in a breathless voice.

Caine's penetrating gaze snapped to hers. "That's lust and desire. I want you."

His declaration slammed her hard in the stomach, making

her feel light-headed. Emma opened her mouth to speak, but nothing came out.

What does all this tell you about me? About us? he demanded, suddenly serious.

Emma blinked. She had just heard him speak in her mind. It wasn't some drug-induced imagining when he'd rescued her. How was that possible? Her pulse raced and she searched his gaze for some clue as to what he wanted her to say. She had a feeling that whatever words she spoke next would be very important. "That you're different."

His expression hardened. "*We're* different. You and I. Tell me, damn it!"

The ferocity in his expression scared her, not because she was afraid, but because she thought he was going to push her away. She tried to blink back the tears of frustration that burned behind her eyelids and answered him as honestly as she could. "You're unique, and we have a connection that's undeniably mind-blowing, but…" Tears began to roll down her cheeks anyway. "I don't know what you want from me!"

Caine's hand encircled her neck. He'd moved so fast, she didn't have time to react other than to wrap her fingers around his wrist. His firm hold locked her in place as his thumb slid along her throat, stopping at the hollow where her pulse thumped a staccato beat.

His steady gaze held both frustration and desire. Emma remained still. She didn't take a breath. If he wanted, he could apply pressure to that spot and cut off her air. Permanently.

Survival instincts demanded she push his hand away, but she refused to act. Instead, she listened to her heart. Her hand slipped away from his wrist and she closed her eyes, tilting her head back.

What do I want? The raw hunger tapped into her primal senses. He was on a ragged edge, barely hanging on, despite his langour. She forced herself to remain calm as his thumb rubbed lightly on her pulse. *For now...this.*

Emma gasped when his lips replaced his thumb. He nipped at her collarbone, then kissed a hot trail along her chest, branding her skin with tingling, fiery kisses. She bit her lip to keep from moaning. His warm mouth felt so good on her skin. Placing her hands on the bed behind her, she arched her back and murmured his name.

Large hands encircled her waist through the covers, cinching tight. "Never whisper your desires, Emma. Always demand them!"

Emma was shaking inside with the need to feel his lips and hands caressing her skin. Her body felt like it was on fire. Tilting her head forward, she met Caine's gaze. His fingers flexed against her waist and his musk grew stronger. The evocative scent made her skin prickle and her breasts tingle in response.

Caine slid the sheet down until only her nipples were covered. His hungry gaze lowered to her chest, then lifted back to her face. "Once we start, our primal natures *will* take over. Are you prepared for that?"

Emma gave a nervous laugh. She was afraid to tell him she'd never been with another man. What if the thought of her inexperience was a major turnoff? "I'm as prepared as I'll ever be. I want to feel the electricity sparking between us. Everywhere."

Caine's warm hands moved up the sides of her rib cage at the same time he lowered his dark head to press his lips to the curve of her breast. Electricity zinged through her as he slid his lips down her cleavage, his movements slow, reverent and achingly tantalizing.

Cool air brushed her nipples as the sheet slipped away, baring her breasts. The sensitive tips puckered and her stomach fluttered when she felt his warm breath bathing her responsive skin. He slid the sheet the rest of the way down her waist and said in her mind, *You're beautiful and...all mine,* right before he ran his tongue around a hard pink tip.

Emma's sex began to throb from his intimate attention. She crossed her legs to keep from crying out and demanding he make the thrumming ache go away. She arched closer and moaned low in her throat.

His hot breath rushed over her nipple once, twice, a third time to the point she thought she might go insane. And then his lips grasped the aching pink tip tight. Emma cried out and dug her fingers into his hair, clutching him close. The spark sent tremors all the way down her limbs. When he began to suck in long drawing pulls, she moaned and gripped his shoulder, digging into the muscle. "More," she begged.

He grunted his approval and his thumbs pressed on the sides of her breasts as he moved to her other nipple and gave it the same provocative treatment. *You taste so good, I could kiss your breasts for hours,* he murmured in her mind.

When he nipped at her nipple, Emma mewled in her throat. *You're purring.*

Of course she sounded like she was purring. The man made her hum on many levels. Emma folded her legs to the side and arched her back. Pressing forward, she lifted up on her knees and wrapped her arms around his neck.

Caine grabbed hold of her arms, and before she knew what was happening, he had her flat on her back with her hands pulled over her head. "Slow down, my little wildcat. Let me love on you the way you were meant to be appreciated."

Emma thought she'd done something wrong, but she couldn't control the urges clamoring inside her. She squirmed under his hold. "I feel like I'm going to crawl right out of my skin if something doesn't happen soon."

His dark gaze narrowed, then turned downright sinful. "Things are going to get out of control between us soon enough. Your scent is incredibly hard to resist. Let's try and take it slow for a bit. Hmm?"

Emma panted as he released her hands and pushed the covers completely back. Oddly, she wasn't embarrassed at all while his hot gaze swept her naked body. Instead, she wanted to touch him as intimately as he had her, to see him free of clothes and trace her fingers across his warm skin and hard muscles.

When he bent to place a kiss on her shoulder, she ran her hand along his biceps. "Aren't you going to take off your pants?"

"Not yet," he said in a rough tone and set his hands on the bed on either side of her, pressing another kiss between her breasts.

Curling her fingers inward, Emma ran her nails down his chest. "I want to see you."

A low growl erupted from his throat and he grabbed hold of her hand. His nostrils flared and he gritted out, "You're not making it easy for me to remain calm."

She raised her eyebrow and ran her other hand down his arm, enjoying the tingling sparks. "I want you to feel what I do. All over."

He gripped her other wrist and pressed it to the bed. "I'm having a very hard time not taking you now. Stop pushing me or what you're going to get is a man who's too far over the edge to go back."

Caine glanced down at his chest and she followed his gaze.

Five red furrows had begun to well with droplets of blood. Emma pulled free of his hold, her shaky hand moving to investigate his wounds. "Dear God, did I do that?"

Caine grabbed her hand and lifted it to his lips, kissing her knuckles. "I'll be fine, but you're making it difficult for me to maintain my cool. Let me enjoy your reaction first for a bit before we move forward."

Emma bit her lip and nodded. She felt horrible for what she'd inadvertently done to Caine's chest. He smiled and ran his knuckles down her belly. "You have a body of sheer beauty, Emma. It was made to be worshipped…every single inch of you."

His compliment flooded her cheeks with heat, but when his fingers reached the bit of hair between her legs, her gaze locked with his and she held her breath. She'd never ached to be touched as much as she did at that moment.

Caine leaned close and grazed her jaw with a kiss at the same time his fingers slid between her legs. Slow, assured… teasing. Emma arched her back and rocked her hips. Anything to assuage the aching need deep inside her.

"Your primal smell is driving me insane. I want to taste every part of you, to suck and nip at your sweet body until you're screaming for me to make you come." He looked at her and his eyes were a lighter green. "And then you'll beg me to do it to you all over again."

Emma began to pant and she arched her back once more before she finally gripped his wrist to stop his teasing. She'd grown wetter with each passing swipe of his fingers along her sex. He moved so close but didn't touch her where she wanted—no, needed—him to. "Touch me. I can't stand it anymore."

The dark look in his eyes made her heart hammer as he slid his finger along her damp folds, then plunged it deep inside her. Emma yelped at the surprising pain and Caine's hand froze inside her. Cupping his palm against her mound, his eyebrows drew downward. "Are you okay?"

Emma winced, then nodded.

"You're so tight and…" Caine closed his eyes, his entire body tensing. His gaze jerked back to hers. "Why didn't you tell me you were a virgin?"

She bit her lip. "I thought it might be a turnoff to you."

"That couldn't be further from the truth—" he started to growl in a harsh tone.

Emma was surprised when he withdrew his hand from her body and leaned forward to bury his nose along the column of her neck. His voice was ragged with emotion as he gripped her inner thigh. "Say the word and I'll stop if you want me to, but damn it to hell, Emma, the last thing I want to do right now is to move away from you."

Emma desperately wanted him to stroke her back to the heightened arousal she'd felt seconds ago. Caine's heartfelt request and the need in his voice only made her want him more. She cupped his face so he would have to look at her. "I want whatever this amazing connection is between us. Very much. Never doubt it."

Her golden eyes shimmered in the dim morning light with honest passion, stealing his breath. For several seconds, Caine just stared. She completely enthralled him. As he rubbed his thumb along her inner thigh, her skin felt so soft and feminine, a knot formed in his throat, locking the words inside. The complete trust Emma gave over humbled him, obliterating his doubts as to her motives. Her attraction was as sincere and heartfelt as his. When their secrets finally came to light, they would face them together. That's all that mattered.

As if she knew he had a hard time voicing his thoughts, she gave a shy smile and ran her fingers across his shoulder. "Say something in my mind. I like the closeness."

Emma, I—

A deafening crash slammed the cabin's front door open, nearly ripping it off its hinges. Emma screamed and Caine whirled around to see three men standing outside the door. One of them took a step through the doorway and fury engulfed him. The need to protect Emma sent him leaping across the twenty-five-foot distance in one single bound. As he sailed through the air, his wereclaws unsheathed while his spine and rib cage began to pop.

Without a second thought, Caine instinctively called forth his Musk form, welcoming the enlarged chest and the searing pain as his jaws started to elongate. When he landed, he hadn't yet fully shifted to a werewolf, but that didn't stop him from instantly attacking the first man who dared to invade his home.

The short stocky man flew backward through the opened doorway with one swipe from Caine's deadly claws. Caine snorted in satisfaction at the blood dripping from his fingers, then started to stalk through the door after the intruders when a dark-haired man of medium height stepped from a hidden spot outside the door and rammed his fist into Caine's chest.

His surprisingly powerful hit sent Caine flying backward to land with a heavy thump on the wood floor. Caine heard Emma call his name in the background as he howled his rage. He recognized the man who'd attacked him as the guy Caine wouldn't let exit out the club's back door last night. Snapping to his feet, he started to go after the guy when the bastard lifted a crossbow-style handgun toward him and pulled the trigger with a snarl. "Down, dog."

Something zinged through the air. The impact threw Caine several steps back and pain exploded in his left shoulder right before a similar jolt slammed into his right arm. Caine roared his rage and tried to yank the silver arrows out of his chest and arm, but the flange on the ends suddenly spun, slicing his hands. Blood spewed from his hands and wounds while the metal shafts drilled deeper into his flesh.

Growling, he fell to his knees in sheer agony, running his claws down his skin, anything to dislodge them. When the flange tips stopped spinning, then curled inward and imbedded themselves into his muscles, the silver began to poison his body with vicious, deadly purpose. Caine fell back against the end of the twin bed, breathing with heavy painful snarls as the silver forced his body to revert back to his human form.

"Damn, he's a tough sonofabitch." A man with thinning blond hair stepped beside the man who'd shot Caine, his own weapon held out, ready to shoot. "It took only one shot each to take down the other bastards."

They're the ones who killed the zerkers. I'll rip them to shreds. Caine snarled and tensed his body, preparing to fight. Despite the pain making him see double, he pushed his shoulders off the bed and fear shot across the blond man's face at the same time his hand tensed on his weapon.

A dark shadow appeared over Caine a split second before a panther landed in a crouch on all fours. Its paw planted on the floor between his feet, while its bulky body blocked Caine from the shooter's line of sight. The animal twitched its long tail and let out a deafening, high-pitched roar, full of anger and warning, daring the men not to get any closer.

Emma! *How had she shifted without an injection?* Caine wondered. *Had she been shot with one while he was fighting?* His worry for her spiked. She was definitely challenging the men, despite the weapons they held. Caine grabbed her tail and yanked her backward slightly. "No!" he growled.

A third man stepped to the leader's other side and raised a different gun toward Emma, a look of worry flashing through his eyes. But the dark-haired man in the center waved him back. Closing his eyes, the leader inhaled deeply, then said in a reverent whisper, "Listen to the sheer beauty. It has been so long since we could unfurl and give a battle cry out in the open like this."

The man beside him tensed. "Her roar will alert the Lupreda to our presence, Malac."

Malac opened his eyes. Lust and covetous desire reflected in their brown depths as he stared at Emma in her panther form. "We'll be gone before they can reach us," he said to the blond man once Emma quieted. Her rib cage heaved as she snorted out warning clicks and snarls through her bared fangs.

The leader lifted his hand toward her. "If you come with us, we'll let him live."

The panther lowered her head. A deep growl rumbled in her throat, while her claws flexed against the wood floor and her long black tail twitched in Caine's hand. Caine squeezed. "No, Emma!"

Malac tsked. "Debating your chances? Remember, I still have the old woman."

The panther's head came up in a fast jerk and the growl in her throat rose to menacing levels. Pulling free of Caine's hold, she turned toward him. Her beautiful yellow eyes reflected sadness as she lowered her mouth to his shoulder.

Caine shuddered when she used her teeth to pull out the silver bolt. Before he could speak, she'd removed the other one from his arm, as well, dropping it with a heavy thunk on the floor. He gripped her ear as she laved at his wounds with her warm tongue. "Don't do this."

"We leave now!" the man demanded behind them.

Emma turned toward Malac and gave an annoyed snort before she returned her attention to Caine and ran her whiskers along his cheek. *Don't go, Emma! I can't protect you if you go with them.* Caine touched her head and started to slide his hand down her neck. She grunted out a little growl and quickly pulled out of his hold before his touch could lock her in place.

Emma walked with a stealthy gracefulness toward the men, but when the blond man raised his gun toward Caine, she bared her teeth and moved with lightning speed, slicing his wrist with a swipe of her extended claws.

The man yelled and held his hand over his gushing wounds, looking to Malac. The leader shrugged and shook his head. "You should know better, Scott." His gaze shifted to Emma as he squatted to pick up the gun the man had dropped. "It's only a tranquilizer gun. The one we'd planned to use on you."

"Emma, no!" Caine's entire body shook from the fever the silver spikes left behind.

When Malac raised the tranquilizer gun toward him, Emma hissed, but she didn't attack. Caine roared at his body to ignore the nausea and pain. *Move, damnit.* He began to slide across the floor, willing his muscles to respond…to react. He'd shifted only a couple of feet when a sharp pain jabbed him in the chest.

I will come for you, Caine vowed in Emma's mind as he struggled to stay conscious through the heavy tranquilizer. The last thing he remembered was Emma lifting up on her hind legs to scoop her aunt's medicine container from the table with her jaws.

Chapter 7

After they ran through the woods for about a mile, the men pointed their guns at Emma and told her to jump into the back of what appeared to be a moving truck. She heard radio squawks as they closed the doors on her and locked them. "We've got her. We're heading home."

Emma's legs began to tremble and all the bravado, fear and adrenaline that had kept her moving through the woods fled her body. She released the pill container onto the truck floor, collapsing onto her belly with a heavy thump as her mind raced with chaotic thoughts.

Emma stared in shock at her fur-covered arms—paws—stretched out in front of her. Not only could she see in the total absence of light, but she blinked several times as she flexed her fingers and her panther claws extended. *I'm having a nightmare. I'll wake up soon,* she told herself as she set her chin on her trembling arms and closed her eyes.

The truck started up underneath her, its loud rumble refusing to let her block out everything that had happened. She'd shifted. To a panther. *God, I'm not human, but I felt human.* Why had her aunt lied to her, raising her as a human and never telling her of her true nature? Did her aunt not know what she was? Or was her aunt a panther, too? So many questions flooded her mind, making her tense with worry that the one person she trusted above all others might've lied to her all her life.

And Caine…her heart sank with worry for him. She hoped she'd saved him. What was he? When he'd started to shift to some kind of half-man, half-creature form, she bit back a cry of shock, but nothing scared her as much as those men shooting at him and disabling him with their strange, deadly silver arrows. She'd both cried and seethed when she saw him sitting there, wounded but still snarling and ready to fight them, even once he'd shifted back to his human form.

Instinctively, she knew the men were there for her. Maybe it was because of the way Caine had fought, refusing to go down. When he fell to the floor, something inside her snapped. Anger and worry had curled in her stomach as she watched the violent scene unfold in front of her. Guilt rode her spine, sending ripples up and down it. Maybe her hackles were actually raising and because she was unaware of her true primal nature, she didn't recognize the sensation for what it was—her body readying itself to shift.

Instantly.

She didn't feel a thing, not a twinge. It was so surreal. One moment she was shaking on the bed, fearful for Caine and furious at the men, and the next she was diving out of it to protect Caine, to yell at the men to stop. Then her body felt like she'd slipped into the skin she'd been born to wear, even if shifting like that had scared the hell out of her.

Hearing herself roar stunned and frightened her, but once her panther's battle howl came out, all her primal instincts took over. She would've taken out any man who went near Caine without a single ounce of regret. No matter what truths she was sure she'd discover about herself and Caine, he'd saved her when she needed him and she would do the same for him. She owed him that much, regardless of the beasts that lay underneath their human skin.

Caine knew, she realized suddenly as she thought back to what he'd said. *"We're different. You and I. Tell me, damn it!"* He'd been trying to get her to tell him that, as if she knew what she was and even what he was. Shaking her head, she snorted. God, she had no freaking idea!

The truck's back door opened and the leader, Malac, hopped in. When she saw he was alone, the need to rip him to shreds for taking her aunt, hurting Caine and kidnapping her rose within her. A low roooowwwl rumbled in her throat.

"Music to my ears," he said in a calm tone before he sat with his back against the wall diagonally across from her. "We're going to chat while we drive home." Placing his elbows on his knees, he leaned back in a relaxed pose as the truck began to move.

Emma didn't miss the gun he held casually in his hand. She narrowed her eyes and opened her mouth a little to let free her threatening snarl.

"We've been searching for you for a very long time."

When he looked directly at her, she saw his eyes for the first time in the dark. Even though they were brown, they glowed like Caine had said hers did. He was a panther, too. Why couldn't she catch his scent like she did Caine's musky one? And why didn't he shift earlier when Caine had gone after him?

She stared him down. *You're not the man who kidnapped me from the club. Tell me why you've been looking for me.* She wished she had Caine's ability to speak in the bastard's mind, but as much as she would've loved the ability to rail at him, there was no way in hell she was letting go of this panther form. It was her best defense. She didn't blink as she waited for him to continue.

He tilted his head to the side, contemplating her. "Your roars in the cabin...they sounded beautiful but stiff, like you've never done them before."

Emma tensed. She didn't want the man to know that she'd just discovered what she was...what she could do. She could hardly believe it herself. Right now he seemed to know a hell of a lot more about her panther half than she did. She didn't like being at a disadvantage.

He inhaled and nodded, understanding dawning on his narrow face. "Ah, that old woman kept you in the dark."

When Emma didn't react, his gaze narrowed. "You are Velius, Emma. A panther, like me and the others. Don't believe the lies I'm sure they tried to tell you about me, however indirectly."

Who might've told her lies about him? Was he referring to the people who kidnapped her from the club? Weren't they all from the same group? And that word...Velius? Why did that sound familiar to her? She racked her brain trying to remember where she'd heard the term before.

"We were created by the Lupreda, ones like that nasty dog you just defended back there."

Emma gave a low growl. She didn't like the contempt in his voice when he talked about Caine.

He clenched a fist on his knee. "He's your enemy! Meant to hunt you down and tear you apart. That's all you are to him. His kind created you for prey!"

No! He didn't hunt me. Instead, he protected me from the likes of you and the others who kidnapped me. Emma quieted and tilted her head to let him think she was beginning to listen to him. She needed as much information as possible if she had any hope of escaping.

Malac gestured toward her. "Don't you see? You're special and that's why he took you. To keep you from us. From your own kind. To keep us weak," he finished with a snarl of disgust.

Emma's ears perked. What made *her* so special? And how were the Velius weak? It suddenly struck her where she'd heard the term Velius before. Caine was on the phone talking to his friend Landon when she was half out of her mind from the drugs. He'd said something like, "If you want the Velius, they're here," before he gave an address. Why did Landon want the Velius? Caine had saved her, so why had he sent Landon after the other panthers? Were they—the Lupreda—trying to destroy her panther race? Was the man right? Did Caine save her because she was special? Whatever "special" meant.

"We need to reinforce our army. And you're the key, Emma."

Malac's comment drew her out of her musings. An army? Were they at war? Where in the world had the Lupreda and Velius come from? And how did the humans not seem to know they existed? And, damn it, *how* was she the key? She grunted to encourage him.

Malac gave her a calculating smile. "I'm the Velius' leader, but my rule will be fully solidified now that I have you. Unlike the rest of us, you're the only one who can shift at will. If you mate with a Velius, chances are that the offspring will be able to shift like you, without the need for an injection. That would give our army a definite advantage when fighting the vampires and werewolves."

Ah, that's why he didn't shift when Caine went after him! But an army against vampires and werewolves? He was psychotic on all counts. She couldn't produce enough children for an army! And something like that would take decades. Not to mention the most important fact—He. Was. Not. Touching. Her. Emma began to growl, low at first but the growl of outrage steadily grew.

Malac scowled. "You act like you have a choice in the matter. You don't. I'm taking you to our facility where our doctor will check you out and make sure you're physically fine and then we'll proceed with my plans." His frown slowly curved into a deadly smile. "The Lupreda may have engineered us to mature very quickly so they could have quick replacements for the ones they killed, but in the end, our rapid reproduction will be to our advantage this time around. Any offspring of yours will be physically mature by age four and ready to wage a war."

Emma snorted and shook her head back and forth. Age four? Going to war? He *was* insane. She could only guess he was referring to the Lupreda when he spoke of werewolves, since he'd called Caine a dog and she'd seen him start to morph, but what of the vampires? They existed only in history books, a bloodthirsty race who'd attacked humans. Wait, there was that article in the paper a few months ago about vampires returning. Was it true? Were the vampires never really extinct? And if so, Malac wanted to wage a full-on war against these two other powerful species? He was a power-hungry nutcase.

Pulling something out of his pocket, Malac popped the lid on a pill bottle and scattered the contents on the floor between them. "Soon there will be no more need for these." His upper lip curled in disdain as white pills pinged everywhere.

They looked like the same vitamin pills she'd taken all her life. Emma's gaze snapped to his and she stood on her feet to slowly push one of the pills over with her nose. When she batted at it with her paw, he gave a harsh laugh.

"Those are how you've stayed hidden for so long. If you didn't know you were a panther, what did the old woman tell you that you were taking?"

Another lie. Why, Aunt Mary?

He waved his hand and continued in a dismissive tone. "It doesn't matter. The pills mask our scent, keeping us hidden from the vampires' and werewolves' detection. But when that bitch stole you away, the pills worked too well. *We* couldn't find you either."

Stomping on one of the pills with his shoe, he ground it into the truck floor with relish, showing just how much he resented having to take them. "An unfortunate side effect for an immature panther like you was that the medicine slowed down your maturity." He met her steady gaze. "Which is why, unlike many of us who were already mature before we started taking the pills, you grew up at a similar pace to that of a human child and not as fast as a panther should've matured."

Now what he said earlier made a bit more sense. *By four her offspring would be fully matured and ready to fight—the panthers have one hell of a metabolism!* He was still crazy. She didn't want to wage war. She didn't want to mate with him or any other Velius for that matter. She wouldn't. Emma backed up and began to growl, the rumbling in her throat

elevated with her rising anger. She wasn't going to be any-
body's chess piece to move to whatever strategic advantage
they thought she could provide them.

Malac narrowed his gaze and held the gun toward her.
"You would choose the hard way. At least you'll produce
strong, willful panthers. Just don't think you'll ever rule me,"
he said right before he pulled the trigger.

The tranquilizer stung her shoulder, embedding deep into
her skin. She roared and leapt toward him, but he rolled out
of the way of her claw's swipe and slammed his fist against
her snout the moment he came to a crouched position. Pain
exploded across her jaw and she saw bright flashes behind her
eyes as she flew back and slammed against the truck's wall.
Infuriated, she started to jump up and attack once more, but
her legs wobbled. The strong tranquilizer was already doing
its job. Toppling to her side, Emma's panther roar slowly
changed to a human moan. "No!" she said in a fading voice
before she lost consciousness.

Caine wondered if he'd been thrown from the roof of a
building. His eyes were heavy and his chest and body ached
like a son of a bitch.

"Wake up!"

Who the hell was slapping him in the face? His eyes jerked
open at the same time he snarled and grabbed the bastard's
arm, ready to snap the bone in two.

Landon grasped Caine's forearm and said in a deadly tone,
"Are you ready to find out who would win in a wrestling
match, wolf?"

"Are you?" Caine shot back, even though he felt weak as hell.

Snorts of amusement drew Caine's attention to the group

of Lupreda who were standing behind Landon's crouched form. As soon as he smelled the panther's lingering earthy scent, everything came back to him.

"Emma!" Caine instantly tried to sit up and fell back to the floor. Dizziness blurred his vision for a second, while buzzing filled his ears. Damn it to hell, his brain was swelling inside his skull.

Landon put a hand on his chest. "Lay there for a minute until you get your bearings. The tranquilizer dart we pulled out of you is going to take a bit to wear off. Your body's already fighting its effects."

Glancing at the wood floor around Caine and then over his gouged chest, Landon frowned. "There aren't any weapons around, but I see the blood and your wounds are healing slower than usual." His gaze narrowed. "Silver?"

Caine nodded and sat up, grunting through the wooziness in his head. "The bastards must've taken the spikes they used on me. It was some kind of arrow that, once it finds its target, embeds itself deep in the tissue. If it weren't for Emma pulling them out, I'd be dead by now."

"If it weren't for Emma, they would never have dared to come on our land," Landon said.

Caine's gaze narrowed. "They're the ones who ambushed the zerkers. They bragged about how it took only one of their silver bolts to take down each of the 'others.'"

Landon's jaw clenched before he straightened and folded his arms across his chest. "She's *still* Velius."

Caine stood and tied the blanket someone had thrown over him around his waist. Clenching his fists by his sides, he grated out, "Emma's obviously valuable enough for them to take the risk and come back here. She didn't go with them willingly. The only reason she went was because they have her aunt."

Glancing from Landon to Kaitlyn, he continued. "Because they still have her aunt, I take it you were too late when you went to the address I gave you."

Kaitlyn nodded. "The place was stripped bare by the time we got there."

"Several humans left residual smells behind, including the human who took Emma from the club," Laird said, sliding his hand through his auburn hair.

"We didn't detect Emma's aunt's scent. I don't think she was ever there," Landon finished.

Caine tensed. *Emma's aunt wasn't there?* Frowning, he rubbed his overnight beard. "I'm beginning to wonder if there aren't two groups after Emma. A human stole her from the club, but the leader of the ones who came here, Malac, he's panther. I slammed into him back at the club. He was pissed as hell. You'd think if he *was* with the people who'd successfully taken her, he'd have snuck out of the club without drawing attention to himself."

"It's possible. Then again, he could've been trying to distract you to let them get away with her." Landon gestured toward him. "Get dressed. We're going home to regroup."

Lowering his hand to his side, Caine curled his fingers inward until his knuckles popped. He didn't want to think what they might be doing to Emma. There was no mistaking the lustful, possessive sweep of Malac's gaze over Emma's sleek panther form or the scent of testosterone rising in the man when she'd moved past him to retrieve her aunt's pills. "I'm going after them. I won't rest until I find her."

"This team has been going all night with no sleep."

Landon's green eyes slitted. "You'll rest. At home. With your pack."

Landon's steady stare was hard to resist, like he'd wrapped an invisible chain around Caine's chest and yanked. Hard. Caine rolled his head from one shoulder to the other and gritted his teeth, fighting his physical response to the Alpha's powerful influence. Landon's low growl made the chain cinch tight, closing off his air, burning his lungs. Any other time he'd be able to fight it, but the silver had weakened his body too much for him to challenge Landon's dominance right now. "Fine," he gritted out.

When Landon grunted in satisfaction and turned to walk away, Caine's own alpha nature roared from deep inside, fighting like a junkyard dog, despite his weakened state. "I'll stay for an hour and then I'm heading back to town," he grated out.

Emma's shoulder ached a little as someone shined a pen-light in her eye. She instantly shoved the light away and jerked back from the person, nearly toppling off the table she was on. Her heart raced at the near miss as the petite woman, with glasses and pale shoulder-length blond hair, grabbed her wrist and steadied her.

"Take it easy," she said in a calm voice. "I'm all done now." Releasing Emma, she backed away and picked up a clipboard from the counter. Squinting, she pushed her glasses up on her nose and began to jot down a few notes.

Emma breathed in an out of her nose, trying to calm her nerves. She quickly glanced down to see she was on an examining table and wearing nothing more than a thin hospital gown with tiny blue flowers.

Her gaze jerked to the woman, noting her crisp white

coat and the name Doctor Thurman embroidered on the pocket. Malac had said he was going to have her checked out. Emma scanned the tiny exam room, her heart racing. On the counter, a vial of blood sat on top of other paperwork. Rubber gloves turned inside out and a couple other personal instruments were lying in a metal pan. Emma ground her teeth and panic knotted her throat. "What have you done to me?"

The woman glanced up from the chart, her green eyes sympathetic. "I didn't do anything to you other than check that you weren't violated."

"*You* violated me!" Emma quickly sat up and swung her legs down the side of the table, her cheeks flaming with indignant heat. "How dare you!"

The woman's gaze darted to the door and her voice lowered. "I insisted on doing your physical instead of Doctor Thurman."

Emma's eyes snapped to the name on her coat. "You *are* Doctor Thurman."

"The other Doctor Thurman is my father. Would you rather a male have done your exam?"

Before Emma could respond, the door opened and Malac stepped into the room. He put his hand out and the woman instantly handed him the clipboard, saying, "She's perfectly healthy."

He flipped the first page over and his dark gaze narrowed. "Did he touch her?"

The doctor shook her head and her tone held a tinge of warning. "She's a virgin."

He raised a dark eyebrow and a pleased, calculating smile creased his narrow face. "An interesting development I hadn't expected." Snapping the page closed, he handed the clipboard back to the doctor and addressed Emma. "Eat and then you'll be allowed to see the old woman to know she's still alive."

"The 'old' woman is my aunt, and she'd better be in good health or I'll claw your eyes out," Emma hissed.

Malac chuckled, but amusement didn't reflect in his brown eyes. "So protective. You really believe she's your aunt, don't you? What other lies did the old bat tell you? You do realize she's human, right?"

Now I know.

When the only answer he got from Emma was her growling stomach, his chuckle turned to a full-out laugh before he sobered. "This is rich. Your reunion would be interesting to observe. Too bad I have business to deal with."

The tips of her fingers tingled, curled tight underneath the examining table. Emma realized her claws were ready to unsheathe, while an angry growl rumbled in her chest. It was so much easier now to feel the panther lying in wait under her skin. This time she wasn't afraid or scared. She welcomed her panther's strength. Apparently, all it had taken to bring out her primal side was seeing someone she cared about threatened.

Malac ignored her hostile sounds and spoke to someone in the hall. "Once she's eaten, escort her down to the old lady. Give her five and then bring her to my quarters."

"What about my aunt's medicine?" Emma snarled after him when he started to leave.

He turned back to her, his expression suddenly serious. "It'll be up to you whether or not she gets her meds."

The moment he turned away and walked out of the room, Emma was off the table, intending to go after the manipulative bastard. But a big man with light brown hair tied back in a severe ponytail stepped in front of her, blocking her way.

She realized he was human, like the doctor, because he *had* a scent. "Eat, then we'll go," he said in a curt tone.

Emma glanced at the gun strapped to his side, then narrowed her gaze after Malac's slim form walking down the hall.

"You need to eat." The blond woman held out a plate that had been wrapped in aluminum foil on a far counter. An apple sat next to a ham-and-cheese sandwich.

Even though her stomach rumbled, Emma didn't want to waste time. She shook her head. "I want to see my aunt."

The woman shoved the plate toward her. "You won't be allowed to see her if you don't eat."

Glaring at her, Emma jerked the plate from her hand and sat back down on the exam table. It took her less than five minutes to devour the food. The stem was the only bit of food left on the plate.

"Let's go." The guard grabbed her upper arm and escorted her out. Emma's bootie-covered feet shuffled quietly, while his shoes made heavy tapping sounds on the hall's gleaming white floors. She squinted at the fluorescent lights shining brightly on the stark white walls. Behind them, at one end of the hall, a young blond-haired man stood with a pulser gun in his hand, obviously on guard. Everything about the space felt sterile and pristine—like a lab. Except for the presence of the guard and pulser guns. They made it feel like a military facility.

A man with shoulder-length dark hair exited the elevator at the opposite end of the hall and walked toward them. As he passed, the diamond stud in his ear caught Emma's attention. Her gaze caught his for a brief second. The coldness in his deep green eyes surprised her. He was too young to appear so detached. She noted the gun strapped to his hip and tried to catch his scent, but couldn't. He had to be another panther.

He appeared to be of similar age to the young sentry down the hall. No more than seventeen or eighteen.

They reached the end of the hall and went through a door on the left which led to a stairwell. Emma's heart raced while they walked down two flights of stairs to the ground floor. They turned down a long, carpeted hall with several doors lining the right side, reminding her of a hotel.

When they stopped in front of the third door on their right, the guy swept his card through the reader and pushed her inside, saying in a gruff tone, "You have five minutes."

Her aunt turned from staring out the barred windows. "Emma!" she called, holding out her arms. She was still wearing her nightgown and slippers, but they'd at least allowed her to slip into her coat when they kidnapped her, Emma realized when she saw the gray wool overcoat lying on the bed.

"Aunt Mary!" Emma hugged the only family she'd ever known as tight as she could. "I was so worried." Emma cupped her aunt's pudgy cheeks and leaned back to look at her. "How are you feeling?"

Mary's wrinkled fingers ran gently across her hair, then touched her gown. "Where are your clothes, child? Are *you* okay?" Her expression hardened and her blue eyes slitted. "Have they hurt you?"

Emma gripped her aunt's hands to stop her fidgeting. "Are you feeling okay? How's your heart?"

Mary pulled her close and whispered, "Don't worry about me. The young female doctor has been checking my vitals." Leaning back, she gave Emma a smile meant to eliminate her worry. "Really, I'm okay. Where are your clothes?"

Emma knew she didn't have time to go into everything that

happened to her so far, so she went for blunt honesty. "I know what I am now." When Mary started to speak, she shook her head. "Don't worry, I'm not angry with you for keeping the truth from me all these years. We'll talk about your reasons later. I just wanted you to know I'm going to do everything I can to get us out of here."

Mary's worried expression softened and tears filled her eyes. "I did it to protect you and because I love you as if you were my own."

Tears spilled down Emma's cheeks and her heart ached for their situation. She hugged Mary tight. Trust was a little hard for her right now, but she cared very much for this woman who raised her all her life. "It's okay. You don't have to expla—"

"No, I want to tell you so you'll understand…in case I don't make it."

Emma's heart jerked. "Don't talk like that. We're going to get out of here. It doesn't matter to me that you're human and I'm panther. You'll always be my family."

Mary sniffled and pushed Emma's hair away from her face with a gentle caress. "Hush and just listen. My brother and I didn't have a normal life growing up."

Emma listened intently. Mary had only mentioned her estranged brother once in passing, but she'd never told Emma why they didn't speak anymore.

Mary's lips compressed into a hard line, then she continued. "Our parents had a nasty divorce. Throughout our childhood, Roland and I were shuffled back and forth between them for years. Mom and Dad each did and said horrible things, trying to turn us against the other parent, which actually made Roland and me closer. We had only each other, and as kids, we promised ourselves that we'd never have children of our own so they wouldn't have to go through what we did with our parents.

"When Roland met Jade, everything changed. I could see his devotion to her right off the bat. No matter our promises about not having children of our own, this young woman instantly became like a daughter to my brother. Only, she wasn't human."

Emma's heart thumped. "Jade was Velius?"

Mary nodded. "My brother helped Jade by creating the medicine that masks the panthers' scent from their natural enemies. I joined their group to be by Roland's side and just like my brother—" the old woman cupped Emma's chin, her smile full of love "—I quickly grew attached to a little girl in the Velius pride. The day before I decided to take you away was the last time I spoke to my brother." Her smile faded and she gave a self-deprecating laugh. "I suppose it's life's ironic justice that Roland and I had become so hopelessly devoted to our 'children's' happiness, to the point our dedication has kept us apart all this time. You see, if he had ever learned where I'd taken you, he would've brought you back to make Jade happy."

"Why would you take me away?" Emma asked, her mind racing in confusion.

Mary's lip curled in contempt. "Malac had splintered off from Jade's group, taking young Hawkeye with him. I was very unhappy about that, but when I later learned that Hawkeye had run away, I knew something had to be done. Even though Jade acted as your guardian and her intentions toward you seemed honorable, because you were special, I knew you'd always be at risk of becoming a pawn in Jade's and Malac's constant power struggle, just like poor Hawkeye. I wouldn't allow that. I wanted you to grow up without strife, to have a happy childhood—at least the best I could provide for you." She touched Emma's cheek. "You're a bit older than I led you to believe, but as far as I was concerned, your life started the day I took you with me."

Emma stared in shock. "How old am I?"

"The medicine slowed your maturity considerably. You're twenty-six."

Emma didn't really remember any other life than that with her aunt, though she felt sorry for Hawkeye having to live with Malac. She'd have run away, too. Tucking all of the truths raining down on her into the back of her mind for future contemplation, Emma gave an apologetic half smile. "I ran out of my pills and forgot to mention I needed a refill. I think that's how the Velius finally tracked me down." When her aunt nodded her understanding, Emma plunged on, needing to know the whole truth. "Malac told me I was created. Does that mean I never had a mother?"

Mary nodded, her smile sympathetic. "I'm the closest thing to a mother you've had."

Emma's head spun with all the new information, yet finding out there were two groups of panthers answered a few questions, while triggering a vague, nagging memory in her brain. She squeezed her eyes shut for a second, trying to process everything. Then the memory suddenly flooded her mind. She gripped her aunt's hands and pulled her over to sit down on the bed. "Has anyone ever called you Margaret? Is that your real name?"

Mary chuckled. "Roland always calls me that, even when everyone else calls me Mary. How did you know about Margaret?"

Emma was excited to share some news of Mary's brother.

"I believe I spoke to him. I was waking up from being drugged, so I never saw his face, but I heard him ask me about Margaret. He was worried for you. He's the one who took me from the club last night." *And the female talking to Roland about me had to have been Jade!*

Mary's blue eyes lit with hope. "Then he knows they have you! They'll come for us!"

Emma shook her head. "It's a little more complicated than that. He doesn't know Malac has taken me, but I'm sure others are searching for me."

Worry pulled at Mary's soft features. "What others?"

"I met a man. Malac says he's Lupreda—" Emma started to tell her about Caine when the door opened.

The guard walked into the room. "Time's up. Let's go."

He stalked over and grabbed Emma's arm, pulling her to her feet. Mary gripped Emma's hand tight, her brow creased with worry. "You can't trust that man you met. Don't trust anyone other than my brother or Jade. No one else has your best interests at heart, Emma."

Chapter 8

Mary's parting words kept echoing in Emma's head as the guard hauled her to the end of the hall, then used his key card to open an elevator to her right. Once they were inside, the man pushed the button and they rode the elevator to the third floor.

Whom could she trust? Everyone seemed to want something from her. First, Roland and this unknown Jade had kidnapped her, and now, of course, Malac.

But what about Caine? Did he also have an ulterior motive? Was their attraction just another lie to get something he wanted from her? To keep her from her people? Her people? She didn't even know what that meant! Mary might love her, but she was human. Emma had never felt more alone or scared. Her heart raced when the elevator pinged and the silver doors slid open.

"Come in, Emma," Malac called from somewhere in the

room. Piano music played off to the right; it was a classical piece. Straight ahead was a huge mural painting of New York City's skyline on the far wall directly across from the elevator entrance.

When a cool breeze blew up her gown, making her skin prickle, she said to the guard, "Don't I at least get to change clothes or something first?"

His answer was to shove her onto the thick Persian rug right outside the elevator and punch the elevator button. As the doors slid noiselessly closed, Emma dug her toes into the soft carpet and turned to see Malac sitting at the piano, his fingers running across the keys flawlessly.

"Ah, there you are." The music suddenly stopped and he stood, grabbing his glass of wine off the top of the grand piano sitting all the way across the three-thousand-square-foot space.

As he passed through the sunken living room area, decorated with an oversized couch covered with opulent pillows in similar earth tones to the area rug under her feet in the foyer area, her stomach tensed. Malac was a wiry, slightly built man, but what his smaller frame lacked, his eyes more than made up for in terms of sheer power and determination. The penetrating way he looked at her as he approached could only be described as cold and calculating. She could almost see his diabolical mind working through the numbers, considering all the strategic angles…how best to use her to his ultimate advantage.

From the way he'd decorated his living quarters to the clothes he wore—a black silk shirt, dark gray slacks and custom leather dress shoes—it was clear Malac liked to surround himself with the finer things in life. Emma didn't doubt for one minute that that skyline painting on the wall to her left held some deeper significance for him…something far sinister than a general appreciation of the city. Malac was maniacally ambitious.

Sheesh, I'm reading all kinds of things into this creep. All she knew for sure was the man made her skin crawl and he definitely had a God complex. She resisted a shiver of revulsion when he stopped a few feet away from her.

"Now that you've seen that the old woman is alive and well, we're going to talk."

"My aunt needs her meds," Emma stated.

"Still clinging to that human?" Malac tsked and walked over to a side bar where he poured himself some more wine. "Want some?" he asked as he took a sip and faced her.

Emma clenched her fists. "I will not be a part of this 'war' insanity you mentioned in the truck. Nor am I mating with you or any other Velius."

Malac leaned casually back against the bar. "My team of scientists and doctors assure me that they can successfully extract your eggs, fertilize them and implant them in surrogate mothers." His dark gaze swept appreciatively down her bare legs, then back up to her face. Closing his eyes briefly, his nostrils flared. "I smell the change in your musky scent. You're heading toward your fertile cycle. Before we extract your eggs to build this army, *my* offspring will come the old-fashioned way, conceived and carried by my mate."

He was going to violate her, then make her his broodmare? Horrified shock slammed through Emma in waves of fury and fear. A chill swept down her spine and bile rose to her throat as her disgust built. "You won't get within an inch of me and neither will your doctors!" she snapped.

Setting his wineglass on the bar top, he turned an unconcerned gaze her way. "And what about your 'aunt'? Doctor

Thurman informs me that she'll need her meds very soon for her health to remain stable."

God, Aunt Mary. You've given up so much for me.

When she didn't answer, his smile held an icy ruthlessness that sent a jolt of fear splintering through her. "You *will* cooperate."

Emma stood there in that thin hospital gown, feeling the most vulnerable she'd ever been in her life. If she said yes, in two seconds he'd have the damn flimsy thing torn off her body. If she said no, Mary might die and she would be responsible.

She glanced around the open living space for an escape path. A huge glass window, farther down the same wall as the mural, led to some kind of concrete patio partially covered in snow. It dropped to nowhere as far as she could see from her vantage point. The elevator to her right needed a key, so she couldn't leave that way.

Every fiber in her being screamed out against the choice she was having to make…and she thought of Caine. How she wanted her first time—her only time—to be with him. Was he sincere in his feelings for her? She desperately wanted to believe *he* was real. *I will come for you,* was the last thing he'd said to her. In that, she believed.

His strength, while fighting his wounds and the tranquilizer, reminded her that she wasn't completely helpless. "Fine." She yanked the front of the gown, and the snaps popped open. Cool air hit her spine and she slid her arms out of the gown to let it flutter to the floor. Standing naked in front of him, she tilted up her chin. "You want me?"

Malac's white teeth flashed in victory. "Faster by the second," he murmured, his gaze slitting with lust as he began to unbutton his shirt with quick flicks of his wrist.

Emma kept her expression calm while her insides quaked. She curled her finger inward in a come-hither movement. "Then you're going to have to work for it."

When he took a step toward her, she turned and fell toward the floor at the same time she let all her anger for her aunt's current situation, for the impending loss of her own innocence—both mentally and physically—and for what Malac had done to Caine well up inside her. All the strong emotions merged into a brewing storm, fast and furious—ready to unleash its wrath.

Her panther form hit the floor on all fours. She turned to face him, her roar shaking the pictures hanging on the walls and rattling his glass of wine on the bar.

"Shift back!" he snarled, his face distorting in fury.

Emma blew air through her nostrils, then swiped her paw across the wood floor, purposefully digging gouges. Like a bull preparing to charge, she planned to make sure he didn't come away from their altercation unscathed.

Sweat coated his forehead. He quickly flipped open a gold engraved box on the bar top. "You'll pay for this," he gritted out over her panther roar.

When her bellow slowed to a steady growl, Emma smelled the beginnings of fear edge his scent, pungent and sharp. She'd almost forgotten he couldn't shift at will. Now, she was the predator and he was the prey. He was still stronger than a human man, but the fact remained that she was a force to be reckoned with in this form, and with no tranquilizer gun at his disposal, he was as trapped as she'd been a minute ago. The air hit her canines with sweet biting sharpness as she smiled and slowly walked toward the bar, her muscles flexing sleekly with each step she took.

He jammed some kind of short needle into his neck and closed his eyes with a hiss as if he'd just shot himself up with his favorite drug. When his eyes snapped open, his pupils had dilated to the same size as his dark irises. It was like staring into a soulless being.

He gave her a pleased smile. "Taking you this way will be harder and bloodier, but I'm up for the challenge. It's probably the best way to show you that my panther rules you just as much as the man does."

His threat brought her survival instincts out full force. Emma curled her upper lip back, bearing her teeth once more. She dug her front claws into the wood flooring, then crouched on her back legs, ready to pounce before he shifted to panther form.

She'd learned Malac's tactics the last time she'd tangled with him. This time she didn't leap for his face; instead, she lunged forward and used her strong paws to grab his legs, pulling him to the floor.

He fell over onto his side, hitting the floor with a hard thud. As her claws dug deep, ripping his calf muscles, his yell of pain deepened to a vicious growling roar. Emma didn't have time to dodge his blow before his powerful front paw swiped at her shoulder, shredding skin as he sent her flying through the air.

She hit the back of the couch and her momentum toppled the heavy piece of furniture. Fire raged across her shoulder where he'd wounded her. She panted and quickly rolled off the couch's plush cushions onto her paws. The smell of her own blood filled her nostrils while she crouched and twitched her ears back and forth, listening for Malac's approach.

Before she heard him coming, Malac soared over the couch and knocked her hard, sending her skidding on her side across the floor. She slammed into the legs of a console table and a vase shattered, spewing flowers, water and ceramic bits all around her.

Malac let out a triumphant rrrrooowl and slowly stalked toward her, his head bent low, his growl promising retribution. His panther body was bigger than hers, easily outweighing her by sixty pounds, but he was still slim in stature, just like his human form. His slightly larger size gave him brute strength, but it probably also slowed him down in agility.

If she could just get on her feet, she might be able to evade him. Emma tried to scramble to her feet, but the water and pottery bits made her paws slide out from underneath her. She slipped back to the floor, banging her chin hard.

Panic closed her throat, keeping her from roaring the way she wanted to. Instead, the sound that came out of her throat was a low, warning rumble.

When Malac reached her side, his roar slowed to an almost evil-sounding snarl as he reached out with his forepaw and batted her body out of the mess underneath her and into the middle of the floor.

Emma spun with his forceful blow and dizziness rattled her mind for a second before she could get her bearings. The moment her head cleared, she jumped up, only to feel Malac's heavy weight slam over her back.

The dominant position sent fear spiraling through her belly. She tried to scramble out from underneath him, but he bit down on her neck. Hard.

Emma howled in pain and her legs began to shake when his hot breath rushed out his nose in a growling grunt. She jerked forward slightly when his hips pushed against hers. As his musky scent elevated several levels, she couldn't mistake what his vise hold meant.

She tried to jerk free, but he deepened his bite, sending pain shooting down her neck. Despite her fear, she hissed and tucked her tail underneath her in an act of rebellion.

He snarled his anger at her defiance, then jammed his right forepaw on top of hers, digging his claws deep.

At the same time Emma let out a yowl of pain, something big burst through the huge picture window across the room. Glass flew everywhere as an enormous panther barreled straight for them.

Malac barely had time to release her before the other panther rammed his huge head into Malac's side.

Emma heard ribs crack right before Malac careened all the way across the room. He collided with an oversized wooden trunk against the far wall, the piece of furniture exploding on impact. Lying among broken planks and splinters of wood, Malac shook his head to clear it, then jumped to his paws with a roar of fury.

The panther who'd attacked Malac stood there. Waiting. The only indication he was on high alert was the slight twitch at the end of his long tail.

Emma backed up when Malac bared his canines and claws and leapt across the room toward the taller, broader panther, who probably outweighed him by at least forty pounds.

As Malac's form began to descend in the air, in a motion that defied his bulky size, the panther moved with grace, rolling forward to land underneath Malac where he hammered his back paws into Malac's underbelly.

Malac's body bowed from the impact before vaulting across the entire room's expanse to land with a sickly thud against the grand piano. Eerie notes played as he slithered across the keyboard. The bench fell to its side before he landed with a solid thump on the floor, lying completely still.

Emma turned frightened eyes to the panther who now approached her with sure-footed steps. Not once did he make a sound. No growl or roar of fury erupted from him while he'd attacked Malac. He'd just taken out the bastard as if he were a weak-limbed rag doll, full of fluffy stuffing.

When the panther reached her, he lowered his head and pushed at her shoulder.

Emma stumbled back, unsure what he was telling her. He did it again, this time more forcefully and she realized he was trying to direct her toward the window.

She shook her head. She wasn't leaving without her aunt. The lights on the elevator began to move. She waited, watching them. Once the elevator finally reached the floor and the doors slid open, she'd force her way in, taking out whoever was in her way.

When she tried to sidestep him, the panther's low warning growl surprised her. She dodged, then attempted to dive past him, but he was much faster than she expected. Before she knew what had happened, he'd grabbed her wounded scruff with his teeth, then hurled her across the room toward the window.

Emma landed on her side, sliding across the floor. She quickly rolled to her feet and started to charge toward him, but bits of glass had embedded in her paw pads. As she yelped and tried to shake the glass from her paws, she was surprised to see him run toward her, then turn onto his side and skid across the floor in front of her.

He stood up and shook the bits of glass from his fur, then looked at her and jerked his head toward the window with a commanding grunt. He'd just cleared a path for her to the window and he wasn't going to let her go in any other direction.

Emma was torn. She didn't want to leave Mary behind, but this panther wasn't giving her a choice. The elevator dinged, and three men stepped out holding pulser guns. Damn it, they weren't giving her a choice, either.

One man yelled and pulser fire zoomed past Emma, jolting her into action. She ran a few steps and vaulted toward the window. Something pinched her side as she crossed the windowsill, but she didn't pause once she'd landed on her feet on the concrete patio—which turned out to be a flat roof. Following her rescuer's lead, who'd landed beside her, they took off in a fast run. Pulser fire singed the snow-covered cement around them as she headed toward the edge. Emma's heart jumped to her throat when the panther in front of her bunched his long powerful legs and easily cleared the six-foot distance to land on the flat roof of an adjacent building.

She came to a skidding stop, sending snow scattering over the building's edge.

The panther impatiently pawed at the cement under his feet, then let out a bellow, commanding her to follow.

Pulser bursts zipped past her ear, elevating her heart rate several notches. Emma backed up several feet, then sucked in a deep breath before bolting forward. Her heart nearly stopped as she took the flying leap between the buildings. When her paws landed on the roof, the shock sent jabs of pain shooting up her legs, making them as useless as rubber. She came to a jolting stop for a second, trying to regain strength.

The panther nudged her with his snout and a low purr of encouragement against her jaw, combined with his familiar scent, evoked a strong feeling of support. She took a deep breath and put one paw in front of the other in order to shrug off the pain in her shaking legs.

Emma followed him inside the building where a rock had been wedged between the rooftop door and the frame, holding it ajar. Her right side stung like someone held a match against her skin, but she pushed forward. Their paws made no sounds as they trotted down the three flights of stairs and then out another door the panther shoved open once he'd pushed down on the metal bar with his front paws.

As soon as they were free of the building, he began to run on the pavement, his sleek, large muscled body both powerful and graceful in his movements. Was that how she looked? She doubted it. Emma gave a self-deprecating snort as she clumsily tried to match his smooth gait. She at least kept up with his pace for a good five blocks while they weaved through what appeared to be a snow-covered, run-down industrial area of town.

She didn't have time to look at street signs, they were moving so fast. The panther seemed to know where he was going. The way she was starting to feel—run-down and weak, her side stitching and throbbing with each pounding brush of her paws across the snow-covered pavement—she hoped he didn't suddenly take off or she'd be lost forever in the maze of buildings and streets around them.

Only, her body had decided it had had enough, even if her mind screamed for her to continue. Emma's rapid run slowed to a trot, and she finally managed to mewl a tired growl before she stopped and fell over onto her left side. As she lay on the freezing asphalt, her nose deciphering car oil and gas aromas under the heavy layer of snow, her ribs heaved up and down with each wheezing breath.

Emma's racing pulse spiked when her vision began to fade in and out. She couldn't pass out. Not now.

A dark-haired man with deep green eyes came into view. His forehead creased with worry and he leaned over her to run his hand across her shoulder. "What's wrong—" he started to say, then swore under his breath. His high cheekbones hollowed with his swift intake of breath when his palm reached something sticky wet on her side.

Bright red blood coated his hand. "Why didn't you tell me you were hurt?" he said in a harsh tone.

Emma grunted her annoyance. How could he give her a hard time about speaking up? It's not like she could at the moment. But if she were in human form...

As if he knew what she was thinking, he ordered, "Don't shift!" while he moved behind her. One big hand slid under her hips and another under her shoulder. "You've lost too much blood as it is. Your human form couldn't handle a wound like this."

She whimpered as he lifted her. Cradling her body against his broad chest, he whispered against her ear, "Hang on. We're almost to my truck."

A few minutes later, he rounded a building and stopped behind a truck. Emma let out a tiny yowl when he shifted her so he could open the covered tailgate.

Sliding her body gently onto the truck bed, he said, "The hard cover above you should keep off the wind. I'm going to slide you forward a little bit so I can talk to you through the cab window."

Emma could only moan her approval. Her eyes rolled in her head and she was having a hard time staying awake, the pain hurt so much. As he pushed her forward, she bumped into rolls of paper. She blinked and tried to focus. Maps. Tons of maps were all around her. One had unrolled near her nose and she saw trails among mountain ranges and trees; they had all been intricately hand-drawn.

He'd disappeared for a second and then he was climbing into the truck bed beside her. She lifted her head at the sound of material ripping. Bare-chested, he sat on his knees in a pair of faded jeans and no shoes, ripping open a T-shirt at the seam. He must've grabbed the jeans and T-shirt from the front of the truck.

Moving at a rapid pace, he cinched the T-shirt tight around her waist, covering her wound. After he jumped out of the truck, he put his hand on her hip and murmured, "That's all I can do for now, Emral."

Emral? The name stirred something familiar deep within her. She knew this man…somehow. The truck started and Emma closed her eyes, trying to remember.

The vehicle began to move and a window slid open at the same time he barked in a gruff voice, "Stay conscious!"

Yeah, yeah, she thought even as his commanding tone jerked her eyes wide open. It was an involuntary response, but one she felt must've happened often in her past for her body to instantly react like it did.

"You don't remember me, do you?" he called through the window.

Emma sighed, wishing she could talk.

"I couldn't let Malac do it to you—I had to save you from the same fate," he ground out. "I promised you I'd always protect you. When I found out Mary had taken you and even Malac didn't know how to find you, I thought you were safe, but I always kept tabs…" He flipped on what sounded like a radio. Airwave static filled the air, then angry squawks came through.

"That traitorous bastard has taken her. Find Hawkeye, no matter the cost," Malac's enraged voice shot through the truck's cab.

"Do you want us to take him alive? His DNA—"

"I don't give a damn about him," Malac snarled. "Kill him on sight, but I *want her back*."

So this was Hawkeye. But why did he call her Emral? Her name was Emma. The hitching pain in her side kept her from thinking about anything for very long. Her stomach knotted and the burning wound on her side seemed to grow even hotter while the pain throbbed incessantly.

They swerved around a corner and she rolled into some of the maps. Emma moaned. "You okay—" he started to ask through the window, then hissed, "Sonofabitch." Two seconds later, she heard a cell phone being dialed.

"I need the address for Landon Rourke Private Investigations in New York City."

Emma's ears perked up. Landon was the name Caine had mentioned.

"That'll do."

When he snapped closed his cell phone, he gunned the engine and the truck shot forward. Several minutes passed, or was it a half hour—she'd lost track of time as her eyes opened and closed—before the truck rolled to a stop?

The tailgate opened and Hawkeye slid her out of the truck, lifting her into his arms. All she could tell was that they were in some kind of alley. "Let's hope he has this place on an alarm," Hawkeye mumbled. Emma jerked when he lifted his foot and rammed it into a door, splintering it off the hinges.

He carried her inside a storage room and through another door to lay her on the carpet. A desk, a rolling chair and a lateral filing cabinet was all she could see from her vantage point on the floor while he scribbled something on the desk.

An annoying beeping sound invaded her mind as he went down on his knee and ran his hand across her forehead and over her ears. An alarm was going off. "You're bleeding too much. For obvious reasons, I can't take you to the hospital." He glanced toward the front door and her gaze followed his. Landon Rourke Private Investigations, she read the backward words on the glass as Hawkeye finished, "This man saved us once. He might be Lupreda, but he's proven he has a conscience. Right now, he's the only one I trust."

He stood up and Emma made whimpering clicks. She didn't want to be left alone. Crouching beside her once more, he ran his hand over her pelt. "I'll be watching from a distance to make sure he takes care of you."

With a sigh of relief, Emma quieted and closed her eyes.

"Stay conscious," he reminded her in an authoritative tone not to be ignored.

When her eyes flew open, he was already gone.

Chapter 9

Caine jerked his gaze to the rearview mirror. Something heavy had landed in the back of his truck. Landon knocked on the glass behind him, then made a thumbing motion to the side of the road.

Gritting his teeth, Caine gripped the steering wheel tight and for several seconds considered swerving to the side, just to knock the Alpha on his ass. He was so pissed at Landon for waiting an hour and a half to wake him, he could feel his Musk form howling to be free, itching for a fight. The tips of his fingers tingled, his wereclaws scratching just below the surface.

When Landon pounded a dent in the roof above his head, he finally pulled his truck to the side of the interstate. Laird drove up behind him in Landon's truck with Kaitlyn in the seat beside him. Roman stood in the bed of their truck, his hair windblown to hell, grinning like a fool at the icy wonderland around him. The idiot.

Why had Landon chased him down? He was almost to the city at this point. He sure as hell wasn't going back to Lupreda land.

Before he could say a word, Landon had jumped down and climbed into the passenger seat. "I told you not to leave without me," Landon snarled.

"And I told you to wake me in an hour," Caine challenged, pulling the truck back onto the road.

Landon's low growl was interrupted by his cell phone's ring. Grabbing the phone from his belt, he flipped it open and read the text message.

"Hell and damnation," he mumbled, then hung up and called another number.

"What is it?" Caine's shoulders tensed.

"My office has been broken into again," Landon said before he spoke into the phone. "Gabriel, I got an automatic call. Can you pull up the monitoring system and tell me what body temperature the sensors are registering?"

Caine heard Gabriel's rumble across the line. "One hundred and three, Landon. Definitely not human, unless the human's sick as a dog." Gabriel snorted at his own joke, then quickly sobered. "You want me to cut the backup call to the police?"

"Cut it," Landon said in a brisk tone before he closed the cell and addressed Caine. "Gotta be Velius. Let's see how fast this souped-up rig of yours can go."

When he gunned the truck, Laird honked and followed suit. Caine glanced in his rearview mirror to see Roman now hanging out the passenger window, shaking his fist and yelling, "Yeah, baby! Go!"

Caine shook his head. "We can't take him anywhere."

"At least he's a talented nut," Landon grunted, then glanced his way. "If we can catch one of them there, we'll do whatever it takes to find out where they've taken Emma."

Landon had just given Caine his full support, surprising the hell out of him. Caine gripped the steering wheel hard and dipped his head in a curt nod, swallowing the lump of appreciation in his throat.

"You will follow my lead. Understood?" Landon ordered when they entered the outskirts of the city.

Every fiber in Caine's body howled in protest. He knew Landon was trying to control the situation so Caine wouldn't use his Musk form. He didn't like it, but right now Landon had the advantage—a lead on finding the panthers. And Emma.

Setting his jaw, Caine stared straight ahead. "Got it."

The moment he stepped out of his truck, Caine smelled Emma's earthy scent and blood. A lot of blood. Panic knotted his stomach. He started to take off for the front door, but Landon was by his side in a millisecond, grasping his arm.

"My lead," the Alpha reminded him as Laird, Roman and Kaitlyn joined them. Releasing Caine, Landon jerked his chin toward the front of the building. "Laird, you and Roman make sure to shield Kaitlyn as you approach from the front. Caine and I are going around back."

Laird nodded his understanding and Kaitlyn pulled her gun, rolling her eyes and mumbling about overprotective wolves.

Narrowing his gaze on Caine, Landon said, "We go in together."

Tension rode Caine's spine, raising the hairs on the back of his neck. He gritted his teeth but dipped his head in agreement.

Landon and Caine headed to the side of the building and rounded to the alley behind it in mere seconds. When he saw the condition of his back door, Landon growled, clenching his fists. "Let's go."

Caine prepared for a fight as he walked into the back room, but no one was around. He and Landon made their way to the front room. The moment he stepped through the doorway, he saw the blood-soaked T-shirt wrapped around Emma's bloody wound. She was breathing with such shallow pants and her pulse sounded slower than it should; his heart nearly stopped. He rushed forward and fell to his knees by her side.

Running his hand over her snout and then down the soft fur along her shoulder, he was so racked with fear she wouldn't survive that his words came out in a guttural grunt. "Emma, it's Caine. I'm here. Stay awake for me, sweetheart."

She whimpered and her forepaw jerked slightly, giving him hope that she recognized him.

"I have the panther's scent." Caine looked up at Landon. "I'm going to rip the bastard who did this to her apart one limb at a time."

"I think you've got it all wrong." Landon approached and with a grim expression turned the piece of paper he held around so Caine could read it.

Save Emral!

Caine frowned. "Who's Emral?"

Landon glanced down at Emma. "*She's* Emral, or Emerald rather. The Lupreda who created these panthers named them after gemstones—Jade, Emerald, Hawkseye, Malachite, Jasper, and so on."

Caine snarled at the note, mentally plotting his vengeance. "It doesn't mean the panther I'm scenting wasn't responsible."

Landon went down on one knee beside Emma and spoke to her. "It's Landon Rourke. I recognize your scents now that I smell Hawkeye's, too. Did he bring you here?"

Emma turned toward Landon's voice and nodded before letting her head roll back to the floor.

Caine had so many questions, but right now Emma's dire condition needed to be addressed. He bent down to run his tongue along a wound on her shoulder and was surprised when it didn't instantly start to heal.

He jerked his gaze to Landon. The Alpha was shaking his head, his jaw set in a hard line. "Apparently our saliva doesn't heal them like it can humans and our own kind."

Caine pressed his hand over the largest wound on Emma's side. "She'll bleed out if we don't do something soon."

Kaitlyn stepped forward to stand beside her mate who was still crouched beside Emma. "Obviously we can't take her to a hospital and because there aren't any doctors among the Lupreda…" She placed her hand on Landon's shoulder and continued. "I have a suggestion. You told me about the vampire leader's sister saving his human mate, Ariel. Do you think his sister might be able to help Emma?"

"A vampire?" Caine growled low in his throat.

"This might be our only option. None of the Lupreda have ever needed someone with medical knowledge." Landon stood and retrieved his cell phone from his belt. Flipping open the cell, he reached into his jeans' front pocket and held his hand toward Caine. "I'll make the call to Jachin after you agree."

Emma had started to bleed again. The warm blood seeped under his fingers, soaking the makeshift bandage. Jerking his gaze to Landon, Caine saw the lone silver chain curled innocuously in the palm of the Alpha's hand.

Returning his line of sight to Emma, Caine couldn't believe Landon would blackmail him like this. Anger and resentment boiled in his chest, building steam. He couldn't lose her. Grinding his teeth, he snarled, "Just do it."

Landon dropped the chain around Caine's neck, then started dialing.

After a few seconds, Caine's keen hearing picked up Jachin's voice across the line. "Rourke. Haven't heard from you in a while."

"I'm calling in my marker for helping you take over leadership of the Sanguinas," Landon said in a matter-of-fact tone.

Shocked, Caine jerked his gaze back to Landon.

Jachin remained silent for a second. "Must be pretty important for you to ask for a debt owed so soon."

The Alpha returned Caine's steady stare and continued in a calm tone. "It's a matter of life and death."

"Whose?"

"I'll tell you everything when you get here. Can you bring your sister to the city? We need her medical expertise."

While Jachin responded on the other end, Kaitlyn put her hand on Landon's arm. Then Landon nodded and went on. "Fine. Meet us at my mate Kaitlyn's house after dark."

After Landon gave Jachin directions to the suburbs and hung up, Caine shook his head. He couldn't believe Landon had just played the pack's most important chess piece for his sake—a wolf no longer with the pack—yet his worry for Emma overrode the varied emotions of guilt, shock and deep appreciation tightening his chest. "We can't risk moving her. She's losing blood."

Landon squatted next to Emma and put his hand on her

head. "The last time I saw you, you were just a cub, so tiny you fit in the palm of my hand." Glancing up at Caine, his green gaze hardened. "If you want her to live, we have to move her."

Caine set his jaw, then pulled off his T-shirt to begin re-binding her wound.

The moment he heard a car pull into Kaitlyn's driveway, Caine tensed. Kaitlyn had put him in a guest bedroom, and he'd sat there for two hours with his back against the head-board, holding Emma on the bed between his legs, her head propped on his thigh. While time had ticked past, Caine realized those two hours were far more agonizing than his own experience a few months ago, waiting to see if he'd shift back to human form from his Musk one. In comparison, that was nothing. He could not lose Emma.

As voices filtered up from the hall downstairs, he stroked her head and the soft fur down her neck for the thousandth time and whispered, "They're here. Hold on just a little longer, Emma."

Emma had stopped responding to his encouraging words fifteen minutes before, tearing him up inside. She was con-scious but barely.

Landon and Kaitlyn appeared in the doorway, followed by a tall, dark-haired man, an equally tall and broad-chested blond man and a petite woman with fine features and long black hair. The woman immediately pushed her way past everyone and approached the bed, a look of concern in her blue eyes.

"She's a shapeshifter, yes?" she asked Caine. Kneeling beside the bed, she ran her hand gingerly over Emma's fur.

Caine tensed when her vampire scent slammed into him. It took every ounce of willpower in his body not to rip the woman's hand away from Emma—his distrust in vampires was too ingrained. Gritting his teeth, he jerked his gaze to Landon's.

As Landon nodded his permission, the woman spoke again. "I'm Mira, what's her name?"

Caine's grip on Emma tightened. "Her name is Emma and yes, she's a shapeshifter. She's lost a lot of blood. We've been unable to heal her wounds."

"You said you'd explain when we got here." The dark-haired man gave Landon a sharp look. "Now would be a good time."

Mira spoke to the blond man. "Talek, please bring all my supplies from the car, quickly." As Talek left the room, she cast her gaze to the dark-haired man who'd come in with her. "Take it into the hall if you want to talk, Jachin."

"I believe the second part of the prophecy referred to the Lupreda," Landon said as he and Jachin stepped outside the room.

Caine listened while he watched every move the female vampire made. Landon appeared to trust them, but damn, it was hard for him.

"The first part of the prophecy was fulfilled by Ariel and the second part is about us, but it—"

"Has something to do with that panther lying in there, doesn't it?" Jachin cut off Landon in a grating tone.

Caine felt Landon's Alpha anger rise and Kaitlyn must have, too, because she walked into the hall and stepped between the men. "No fighting or I'm kicking you both out of my house."

Jachin glanced down at Kaitlyn, then met Landon's gaze. "Only you would pick someone as stubborn as you for a mate."

Landon laughed outright. "Hello, pot."

"So glad I can help put you two back on common ground."

Kaitlyn snorted at them before she walked into the room and approached the bed. "I'm Kaitlyn. Can I get you anything, Mira?"

Mira twisted her hair up in a knot on her head. "Do you have something we can put under her? There's going to be a lot of blood and fluids when I start to clean the wound." Before Kaitlyn turned to get the items, Mira listed a few more things she needed.

Caine tuned in to Landon and Jachin as his Alpha spoke of the prophecy. "It's not our proudest moment by far, but some of the Lupreda used the abandoned lab to create their own prey to hunt. The Velius."

"While you were still under our rule?" The annoyance in Jachin's tone made Caine smile.

Smugness laced Landon's response. "We were far smarter and more stealthy than the Sanguinas ever gave us credit for."

"And you condoned this?" Jachin challenged.

Landon's testosterone levels elevated. "Hell no, I didn't. When I found out, I destroyed the lab and set the few panthers free." Snorting his annoyance, Landon continued. "I didn't expect them to rally and try to start a war between the vampires and werewolves."

"Ah, so the panthers are the ones who killed your zerkers."

"Yes," Landon ground out.

Jachin glanced through the doorway at Caine and Emma. "Yet, you're trying to save this one. Why?"

Landon met Caine's gaze briefly. "Because I think the panthers are part of the prophecy, as well."

Kaitlyn walked up carrying blankets and what appeared to be plastic trash bags. As she passed the men, she addressed Jachin. "I'd like to hear this prophecy. Landon mentioned it to me but not in detail."

Landon and Jachin followed Kaitlyn inside the room, and once Talek returned and handed Mira her supplies, Jachin told them the full prophecy.

A human will speak of our demise.
Her purity and intelligence will help us survive.
A mate she becomes to the leader of vampires
Joining our races, fulfilling our ultimate desire.

The hunted becomes the hunter, no longer the prey.
An enemy in your midst is less dark and more gray.
Examine your failures and there you will find
The answer to all your questions in time.

A leader is needed, you know this is true
Look not to one, but two.
A lesson was the goal you sought
You too must learn from what you taught

Layers of deception must be unveiled
For three to become one and peace to prevail.

"It fits," Caine mused once Jachin finished relaying the full prophecy. He'd heard it before, but now with all the context of what had happened in the past six months, his mind pieced it together. "The part about the human was obviously about Ariel writing her book about vampires and then Jachin and Ariel becoming mates. The 'hunted becomes the hunter, no longer the prey' part refers to the Lupreda creating the Velius to hunt. And 'an enemy in your midst is less dark and more gray'…that would describe Emma, but I can't say that's true of the other panthers we've tangled with so far."

"'Examine your failures…' I made sure the Lupreda failed with their panthers project," Landon finished.

"We'll figure it all out eventually," Mira murmured, her focus on the panther as she pulled out a scalpel.

Caine quickly dropped his ponderings about the rest of the prophecy when Mira moved close to Emma with the sharp instrument. Protective instincts flared and he grabbed the female vampire's wrist, giving a low growl.

Talek was by Mira's side and gripping Caine's shoulder in a crushing hold. "Release her or I'll break every bone in your body, wolf."

Caine's growl intensified. His fingers tightened around Mira's arm as he met Talek's angry gaze. The tension in the room spiked until Emma gave a low mewl and lifted her paw. Placing it over Caine's hand on Mira's wrist, she tugged.

Caine met Emma's pained yellow gaze and sheer worry filled him. Letting his hand slip from Mira's wrist, he grated out, "Don't hurt her any more than she's already been injured."

Mira nodded to Talek and he released Caine with a grunt and a warning glare. As the healer began to cut away the T-shirts binding Emma's wound, she spoke to her in a soothing voice. "Emma, I need you to shift back to your human form so I can see exactly how deep your wounds go."

"She should've shifted back by now," Landon said. "The drugs the Lupreda used to make them shift only lasted a couple hours."

"They could've developed a longer sustaining drug," Kaitlyn suggested.

Emma whimpered and her eyes fluttered open and closed as she shook her head. Caine's heart seized with panic when Mira's concerned blue gaze locked with his. "I can't help her if she doesn't shift. I'm not familiar with panther anatomy. Talk to her. See if it's some kind of mental block." Standing up, she backed away from the bed to give them privacy.

"They can't control their shifting," Landon said when Mira moved to stand beside her brother.

While Caine slid out from underneath Emma, Kaitlyn walked up with a lightweight blanket. Handing it to him, she said, "All you can do is try. We'll be in the hall when you're ready."

Caine took the blanket and nodded his appreciation while everyone filed out. Once he spread the cover over Emma, he went down on his knees on the floor and ran his palm over her head and along her neck and shoulders in a rhythmic, soothing motion. "Emma…" Caine choked on his worry. He tried to act calm, even though his gut felt as if it were jamming up his throat. He couldn't lose her nor could he let her know just how bad off she was.

Instead he spoke in her mind, giving them true privacy. *I didn't get to tell you how much you mean to me before Malac took you. I hope you felt it in my touch.* His fingers shook as they traveled along her pelt and met bloodied, matted fur. Caine worked hard to focus. *I don't give a damn that you're a panther and I'm a wolf. I want you…us very much. If I can overcome decades of hatred for the vampires, enough to let Mira help you, know that it's only because I care very much what happens to you.*

Emma released a heavy sigh and she instantly shifted back to human form. Caine blinked at the lightning speed of her shifting. He'd never seen anything like it. Even shifting to his full Musk form took at least thirty seconds.

"You really didn't know I could control my shifting, did you?" she said in a tired voice.

Caine was surprised to see her smile slightly before her eyes fluttered closed as she lost consciousness.

Chapter 10

"Mira!" Caine yelled, his heart thumping in fear for Emma.

The vampire was by his side in an instant, saying in a commanding tone, "Go to the other side of the bed if you want to be near her."

Caine swallowed the retort that came to his lips and did as the healer commanded. Emma looked so pale and the claw marks marring the soft skin across her neck, her shoulder and down her collarbone made him see red. His Musk form howled for vengeance just below the surface.

Clasping Emma's limp hand, Caine laced his fingers with hers and held on tight, blinking back the moisture blurring his eyes. He refused to look at the gaping wound on her side or he'd lose it completely. Seeing the damage to her fragile human body tore him up even more inside, leaving him raw and shaken. He plotted the many ways he would repay the favor to Malac before he killed him.

Mira began pulling tubes out of her bag, then beckoned Jachin over and asked him to roll up his sleeve. Caine's entire frame tightened with suspicion. "What are you doing?"

Her blue gaze met his. "Your friend has lost too much blood. We must replace it or she will die. While I'm sewing her wound closed, my brother's blood will help her heal."

Caine gritted his teeth and began to roll up his own sleeve. "I'll give Emma the blood she needs."

"Landon said you couldn't heal her wounds," Mira reminded him.

Caine's jaw flexed. "My saliva couldn't heal her wound, but if it's blood she needs, I want her to have mine."

Mira set her lips in a firm line, then nodded.

Jachin moved out of the way and Caine retrieved a chair, setting it next to the bed.

Caine heard Jachin speaking in a low tone to Landon while Mira connected Caine to Emma via the tubing. "Did you hear the panther before she passed out? She said she can shift at will."

"She and the other panther were just cubs when they were released. Their abilities hadn't been tested yet, but if it's true that she can control her shifting, she'd be a valuable asset to the panthers."

An asset worth fighting over, Caine realized, staring at Emma's pale face. He stood at Mira's urging to let gravity help the blood flow from his body to Emma's. Caine stared at Emma's wan features and mentally yelled for his blood to flow faster. *Help her heal, damn you!*

Mira began to sew Emma's gaping wound closed, first on the inside and then moving to her outer skin with rapid speed and precision. Caine's heart squeezed tighter and tighter as time crept by. It felt like an eternity. He watched his deep red blood flow to Emma and realized if it took every last drop of blood in his body to save this woman, he'd give it to her without a moment's hesitation—the young panther had her whole life ahead of her, while his human life could end the next time he shifted to Musk form.

Mira smiled up at him from her seated position on the bed. Snipping the thread, she set down the scissors and held two fingers around Emma's wrist, checking her pulse. "The wound is already healing ahead of my stitching and her heart rate is leveling off. Your blood was exactly what she needed."

Caine's gaze jerked to Emma's wounds. They were closing and light pink scars were forming in their wake. Color had begun to spread across her cheeks.

Emotional relief tightened his chest. After Mira removed the needle and tubing from his and Emma's arms, he helped her take the plastic out from underneath Emma. When they were done, he put his hand out. "I can't thank you enough for your help."

Holding up her bloodied hands, Mira's smile was apologetic. "I'd shake your hand, but mine are a bit messy at the moment." She nodded to Emma. "Sit with her. I have a feeling she'll be waking up in a bit and she'll want you with her."

Caine watched the woman walk out of the room with a regal, assured bearing.

"Mira?" Talek jumped up from the sofa the moment she passed by the office.

Mira expelled an inward sigh. Somewhere along the way, Talek had assigned himself as her personal bodyguard, and her brother fully supported such nonsense. Damn Jachin's hide. She didn't need a babysitter. "I'm fine, Talek," Mira said. "Just need some air."

"And Emma?" Kaitlyn asked once Talek zoomed past Mira to open the front door for her.

Mira smiled at the attractive redhead, liking the woman's straightforward approach. "She hasn't awoken yet, but her heartbeat's strong. She'll be okay."

When Talek tried to follow her outside, Mira shook her head. "I'd like to be alone."

Talek set his jaw and stubborn concern hardened his strong features.

"I'll be fine," Mira assured him.

His gaze dropped to her blood-covered hands. "Don't you want to wash up first?"

She shook her head. "Back in a few minutes."

With a look of doubt, Talek gave her a curt nod and slowly pulled the door shut, leaving her alone on the porch that spanned the entire front of the house.

Mira sighed and rolled her head from one shoulder to the other to relieve the tension that had built inside her as she dealt with suspicious Lupreda and operated on Emma. She moved to the edge of the porch and leaned over the railing to stare into the unusually clear night sky above her. No more snow was coming. Stars twinkled all around her, and one seemed suddenly brighter than the others until she realized it was moving.

A shooting star! Mira stared in wonder, wishing she believed in fanciful dreams enough to make a wish upon the star. But she didn't. Glancing at her bloodstained hands, she stared at the signs of both life and death coating her palms and fingers and thought about how easily it would be to let herself slip away from this life, like she'd wanted to do while saving Ariel. All she had to do was stop taking blood from her clan members. Eventually she'd fade away.

A sound in the woods drew her attention. She glanced into the darkness and saw a tall, black-haired man standing on the edge of the woods. Stark naked, his broad-shouldered body formed a perfect muscular V down to his trim waist. Mira blinked and gripped the railing to remain calm. She knew he wasn't human and she doubted he was Lupreda, either. Her gaze locked with his steady one at the same time she caught his earthy, primal scent on the light wind blowing around the house. He smelled like the blood on her hands.

His black eyebrows slashed downward. "Her heartbeat is steady. Did you save her?"

Mira nodded. "With Caine's help. Yes, we saved her."

Not a flicker of emotion crossed his face. Instead, he bowed his head in acknowledgment and immediately turned, falling toward the ground. Before his human hands hit the leaf-covered underbrush, he'd shifted to a sleek black panther, then took off into the forest.

Wondering about the man's swift retreat, Mira stared into the dense woods for several minutes before she finally walked back inside the house. Talek stood once more and she waved him back, addressing Landon. "I just saw another panther."

Landon jumped up from the office chair he'd been sitting in behind the desk. His green gaze narrowed. "Where?"

Mira waved to the front door she'd pushed closed with her foot. "He emerged from the woods and asked if I had saved Emma. When I told her she would be okay, he shifted back to his panther form and ran off."

Landon's tense stance relaxed and he rubbed the back of his neck as he came around from behind the desk. "Damnit, I want to talk to him. Hawkeye could provide some much-needed answers."

He didn't seem to want to interact...with anyone. I understand that feeling sometimes. "Maybe Emma can help when she wakes. I'm going to wash up and then check on my patient," Mira said.

Emma awoke to the scent of honeysuckle and the sensation of soothing warmth gliding over her body. The softness disappeared, followed by the sound of water falling into a container. Then the wonderful heat was back, stealing over her skin. It felt so good, she peered through half-closed eyes to see Caine leaning over her with a sponge, his black hair falling across her brow creased in concentration.

Her heart melted when she realized Caine was bathing her body. Her side was a little sore, but other than that, Emma felt rejuvenated. For a split second she wondered if everything had been a dream, if she was still in the cabin with Caine.

But when he looked up and his hazel eyes were shot with streaks of light green, she remembered everything that had happened to her—from Malac kidnapping her, his crazy plans for the Velius, her near-rape and Hawkeye saving her, to the memory of a beautiful vampire doctor trying to save her life as she bled out from a gaping wound that could've killed her.

"You knew what I was, yet you rescued me. Why?" she asked in a whisper.

Caine dropped the sponge in the water, then ran his warm hand up her belly, creating a sparking, heated path in its wake. He cupped his hand over her heart, the edge of his fingers resting just below her breast. "I didn't know what you were when I met you in the club, but the electricity between us... was and still is...undeniable."

His brow furrowed as he ran his thumb along the inside

curve of her breast. "When I went to your house and learned what you were, that you've been hiding yourself with those damned pills, I felt as if someone had ripped me in two. I hated how betrayed I felt." His gaze snapped to hers. "But what I hated worse was that it didn't matter—that I still felt the same way about you, regardless of what you were."

Emma's eyes watered with tears. She gripped his hand and brought it to her lips. Kissing his palm with reverence, she kept her gaze locked on his as hot tears streaked down her temples. "This is what you were trying to get me to tell you in the cabin, wasn't it? That I knew what you were and that I was a panther."

She shook her head slowly and she gulped back a sob. "All my life I've been told I had a vitamin deficiency and that's why I had to take a daily pill. When Malac took me, he told me the pills' true purpose was to mask my panther scent— and that the medicine was what kept him from finding me all these years. He has such horrible plans, Caine. He wants me to be his broodmare, to produce a legion of panther offspring who can shift at will."

Fury swept across Caine's face and his eyes stormed, turning even greener. Worry filled her when he began to growl deep in his throat. Pushing aside her fear, Emma touched his stubbled jaw and continued in a trembling voice. "I only discovered what I was when I shifted to protect you. Please, please believe me."

Caine touched her hair where her tears had left damp trails. He vibrated all over with tension. "Did. He. Touch. You?" he bit out through clenched teeth.

His slowly spoken words scared her. Emma worried if she told him what almost happened to her, he might go after Malac alone. She didn't want anything to happen to him.

Mira walked into the room, distracting her from answering right away, which was apparently too long for Caine.

He let out a growl and punched his hand straight through the bed's headboard. "I'll shred him to pieces. I'm going to—"

"Hawkeye saved me in time, Caine!" Emma panicked and quickly sat up, pulling the covers against her chest, speaking as fast as she could. "Malac...didn't get a chance to do anything—"

"What is it?" Landon came barreling into the room, his expression alert, wereclaws on full display. Jachin and Talek were directly behind him, fangs and vampire talons extended. Laird and the blond man from the club quickly followed, looking equally intense. Kailtyn stepped into the room behind them. Everyone was on alert. Ready to battle.

Mira stood frozen in the center of the room, while her brother and Talek glanced at her for acknowledgment that she was okay. Tension arched through the air, and the men glared back and forth between each other, testosterone rising. The fierce looks on the vampires' and werewolves' faces made Emma's heart pound with anxiety. Did their hatred run so deep?

The sudden ringing of a cell phone sliced through the thick adrenaline hanging in the air between the different species.

Caine's chest heaved and his eyes glazed as his fists opened and closed reflexively. Landon growled at Caine, "Answer the damn thing before a fight breaks out."

Caine pulled his cell phone from his pocket and looked at the caller ID. His gaze snapped to Landon's. "It's the Velius bastards who kidnapped Emma from the club."

He flipped open the cell phone and tilted it so Emma could hear a woman speaking. "Hello...I'm assuming this is the

Lupreda who took Emral from us. Because you used Roland's number to find us, I'm returning the favor. My name is Jade."

Caine's eyes instantly narrowed. "This is Caine. What do you want, Jade?"

"To talk."

Jade? Emma's heart thumped. She pulled her knees underneath her and gripped his hand. Once Caine muted the phone, she said, "Jade's not with Malac. Before Hawkeye rescued me from Malac, my aunt told me the panthers splintered into two factions a while back. She said I could trust Jade, that she wouldn't mean me harm."

Caine's jaw tightened, suspicion in his hazel gaze. "They kidnapped you!"

Emma ran her hand through her messy hair. "I—I'm beginning to think they did it to keep Malac from finding me first." Expelling her pent-up breath, she continued. "It's a long story."

"Caine?" Jade called. "Are you there?"

Caine unmuted the phone. "Yeah."

"I think we should discuss this in person."

"Discuss what? The fact I'm going to tear every single one of you apart for drugging and kidnapping Emma? Your man tried to kill us," Caine gritted out, his gaze snapping to Emma.

"He was trying to protect Emral," Jade said, concern in her voice. "Can I talk to her?"

Caine gripped the phone tight. As he laced his fingers with Emma's, she could see the complete distrust on his face. "No, and her name is Emma."

The woman on the other end of the line sighed. "This is why I think it's best that we meet in person. And because they're there with you, we'd like the Lupreda and Sanguinas representatives to come with you and Emra—Emma."

Caine tensed and glanced toward the curtain-covered window. "How'd you know they are with me?"

"Hawkeye told me when he called to say Emma was safe."

Caine narrowed his gaze and Landon dipped his head to acknowledge that Hawkeye had been around, then the Alpha and Jachin exchanged meaningful looks. Tense shoulders relaxed and wereclaws, talons and fangs retracted. Returning his gaze to Caine, Landon gave him a curt nod and mouthed the word, "Trap."

"We'll meet, but we choose the place," Caine said.

"Fair enough," the woman replied in an appeased tone. "Call me back with the location and the time."

The moment Caine snapped the cell phone closed, Kaitlyn stepped forward. "All right, everyone, please go to the living room. We obviously need to talk, but Emma must get cleaned up and put on some clothes first. She can meet us downstairs when she's ready."

Once everyone but Caine left, Kaitlyn looked at him and raised her eyebrow.

"You expect me to leave?"

Emma almost smiled at the surprise in his voice. Kaitlyn put her hands on her hips and sighed. "Yes, you, too. Emma needs some time to herself."

Caine's fingers tightened around Emma's. "But she might need help—"

"And that's why *I'll* be here if she needs anything."

"I'll be fine." Emma squeezed Caine's hand, then untangled her fingers from his. "But she's right. I'd like to take a shower and put on some clothes." Letting her gaze slide over his bare chest, she chuckled. "Maybe they can find a shirt for you to wear, too."

Caine glanced down at his naked torso and snorted. Leaning over, he kissed her forehead, then whispered in her ear, "I'll be right downstairs if you need me."

Emma nodded and pushed at his hard chest, her heart pounding at the muscles underneath her fingers. "Go on. I'll be fine."

The moment Caine walked out of the room, Kaitlyn shut the door. Facing Emma, she shook her head and mumbled, "Lupredas and their strong protective streaks," as she walked over to the chest of drawers near the closet and rifled through them.

Once she'd pulled out a few articles of clothing, Kaitlyn carried them over to the bed and sat down with the bundle in her arms, her expression sympathetic. "I know you're probably feeling a bit outnumbered, surrounded by a bunch of werewolves and vampires."

The truth was Emma was completely torn. She trusted and cared for Caine, but she didn't want the werewolves to attack Jade and her people. "I am a bit confused at the moment."

"These clothes should be close enough to your size." Kaitlyn handed her the bundle, then smiled. "I grew up living a human life for twenty-four years. I didn't know that my father had been bitten by a werewolf before I was born and that as his offspring I carried Lupreda blood in my veins." She gave an ironic chuckle. "At least not until I met Landon. My point is, I totally understand how you feel, because I was in your position not too long ago."

"I might be a panther," Emma said, her voice trembling, "but I was also raised thinking I was human all my life. I only discovered what I was when Malac took me, but the fact remains, I *am* Velius. I don't want to go to this meeting with a plan to ambush those of my own race. It's not right. My aunt said Jade can be trusted. I have to give her the benefit of the doubt. She might be able to help me rescue my aunt. I passed out before I could get a feel for the area of town where Malac resides…and Jade may know."

Kaitlyn squeezed Emma's hand. "When you come downstairs, you can help fill in the missing pieces. Then we'll discuss all the options."

"I don't believe Jade would harm me," Emma insisted.

"That may be true, Emma, but the panthers have had no problem murdering three Lupreda zerkers and in doing so—"

"Zerkers?"

Kaitlyn nodded. "Lupreda who are permanently caught between human and wolf form."

Emma's brow furrowed. "Are you talking about a werewolf?"

"Yes, the Lupreda call it their Musk form. The Lupreda discovered too late that only mature wolves can handle shifting in and out of their Musk form. Once those three Lupreda went zerker—unable to shift back to human form—the wolves declared that no Lupreda can use their Musk form until they've fully matured. The Lupreda are bound to their wolf form during the three nights of a full moon. That they can't control, but the older ones can call forth their Musk form at will any other time."

Emma thought about the fight she'd witnessed between Malac and Caine. "When Malac shot Caine, Caine was shifting to what must've been his Musk form. That arrow forced him to shift back to human form at the same time it seemed to literally destroy his strength. What was in that weapon?"

"Thank goodness for small favors," Kaitlyn mumbled,

piquing Emma's curiosity, but she continued on, distracting Emma from the question she wanted to ask. "When the vampires first created the Lupreda, they used silver collars to keep them from shifting to their wolf form until the vampires were ready to hunt them. Over time the werewolves developed a deadly allergy to silver. So silver around their neck keeps them from shifting from their human form and if infused in their system, the metal can kill Lupreda.

"Apparently the Velius have figured that out and are using those silver arrows on the Lupreda to their complete advantage. They kidnapped the zerkers, then left their burned bodies in strategic places meant to incite a war between the vampires and wolves. It probably would've worked, too, if Jachin and Landon hadn't been on speaking terms."

"Um, the Lupreda and Sanguinas still seem wary and distrustful of each other," Emma said with a frown.

Kaitlyn sighed her agreement. "They have decades of hatred to overcome, Emma, and the panthers' devious and murderous acts aren't making that any easier."

"That was Malac's doing," Emma interjected, finally piecing together the conversation between Caine and Malac in the cabin. "He admitted his role in killing some of the Lupreda to Caine before he kidnapped me."

"It might just be Malac, but all the panthers have been masking their scents, and until their motivations are clearly understood, Landon and Jachin have to look out for the best interests of their pack and clan. Their truce is tenuous enough."

When Emma tensed, Kaitlyn tilted her head, an encouraging look in her hazel-blue eyes. "No matter whether you're panther, werewolf, vampire or human…it's always in your best interest to be prepared for anything. Wouldn't you agree?"

The woman had a valid point. Emma was going purely by what her aunt told her about Jade. The female panther could've changed over the past twenty years. Malac was definitely insane, and even if Jade might not want to hurt Emma—as she claimed—her intentions toward the Lupreda and Sanguinas could be completely different. Emma didn't want to put Caine, his pack or the vampires who'd helped her in jeopardy. She nodded mutely while her stomach churned in turmoil.

Kaitlyn smiled. "Good. As long as you're willing to consider a contingency plan, we can make sure those testosterone junkies downstairs hold their primal instincts in check."

Emotions welled within Emma. The thought of going against a race she barely knew, yet one she was very much a part of, weighed heavily on her chest. She impulsively hugged Kaitlyn. "Thank you for understanding."

Landon's mate hugged her and leaned back with a wink. "We women have to stick together to keep these alpha men in line. Do you think you can get a shower on your own? There's plenty of extra supplies in the linen closet."

Emma gripped the blanket and stood up from the bed. She felt a little woozy for a second, but her mind quickly cleared. "I'll be fine. Fill everyone in on what we've discussed and I'll be down as soon as I'm presentable."

The moment Emma entered the living room, all conversation stopped. Everyone stared at her, making her feel like a bug under a microscope. She resisted the urge to fluff her damp hair, but couldn't quite stop herself from biting her lower lip.

Caine jumped up from the wingback chair he'd been sprawled across sideways and was by her side before she dug her teeth too deep into her lip. He looked sexy as hell in a thin, black V-neck sweater. Clasping her hand, he pulled it to his mouth and kissed her knuckles. "Hey, beautiful," he said in a soft tone and finished in her mind, *Are you feeling okay?*

Emma blinked away the emotion that swept her heart when his deep voice, full of worry, entered her mind. His intense hazel gaze held hers for several seconds until she realized he was waiting for a response. She gave him a tremulous smile and nodded. "Thanks to you and—" Emma swept her gaze to Mira sitting on the formal couch between Talek and Jachin "—Mira. I can't thank you both enough for all you've done."

Mira inclined her head and smiled. "If Landon felt strongly enough about you to ask for our help, that was enough for us."

Caine released Emma's fingers and settled his hand against the small of her back as her wide gaze locked on Landon. He was leaning against the side of the other wingback chair Kaitlyn was sitting in. "Why *did* you help me?"

"Apparently, I'm not the only pack member who does crazy things," a man with longish blond hair snorted from his position near the window.

"Shut up, Roman!" Laird elbowed the blond in the arm.

Landon's gaze held Caine's as he addressed her. "Caine is the pack's Second. He cares for you. That's why I helped."

Caine was Second to the Alpha? Emma glanced at Caine to see him shaking his head. Banked tension vibrated in his edgy tone. "I'm no longer Second."

Landon instantly straightened from his relaxed pose. "The hell you aren't—"

"Emma, why don't you tell us why you think Jade can be trusted. We want to help you and your aunt if we can, but we need to know everything you do before we meet with the other Velius," Kaitlyn said.

Emma had seen the anger flash across Landon's face when Caine said he wasn't the Second. She wondered what that was all about, but was thankful Kaitlyn had intervened. They needed to stay focused, not fight. Time was ticking and she hoped that Jade could help her find and rescue her aunt. Nodding to Kaitlyn, she began with the story Mary told her about the panthers splintering off and the fact Malac took Hawkeye when he left and she stayed with Jade. She told them about Mary and her brother Roland's history, how Roland created the pills that masked the panthers' scent and how Mary hadn't seen her brother since she took Emma to hide her from all the panthers. "She didn't trust that they wouldn't begin to fight over me."

"Because you can shift at will?" Landon asked.

Emma nodded.

"Malac is certifiable. I have no doubt he's the one behind for trying to start a war between the vampires and the were-wolves. *He* wants to go to war with both your races, but he needed me to help make that happen."

"The sonofabitch wants her ability to shift at will," Caine snarled.

Emma curled her lip in a derisive snort. "He wanted to take my eggs so he could create an entire army of shape-shifting Velius."

A growl emanated from Caine and his hands fell to his sides, clenched in tight fists. "His death will be very painful."

Caine's dark tone sent a chill across Emma's skin, making her glad he was on her side.

Landon narrowed his gaze. "If Malac had gotten what he wanted from Emma, combined with the Velius' swift maturity rate, he feasibly *could've* produced a formidable army in a few years. As to whether or not they'd be shape-shifters..." He shrugged.

When Landon trailed off, it suddenly occurred to Emma what Hawkeye had alluded to; Malac had already done something similar to him—or tried to. *"I didn't want you to suffer the same fate."* She closed her eyes and her heart ached for the little boy who'd been forced to live with Malac. The memories came flooding back to her. Of how Hawkeye had always watched over her, worried about her.

Glancing up at Landon, she said, "Now I know why Caine's smell intrigued me when I first met him—because, even though I didn't remember your saving Hawkeye and me when we were cubs, your Lupreda smell has lingered with me."

When Caine's expression went blank, Emma realized he'd taken what she'd said the wrong way. The devastated look in his eyes slammed her in the stomach. She wanted to grab hold of his hand and reconnect with him, but she forced herself to focus. "Where do you want to meet with Jade?"

Jachin's dark blue eyes stared at her. "You don't know what Jade's true intentions are. We have to plan for the worst." He glanced at Landon. "Especially because she wants us there."

"But she could just want to talk," Emma insisted, feeling desperate. "Can't we meet somewhere in public, where we can discuss without worry of a surprise attack? I don't know how to get in touch with Hawkeye. Jade may be my only connection to finding my aunt. I have to help her!"

Caine soothed her before she could get too worked up. "We'll find your aunt, Emma."

"We could tell them to meet us at Jamie's Pub," Landon said, rubbing his hand along his stubbled jaw.

Jachin nodded slowly. "It's crowded and loud enough to cover whatever we might discuss."

"Not to mention…it's dark in there." Landon's lips tilted in a feral smile.

Kaitlyn looked at her mate and understanding lit in her eyes. "That could be advantageous."

Emma frowned. "Why would dim lighting be to our advantage?"

Caine looked down at her. "The pills the panthers are taking to mask their scent leave behind a glittery, iridescent residue on anything they touch. They're unaware that Kaitlyn and Landon have the ability to see this substance, which could clue us in as to how many panthers are present among the crowd."

"Taking their element of surprise down considerably." Jachin nodded, a dangerous smile on his angular face.

Kaitlyn stood. "Come in my office across the hall. We can look up the city maps and check for places around Jamie's they might try to hide."

Jachin unfolded his tall frame from the couch. His long black coat fell past his knees in a quiet whisper of leather as he pulled his cell phone from his pocket. "I'll call my Sanguinas Sweeper unit. Instead of hunting for rogue vampires, tonight they'll be our backup."

As everyone brushed past her standing in the living room doorway, Emma felt a rush of panic that Caine had moved to walk away without a word to her. "Caine, wait!" she called. Turning to the blond Lupreda, who was about to leave the room, she quickly grabbed his hand, and said in a hushed voice, "It's Roman, right?"

Roman's gaze locked with Caine's, then a brilliant, sexy smile tilted his lips. "At your service, Emma. I guess this is a formal introduction."

Emma felt Caine's tension behind her. The spiked wave of heat and testosterone was that powerful. Her pulse skittered as she squeezed Roman's hand and asked, "What do you feel?"

Roman didn't even miss a beat. "Horny."

Caine's snarl of fury made the tiny hairs on Emma's neck stand on end. Before she lost her nerve, she held fast to Roman's hand at the same time she quickly turned and grabbed Caine's fisted one. The moment her hand touched Caine's, his fingers unfurled and clasped hers tight in a crushing, possessive hold. Electricity flew, whirling so fast and furious between them that it knocked Emma slightly off-kilter. All this happened in milliseconds, yet she had to practically tear her gaze from Caine's to address Roman once more. "What about now—"

"Sonofabitch!" Roman instantly jerked his hand from hers, his brow furrowing. "What the— What was that?" His confused dark brown gaze darted between them as he opened and closed his hand. "Are you trying to electrocute me?"

"You didn't feel that when Emma shook your hand?" Caine's words were measured.

Roman's blond eyebrows elevated. "Hell, no! Only when—" His eyes lit up and he reached for her hand once more, a sly grin tilting his lips. "Let's try that again—"

At the same time Caine's muscular arm curled around Emma, pulling her against his hard chest, his palm slammed into Roman's chest, sending him back against the doorjamb with enough force to shake the whole house. "Back off, wolf!"

Chapter 11

Emma had never felt so protected and wanted. It thrilled her to her toes. "I'm sorry," she whispered to Roman. She felt a bit guilty for involving Roman, but he'd seemed good-natured enough, and she didn't think any other way would've proven her point as effectively to Caine.

"Is there a problem?" Landon's hard voice sounded from the office doorway.

"Why don't you go do some recon with the others," Caine said to his packmate in a less forceful tone. "I need a minute."

Roman rubbed his chest and snorted. "You two need more than a minute. A room would be better."

"Go!" Caine barked, sounding ready to snap off the other werewolf's head.

The moment Roman walked away, Caine hauled Emma into the living room and set her back against the wall. Caging her in with his hands on the wall beside her, his black eyebrows slashed downward as he growled in a low voice, "That was a hell of a risk you just took!"

Emma met his intemperate hazel gaze with determination. "You took what I said about your Lupreda scent the wrong way. I saw it in your eyes. You'd closed up and were already shutting me out."

"If Roman had felt that same charge when you first touched him, his wolf would've instantly challenged me for you, Emma. You just riled his rocks, sweetheart. What happens between us is *that* intensely sexual."

Heat shot up her cheeks at his comment. "Are you saying I just—"

"Sent a jolt that bypassed his brain and went straight to his cock."

Emma closed her eyes and groaned with embarrassment, but her breath quickly caught when she felt Caine's musky heat, hot and thick, envelope her as he leaned close and whispered near her ear, "Is it any wonder why I can't stop touching you every chance I get?"

As if to prove his point, his warm hands slid under her cardigan and tank top and up her sides, sending electric shimmers in their wake. His fingers gripped her rib cage in a fierce hold and he yanked her against his hard chest. Emma barely had time to take a breath before his lips covered hers.

From the moment his lips slanted across hers, Caine staked his claim, tasting her instantly as he spoke in her mind. *I've never been so scared in my life when I thought you might die.* His tongue delved deep, sliding along hers in a provocative, possessive dance. His seductive intensity demanded her participation and Emma was more than willing to accommodate him.

"After everything that's happened, having you there—fighting *for* me, and not *over* me—was the only thing that kept me from giving up," she confessed and encircled her arms around his neck, locking him tight against her. Emma never wanted to let him go.

Caine's arms locked around her and he planted a kiss along her jawline. "No matter what happens tonight, know that I'll always be there to protect you."

Tears burned the back of Emma's eyes when she thought of the tension she'd seen in the bedroom earlier between the vampires and the werewolves. The history and distrust between their races went deep, as did the history between the werewolves and the panthers. Would their differences eventually come between Caine and her, too? Her arms cinched tighter. She wasn't going to let that happen to them.

"Caine, we're ready to call Jade back whenever you are," Kaitlyn called from the office.

Emma sat in Caine's truck, her stomach knotted so tight she felt like she might throw up the food Kaitlyn had forced her to eat before they left. "You must eat, Emma. You look way too pale."

She looked pale because she was worried about her aunt. Plus, she didn't know if the meeting they were getting ready to leave for would end in an all-out war between the panthers, vampires and werewolves. Where would that leave her and Caine?

Landon leaned his elbow on the driver-side door as he spoke to Caine. "We'll meet you there."

While Landon talked, Caine started to lift the silver chain over his head.

Landon grabbed his wrist, his tone harsh. "We made a deal."

Caine's jaw worked for a second before he gritted out, "We don't know what we're walking into. Emma's life could be in danger."

"It's not worth the risk. I've got your back. I'll keep Emma safe."

Lowering the chain back on his neck, fury emanated from Caine. "She's mine to protect."

Landon glanced Emma's way and the curt edge in his tone softened. "Exactly why it's not worth the risk."

When Landon walked off and slid into the car with Jachin and his Sweeper unit—who'd shown up only minutes before, allowing Talek to take Mira home—Emma asked, "What was that about?"

Caine started the engine and stared straight ahead, his face impassive. "Nothing."

As he pulled away from the curb outside Kaitlyn's house, Emma's gaze drifted to his necklace. Kaitlyn had told her that silver kept the Lupreda from shifting. It wasn't quite a full moon tonight, but Landon's mate had also said the Lupreda did have control over their Musk forms—at least the older ones did. Which meant they could shift whenever they wanted as long as they weren't hampered by the silver.

"Are you too young to shift to your Musk form?" Emma asked.

Caine's hazel gaze glinted sharp and dangerous in the darkness between them. "Do I look like a young pup to you?"

He looked on edge, but Emma wasn't about to let him intimidate her. "What you 'look' is angry. Kaitlyn told me the Velius killed some of the Lupreda—zerkers she'd called them. If you're not too young, why did Landon make that deal with you about wearing the necklace before he called Jachin to help me?"

Caine turned a corner faster than necessary. The truck's tires skidded in the slushy snow, then caught on the pavement, squealing in protest. His fingers gripped the steering wheel tight, while a vein thumped along his temple. Emma's chest weighed heavy with worry. "Why doesn't Landon want you to shift?"

"Because I'm the last of them, Emma!" Caine shouted. Jamming his hand through his dark hair, he continued in a calmer voice. "I'm the only one left of my generation who hasn't gone zerker. The pack learned from our mistakes."

Silence, thick with tension, descended in the truck and several seconds ticked past. Emma chewed her bottom lip, trying to understand. "He doesn't want you to shift because it could be permanent the next time?"

His narrowed gaze sliced her way. "I'd be neither human nor wolf, forever." Staring at the road once more, he continued, his words cold and grating. "No one wants that. We called them zerkers for a reason. Not being able to shift back eventually screwed with their minds. They became dangerous, their urges more primal, their reactions unpredictable. That's why they didn't live with the pack. They used to live in the cabin we stayed in."

Tears threatened and Emma's throat burned with the effort to hold back a sob, but she had to know the rest. "The cabin… But you called it *your* home."

"It'll be my home when I finally go zerker," he said, his words flat and final.

Reaching out, she dug her fingers into the corded muscles that ran along his forearm. "If going zerker would force you to stay away from me, then keep your promise to Landon. Never take the damn necklace off—"

"I'll do whatever it takes to keep you safe." He cut her off with a low rasping growl.

"You can protect me just fine. You've proven that already. I'm not worth losing your humanity over." Panic swelled her lungs, pushing the air out of them until she could barely catch her breath. "I don't want to lose you," she finished in a whisper.

Caine quickly grabbed her hand and pressed his warm lips against it. The roughness of his five o'clock shadow, combined with his tingling kiss, skittered along her skin, sending tingles scattering down her arm. "I'm here, Emma. Don't worry."

Emma laced her fingers with his, gripping his hand tightly. "I want to believe you're listening to me, but I know you're too stubborn. You'll do what you want to regardless of my wishes."

Once Caine slowed his truck and parked it along the side of the road, his hazel gaze met hers. "I'll grant your every wish if I can, but your safety comes above my own."

Emma shut her eyes and tears squeezed past the corners. Caine's fingertips brushed away a tear and she opened her eyes to see his hungry gaze on her face. "I'm on shaky ground as it as, Emma." His low, tortured voice slid over her like a velvet caress, while his fingers cupped her face, tilting her chin so she had to look at him. "It would rip me apart if anything happened to you."

How could she argue with that without sounding ungrateful? Appreciation and respect combated with guilt and anger at their situation. Emma pressed a kiss on his palm, then cupped the warmth against her cheek. "I've never felt more blessed than to have met you." She spoke from the heart, even as she wondered what the outcome of this meeting would bring.

Would seeing her among her people highlight their differences in his mind? She knew he felt protective of her, but would Caine's loyalties to his pack and his own kind eventually pull him away from her, making him want to be with a Lupreda woman instead? Her chest ached at the thought. A knock on Caine's window made Emma's heart jerk. Caine's hand fell away when Landon thumbed for them to accompany their group inside the pub.

The moment Emma slid out of the truck, Caine wrapped his arm around her and pulled her close as they walked along the sidewalk. Dark shadows hid in nearby alleys, filled with day-old trash and dirty snow. Bums, stray dogs and cats foraged in and around the Dumpsters, looking for scraps. If a Velius jumped out of the alley in its panther form now, would Caine be able to inflict enough damage with his were-claws and superhuman strength to protect Emma?

He gritted his teeth and tensed in anger and resentment at the truth. Hell, no! Without his Musk form, he'd always feel as if he weren't giving his all, using everything within himself to defend the woman he cared deeply about. Landon and his brethren wouldn't always be around to help defend her, nor would Caine let anyone fight his battles for him. Ever. Was it fair to shackle Emma with a man who couldn't defend her as he should? No, yet he curled his lip in a snarl at the idea of any other man touching her.

By the time they neared the pub, Caine's testosterone levels had elevated considerably. He was ready to take down anyone, in any form necessary. Several more Lupreda converged with their small group, and Caine didn't miss their rumbles of discontent. Some of the weres curled their lips in a low growl at the members of Jachin's Sweeper unit who'd accompanied them from their vehicles.

"Enough," Landon snapped. The dozen Lupreda before him quieted and instantly splintered off, disappearing into the darkness to take the positions Landon had given them via his cell before they'd left Kaitlyn's house. Once the Sweeper unit of six men dispersed to take up their own sentry duties on the rooftops and at the building corners, Landon, Kaitlyn and Jachin entered the pub, followed by Caine and Emma.

Only a few steps into the crowded, dim pub, Kaitlyn looked at Landon. Placing four fingers at the corner of her eye, she signaled that she saw four Velius in the place, then she nodded to a man in a baseball hat and a woman with short dark hair sitting alone at a table in the far corner of the room. Caine inhaled in the direction of the table and instantly recognized the human man's scent as the one who'd taken Emma from the club. The other four panthers must be positioned elsewhere in the room on guard duty.

Steeling himself, Caine's hand cinched tighter around Emma's rib cage. Just because Kaitlyn saw only four Velius with iridescent sparkles on them in the crowd didn't mean there weren't other humans helping the panthers. He mentally cursed the "unknown variables" of the situation and followed Landon, Kaitlyn and Jachin's lead toward the back of the bar. As they weaved around the various tables, filled with patrons watching the latest game and talking, drinking and laughing among themselves, Caine scanned the room for all possible exit points in case they had to get out of there fast.

The moment he smelled Roman and Laird's presence in the room several feet behind him, some tension eased from his shoulders. Knowing the weres would merge into the crowd to keep a general watch helped him move to an "aware and focused" mode from his "jacked-up and ready-to-battle" one.

They'd just reached the table where the man and woman sat when the man pulled off his baseball cap and ran a hand through his spiky graying hair.

"Sonofabitch!" Jachin froze and stared at the man. "I thought you were dead."

The man, now free of the beard Caine remembered seeing on him in the club, smirked. "That was the whole point, Jachin."

Seeing Mary's same facial expressions on the man's face, Emma knew she was staring at her aunt's brother. She gripped the back of a wooden chair and glanced at Jachin. "You know Roland?"

A muscle twitched in the vampire's jaw. "Yes, but I knew him as a surly, extortionist named Roach."

The man's steady gaze locked with Jachin's. "Who kept you alive for ten years."

"What the hell is going on?" Landon growled.

The dark-haired woman gestured to the chairs in front of the table and spoke in a calm tone. "It's good to see you again after all these years, Landon. Why don't you have a seat and we'll talk."

"We prefer to stand," Caine snarled. He didn't like this new surprise—the Velius' connection to the vampires.

The woman glanced toward the crowd. "You're drawing attention to us by standing."

"And growling," the man added with a snort.

"Start talking," Jachin demanded through clenched teeth. Yanking a chair out from under the table, he sat down and pinned his gaze on Roland. "You have one minute before I rip out your throat. I don't give a damn who's watching."

"And here I thought you might've missed me just a tiny bit these past six months," Roland said in a light tone.

"Forty-five seconds," Jachin shot back, curling his lip briefly to show that his fangs were fully extended.

Emma couldn't stand the tension crackling across the table. Pulling from Caine's tight hold, she sat down in a chair beside Jachin and put her hand on the vampire's tight fist sitting on the table. "Let's hear what Roland has to say before you tear him apart."

Heaving a heavy sigh, Roland said, "Actually, despite our barbs, I've only had Jachin's best interests at heart."

"By gouging me for ten years? Making me think you were dead? Leaving me without food?" Jachin challenged.

Roland gestured toward him. "You had Ariel. She was the answer to your prophecy."

Jachin's gaze slitted. "You never believed in the prophecy."

Roland pointed to him. "Ah, but *you* did…and that's all that mattered. We thought we were going to have to convince you there was a better way for the vampires, but then you told me about the prophecy and you were so convinced…your survival became very important to us."

"None of this is making any sense." Landon's voice was cold and hard as he moved to stand to Emma's left.

"Start from the beginning, Roland." Emma spoke quickly, hoping to tamp down the rage she felt emanating from the vampire and werewolf leaders on either side of her.

Roland looked at Jade and the female panther inclined her head to acknowledge Emma's request. "It's good to see you again, Emma. I wish the circumstances were less—" she glanced at the group of people surrounding Emma "—intense."

"You drugged and kidnapped her! What do you expect?" Caine stood directly behind Emma, placing a hand on her shoulder.

Jade stiffened in a defensive posture. "We were trying to get her out of there quickly. Emma ran out of her pills and had called Roland's number, trying to fill the prescription. We knew something had to have gone wrong with Mary if Emma was calling us, thinking we were a pharmacy and that it was only a matter of time before Malac or one of his team scented her. We tracked her cell phone to the club."

"What does all this have to do with the Velius' involvement with the vampires?" Emma asked, feeling Jachin's fury winding tighter and tighter beside her.

"The Sanguinas have everything to do with it, Emma," Jade said in a quiet voice, her gaze snapping nervously between Landon and Jachin as the two men exchanged a look.

Before anyone could say a word, Jade continued, speaking at a rapid pace. "After Landon freed us, we were few in number compared to the vampires and the werewolves. We barely kept it together, trying to survive while hiding from the vampires who ravaged the city each night. Then I met Roland." Patting Roland's shoulder, she plunged on. "With his background in chemistry, he helped us devise a plan that would make the humans' blood unpalatable for vampires, therefore freeing the humans from the vampires' vengeance."

Jachin snarled and slammed his fist on the table, sending a hairline crack all the way across the wood's surface. "You tried to wipe out my race!"

Emma glanced around the pub, thankful the patrons were so into the game that no one noticed Jachin's outburst.

"I *told* you the Lupreda weren't responsible." Landon cut his gaze over to Jachin. His casual comment belied the tension that had vaulted within him. Emma knew he wasn't as calm as he let on, because Kaitlyn clasped her mate's left hand and Caine's hold on her shoulder had tightened.

Roland shook his head, seemingly unfazed by Jachin's anger and oblivious to Landon's reaction. "We had to take drastic measures. Too many innocent humans were dying while the Sanguinas' numbers were inching upward."

"Many of us were moving toward peace." Jachin's low tone held a defensive edge.

"But the majority of the Sanguinas weren't and humans were still being slaughtered. How many people had to die before the vampires realized this wasn't the way? How long would it have gone on?" Roland countered. "Our goal was to slow down the Sanguinas, not destroy them. But your race was stubborn and many vampires succumbed to the effects of the tainted blood before the clan finally withdrew from human society. When you came along ten years ago, we realized our ultimate goal might finally be accomplished."

"What goal was that?" Jachin bit out, his temper simmering.

Sympathy filled Roland's gaze. "You were outcast, Jachin. You were barely hanging on, and we saw an opportunity. It was risky, yes. You could've killed me when I purposefully put myself in your path so you'd attack me. But it was the only way I figured that you would accept my offer to provide the blood you needed—if you thought the only reason I came up with the idea of a partnership was because I was desperate and didn't want to die."

"You didn't make it easy for me."

Roland snorted at Jachin's surly tone. "I knew that whatever I said or did, you'd take the opposite stance. You hated humans *that* much. If I simply gave you the blood, you'd throw it aside out of distrust. But if you had to work hard for it…" He trailed off and his eyebrows elevated. "The same was true for your belief in the prophecy. My comments to dissuade you from believing were because I knew you'd only dig your heels in deeper, holding on to your prophecy's promise even more."

"Don't try to bullshit me, Roac—Roland. You never gave a damn about the prophecy."

Roland's shrug was unapologetic. "Whether the prophecy was true or not didn't matter to us in the beginning, but *your* belief in it did. Every time you spoke of it, I heard 'desire for peace' in your voice, saw it in your eyes. That's ultimately what the Velius sought. Peace. And that's the reason I helped them treat the water system to turn the humans' blood poison-ous to vampires all those years ago."

"You had no way of knowing that things would unfold the way they did—that Ariel would write a fictional book about vampires, that Jachin would discover Ariel's blood was pure or that he'd want to take her for his mate and become the new leader of the Sanguinas." Landon sliced his hand through the air between Jachin and him. "And there's no way in hell you'd know that he'd forge a truce with me."

"That's true," Jade jumped in with a nod. "But Jachin followed his own heart and did what he felt was right and that included his interactions with you. As far as we were con-cerned, the Lupreda weren't a threat to the human population. Only the vampires were."

"You *had* to hate us." Suspicion laced Landon's comment.

Jade shook her head. "No, I didn't, because you freed us, Landon." Sighing, she continued. "But Malac never could let go of his hatred. We splintered off in our beliefs a long time ago. The only reason he stayed in check for as long as he did was the fact we manufactured the pills and he didn't know how to replicate them. If he went after the vampires or the werewolves, we would have cut him off from his pill supply. He would've been exposed and very easy to hunt down."

"We've had the upper hand with him all these years, until recently." Roland curled his lip in disgust. "Malac had always had underworld dealings with the Mafia, but his connections grew stronger and he formed his own team of scientists. A few months ago, he stole my formula." The man's gaze locked on Jachin. "The attack in my house—on me—was real, Jachin. The only difference was that I realized it was probably in your best interest to let you think I was gone. You'd eventually discover Ariel's generation didn't have tainted blood. We'd stopped treating the water fairly early on, but ironically the older humans' blood stayed poisoned, while the younger ones' blood seemed to be able to adapt and resist the treatment, eventually eradicating its effects on their blood. I knew your goals for peace would set you on the right path from there."

At the look of disbelief in Jachin's eyes, Roland snorted. "It was all over the news that Ariel Swanson who'd written a book about vampires had been kidnapped. I knew how obsessed you were. I was fairly certain you were responsible."

"Malac was aware of your belief in the prophecy, too, Jachin," Jade said. "And when you kidnapped Ariel, the prophecy appeared to be coming true. That's when he broke into Roland's home. He wanted that formula and his freedom from us, so he could inflict as much damage as possible to both the Sanguinas and the Lupreda without any repercussions."

"He wants an all-out war, not just skulking-behind-the-scenes-wrecking-havoc scenarios." Emma finally broke her silence.

When Jade stared at her in shock, Emma quickly told her of the plans Malac had for the future of the Velius—at least how he saw it.

Jade's forehead pinched with fury. "He was going to take your eggs?"

Emma nodded. "Malac's insane. He has to be stopped." Turning to Roland, she conveyed the rest of what she knew. "He has your sister, Margaret, and he's keeping her a prisoner to blackmail me into cooperating with his plans. The only reason I agreed to come and meet you tonight was because Mary said I could trust you. Tell us where Malac's place is so we can get my aunt out of there."

Roland shook his head. "We don't know where he is. He's always kept himself well hidden."

Emma's brow furrowed in frustration. "I was wounded and the snow covering everything kept me from seeing land-marks the way I might've when Hawkeye helped me escape the facility, but…he should know. If we can contact Hawkeye, he'll tell us how to find Malac."

Roland's lips thinned. "We tried a trace, but Hawkeye called us from a pay phone. He doesn't trust us. Why do you think he brought you to the Lupreda instead of us?"

Emma's gaze narrowed. "Why *doesn't* he trust you?"

"Because we let Malac take him when he splintered off from us all those years ago. Hawkeye's never forgiven us," Roland said with a sigh.

"Then why did he bother to call you at all?"

"He called to let us know that the Sanguinas and the Lupreda were with you and that they had helped you. He said if we believed in the prophecy at all, now might be a good time to finally reveal ourselves," Roland grunted, then mumbled, "Damned arrogant panther."

"You didn't come tonight because you wanted to be with us, Emma? To be with your pride?" Jade had been quiet through Emma and Roland's exchange. Emma shifted her attention to the female panther. Disillusionment filled the woman's expression. Her green eyes glistened with unshed tears, yanking on Emma's conscience.

"I—I'm here about my aunt." Emma straightened her shoulders and Caine's hold tightened on her. "She's my priority right now. How can you two sit there so casually when her life is in danger?" Her gaze jerked to Roland. "She's your sister, for God's sake!"

"Aw, man!" Several men in the bar began yelling at the referee on TV, who apparently had the nerve to make a bad call.

Pain and sorrow reflected in Roland's eyes when he turned them back to her from watching the fans. "I *am* worried. I got a call from Malac earlier today. He assumed Hawkeye brought you back to us. Malac wants to trade my sister for you— manipulative sonofabitch! He won't let anything happen to her or his advantage is lost."

Emma's chest tightened and her breathing came in pants. "Aunt Mary is not some bargaining chip to be shuffled back and forth. She's a human being with a frail heart, arthritis and—"

"And she gave up her life so you could have one!" Roland's harsh words cut her off, notching her guilt up considerably. "An hour ago, I got a whispered call from a female doctor who's in Malac's facility. Unfortunately, I couldn't trace the call because she hung up too quickly, but she wanted me to know she's been slipping Mary the meds she needs. I'm worried about my sister, too, Emma, but do you really think, after giving up twenty-plus years of her life for you, that *she'd* want you to walk right into some trap that Malac has set without careful planning? You know as well as I do that he's not going to give my sister up—you said so yourself, she's his only leverage with *you*. He's planning something. I guarantee it. With his own group of panthers and his Mafia people, he outnumbers us at least five to one."

"Not anymore, he doesn't," Caine said.

Emma glanced up at Caine, to see his sharp and ruthless gaze locked on Roland.

Were the Lupreda offering their help? She jerked her attention to the Alpha, who placed his hand on the table and leaned forward. "You've got our support. When and where does Malac want to make the exchange?"

"Tomorrow night on the west side of town. He said he'd call with the specifics tomorrow morning," Jade said.

"He *would* pick tomorrow," Caine snarled.

"What's wrong with tomorrow?" Emma asked. The sooner the better as far as she was concerned.

"It's the first night of the full moon, Emma," Kaitlyn supplied with a concerned look at Landon.

"The moon's pull will force the Lupreda to their wolf forms tomorrow night. We won't be able to shift to our Musk forms to use to our advantage at all," Caine gritted out, his face turning dark.

"But Malac doesn't know I'm with the Lupreda. He thinks I'm with Jade," Emma argued.

"He knows I won't give up looking for you. It's the perfect time to make an exchange. He expects me to stay close to home while I'm bound to my wolf form," Caine said.

"The bastard definitely has something planned," Jachin cut in. "The Sanguinas will offer their support, as well. There's enough distrust between our races as it is. This prowling menace needs to be eliminated."

"We don't want to go to war with our own kind," Jade argued, sadness making her voice quaver. "There are so few of us as it is. Many of the Velius are just confused, unsure who to follow."

Emma's heart wrenched for the panthers. They seemed so divided and torn by Malac's vengeful aspirations. "Malac won't stop until he's destroyed everyone involved, including you."

When Jade's eyes widened and she began to shake her head in denial, Emma nodded. "It's true. He told me he planned to rule the Velius. *All* Velius. No matter what it took." Nibbling her bottom lip, she thought about how things might unfold tomorrow evening. "There might be a way. During our meeting with Malac—"

"He doesn't intend for it to be a sit-down discussion, Emma," Caine warned.

She nodded to acknowledge Caine's comment, then returned her focus on Jade. "If, during the battle with Malac, we can get to him and take him down, the others may then follow your lead instead."

"My lead?" Jade laughed, her green eyes glinting in the dim light, full of amusement.

The bar crowd suddenly uproared. The game was almost over. Some yelled at the referee, while others cheered him on.

"Emma, *you're* our leader," the Velius woman continued. "You and Hawkeye can shift at will. That gives you the highest rank, the most respect and the most responsibility for our panther pride. *You* two are our leaders. We've waited a long time for you. Now that you're back with us, you can convince Hawkeye to rally the panthers under Malac to his lead. He can help bring our divided pride back together by taking his rightful place at your side."

"But you've led the panthers just fine all these years," Emma insisted, while twinges of panic began to swell in her chest. *This is wrong. I'm no leader.*

Jade shook her head. "I'm not as respected as you might think or I wouldn't have lost some panthers to Malac. Don't you understand? Your 'pure-blood' leadership is needed. You and Hawkeye are the key to not only merging our groups, but also to helping us build a 'pure' pride of panthers."

With each word that slipped from Jade's lips, Caine's fingers cinched tighter and tighter on Emma's shoulder. He wasn't hurting her, but the tense pressure was there. Emma glanced at him. He'd lost some of the natural color in his face and his eyes held a stormy, tortured expression.

"It all comes down to the prophecy," Jachin murmured, drawing Emma's attention. The vampire's deep blue gaze was locked on Roland and Jade. "Before I left, Ariel reminded me that it involved others."

"Yes, the prophecy." Roland nodded solemnly. "After everything that's happened these last several months, we have come to believe it is true, and that the last part was about the Velius."

A leader is needed, you know this is true
Look not to one, but two.
A lesson was the goal you sought
You too must learn from what you taught

Layers of deception must be unveiled
For three to become one and peace to prevail.

While Roland recited the last part of the prophecy—that Emma remembered hearing Caine, Jachin and Landon discussing while she was injured—she'd already gone over the entire prophecy in her mind three times. *"Look not to one, but two,"* she whispered in a hushed voice.

"Yes, two. You and Hawkeye," Jade said with excitement.

"A lesson was the goal you sought. That fits with the Velius hoping to slow down the vampires, not destroy them," Roland added.

"You too must learn from what you taught." A derisive smirk lifted the corner of Jade's lip. "We've certainly had our own issues with Malac—who apparently wanted to rule *everyone.* It's ironic, I know. I'd hoped he would come around to our way of thinking once we found you, but now I know that'll never happen."

"For three to become one and peace to prevail." Roland repeated the last line of the prophecy and spread his hands wide, staring at each of them across the table. "And here you are side by side—Lupreda, Velius and Sanguinas—discussing strategy to keep the peace. I think a round of beer is in order while we discuss how I'm going to help Sanguinas and Lupreda arrive at this meeting without being detected."

Emma met Caine's gaze briefly and put her hand over his on her shoulder. Tension flowed from him in intense waves of musky heat. He'd curled his hand into a fist and strands of her long hair were tucked in a possessive hold between his fingers. The moment her skin touched his, electricity zinged between them and her stomach knotted.

Duty and desire twisted and tugged her heart in two very different directions. *This can't be happening. My race needs to propagate or risk extinction. To strengthen our pride, they want—no...expect—pure panthers from me...and I want only Caine.*

Chapter 12

"I'll meet you back at the house," Landon said, tapping the open truck window next to Caine.

Caine rested his wrist on the steering wheel and stared straight ahead. "We're going to my cabin."

Emma put her hand on his thigh, hoping to dispel some of his tension. He'd stayed tightly wound the entire time they were in the pub. Caine didn't look down as he reached for her hand and gripped it tight.

"Your cab—" Landon dipped his head and stared past Caine to their clenched hands for a second before he spoke. "I'll post guards around the cabin's perimeter. Come by the house tomorrow morning so we can discuss more details about how we want to approach this meeting with Malac. By then we should know the location."

Lifting his gaze to Emma, Landon grimaced and pushed a

fist against his chest. "That pill you took didn't make you feel like there was a lump sitting in your chest?"

Roland had given them enough pills for every Lupreda and Sanguinas who planned to be involved in the meeting with Malac tomorrow, saying, *Take them now and have the others take theirs as soon as you arrive home. It'll take the pills eighteen hours to neutralize your scents. The medicine will start to leave your systems once another pill hasn't been taken within twenty-four hours of taking the last one.*

"Roland said it was safe for the Lupreda and Sanguinas to take—" Emma started to say.

"The *rest* of us took it with our beers." Kaitlyn stepped close to her mate, gazing at him with a smirk. "You're the only one who swallowed it without anything."

Caine snorted and tossed Landon a spare bottle of water from inside his truck door. Landon caught the bottle with a grunt, his gaze zeroing on his Second. "Be at the house by ten."

The Alpha and his mate walked back to their truck. Kaitlyn was talking to someone on her cell phone as they met Laird and Roman, who were waiting for them beside their vehicle. All the other Lupreda, Jachin and his Sweeper team had already left.

Caine started the truck, and as the engine rumbled to life, he gripped Emma's hand and kissed the back of it. Soon, the truck was sloshing through the dirty, partially plowed snow, eating up the miles back to the mountains. There was so much Emma wanted to say, and yet she was afraid to speak. Her emotions were all jumbled. Like a ball of yarn batted by a playful cat, her insides were knotted and twisted up beyond hope of ever being straightened out again.

Caine seemed deep in thought the whole time he drove. Yet even though he didn't smile, didn't say a word, he never let go of her hand. Instead, he conveyed his feelings about them through his touch, running his thumb along her palm in slow, mesmerizing circles. Each circular swipe sent erotic tingles flowing through her, shooting to her breasts and her core, spiking her need for his touch. If he paused, even for a second, her heart dipped a little. Emma realized with a start that she'd become addicted to their electric connection, like a junkie, looking for her next rush.

By the time Caine pulled his truck up to the cabin, Emma's heart felt truly ripped in two. *How can I feel so divided? I've known Jade for even less time than I have Caine, yet I still feel deeply responsible for the Velius' future and for my aunt's well-being. They're depending on me.*

They sat for a moment in the quiet darkness of the truck's cab. When she looked at Caine, his brooding hazel-green eyes were staring back at her and her heart swelled with deep emotion. She'd come to care deeply for this man, more than she ever thought she was capable of. They would find a way to make it work.

Caine climbed out his truck door, opened the passenger door and lifted her down in his arms in mere seconds. The frigid wind whipped around them and Emma wrapped her arms around his broad shoulders, tucking her nose under his chin.

Kissing the top of her head, Caine cradled her close and carried her inside the cabin. When Caine kicked the door close behind them, they both stared in shock at the transformation the cabin had undergone.

A new rug had been added to the entire expanse of the room and the exposed wood flooring around it had been polished to a shiny sheen. The single bed was gone and a couple of end tables and lamps—which currently gave off a soft yellow glow—flanked either end of the couch. The set of furniture had been rearranged on the new carpet, making the living room look much larger. Soft jazz music played on a stereo against a far wall and a fire roared in the stone fireplace, giving the room a cozy, lived-in feel.

"Wow, talk about a transformation," Emma murmured as Caine set her on the floor.

Caine hadn't said a word. She looked over to see his throat working, his expression full of surprised, pent-up emotion.

Shrugging out of her heavy coat and the cardigan, Emma set them on the back of the couch. Gripping his biceps through his sweater, she said, "Hey, are you okay?"

"Kaitlyn," he mumbled, his attention focused on the transformed room.

She tried to be lighthearted. "I wish I could command a remodeling team like your Alpha's mate apparently can. Man, what Aunt Mary and I could do with our small house."

Caine's gaze finally pulled away from the room, but before his hazel eyes locked with hers, he'd moved with lightning speed. Emma found her face pressed against his hard chest and his hand fisted in her hair. Inhaling along her jawline, as if he couldn't get enough of her scent, he rasped, "You'll have an entire pride at your beck and call very soon, sweetheart."

His comment made her tense before her body instinctively yielded to the possessive slide of his other hand down her spine. Emma folded her arms around his wide shoulders, reveling in his hard-muscled frame and the arousing feel of his erection pressing against her. Caine's belief in her as the leader of the Velius kept echoing in her head until she finally confessed, "I'm no leader. Jade—and the other Velius—they've got it all wrong."

Caine wrapped a strong arm around her waist, fitting her

body fully against his. He kissed her nose, then her chin, before moving to her jaw, leaving tiny sparks behind. "Leadership radiates from you in every action you make, Emma, whether you realize it or not," he whispered in her ear.

"Wh-what are you talking about?" She tried to pull back, to meet his gaze, but Caine held fast, refusing to let her budge. His lips slid down from her ear and along her throat, sending tantalizing fiery sparks zinging through her body.

Sliding his hand up the back of her shirt, he flattened his palm against her back. Skin to skin. "You stepped in and took over when your aunt needed interference to keep her healthy and safe, you run the show at work in the café—the workers there looked to you for direction. You kept Jachin from killing Roland on the spot, you refused to let Jade believe Malac can be redeemed—"

"I've seen—experienced—what that sadistic maniac is capable of," Emma shot back as Caine's touch continued to turn her body to butter.

His fingers cinched tight in her hair and he growled, "No more after tomorrow. No matter what, I promise you Malac won't make it out of that meeting alive!"

His vow scared her. He almost sounded like he didn't plan on surviving tomorrow night's encounter with Malac, either. Emma's heart jerked and she tried to pull back, but Caine held her against him while he nipped at her collarbone. Her heart thumped in fear, even as her body betrayed her mind, responding to his dominant aggression. "Caine, I want to talk to you. Let me go."

"I can't. Not right now," he grated out, his voice rough as his fingers dug into her rear, tilting her hips, hitching her closer. "Tonight is all we have."

True fear rippled through her, the kind that left her hollow inside. Emma gripped his shoulders and pushed back until she met his gaze. "What are you talking about?"

She saw streaks of light green in Caine's eyes before he lowered his gaze to her lips. "I might not be able to use my Musk form tomorrow night, but I *will* make that bastard pay— for you, for your aunt, for the zerkers—"

When he trailed off, Emma cupped her hands around his stubbled jaws. "Don't you dare put yourself in harm's way or go and get yourself killed. I told you, I need you. Nothing has changed!"

Caine's lips kicked up just a bit and his gaze slowly lifted to hers. The sadness in his eyes tore at her heart. "Everything has changed. Your pride needs you more, Emma. You know it. And I know it. I'm an Alpha to the core, and if it weren't for the fact I could go zerker at any time, I'd be the next Alpha of my pack." Big warm hands encircled her wrists and his black brows knitted together. "I understand duty and responsibility to those in your care…and that's why I can see it in you. I felt it in your reaction to Jade when she told you that you were their leader, expected to help carry on the pureness of your breed. I saw it in your eyes when you looked at me. I know your heart will lead you to do what's right by your pride. It's ingrained in you."

Tears burned Emma's eyes and the pressure inside her chest was almost unbearable. "How can you just let me go? My heart hurts so much I can barely breathe!"

Caine closed his eyes and planted a tender kiss on her palm. "If I were a whole man, I'd be one selfish bastard, demanding we find another way. We'd merge our races…I wouldn't give a damn—" Fire lit in his eyes when they met hers. "I'd rip any panther apart who dared touch you or think for one second you'd agree to be his mate. But I'm not a whole man, Emma. I could go zerker any day. My Musk form is *that* much a part of me. I won't tie you to me. You don't deserve that and neither does your pride."

Tears spilled down her cheeks and her voice quavered with desperation. "Did—didn't Jachin mate with a human? And isn't Kaitlyn human, as well?" Emma argued, feeling as if she were stepping into a pool of thick quicksand that was sucking her down into suffocating darkness. "Hybrids are a possibility."

Hard lines creased either side of his mouth. "Your pride needs your offspring. I can't promise you a future, which children should be a part of." Touching her chin, he ran his thumb along her bottom lip. "All I can offer you is now."

It sounded so final, Emma had been breathing so hard, she suddenly lost her ability to catch her breath. She just stared at Caine, her chest caving in on itself, her heart shattering. "I—" She wheezed, trying to catch her breath.

"Emma?" Caine tilted her chin upward, concern etched in the hard lines of his face.

"I—can't—" She tried to inhale, but her breath just wouldn't come.

"Emma!" Caine scooped her up and carried her to the couch. Sitting down, he cradled her with one strong arm while he gripped her jaw, his fingers turning her face to his. "Breathe, damn you!"

He looked so angry and all she could think of was losing him. He was her rock in all this chaos. "Can't—" She shook her head and clasped his wrist, gasping for air again.

Caine kissed her and sparks shot between them. His fingers speared through her hair at the same time his lips pressed hard against hers, forceful and dominant, just as dominant as the voice in her head. *Breathe, sweetheart!*

His intimate kiss opened up her chest and Emma inhaled through her nose as she kissed him back with all the passion, all the wrenching physical connection she could give.

When she sobbed her happiness, Caine nipped at her bottom lip, making her gasp with pleasure. He took advantage and slipped his tongue inside her moist lips, thrusting deep, tasting, taking, exploring and seducing her with every sensuous swipe, every decadent thrust and parry.

Emma melted into Caine's fierce embrace. She ran her fingers across his stubble and memorized every contour of his face with her hands before threading her fingers into his thick black hair to pull him closer. And when she did, his kiss slowed, turning seductive and enticing as his hand slid up her rib cage, his palm grazing the side of her breast.

Kissing the side of his mouth, Emma tugged at his sweater, whispering, "I can't lose you… I…can't."

Swiftly pulling off the sweater and tossing it to the floor, Caine smoothed his hand along her face, pushing back her hair. "Shh."

Emma couldn't stop touching him. She ran her hands over the muscles in his shoulders and along his arms and down his chest as he kissed her temple. "I'm here, Em." Moving his lips to her ear, his voice lowered to a husky register as he slid his thumb over her sensitive nipple. "Slow down, my little wildcat."

Emma moaned and arched her back, pressing her breast into his hand.

Caine's low laugh made goose bumps skitter across her body. But he didn't take any prisoners when he suddenly rolled her onto her back and settled his hips between her legs. Pulling her hands above her head, he locked her wrists with one hand in a vise hold.

Emma panted in anticipation, butterflies of excitement dancing in her belly as he ran his teeth along her shoulder and rocked his hips in the cradle of hers, pressing his hard cock against her sex. "Damn, I can smell your sweet musk. You're ready."

"I never stopped being ready." A desperate gust of breath rushed out with her honest words. Her sex was already throbbing, her breasts tight and swollen, and with only a thin tank top separating her breasts from Caine's hungry gaze, his enticing touch and warm mouth, her nipples were more sensitive than they'd ever been.

Emma pressed closer, enjoying the pressure of his rock-hard chest against her nipples. Pushing her back to the couch, Caine's teeth blazed a teasing trail along her neck while the intimate slide of his thumb under the curve of her breast sent arousing jolts through her body. "All I've thought about is feeling your hands on me, your nails digging deep into my skin and that sexy purr growing louder right before I make you come again and again," he said, the rough rumble of his voice vibrating against her throat.

Emma's fingertips tingled as if her hands weren't getting enough blood flow, but this time she recognized the sensation for what it was. "Then let me go so I can accommodate your wishes," she said in a husky voice, tugging against his steel clasp.

His gaze darkened and a dangerous smile tilted his lips. He cinched his hand tighter around her wrists. "Not yet, my sexy little kitten." When Caine dipped his head and bit at her nipple through her shirt, sharp desire shot through her, centering between her legs. Before she could react to the pain, his lips latched on to her nipple through the shirt, sucking hard, rolling her nipple with his tongue. Emma mewled her pleasure, rocking her hips against him while her body clenched in heated response.

Her heart rate thundered in her ears and just when she thought she couldn't take his teasing torture any longer, Caine moved to her other nipple and began the pleasure-pain all over again.

Emma panted and pressed her sex against his erection to relieve the tingling painful throb building inside her. She couldn't get close enough, anything to relieve the pressure.

When Caine groaned and shoved her hips back down to the couch with a downward thrust, his heavy weight pinning her still, the pressure felt so good, Emma whimpered.

Caine lifted his head from her breast and stared at the two wet spots his kisses had left behind on her cotton shirt. The air cooled the damp material clinging to her, making Emma shiver and her nipples stand out, hard tips begging for more. Male satisfaction flitted across Caine's face right before he leaned close and breathed out across one damp tip.

Warmth skittered across her breast, flitting through her body. Emma quaked with pent-up arousal. "I—can't take it. I'm on fire, Caine. God, do something!" she demanded, her voice pleading and frustrated at the same time.

Eyes locked with hers, Caine's thumb slid slowly down her belly and then his hand was on the waistband of her jeans. He moved so fast, Emma barely felt the yank, but all that was left of her pants and underwear was shredded denim around her thighs.

"My clothes," she gasped. Yet the moment Caine had released her hands to pull her pants off her body, Emma immediately tugged off her tank top and tossed it to the floor.

"You have an extra set in the dryer," he curtly reminded her as he trailed his fingers past the trim dark bit of hair between her legs and teased her with stimulating skin-to-skin sparks of pleasure.

Emma moaned and canted her hips, trying to encourage his deeper exploration of her body, but Caine just brushed his finger lightly along her skin, then moved back to circle the bit of sensitive flesh with her own moisture. His electric touch sent splinters of pleasure vibrating through her, making her temporarily forget everything but the hungry desire clawing inside her sex. Her body demanded to be taken and assuaged with hard powerful thrusts, to be battered with fierce, all-consuming roughness, the kind that she was sure would make her heart threaten to explode from her chest.

She was surprised when Caine didn't remove his jeans, but instead put one knee between her thighs and walked his hands up the cushions until his face aligned with hers. His sexy mouth was a breath away and her body literally vibrated, needing their connection—the pull was that strong when their skin was this close.

His earthy, musky scent invaded her senses, making her feel light-headed and thoroughly seduced. Placing her hands on his hard pectorals, she enjoyed their humming physical bond and was ready to experience every part of Caine exploring her body inside and out. "Take off your jeans."

Caine's warm hand slid between her thighs, fingers tracing upward along her inner thigh. "I'm not going to remove my pants."

Apparently he needed to be talked out of this whole "slowing things down" idea he had in his head. Emma glanced at their bodies and raised an eyebrow. "That's going to make this a little difficult, isn't it?"

Caine shook his head and his fingers sent waves of excitement scattering through her body. "I meant what I said earlier. I'm almost zerker, Emma."

He couldn't be saying… Her voice trembled. "But when we were together before you were willing—"

"That was when I thought we could live a human life in the human world, but as the Velius' leader, you'll be expected to take charge and in doing so you'll be constantly challenged by your panthers. I would naturally defend you."

"And it would only be a matter of time before your Musk form became permanent," she finished for him, feeling bereft. She would never put him at risk of going zerker for her own selfish need to keep him close.

"Your pride doesn't need offspring with the taint of zerker potential in their blood, and because I don't know if this is something I can pass on, I won't take that risk with you."

"We'll use a condom."

"Which isn't foolproof." He shook his head and the determined set of his jaw made her stomach twist and her heart sink.

Emma hammered her fist on his shoulder, sobbing her frustration. "If all we have is this brief time, you're the only man I want to share my virginity with. You're the only man I want, damn it!"

A dangerous shadow crossed Caine's face and he quickly clasped the back of her neck, his power over her obliterating Emma's ability to fight him. When her fist froze on his chest and her attention zeroed in on him, Caine leaned close, his low voice dark as sin. "You might walk out of here tomorrow technically still a virgin, but I guarantee you after tonight... you won't feel like one."

Chapter 13

Caine stared into Emma's luminous golden eyes with resolute regard, even as his body shuddered deep inside. Her black hair was spread along the couch cushions and her cheeks were still flushed in arousal. She was biting her lower lip, trying not to cry, shredding his heart. The idea of another man having sex with Emma, touching her intimately, sent his mind in a vicious tailspin. He gnashed his teeth, already hating the bastard.

But Emma deserved so much more than he could ever give her. All because of his foolish youthful need for vengeance, he'd pay for the rest of his life. Ironically, he'd spent the last decade thinking nothing was worse than going zerker. Even death paled in comparison. He was wrong.

The thought of walking away from Emma, of not sliding inside her and bonding with her the way a Lupreda wolf would, was mentally and emotionally devastating, yet he couldn't let her know how much he suffered, couldn't share that his stomach burned and his heart felt like it was being ripped from his chest. He wanted the freedom to stand outside and howl, "She's mine!" across the entire Shawangunk Ridge, to snarl at any man who looked her way. And heaven help anyone who tried to touch her—if Emma hadn't been standing between them, he'd have beaten Roman senseless for daring to touch her. The dumb ass!

Sliding his fingers down from her neck to her shoulder, Caine released Emma from his hold and felt the slight tremor in his hand as he traced his thumb along her collarbone.

Tears filled her eyes, spilling down her cheeks. "Why does your touch affect me that way? Why can you lock me in place? No one else can do that."

Caine chuckled and shook his head in wonder, skimming his fingertips across the curve of her breast. "Maybe because you completely trust me and know that I would never hurt you."

Emma glanced down as her warm fingers slid along his chest. Arousing electrical currents slammed straight to his engorged sex when she pressed on his nipples, then rubbed her nails across the tiny tips. "I think it's because of this magnetic link you and I have." Her gaze snapped back to his at the same time she dug her nails into both nipples. "It's *that* powerful."

Caine ground his teeth at the erotic sensations blasting directly up his spine. Growling, he leaned forward and captured her nipple, rolling his tongue around the pink tip as he sucked hard. Not to be outdone, he captured her other nipple with his fingers at the same time, twirling the tip before he pinched, squeezing hard.

Emma's head fell back with her excited gasp. Her grip

moved to his shoulders and she rocked her hips, moaning in pleasure. Caine took full advantage of her distraction. Releasing her nipple, he continued loving on her breast with his mouth at the same time he slid his palm down her rib cage and stomach until he found her center.

Emma bucked against his hand, her fingers digging into his shoulders. Her nails marked his skin, sending his inner wolf through the roof. Damnit to hell, he wanted to slide inside her sweet body. To fill her up and never let her go. Remembering how small she was the last time he'd touched her, Caine ran his fingers up and down her slick sex, teasing her sweet clit and touching every precious pink fold to the point of driving her as insane as he felt. Emma's fingers jammed into his hair and she tugged hard, pulling his mouth off her breast and his body along hers until his chest crushed hers. "I can't stand the tingling pressure. It's almost painful. Touch me!" she panted.

Caine set his jaw and groaned. Her feminine smell had sent his senses into hyperalert, making him want her with a fierceness that would leave his brain sheer mush when he was done. She was so beautiful and uninhibited, her head thrashing back and forth in wild abandon. His own insides felt as if his wolf was shredding his guts from his chest all the way to his rockhard crotch. He was burning from the inside out. Damn, he wanted nothing more than to fulfill her request and thrust his fingers inside her, deep and hard. But he had to keep it together for Emma.

He started to push his finger slowly inside her, but Emma bucked and his thick digit dipped inside.

Emma's breath caught on a pained gulp and Caine cupped his palm on her mound to keep his fingers from going to deep. Pinning her still with a tight hold, he spoke as calmly as he could. "Open your legs, sweetheart, and let me help you get used to me touching you."

As the tension released from her legs, her soft wet channel contracted around his finger, making his gut cinch and his body flash with heat. Caine clenched his teeth and closed his eyes for a second so he could focus. Slowly, he moved his finger deeper, pulling out and then sliding back inside.

Emma's hips began to move and she let out tiny whimpers of pleasure, begging, "Deeper."

Once Caine had plunged his finger to the hilt a few times and Emma changed her demands to, "Harder," he knew her body had finally adjusted.

Sweat coated his skin and Emma's, too, as he began to pump his finger in and out of her sex, adding another finger to the mix. Her smell was playing havoc with his mind. Caine planted kisses and then slid his tongue in a leisurely lap along the sensitive crease where her leg met her body. He needed to taste her, to implant her unique flavor in his memory so he could keep a tiny part of Emma to himself.

Emma cried out when he withdrew his hand, ceasing their intimate connection, but Caine's pulse thrummed in his head, a steadily increasing beat, drowning out everything but his desire to pleasure her in the most passionate and carnal way possible.

Dipping his head, he ran his tongue up her slick sex and shuddered, closing his eyes as her arousing taste exploded in his mouth and set his body on a knife's edge. Sharp and alert, he would readily accept the pain of holding back while he pleasured her. Spreading her thighs wide, he dove back for more, groaning as he slid his tongue inside, wishing like hell his cock could follow suit. Emma moaned and her musky sweet flavor coated his tongue, tasting like the most decadent dessert. She was pure heaven.

"Feels so good. More!" she demanded.

Caine thrust his tongue deeper before moving his lips to explore every intimate part of Emma…not a single place was left untouched. The moment he latched on to her clit, Emma jerked and her back bowed with her wailing cry.

"Don't stop, don't stop," she begged through ragged choppy breaths, her hips rocking at a faster pace.

Her excitement spiked his own and Caine had to mentally steel himself to keep from losing it. He was surer than hell that he'd have the worst case of nauseating blue balls when they were done, but this special woman was worth every ounce of suffering.

Let go, Em. Give yourself to me, he said in a low growl in her mind as he slid his fingers deep inside her and found her G-spot, upping the tension even more.

Emma screamed and yanked hard on his hair at the same time she began to convulse around his fingers. As her warmth flowed over him, Caine experienced a wild, jacked-up rush unlike any he'd ever had before. He counted every flutter around his fingers, relishing in each precious one, and again cursed the fates for keeping them apart.

He'd had his share of Lupreda women, felt their sweet sighs and soft feminine skin, experienced their bites of passion and demanding growls, but nothing came even close to the enthralling, erotic experience of watching Emma's passion unfurl and seeing her turn into the full-fledged wildcat he knew she'd be. Nothing got him off more than knowing he was the man responsible.

Caine moved up her sweet curves and gripped at her waist

with one hand while he pressed his lips against hers. Emma wrapped her arms tight around his neck and kissed him back with a wild fierceness that made his heart soar, telling him what their bodies already knew. They belonged together…like this. Loving one another, wallowing in each other's desires for days until they both couldn't walk, couldn't think, could barely breathe. Then they'd sleep to recover so they could rediscover each other all over again. Hell, yeah, that's what he wanted.

Hot tears stung behind Emma's tightly closed eyelids. Caine's kiss was so passionate and intense, she returned his fervor with every ounce of her soul. She couldn't believe how much she'd felt as he loved intimately on her body. The sparks flying between them, combined with his sexy voice floating through her mind and his talented mouth and tongue loving on her and tugging at her insides as if he were personally strumming them to life, sent her to a semiconscious plane she never knew existed.

"Only you," she whispered in wrenching sobs against his mouth.

Caine surprised her by growling low in his throat and thrusting his tongue deep into her mouth to the same rhythm of his finger still inside her…as if he were trying to imprint apart of himself on her forever. Emma knew she'd never look at herself the same way again. Caine had already left his impression on her, but the thought of being branded by the sexy wolf turned her on, and she met each of his thrusts with welcoming movements of her hips, holding him tighter against her.

When Emma crooned and undulated her hips, Caine withdrew his finger from her and slid his thumb along her slick folds. With each downward thrust back inside Emma's sexy body, he moved his thumb along her folds and applied circular pressure, bringing the tiny bit of flesh into play. The moment she began to purr between pants, the appealing sound rumbling softly in her throat was the ultimate aphrodisiac. He had to grit his teeth and force himself not to react or move or he'd go right over with her.

Instead, he shared, whispering every thought that went through his mind into hers. *I feel your hot body tightening around me, Em. Imagine it's me inside you thrusting deep. That's exactly where I want to be right now. Filling up your beautiful body with mine again and again. Come for me, sweetheart.*

Emma breathed heavily against his neck and then his shoulder as her body spiraled toward another climax. Caine gritted his teeth from the pleasurable pain he experienced as her nails dug deep into his shoulders, gouging him with each hitching breath she took.

Emma screamed and bit down on his shoulder to muffle the sound as she rode the waves of her powerful climax. The moment her tremors slowed, Caine pressed his lips to hers and spoke in her mind once more, his voice sounding hoarse like he'd yelled for hours. *In your heart and mine, you'll always belong to me.*

When Emma wrapped her arms around his shoulders and kissed and laved at the spot where she'd bitten him, his deep love for this woman clogged his chest as if someone had slammed a fist deep inside. He'd wanted nothing more than to bite her back; he'd even felt his canines descend while her body rocked against him, regardless of the silver around his neck. Caine barely held on, but he managed to keep his sharp teeth out of her skin, even though every fiber inside him, from his aching cock to his inner wolf, howled at him to claim her.

Staring into Emma's gorgeous eyes, full of love and passion, he realized he needed to back off for a bit or that's exactly what he would do. Caine ran his finger down her nose and tapped the end in a lighthearted gesture that was far from the intense battle that raged inside him. "Why don't you go sit by the fire and I'll see if anyone thought to stock the fridge for us."

Emma grabbed the soft throw blanket lying across the back of the couch and stood on trembling legs to wrap it around her before she moved to sit on the soft carpet in front of the warm cracking fire. Flames leapt high and sparks flew when a log shifted in the grate. The room held a pleasant smoky smell as she bent her knees, wrapping the blanket around her.

Caine's back was clearly in view while he peered into the fridge. Red claw marks marred his broad shoulders where she'd held on for dear life through her orgasm. Emma's stomach clenched from the vivid memories of the explosive climaxes Caine had given her, not to mention the fact she'd bitten the man. It was bad enough he'd been holding himself back, but why'd she go and tempt him even more by biting him?

Her cheeks flamed and her hands shook. She'd freakin' bit him. Laying her forehead on her arms, she blew out an unsteady breath. What must he think of her? She could still taste his blood and the salt from his sweat on her tongue and her body continued to react, clenching instantly at the memorable taste.

"Hey, are you asleep?"

She lifted her head and her heart jerked when Caine set a mug on the floor and sat facing her. Cinnamon apples and mulling spices wafted in the air while Caine stretched his long legs out beside her bent ones. Leaning back on his hands, he stared at her intently as if waiting to hear her innermost thoughts.

The position flexed his biceps and pulled his chest and stomach muscles tight, displaying his ripped body to perfection. He was beautiful, sleek and sculpted with firelight dancing in his intriguing hazel eyes. Their color appeared a lighter green than usual, but the swirling brown combined with the lighter green definitely affected her, knocking the breath from her lungs.

"You turned out the lights," she commented, blowing her hair out of her eyes.

He smiled and leaned over to brush her hair away from her face. But instead of pulling away, he ran his fingers through the strands, his reverent gaze following in their wake. "I wanted to watch you sparkle."

She lifted a hank of her hair to inspect it and saw the glittery strands. Awkward heat flooded her cheeks once more. "Why is my hair doing this?"

Caine's smile faded and his jaw flexed. "The Velius' fur was engineered to sparkle in the night, taking away their greatest hunting skill—the ability to hide in the darkness. Your eyes are the same, glowing golden in low light. My guess is the medicine you were taking was still inhibiting those attributes, and that's why I didn't notice a difference in you the first night in the club, even though your smell was definitely earthy."

The truthful tidbit of their race's history made her chest ache. Differences. They were different. And she was meant to be his prey. "What do feel when you look at me?"

Caine ran his fingertips leisurely along her brow, then slid his hand through her hair once more. "Aroused."

His honest, sexy-as-hell response made her skin prickle. "So my scent and the way I look doesn't make you want to hunt me?"

His lips tilted in the most devastating smile she'd ever seen—the kind that had "wicked" written all over it—making her toes curl and her body tingle all over. "I definitely want to hunt you. Not for prey, but to sink my teeth into your sweet skin like you did mine."

Mortified all over again, her cheeks burned and she spoke in a stuttering rush. "About that…I'm so sorry I bit you. I— I have no idea why I did that. I—"

Caine pressed his thumb against her lips and his eyes held a feral glint. "In the Lupreda world, biting you is how I would stake my claim and mark you as my mate, Emma."

His comment hit her hard in the stomach. Emma's pulse thundered in her ears. She'd never been more turned on in her life. She wanted him to bite *her*. Fiercely wanted it. More than anything, she wanted to be his mate. But when the hungry look in his eyes faded and his hand fell away, she knew he wouldn't bite her. Ever. How could he resist the sexual pull? She certainly couldn't. She knew he said he wouldn't have sex with her because of his zerker issue, but did he hold back from biting her because she was a panther and ultimately different? Her heart sank at the thought.

Caine picked up the mug of apple cider and handed it to her with a self-deprecating smirk. "Apparently, all I'm ever going to be able to offer you for sustenance is hot liquids."

As Emma sipped the hot cider, her gaze trailed over his beautiful body to the thick bulge pushing against the zipper in his jeans, and a sudden erotic thought shot through her mind. She took another gulp of the warm liquid and smiled behind the cup, plans forming. Being different could be *very* sexy.

* * *

Caine watched Emma drink the cider and his entire body pulsed to the beat of each swallow she took. To keep from reaching for her, he leaned back on his hands once more, loving this intimacy. He stored it up in his mind, inhaling deep and capturing her scent, memorizing all her sexy little movements for those long, lonely nights ahead of him once he turned zerker. It was only a matter of time. He couldn't see himself wearing the silver necklace forever, especially now that being with Emma wasn't an option.

She smiled at him over her cup and his heart soared. She was so damn beautiful and smart and sexy and…not his to have. The moment his mind started to wander down that unsettling path, Emma surprised him by setting her cup on the floor and shrugging the blanket off her shoulders.

Caine's breath literally lodged in his throat as she crawled across his legs and up his body, her luscious breasts still swollen from his kisses and the fire glinting off her soft skin. He suddenly ached everywhere at once, though the true pain centered in his groin—the one place Emma was studying with intense interest.

When she reached for the button on his jeans, Caine's movements were whip-fast. Catching her hand before she connected, he said in a strained voice, "What are you doing?"

Emma tried to pull out of his hold, then frowned when he wouldn't release her. "I'm unbuttoning your jeans."

"Not a good idea," he bit out, barely keeping a rein over his lust for the woman leaning over him.

Emma laughed, her voice washing over him in seductive waves, a siren's song. "Of course it's a good idea. I want to kiss you like you did me."

Caine closed his eyes briefly and ground his teeth, trying his damnedest to erase the mental picture of Emma giving him oral sex. His eyes snapped open and he growled, "As much as I would like nothing better than that, if these pants come off, I can't guarantee that I won't have you on your back in two seconds flat, taking you the way I really want to."

Desire flashed through Emma's golden eyes and they lit up with playful excitement. "Ooh, promise?" She reached for his pants button with her other hand.

"Emma," he warned, capturing that wrist, too.

Emma stared at him for several seconds. He could see her mind working behind those beautiful eyes of hers.

Caine didn't know how much more he could take. His inner wolf was snarling and snapping to get at Emma; her aroused scent was driving him wild with the need to join their bodies. When she sat back with a heavy sigh, parking her sweet ass on his leg, he released her wrists, heaving his own mental sigh, which sounded more like a groaning growl in his mind.

"Don't you want to keep your promise?"

Caine's gaze snapped to hers. "What promise haven't I kept?"

Picking up her cup of cider, she took another long sip, then set it down on the floor again. "The one where you promised me that I'll leave here a virgin tomorrow, but I wouldn't feel like one."

Caine realized she was referring to giving him oral sex as figuratively blowing away her all virginal innocence. Smart woman. Leave it to her to turn his words around on him, and it worked quite effectively as far as his inner wolf was concerned—the deviant, selfish bastard!

His gaze narrowed. "That wasn't what I meant, Emma. I was referring to your body, not mine."

A delicate eyebrow rose. "Are you saying that you want my first time giving oral sex to be with someone else?"

Caine fisted his hands on his thighs. "Hell, no! I don't want you to ever give anyone else—"

"Then what are you saying?" she interrupted, her voice breathless, her eyes wide.

Before she could think to pull away from him, Caine moved quickly, sliding his hand under her hair and cupping the back of her neck. As he held her captive, he ran his thumb along her jaw, tracing the delicate bone. "I'm saying you're dangerous and a worthy opponent in every respect."

A brilliant smile lit up her face, stealing his ability to think. He'd already lost thousands of brain cells during their earlier explosive lovemaking. "Is that a 'yes, you may continue, Emma'?"

Caine released his hold on her neck, his voice ragged and raw, his body raging for her to touch him. "Yes."

When Emma moved to settle between his legs on her knees, bending to unbutton his jeans, Caine's hand shook as he lifted it to her hair. The soft strands slid through his fingers in a sparkling flow of watery black silk, wrenching his gut even tighter. She was precious to him.

Every nerve ending in his body craved her electric touch with greedy anticipation and he found himself pushing her hair over one shoulder, exposing that sweet spot between her shoulder and her neck—exactly where he'd clamp down with his canines if he'd had the freedom to do so. His canines tingled, wanting to elongate. Caine ground his jaw and his fingers fisted in her hair as he mentally worked to keep his fangs from descending.

The sound of his zipper opening jerked his attention back to Emma. She lifted her head and laughed as she tried to tug down his jeans. "Um, a little help would be nice."

Caine gave a strained chuckle and after Emma moved to sit beside him and took a sip of cider, he shoved his jeans and underwear off his body. She sat quietly, her watchful golden eyes above the rim of her cup following his every movement.

The moment he tossed his clothes aside, she set down her cup. Leaning close, she breathed out a warm breath over his tensed stomach, then ran her cider-spiced tongue from his abs all the way up to his chest in one long, decadent lick. Caine held back a shudder of unadulterated ecstasy when she slowed to press a tingling kiss to his hard pectoral.

"You know, there are some benefits to being different," she murmured. Her lips barely grazed his nipple and an electrical current arced between them, shooting through his chest and straight to his rock-hard erection.

Hell, yeah, there were! Caine suppressed a groan of sexual frustration and curled his hands into fists, setting them back on the floor behind him. He wanted nothing more than to touch her, to run his hands along her soft, supple skin, to make her tremble from his sizzling touch, but the moment he connected, their humming attraction might be more than he could resist. He was an honorable man. He wouldn't take Emma against her will.

Then she glanced up and he saw the look in her eyes.

The problem was, it wouldn't be against her will. She wanted him sliding inside, taking her body and soul, biting her. Damn it to hell! Grinding his jaw hard, he locked his elbows to keep from moving one single inch. He refused to inhale through his nose or he'd catch the strong musky sweet notes of her arousal and his rigid control would shatter.

"Are you going to touch me?" she asked as she trailed more magnetic kisses back down his abdomen.

"Not a good idea," he managed to grate out.

A low, sexy laugh bubbled up and she continued her path downward. "You have a beautiful body, hard as a rock and sculpted in *all* the right places. And you taste like pure sin," she finished, planting a kiss along his erection.

His cock flexed and Caine shut his eyes to cut off the evocative picture of Emma bent over him. He jerked when her fingers surrounded his ridged shaft and his breathing instantly turned shallow.

The moment her tongue lapped up the moisture along the tip of his erection, Caine's head fell back and he growled toward the ceiling, tendons flexing in his neck.

But nothing prepared him for Emma's enthusiasm. The heat from her drink made their shocking connection even more erotic, and before he realized it, his hand was sliding through her hair, cupping the back of her head. Silk and heat made a heady aphrodisiac.

Caine groaned and rocked his hips, pressing deeper into her warm mouth, whispering encouraging words. At first Emma complied, taking direction, but she quickly adapted her own method—one that included a very talented tongue and strong-as-hell suction. She blew his mind, ratcheting up his heart rate, winding his insides tighter and tighter to a painful, pulsing throb.

Just when he thought he couldn't take it anymore, when he was sure he was going to explode, Emma began to purr; a deep, throaty vibration that rocked his world. The fast-paced sensations surrounded him, and the physical proof that Emma found pleasure in pleasuring him sent Caine right over the edge. He shuddered as his orgasm rushed over him in an all-over-body experience, slamming in thunderous, blistering waves of hot and cold flashes. Each heart-thudding jolt through his system was accompanied by his own groans and growls until he finished with a long guttural howl.

Emma jacked him up even more as she laved and tasted his body with slow reverence once he was fully spent. When stillness descended between them, she lifted her gaze to his, a sexy smile tilting her lips. "Different definitely has its fringe benefits. Wouldn't you say?"

Caine's pleased laugh echoed in the room. He pulled Emma into his arms and rolled her onto her back. "You're killing me."

Wrapping her arms around his neck, she gave an exaggerated sigh. "And here I thought I was entertaining you. I must work on my delivery."

Gripping Emma close, Caine buried his nose against her neck. Inhaling her earthy scent, he brought every bit of her deep inside himself. This beautiful, intelligent, quick-witted panther challenged every part of him—from his mind to his body. A howl of possession rumbled just below the surface, demanding he unfurl it for the whole world to hear. Caine swallowed the primal sounds that rose within him and remained silent, even as he ached to be the only man in Emma's life—now and forever.

Chapter 14

"The street Malac designated to meet with the other Velius is a dead end, flanked on three sides by abandoned buildings. We'll have to enter the buildings via back doors and come out through any open or broken windows," Landon commented as he stared at the blueprints on the polished mahogany table in the Lupreda's huge library.

"You know he's going to have men hiding in the buildings." Caine slid his finger down the paper. "This appears to be a narrow opening between these two buildings. It might be an option. We could slip through here unnoticed."

"Your wolf forms will make it harder to get inside the buildings. My men will enter first and leave doors open for yours while they go off to secure any men Malac may have positioned inside the buildings," Jachin commented from the cell phone's speaker.

As Landon agreed with Jachin's plan, Caine said, "I will be in human form, too, so I can help Jachin's Sweeper unit."

Landon jerked his attention to Caine, his brow furrowed. "You're stronger in your wolf form."

Caine's hazel eyes narrowed. "Once I'm a wolf, I'll stay one until daybreak. I want to take Emma safely to Jade myself. I won't let her out of my sight until I have to. Only then will I join you."

"I can take Emma," Kaitlyn offered.

"Thank you, Kaitlyn, but I would like Caine to take me to Jade." Emma took in all the Lupreda standing around the room. She'd watched them nod whenever Landon or Caine spoke, saw the respect in their eyes, and felt the closeness. Where had the Velius gone so wrong that they'd splintered so drastically? Did the panthers' individualistic nature make it hard for them to work together as one? Addressing the group of Lupreda whose gazes were locked on her, Emma said, "I want to thank all of you for offering your services. Malac will try to double-cross Jade and Roland. He needs my aunt so I'll cooperate with him. He has no reason to give her up, other than to set a trap for the other Velius. But I believe with your help, we'll be an unstoppable force—one he isn't anticipating."

After the meeting was over, several of the Lupreda crowded around the table to further strategize with Landon and Caine. Kaitlyn pulled Emma to the side. "I know you two are getting ready to go back to Caine's place. I have a request of you."

Emma nodded. "Anything. I appreciate everything you've done for me."

Kaitlyn's hazel-blue gaze shifted to the group at the table before she spoke in a low whisper. "I want you to talk to Caine. To convince him to come back to the pack."

Emma's eyes widened. "He's not part of the pack?" She'd seen the respect in the other Lupreda's eyes, the way they deferred to him, second only to Landon.

Kaitlyn shook her head. "He left over a fight with Landon about wearing the necklace. That part seems to have resolved itself, and I believe out of respect for what Landon has done for you, Caine will come back, but…" Kaitlyn paused then plunged on. "If today's any indication, I don't think he'll resume his role of Second."

"Why not? The other Lupreda seem to respect his opinion."

Kaitlyn shook her head, her expression sad. "I can tell by the way he held himself away from the others today, not approaching the group until it was time to discuss strategy. He's different. He only got involved when you were the center of the discussion, but not until then. In past Lupreda business discussions, he would have been right in there, side by side with Landon, butting heads over issues, giving his opinion. Challenging. Today, he's not the same and I'm worried."

Emma glanced up at Caine and Landon, their heads bent over the blueprints—two strong alpha men working together with a common goal. Peace. Her heart ached. She needed to make it right, to repay Caine for everything he'd done for her. "I'll do my best, Kaitlyn."

The Alpha's mate smiled. "Caine respects Landon, but he cares deeply for you. I know he'll listen to you."

Later that day, Caine entered the cabin via the back entrance, carrying the food he'd caught for an early dinner. When he didn't immediately feel Emma's presence in the house, he tensed. "Emma!" he called in a loud voice, setting the meat on a plate on the counter.

"I'm up here," came a muffled reply. She sounded like she was above him. The cabin didn't have a loft or attic, so there was only one place she could be. Caine washed his hands and walked out the front door.

The snow crunched under his boots as he stepped off the porch and turned his gaze to the roof. "What are you doing up there?" he said with a frown. Emma sat next to the stone chimney in the only spot on the roof that wasn't covered with several inches of snow. The fire from the night before had helped melt the snow near the chimney apparently.

"I found a good spot to enjoy the view before the sun sets."

She looked so adorable bundled in her coat with her arms wrapped around her bent knees. It was a good thing the roof wasn't a steep slope or she'd never have been able to stay perched up there comfortably. Caine started to ask how she got up there when he saw the disturbed snow along the edge of the porch roof. A single set of footsteps led diagonally up the roof toward the chimney.

"Come join me for a minute," Emma beckoned.

Caine stepped back and then took a flying leap. When he landed on the porch roof, Emma clapped. "You'll have to teach me that one! I got here the hard way."

Emma scooted over and Caine settled between her and the chimney. Leaning back against the stone wall, he pulled Emma against his chest and wrapped his arms around her waist, settling her in between his bent knees. "Just in case the pill doesn't work, after dinner, you'll need to take a shower to get my smell off you before we leave for the city."

Nodding, she sighed and leaned into his chest. "Hmmm, this is cozy."

Her soft hair, lifted by the cool mountain wind whipping

around them, ruffled in his face, reminding him of the torturous night he'd spent with her sleeping in his arms. They laid on the rug by the fire all night long. He couldn't bring himself to move her once she'd fallen asleep against him, nor did he want to. Instead, he'd pulled the afghan over them and rolled onto his back. Gathering Emma to him, he'd let her use his arm as a pillow. In turn, Emma had snuggled close and sighed contentedly in her sleep, making his chest wind tight with many regrets.

"It's beautiful and very peaceful here," she commented wistfully, drawing him out of his musings.

Caine took in the view from Emma's perspective. The sun sunk low in the deep blue sky, giving off streaks of vivid orange and purple mixed with muted pink far in the mountainous horizon. Vivid green poked through the snow-covered trees, letting winter know they would survive the heavy white blanket currently covering their limbs. A mixture of pine and Emma's earthy scent wafted around him in an alluring aroma. Kissing her temple, he stared at her profile and murmured, "Takes your breath away."

Emma's sigh sounded sad. She turned her head slightly and met his gaze. "I've been thinking about my aunt. I'm glad that doctor is sneaking her the meds she needs, but I'm still worried about her. I feel like all of this is my fault. She's old and fragile and…" She blinked back tears and Caine's arms tightened around her.

"She did this for you, Emma. I doubt she'd want you to feel guilty. We'll get your aunt back safely."

Emma's small hands fluttered nervously over his for a few seconds, then settled as she rested her temple against his jaw. "Thank you for trying to ease my worries…and for everything."

Strong emotions whipped through Caine, knocking the wind out of him with their intensity. He couldn't speak for several seconds, but his hold tightened around her reflexively.

"It was interesting and awe-inspiring experiencing your pack's dynamics today. I don't think the Velius have anything close to your cohesiveness."

"That's where you come in. They've waited a long time for a leader to show them the way."

Emma met his gaze. "I saw how your pack reacted to you and Landon—the Alpha and his Second giving direction. You both exude leadership, demanding respect with a mere look. It was fascinating to watch."

Caine stiffened. He'd felt so out of sorts among his brethren today, like he had no right to command their respect. "I'm a general member of the pack, yes, but I won't be Landon's Second any longer."

Emma frowned. "Why wouldn't you be? It's obvious how much you're respected."

Caine flexed his jaw and bitterness laced his words. "Because I have to be able to fight to keep that respect. Musk mode is no longer an option for me."

Emma raised an eyebrow. "Are you saying leadership is based on strength?"

"It is for my pack."

Both her eyebrows shot up. "Yet you expect me to lead my pride, and I'm not physically strong compared to some of my people."

"You'll have bodyguards." Caine frowned. He didn't like the direction she'd taken their conversation.

Emma ran her fingers along his jawline, her electric touch tempting him. "Leadership is about responsibility and making tough decisions no one else wants to make. It's about knowing you won't always be popular because of those decisions, even if ultimately they're in the best interest of the group's survival as a whole."

He cut his gaze to hers. "And you said you weren't a leader."

"Your pack looks to you because of your guidance, not because of your strength."

Caine clenched his jaw. "I can never be Alpha."

Surprise flitted across her face. "Are you saying that the Second in your pack is expected to be the next Alpha?"

"No. Neither has to do with the other. The Alpha chooses his Second based on his belief in that wolf's ability to lead in his stead if the need arose. It's a position of trust."

Emma tilted her head and squinted at him. "So why can't you be Second again?"

Because I want to lead, damn it! He shook his head at their circular conversation. As Second he would be leading. Landon always respected his viewpoints. Emma was right and she wasn't afraid to tell him he was wrong, even if she did so by directing him to the answer himself. *And that's why she'll make a great leader.*

Chuckling, he ran his fingers through her hair, letting her alluring scent loose. "I'm jealous your pride will have your shrewd leadership skills all to themselves."

"I'll bask in your compliment, even if I don't think I'm particularly skilled, just very determined." She closed her eyes briefly, purring at his touch.

Caine adored everything about her. Everything. "Although I don't know how our pack would deal with two women as strong-minded as you and Kaitlyn—"

Her eyes opened and amusement danced in their golden depths. "Feeling threatened?"

Caine let out a low growl and snapped his teeth close to her neck, making her gasp. "Try aroused, my little panther."

"Stay between Roland and Jade." Caine's hazel gaze locked with Emma's as they stood outside his truck, waiting to meet up with Jade. Five huge Lupreda paced in their wolf forms in the truck's bed behind them: Landon, Laird, Roman and two other males. Kaitlyn had parked behind them. She'd driven another seven wolves to town in Landon's truck and would stay in her human form to bring the truck into the alley if they needed her. They'd gotten a few strange looks by those who'd noticed the wolves in the dark, but then again, nothing surprised anyone in New York.

When Jade and Roland arrived, their SUV's headlights cutting through the darkness, another two vehicles, presumably more Velius, pulled up behind them. Caine's eyes narrowed. He started to reach for Emma as if planning to wrap his arm around her and keep her close. He stopped himself just short of touching her and spoke to her mentally. *I don't like leaving you in their care. Nothing about Malac is trustworthy. Despite what Jade says, I think she still harbors some hope he'll come around. He's unpredictable and out of control. Shift as soon as you can. You'll be able to defend yourself better in your panther form. We'll be right behind you.*

She nodded but didn't have a chance to say anything because Jade walked up. "Are you ready, Emma?"

Emma followed Jade and Roland back to their vehicle and climbed inside. Sandwiched between her people, Emma watched Caine get back in his truck. Even though she was with those of her own race, Emma had never felt so torn. Her heart ached and her palms began to sweat. *I already miss him, his warmth, his touch. How will I ever live without Caine?* she wondered. She didn't want to think about her future or the fact the Velius would expect her to produce more panthers to help propagate their race. Emma shuddered, despite the warm air blowing through the vents in front of her.

They were a couple of blocks away from the meeting place when a black panther darted across the street ahead of them.

Roland slammed on the brakes and Jade whispered with reverence in her voice, "Hawkeye."

The panther stopped briefly, his eyes and coat glowing in the darkness, before he bounded into a fast-paced run.

Even before Jade spoke, Emma could tell it was Hawkeye by the panther's massive size. As he disappeared between two buildings, she prayed Caine and the other Lupreda would catch his scent and recognize him as an ally. Once again, she found herself wishing the panthers had the ability to speak mentally like the Lupreda did. It would be so much easier to communicate with each other while in panther form.

Dirty snow had been plowed in six-foot piles on either side of the road as they parked their car on the street beside the building. Roland insisted on parking on the main road instead of in the alley. He wanted to be able to get away quickly and not be trapped by another vehicle.

After she'd shrugged out of her heavy jacket and exited the car, Emma shivered and tried to ignore the cold wind blowing around her as eight men exited their vehicles behind them. Her confidence bolstered, she acknowledged the deferential bow of the men's heads when they approached her. "Don't act unless you see me start to shift. Understood?" she whispered. She wanted to get her aunt to safety first before all hell broke loose.

"They're carrying the injections they'll need. They can shift almost as quickly as you. Your panthers will be behind you when needed," Roland assured her.

Once everyone nodded their understanding, Emma turned and accompanied Jade and Roland up the sidewalk that led to the alley.

The moment their group turned the corner, Malac stepped out of a black Hummer parked in the far back corner of the alley and beckoned to someone inside the vehicle.

Emma tensed but continued forward with her group past a few abandoned cars and a couple of Dumpsters. Trash showed through the dirty snow along the edges of the road.

Another man exited the back of the vehicle and helped Mary down. As Mary and the man holding her arm stepped under the streetlight's glow, Emma's temper flared when she saw the reason the man *had* to help her aunt down. Mary's wrists and hands were duct-taped together and a gag was tied around her mouth. Emma glared at Malac and started to stalk forward, ready to rail at him.

Roland's hand clamped tight on her shoulder. "Calm, Emma."

She jerked her gaze to Roland, shocked that he could see his sister treated so horribly and not react. "How can you watch—" Her words died off when she saw the look on the older man's face. Sheer hatred reflected in his eyes as he stared at Malac, who was currently talking to the man holding Mary.

Taking a deep calming breath, she returned her attention to Malac. He'd stepped away from his men and stopped several feet away from her. Sweeping the crowd behind Emma with a derisive look, he smirked. "I see you've brought a large part of the pride with you." Dark eyes flickered to the handguns Emma's men held. "I don't see any reason for such overkill. This is just a friendly exchange."

Emma had counted only three men other than Malac: the driver, who'd gotten out of the Hummer as they spoke; the man standing beside her aunt, holding her upper arm; and another man flanking the rear of the Hummer. Her gaze flicked to the surrounding buildings' broken windows, their kicked-in and broken graffiti-ridden doors.

She didn't think for one minute that Malac hadn't placed other men in strategic offensive positions inside the buildings, probably with guns in their hands. She knew he'd picked this section of town for its seclusion and abandoned environment, yet she was surprised she didn't see any homeless people hanging around. Then again, it was cold. The homeless people were probably huddled in a corner inside the buildings, trying to stay warm.

Running her hands down her thin blouse sleeves to stay warm, she locked gazes with Malac and kept her voice steady. "Once my aunt has reached the safety of her brother's side, I'll come with you."

Malac shook his dark head, his expression determined. He whistled and two sleek panthers jumped from the Hummer's open back window. She was surprised to see a light-colored, spotted jaguar walking alongside the pitch-black one. They quickly moved to flank Mary on either side. "The exchange will be an even one. You come forward at the same time my sentries escort your aunt across to her brother."

Emma recognized the diamond stud winking in the black panther's ear. He had to be the very young guard she'd passed in the hall at Malac's facility. The spotted jaguar must be the other young sentry she'd seen at the end of the hall. She remembered their detached expressions. Nothing but duty had shown in their eyes. Her heart thumped in fear for her aunt.

The wind whistled between the buildings, ruffling Mary's bobbed gray hair and flapping her coat open. Tears welled, spilling down her plump, wrinkled cheeks. The older woman was shaking her head "no," but one of the panthers nudged her forward with his shoulder. "It's going to be okay, Mary. Roland will take care of you," Emma said. *I just need to get her to safety first,* Emma reminded herself.

When Emma began to move forward, two of her own men stepped into place on either side of her, guns at the ready. They escorted her the same as the young male panthers were escorting her aunt.

Right before they were about to pass each other, a shot rang out from the direction of the Hummer. A man had popped up behind the passenger-side window and shot the guard on Emma's right. When the man stumbled back, she tried to steady him, but one of the panthers knocked her to the ground in the process of attacking the injured man. At the same time, the other panther went after the man on her left, who got off one shot before the panther struck.

Emma moved to the balls of her feet. A couple more of her men had rushed forward, only to stop in their tracks when Malac held an automatic handgun to Mary's head.

"You really didn't think I'd let her go, did you, Emma?" Malac taunted.

"Don't do this, Malac!" Jade said, raising her hand as she took a step toward them.

Malac jerked his gun upward with lightning speed and

fired, pegging the center of Jade's chest, saying, "Sometimes the traditional bullet just *feels* better." As the female Velius fell to the ground, blood spreading quickly from her gaping wound, he sneered, "You've always stood in my way. Not anymore."

Jade! Emma's gut wrenched when Roland caught Jade in his arms and fell to his knees. He gently laid her on the asphalt, his voice hoarse with worry. "Jade! God, can you hear me?"

Sheer hatred and rage rose up inside Emma, a rumbling, seething volcano ready to blow. Her claws itched along her fingertips and the tiny hairs on the back of her neck rose, sending a prickling sensation all over her body. At the same time she called forth her panther, she dove toward Malac in mid-shift.

Malac hadn't anticipated Emma's aggressive move. He was too busy enjoying Jade's suffering. The moment Emma slammed into him, her panther paw shoved at his wrist and the other paw landed on his chest. His gun skipped across the icy asphalt and Mary ducked out of the way, running toward her brother. Emma roared, digging her claws into the man's arm and chest as she sent him hurling across the road with a powerful shove.

Landing with a hard thud, Malac bellowed and jammed something into his neck. The second he jumped to his feet, a huge black wolf landed on the road between Emma and the man. Crouching in a battle stance, the wolf snarled and bared his teeth, challenging Malac.

His scent alone indicated to her it was Caine, but when she saw a silver chain hanging around the wolf's neck, she was surprised. *How was that possible?* Emma didn't have time to consider further because two other panthers suddenly attacked Caine simultaneously. They must've been hidden in some of the abandoned cars. One panther jumped onto Caine's back and the other rammed into his side with his shoulder.

Roaring, Emma started to pounce into the fray, when another huge panther shoved her to the side with his massive head, jumping between her and the panthers attacking Caine. Hissing at the panther who'd interfered, she tried to dive around his immense size, but the panther batted her away, blocking her path. Even if his size didn't give him away, Emma recognized his smell and his tactics. He was trying to keep her safe. Hawkeye.

Nodding to Caine, she pawed at the ground and Hawkeye flexed his powerful legs, jumping into the fight. One of the smaller panthers flew to the side, bleeding profusely at the neck, and while Caine fought the other one, teeth snapping and fur flying, Hawkeye went after the one he'd wounded.

Emma was so focused on Caine, she finally heard the roars, howls and guttural snarls all around her. The entire street was now filled with wolves and panthers fighting, claws and teeth ripping at fur, muscle and sinew.

And then her gaze landed on Malac who'd just finished shifting to his panther form.

An enormous black-and-brown wolf stood snarling at Malac. Landon's wolf stance bristled with challenge. He gave the man time to shift, yet he let him know by his bared teeth and fur standing on end that he planned to tear the panther apart.

Emma heard a distinct victory growl and turned to see one of Malac's panthers had a tawny-colored wolf pinned down with a locked bite on his neck. She knew she only had seconds to react or the panther would deliver a deathblow to the wolf's skull, killing him instantly. She wasn't sure how she knew this. She just did. Her instincts were that strong.

Bolting into a fast run, she thundered toward them. Before the panther knew she was coming, Emma leapt onto his back, digging her claws into his sides and grabbing hold of his scruff to yank him off the wolf. Her momentum took them all to the asphalt where they landed hard. Her ribs bruised, but Emma didn't stop. She released the muscle and skin along the panther's neck only long enough to grab hold of his head. Clamping her teeth hard, she crunched down to let him know she'd keep going and kill him if he didn't stop.

The panther thrashed and tried to throw her off, while keeping his hold on the wolf. Emma's claws dug into his sides. He wasn't giving up. He planned to finish off the wolf. He gave her no choice, damn it! She clamped down a bit harder and heard a slight crack—it was enough to get the panther's attention.

The moment he released his death hold on the wolf, Emma yanked her locked jaw and slammed his head to the ground. When the panther let out a grunt before he passed out, Emma loosened her jaws and scrambled to her pawed feet. His blood coated her mouth, and she could still feel how her teeth had embedded in his hard skull, nearly crushing it, but she refused to dwell on the sick feeling knotting her stomach—she'd almost killed someone, even if it was in defense of another.

She glanced up to see some of Jachin's men jumping from open windows. They each carried at least one man in their arms. The humans had to be Mafia working for Malac. The moment the vampires landed, they dumped the humans' unconscious bodies onto the road and then jumped into battle.

How can they tell whom to fight? Emma wondered, until

she saw Jachin nod to Caine, then point and direct his men. They must be speaking to each other mentally, she realized.

With Malac's men's numbers quickly dwindling, Caine, Landon and Hawkeye now stood in a semicircle facing Malac.

The Velius leader backed up a couple of feet, roaring at the panther and wolves to stay back.

Emma was surprised to see the original two panthers who'd flanked her aunt take flying leaps over Landon, Caine and Hawkeye to land between Malac and them. Simultaneously, the two panthers turned and crouched, ready to defend their leader.

Malac's eyes narrowed into slits, clearly pleased by the two panthers who'd put themselves between him and his attackers. He even nudged them until his defenders changed places.

Emma's gut tightened. She padded closer to the group. Something wasn't right, but she couldn't reason why she felt that way. Malac let out a challenge roar, seeming far too cocky as he walked forward a bit and placed himself in between the two panthers who were protecting him. They growled and flanked Malac even closer. Such blind devotion.

Malac let out an almost gleeful hiss right before he used his hind quarters to bump one of the panthers toward Caine and Landon, then quickly used his front paws to shove the black one into Hawkeye's path.

The moment Malac ran off toward the buildings, Emma reacted. She jumped onto Hawkeye's back, throwing him off balance. The huge panther stumbled while in mid-swipe. He'd intended to eliminate the panther in one blow, but Emma's interference lessened the impact of his attack and his paw only knocked the younger panther to the pavement, stunning him. Before Hawkeye could recover, Emma leapt off his back and crouched over the momentarily disoriented panther underneath her.

Hawkeye snarled at her and shook his head. Emma growled back, crouching closer to protect the young panther. She was going purely on her gut instinct with this one, but above all else, she knew she could *not* let Hawkeye hurt this panther.

Emma, Landon has gone after Malac. Do you want me to spare this one, as well? Caine's voice entered her mind. Emma glanced his way. The light-colored panther and Caine were facing off, circling each other, looking for an opening to strike. She nodded vigorously, hoping Caine would know to knock the beast out so he wouldn't be a threat to him or anyone else.

At that moment, the panther leapt toward Caine and the two animals rolled across the ground, ripping and snapping at each other with their claws and sharp teeth. In mid-turn, Caine began to shift and before the roll was complete, he'd fully shifted to his Musk form. Grabbing hold of the panther's muzzle with one powerful clawed hand, Caine slammed his fist into the panther's jaw, knocking out the animal.

Emma blinked at Caine in his Musk form. She'd been told the Lupreda couldn't shift to their werewolf form during the full moon, that the moon forced them from their human to their wolf half, unless they wore silver. When the panther underneath her began to stir and growl as if he planned to attack her, Hawkeye nudged Emma out of the way with his shoulder and slammed his massive head into the other panther's, knocking him unconscious with a satisfied grunt.

Caine gave Hawkeye a curt nod. The panther returned the gesture before he moved to stand beside Emma. Turning his black werewolf muzzle toward Emma, Caine spoke in her mind. *Hawkeye will keep you safe. I'm going to help Landon track Malac.*

After Caine jumped to an open window two stories above them and disappeared inside, Emma glanced around them. The battle appeared to be over. Wounded panthers, wolves and vampires were scattered along the street. Some leaned on cars, others lay on their backs panting and bleeding in the dirty snow, and a few, at least one or two from each race, were very still. Emma tried not to think about the losses as she padded up the road to see how Jade and Aunt Mary were doing.

A loud roar caught her attention right before something heavy landed on her back, slamming her to the ground. The wind wooshed out of Emma's lungs, quickly followed by horrific pain, but when Emma was unable to let out a moan or even move, panic set in.

Malac must've dived on top of her from the building above. Heavy thuds landed on the street next to them and Malac was yanked off her before the panther could do some serious damage.

Jachin, Caine, Landon and Hawkeye surrounded the panther. Blood oozed from several vicious wounds along his feline body, yet Malac didn't give up. He roared and swiped at them all with his deadly claws. Emma rolled onto her side and saw the vengeance in the faces and tense stances of her comrades. Each of them had his own reasons for wanting a piece of Malac, to pay him back for every bit of pain and suffering he'd caused.

When they all began to snarl at each other, Emma's heart jerked with worry. She gingerly moved her paws under her and started toward them when a loud shot echoed through the alley.

Malac paused mid-roar and then the panther crumpled to

the ground, unmoving and silent. A single bullet wound oozed blood from the center of his head.

"For my daughter!" Roland yelled, his frame quaking in anger and anguish. Dropping the handgun, he fell to his knees beside Jade and gathered her limp body in his arms.

Emma followed him and touched her muzzle to her aunt's leg. Mary shooed her toward Jade with a quiet but gruff, "I'm fine." Moving to Jade's side, tears filled Emma's eyes and she rubbed her panther whiskers along the female Velius' cheek. Jade touched her muzzle, then gulped in air. Blood seeped between Roland's hand, despite the pressure he was putting on her wound. Tears trickled down the woman's temples into her hair as she stared from Jachin to Hawkeye and then Landon and Caine, who'd all moved to stand on either side of Emma. Her forehead creased in pain and her words came out broken and winded. "We. Did. It. Right? Worked together for peace."

Emma's heart ached for the woman who'd led the panthers with such dedication and vision. Not everyone agreed with the methods she and Roland employed, but they all shared her desire for peace.

Kneeling down beside Roland, Jachin's blue gaze locked with the older man's and then Jade's as the vampire clasped her hand. "Yes, peace, Jade. We did it."

Silence descended on their small group once Jade took her last breath. No one said a word. No one moved for several minutes. No one could. Only the sound of Roland's soft cries and Mary's comforting words as she hugged her brother's shoulders filled the air.

When Landon jerked his wolf head up and stared behind her, Emma turned to see Kaitlyn in her human form kneeling beside the light brown wolf Emma had saved from the panther earlier. Emma remained in her panther form as she followed Landon and Caine over to Kaitlyn's side.

Kaitlyn's eyes filled with worry as she met her mate's gaze. "Roman's spine was badly wounded. He says he can't move." Tears spilled down her cheeks and she ran her hand over the wolf's head and ears. "He—he wants you to end it for him. He doesn't want to live like this."

When Landon looked up at Caine towering above them in his Musk form, Emma's chest tightened. Without hearing the words, she knew what he was mentally asking of his Second.

Chapter 15

I could end it for Roman with one bite, but in your Musk form, you could make it painless.

Caine glanced at his powerful Musk hands, and then he stared at Roman, the happy-go-lucky guy who wore T-shirts sporting "I'd rather be boarding than bored" logos. He understood why Roman would feel his life was over, but…what if he could eventually heal?

As if he knew the dilemma going on inside Caine's mind, Landon spoke to him once more. *This decision is entirely your own. As leaders, we have to make the tough ones. I consider you my equal in that respect. Whatever you decide for your packmate, I'll stand by you.*

Laird limped over to stand beside him and lifted his auburn wolf head to stare at Caine. *Don't do this. He'll heal,* he said, his tone sad, imploring.

What if he doesn't? He'll never forgive me, Caine said to Laird as he met Roman's deep brown gaze and thought of all the fun times they'd had together as friends.

Well? Roman finally spoke to Caine. *Get it over with, damn it!*

Caine flexed his jaw for several seconds, then shook his head. *You'll heal.*

Addressing Kaitlyn, Caine said, *We'll need to make a stretcher for him when we take him home. His neck needs to be immobilized so he doesn't have permanent damage.*

When Caine turned around, he saw that Hawkeye stood with all the remaining panthers behind him. Some were wounded and some were barely conscious, but their attention was focused on Hawkeye. Emma moved to stand beside Caine in a supportive stance.

In the blink of an eye, the panther shifted to his human form and spoke to the Velius with a deep authoritative voice. "Malac is gone. Too many events have happened for you to deny the prophecy's truth. The prophecy speaks of a leader… 'A leader is needed, you know this is true. Look not to one but two.' I know many of you believe I was the second leader along with Emral—Emma—but I'm feral, a loner who prefers his solitude, and that will always be true."

Sweeping his arm toward Caine and Emma, he continued. "They are your leaders. This wolf has proven he'll do what-ever it takes to protect your Queen, and for that you should be forever grateful. Either choose to follow them or leave, but know that if you try to stir trouble with the other races as Malac has in the past—" Hawkeye's gaze narrowed "—I'll help Caine and the others hunt you down."

Caine was surprised by Hawkeye's declaration and his

support, but before the panthers accepted him, before he asked for Emma's decision, he wanted them to see him standing side by side with Emma—as he truly was…different from them in many ways.

Releasing his Musk form, Caine shifted back to a black wolf. He could never love Emma enough for the gift she'd given him—the ability to shift at will despite the silver chain. He realized what she'd inadvertently done after he'd heard the gunshot and dove out of the building window in his human form to help her. Without conscious thought, he'd shifted on the fly as he flew toward the ground, landing as a wolf to face Malac. He was no longer zerker.

With a nod of approval to Caine's wolf, Hawkeye morphed back to his panther form, and then turned and ran off down the road, disappearing into the night.

Caine slid his wolf muzzle along Emma's panther one. *Is this what you want, Emma? For me to be your mate and help you lead your pride? If you don't wish it, I'll understand and walk way. But if you do, I promise to protect you with every fiber of my being, even as I spend the rest of my days repaying you for the gift you've given me.*

Tears filled the panther's golden eyes staring back at him. Caine's heart stuttered and he waited for a sign. Tears could mean so many things. Stepping close, Emma ran her whiskers along his muzzle and leaned into him before she tucked her nose underneath his powerful jaw.

Caine clamped his jaw over Emma's muzzle, locking her against his neck in both a loving and possessive gesture. The sudden sensation of her purr vibrating against him made his throat knot and his chest swell with love and pride for this amazing panther and her acceptance. He knew they'd have a tough road ahead of them bringing the Velius pride around to a group who lived and breathed as one. But together, he and Emma could make it happen.

When Caine heard the Alpha's howl behind them, quickly followed by the other Lupreda, a bit of tension released from his body. Landon understood his decision and approved. The moment the Velius began their own deafening din of panther roars, Caine relaxed. Lifting his head, he released Emma and together they joined the primal chorus.

Emma stared at Caine as he drove them out to "their cabin" in the Shawangunks. He'd said it would be their getaway house when they needed a vacation from the city. And after the last two days, they certainly needed one.

Between Jade's funeral and those of several others they'd lost in the battle, as well as the various back-to-back meetings they'd conducted with the Velius, Emma and Caine had spent tons of time together—working—only to fall asleep in each other's arms exhausted the past two nights.

Mary had insisted Roland move in with her temporarily—that he needed to get away from the city for a while. According to her aunt, Casper hadn't left Roland's lap since the man had entered the house. Emma was relieved she didn't have to worry about them. Mary and Roland would take care of each other and would join their pride once more when they were ready. Now, if she could just get in touch with Hawkeye. She needed to tell him he had a family waiting for him to return.

After Emma had given Jared her notice, telling her boss that she'd stayed with her sick aunt at the hospital the past several days, she and Caine decided to start fresh in every respect. They would sell off Jade's and Malac's old properties and use the proceeds to build a new facility and a home for the Velius, one that was conducive to group meetings and activities.

The truck's headlights shone on Landon leaning against the cabin's porch railing as they drove up. Emma glanced Caine's way. "Since you called him to let him know you were staying here for a few days, I'm sure he's waiting on you for a reason. I'll go inside and let you two catch up."

Caine reached over and captured her hand as she started to get out. Kissing her palm, he shook his head. "We're a team, Emma. Whatever Landon has to say to me, he says to you."

His comment surprised her. "Are you sure? He's still your mentor in many ways."

He smiled. "He's my friend first and foremost."

As Emma and Caine climbed the porch steps, Landon pushed off the railing and addressed Caine. "You look good, if a bit tired. Those Velius giving you hell?"

Caine laughed. "No more than the Lupreda would when reorganization and reshuffling of duties occur."

Emma smiled at Landon. "I'm in awe with Caine's ability to garner devotion and respect from my pride so quickly—" She paused when another vehicle drove up behind theirs and four Velius men climbed out, looking focused and on guard.

Landon's eyebrow shot up as each man took a post around the four corners of the house. Amusement laced his comment. "I see how well you've gained their trust. That's a helluva security detail."

Caine shook his head. "Emma is precious to them. Even though she's safe here, it's hard for them to let go of old habits and concerns." Stepping off the porch, Caine called out to the men, "Your senses allow you more leeway. Spread out from the house a bit and you'll be more effective."

As the men quickly adjusted their positions, deferring to Caine's direction, Emma smiled. "You've taught him well, Landon."

Landon's green eyes crinkled with his deep laugh. "He's far too stubborn for me to teach him anything, Emma. You're seeing Caine's own leadership skills in action. Over the years, all I've done was to steer him away from crazy extremes."

"I guess that's *my* duty now." Emma snickered.

Smiling, Landon nodded. "Yes, it is. He'll keep you on your toes."

"It's great to hear how loved and respected I am," Caine snorted as he returned to Emma's side.

Emma wrapped her arm around Caine's waist, enjoying the feel of his muscular body against her side. "We're just teasing."

Caine pulled her close. "*He* was serious."

Landon's smile faded to a serious expression. "I've always known you'd make a great leader. I wouldn't have picked you as my Second otherwise. You make sound and fair decisions."

Caine's arm tightened around Emma. "How's Roman doing? He refuses to take my calls."

"He's healing slowly." Landon stroked his jaw, then sighed. "Only time will tell. I would've made the same decision you did for Roman. I told him so the night we brought him home."

Caine frowned. "Then why did you ask me to decide on his fate?"

Landon's gaze remained steady. "Because you needed to know what it felt like to have to make life-and-death decisions as a leader. Roman was your friend as well as your packmate.

Learning to separate yourself from your emotions so you can make that impartial call is the hardest skill to master."

Caine grunted, acknowledging his statement. "While you're here…" Lifting the silver chain off his neck, he held it out to the Alpha. "I'll give this back to you."

Landon curled his fingers around the silver chain, his brow furrowed. "Care to tell me how you were able to shift, not only with the silver around your neck, but in and out of Musk form, even though it was a full moon?"

Moving his arm to Emma's shoulders, Caine traced his fingers along her cheek. "It was the damnedest thing. I didn't know what Emma had done until I shifted on my way down from the second story of that building to defend her against Malac."

Emma glanced up at Caine as he continued. "I think I know what happened, though it's only a guess, because a panther has never mated with a wolf before."

Emma's cheeks heated under Landon's steady regard. He was watching them intently. "Mated? But we haven't. I mean you haven't—"

Caine chuckled and kissed her forehead; a soft electric touch to remind her how right they were for each other. "Remember when I told you that the Lupreda bite to mark their mates? You bit me that night, remember?"

Emma's face flamed brighter. "I have no idea why I did it," she mumbled.

"The desire to mate is fundamentally primal, Emma." Landon's light brown eyebrows elevated with his grin. "I find it amusing that you marked Caine and he hasn't marked you yet. He's always claimed to be a selfish bastard."

"I was *trying* to be honorable," Caine grumbled.

Laughing at Caine's annoyance, Landon's expression

turned contemplative. "It's intriguing that Emma's bite has apparently given you the ability to shift at will, though I guess I shouldn't be surprised. Kaitlyn and I still aren't sure if my mating bite gave her the ability to shift to a wolf, or if she has always had the ability because she was half Lupreda but was hindered by the silver chain she'd worn most of her life. Gabriel has been so busy in the city, he refuses to share anything about his human mate Abby until he brings her home in two weeks. It's driving Kaitlyn nuts not to know what changes, if any, have happened to her friend. It could answer the big debate between us."

Caine snorted, shaking his head. "You *like* thinking you had something to do with Kaitlyn's ability to shift. You're just jealous she can do so outside the moon's cycle."

Landon slid his gaze to Emma. "See what happens when he runs off to lead his own group? Complete insubordination."

Emma smirked. "Um, I think he's always been that way."

"Very true," Landon agreed. "As for you, it'll be interesting to see if Caine's mating bite changes you in any way."

Landon's comment sent heat shooting in rapid bursts throughout Emma's body, spreading to every nerve ending. She'd fantasized about feeling Caine's sharp teeth sinking possessively deep into her skin more times than she cared to count over the past few days, but she hadn't thought beyond the physical pleasure she knew the act would bring. The idea Caine might also be sharing something more of himself with her sent her emotions flying. Emma was left speechless.

The front door opened and Kaitlyn stepped out. "Oh, hi. I was just making sure you two had food since the last time you stayed here—" she cut her gaze to Landon "—someone forgot to make sure to have the Lupreda leave food for you."

Landon snorted. "Caine knows how to hunt."

"Not everyone lives on a steady diet of meat." Kaitlyn grabbed her mate's hand. "Come on, let's leave them to their evening." Nodding to Emma, she continued. "There's a pot roast and a salad in the fridge."

Emma smiled her appreciation, feeling like she'd joined not just one, but two new families. "Thanks, Kaitlyn."

"You're welcome." Kaitlyn stepped around them, tugging Landon off the porch with her. "Come by around ten tomorrow."

Growling, Landon moved with lightning speed, lifting his mate over his shoulder. Kaitlyn landed with an *oomph.*

"Put me down!" She pounded on his rear, sounding more embarrassed than angry.

"In case you haven't noticed, Kaitie, the boys took the truck when they left. I'm going to have to carry you back." Smacking her denim-covered rear, he grinned at Emma and Caine.

Kaitlyn kicked her feet in annoyance. "I can walk! Put me down."

Landon's grin turned downright sinful. "Oh, I will. In a bit." He turned to walk away and called over his shoulder, "Make that noon, Caine. I have a feeling Kaitlyn's going to be sleeping in."

"Landon!" was all they heard as the Alpha shot away in a blur so fast that Emma blinked in surprise.

"Um, wow!"

Caine leaned close. "Never leave a wolf wanting once he's had a taste. It makes us…antsy."

Emma's insides turned to molten liquid. "Have you felt antsy?" she asked in a whisper as she stared into the dark woods, mesmerized by imprint of Landon's blatant desire for Kaitlyn left behind in her mind.

Caine's voice was a husky rasp. "I've felt more than antsy. Each night I watched you sleep, I've burned."

Emma's gaze jerked to him. "You watched me sleep?"

Caine's eyes glowed a much lighter green. Sliding his hand into her hair, he skimmed her features as if he couldn't get enough of looking at her. "You murmur in your sleep and make the sexiest mewling sounds." His thumb slid an electric path across her jaw until it reached her lips. "It was very hard not to touch you."

Caine's touch, his voice, his intoxicating, musky smell and his mesmerizing gaze…everything about him enthralled her. "Why—why didn't you touch me? I thought you were just as tired as me and needed your rest. That's why I didn't—"

He pressed his thumb against her lips to cut her off. "I didn't touch you because I knew that when I did, I wouldn't stop. One night with you wasn't going to be enough for me, Emma. The next day, I'd resent the hell out of the panthers taking up our time. Call me a selfish bastard, but I want at least three uninterrupted days alone with you."

Emma swallowed, feeling a twinge of apprehension tighten her stomach. "Three days?" Caine had stamina unlike any she'd ever seen. More than one of the Velius had backed down during a debate with him, due to her wolf's sheer will. "I won't be able to move or walk or even think. I'll be—"

"All mine!" Caine's lips met hers at the same time he cupped the back of her head and pulled her against him.

Emma's heart raced from the possessive slant of his mouth moving across hers, his taste and the feel of his hard, muscular chest and strong arms surrounding her in a cocoon of steel. She kissed him back, her tongue sliding against his, loving the pent-up tension in his body, the sensation of his fingers fisting in her hair, while his other hand slid lower to clamp her butt hard through her jeans. Possessive, aggressive and all male.

His heart thumped steadily against her chest, slightly faster than it did each night while she'd fallen asleep in his arms. The fact that she could feel the rhythmic beat through their clothes only made her own heart ramp up even more.

Inside, Caine spoke in her mind right before he lifted Emma and carried her across the porch.

Emma didn't remember walking inside or Caine closing the door behind them. She was so caught up in kissing the sexy man, nothing else registered in her brain but him. Every single seductive, muscular inch of him.

Caine lifted his mouth from hers and placed his hand on the door behind her. Staring down at her, his breathing shallow, his voice carried raw emotion. "Lupreda don't often find their true mates, but when we do, the instinct to mark is near impossible to resist. I've fought my desire to make you mine for longer than I thought possible."

He closed his eyes briefly and his jaw tensed. "The thought of you being with someone else, touching another, giving him what I desperately wanted, tore me up inside. You'll never know how hard it was not to spread your sweet thighs and take everything you offered that night." Lifting her chin, he slid his fingers down her neck, his gaze following their path before his eyes returned to hers, serious and intense. "I *will* bite you, Emma, and I can't guarantee that it won't hurt. My feelings for you are too raw to deny you fair warning."

Emma loved this man so much he made her chest hurt. She respected his honor and integrity. She admired how ruthless he could be in the best interests of those he cared for, but more than anything she adored that he admitted he couldn't continue to hold back from her; that his feelings for her were that explosive.

Elongating her panther claws from the tips of her fingers, she dug them into his waist through his clothes. She didn't apply enough pressure to tear the material or break his skin, just enough to make him growl at her. "What makes you think I'm not going to bite you again?"

Not that I'm opposed to your bite—far from it, sweetheart, but it's my turn now. Caine gave her a feral smile and all four of his canines were on full display. Emma didn't bother holding back her gasp of excitement. Hell, she couldn't if she'd tried.

When she started to lift his shirt, Caine folded his fingers along the back of her neck and Emma's hands froze. Her gaze snapped to his, curious as to why he'd lock her in place.

Running his thumb down the side of her neck, Caine used his other hand to unbutton her shirt with slow purposeful determination.

As the cool air hit her, Emma's skin prickled and her desire rose. "Why are you holding me still?"

When the last button was freed, Caine pushed her shirt and jacket down her arms. Once they fell in a heap on the floor behind her, his eyes were the brightest green she'd ever seen them.

"You make me ache too much. I'm having a hard enough time keeping a rein on myself without your fueling my arousal."

"I want to touch you," she whispered, her voice desperate.

Caine gritted his teeth, sucking in a hissing breath before he shook his head. "I smell your desire spiking. It's like a freakin' red flag. If I let you touch me, we won't make it to the bed. I'll take you against this damned door!"

His ferocity and the obvious tension vibrating within him made Emma's stomach tighten and her sex throb. He was like a cobra, coiled and ready to strike. She loved him like this. Uncensored and edgy as hell! Her hands itched to slide over his hard back and heated skin. Her fingers tingled, ready to dig deep into his muscles and pull him as close as she could. A sly grin tilted her lips. "What's wrong with the door?"

Caine's guttural growl rumbled deep in his chest. "I want a chance to touch you, to make you so wet and needy that you can't stand it before things get primal and rough between us."

"I'm already there." Frustration laced her calm tone.

His gaze narrowed. "You're still a virgin and I'm not going to hurt you any more than necessary. End of discussion."

Damn his Alpha hide. Emma opened her mouth to speak, but Caine captured her lips in a head-reeling kiss, obliterating the argument she'd planned to make. *What was it again?*

Emma unleashed all the emotions that had built inside her over the past few days. She pressed her mouth to his and kissed him deeply, sharing the one part of her she seemed to have some control over. "I'm going to make you pay for holding me captive," she panted against his mouth, enjoying the feel of his canines brushing against her as he nipped her bottom lip.

Caine lifted his head and lines creased his forehead, his expression turning serious. "I promised you I would never use my power over you to hurt you in any way, but I *will* use it to keep you safe, Emma. Every damn time. You can rail on me later, if you wish."

Running his lips down her throat, he continued. "My job is to love you and protect you at all costs." He held his lips to the thudding hollow of her throat. *I feel how much you want this and the feeling is excruciatingly mutual, love.*

"Then, do something about it—" Emma cut herself off with a gasp when her bra suddenly fell away into two pieces, exposing her breasts.

Without pause, Caine dipped his head and captured a nipple between his lips. An electric jolt shot through her when his tongue rolled over the hard tip, then he began to suck.

Emma's knees went weak and her fingers flexed slightly, but that was all she could do…other than feel. God, she felt every humming sensation shooting through her system. The pleasure radiated from her head to her toes, pulsing to the erratic beat of her heart, landing with a thud in the center of her body. Need clawed with heavy, digging swipes at her sex, making her mewl and squirm under her skin.

When he slid his hand between her thighs, then cupped her denim-covered crotch with an aggressive hold, Emma whimpered, "Ca-can't take it. I don't care…just take me to—"

Caine didn't let her finish. He swiftly lifted her in his arms and strode across the cabin to the bedroom.

Chapter 16

The moment Caine set Emma back on her feet, she immediately pulled off his shirt. As the cloth fluttered to the floor, Caine unbuttoned her jeans, his hungry gaze lingering on her chest. Emma started to shove her jeans down her hips, but Caine snarled, halting her movements. Yanking hard, he ripped her pants and underwear right down the middle and gave a satisfied grunt as the two pieces slithered uselessly down her legs.

Standing naked in front of him, Emma's eyebrow shot up. "I still have shoes on, though I think it'd be easier on my clothes budget if you just slid them off instead of gnawing them apart."

Caine gave a dark smile and pushed on her shoulders, sending her flopping onto the bed. Emma's heart raced as he picked up her foot and removed her tennis shoe, but what she wasn't prepared for was the slow, sensual glide of his fingers along her calves as he pulled the torn pants and underwear off her legs. Tiny shocks of electricity mixed with heat.

Setting her foot on his chest, he did the same to the other leg, but didn't relinquish her foot when he was finished. Instead, Caine planted a soft kiss behind her toes and in the arch of her foot. Humming ensued between them, sending chill bumps scattering across her skin. Emma's breath caught as her lungs cinched. She was absolutely mesmerized by the site of Caine's sexy dark head bent over her foot, his big hands holding her gingerly, his warm lips traveling to her ankle where he kissed, then nipped at the fine bones.

All amusement fled, replaced by lightning heat snaking through her body in a swift awakening of passion and yearning that set her skin on fire. When he planted a sensual kiss behind her knee, then ran his warm tongue along the same spot, Emma discovered how erotic such reverent attention to her untapped erogenous zones could be.

Her toes curled on his hard, muscular chest and she stared hungrily at his broad shoulders as he moved his lips farther down her leg and nipped at the ultrasensitive skin along her inner thigh. When Caine pushed her foot up over his shoulder and went down on one knee beside the bed, Emma's fingers dug into the soft comforter under her. "Don't you want to—"

But she didn't get a chance to finish. Caine ran his tongue up her sex in a determined yet leisurely lap. When he went back for more, she set her other foot on his thigh and let her thoughts flit briefly onto a plane of blissful pleasure. Caine's growl turned into a groan as he thrust his tongue deep inside her, pressing hard against her body. Emma's heart raced and her pulse thrummed an erratic beat of stair-stepped excitement. Already her body was humming, tightening to a pitch of near orgasm. She didn't want to come without him this time.

Sliding her foot along his pants, she pushed her toes against his erection and whispered, "Take off your pants."

Caine shuddered, his intemperate gaze snapping to hers. *Demanding woman!*

His emphatic thought caused her to take notice and acknowledge his strength and primal urges lurking just below the surface. Emma squirmed from the invigorating power she derived knowing he was barely holding it together and could lose it any moment. The thought made her ache even more. "I'm not telling you anything you don't already want."

When Caine pulled away and stood to unbutton his pants, Emma propped up on her elbows and watched his dark, hooded gaze sweep over her naked flesh. She returned the favor, enjoying the play of muscles moving under his skin, the sexy dips and hollows of his chest and abs, down to the very nice line of dark hair that led to his very well-endowed erection that pushed against his abdomen when he stepped out of his pants.

A little apprehension mixed with her excitement, zipping through Emma as Caine placed a knee on the bed. But instead of moving over her, he caught her by surprise when he grasped her hand and pulled her to a seated position in front of him as he positioned himself at the top of the bed. Leaning against the headboard, Caine reached over and gripped her waist, lifting her as if she weighed nothing, and then settled her in front of him with her knees straddling his thighs.

"Hmmm, perfect," he murmured, his warm hands sliding to her upper back to press her body and therefore her breasts closer.

Not that she didn't enjoy the skin-to-skin contact. Caine's

warm body felt so good against hers, but in this position she was too high for them to—

Caine bent his head and captured a nipple between his lips, sending her concerns flying. Emma's pulse raced and her sex contracted at the exquisite pleasure his hard sucking was doing to her. Sliding her fingers through his silky hair, she clutched him close, then moaned even deeper when he clasped her other breast and ran his fingers teasingly across her nipple, barely touching her.

You're so ready I can smell the difference. Your musky scent is sweeter, his husky voice entered her head, raw and seductive.

Emma rocked against him. Spreading her legs slightly, she tried to lower herself onto his erection, but his arm locked her hips in the position they were, only allowing just the tip of his cock to penetrate her.

Releasing her nipple, he pressed gentle kisses against the inner curve of her breast. "There are other ways to orgasm, Emma. I'd like to show you."

Emma tried to move downward even more, to slide over him and lock them together in the most intimate way possible, but Caine's hold on her hips remained firm. "Why won't you let me go?"

His hazel gaze locked with hers and he slowly drew his thumb back and forth across her nipple, driving her libido through the roof. "Because it's your first time and I want you to be ready so you don't feel any pain. That's why."

Emma was trembling all over. She ached to the core, she wanted him that bad. "I'm in pain *now*. I'm beyond sure. I'm ready!"

Caine's chuckle sounded strained. Good, she wasn't suffering alone.

"Trust me, you'll enjoy this."

"Just let me—" Emma's demand broke into a moan of pleasure when Caine pinched her nipple. Her hips moved intuitively as shocking waves of desire splintered from her breast and straight to her core. Her muscles clenched tight, wanting more.

Caine captured her other nipple with his lips and began to tug, then nip at the tip. Emma's insides quickened with sexual excitement. Ecstasy coiled tight within her, tensing her stomach muscles, She rocked against him and the teasing tip of him barely inside her drove her into a frenzy of gnawing need. She pulled him closer and demanded with breathy gusts, "Feels so good. Don't stop."

Caine pressed his hips upward just slightly, penetrating then retreating in a tease that made her thigh muscles tremble as he spoke in her mind, his voice rough, aroused. *Come, sweetheart.* He gripped her hips and groaned, his own body a tense wire, ready to snap.

Emma screamed as wave after wave of pleasure began deep in her sex, swirling inside her. She rocked against his hard body, pressing herself shamelessly against him, trying to prolong the sensations clamoring through her. Anything to get closer to his magnificent heat and musky scent. Then she felt the slight pinch of him pushing inside her, stretching her walls, but she didn't care. She continued to move, loving every scent, every tremor, every touch between them. Finally she stilled and the only sound she heard was her harsh breathing and thudding pulse rushing in her ears.

A thin sheen of sweat coated her skin and Caine's expression was a study of intense concentration. She felt him, heavy and large inside her, his hands clamped bruisingly on her hips as if he couldn't let her go if he wanted to. "I guess I'm no longer a virgin," she whispered with a trembling smile.

"Not quite," Caine bit out, his voice full of gravel, the tendons on his neck and shoulders taut.

"I don't under—"

A tight, pinching sensation rippled through her walls, making her gasp.

Caine's gaze came into focus and concern etched his brow. His grip on her shifted, holding her up. "Sorry, Em. I meant to hold you in place."

Shock slammed through her when she realized the truth. Granted, she knew she wasn't sitting fully down, but still. Her eyes widened. "You're not all the way—"

He shook his head, his voice rough. "Not yet."

Emma's heart filled with love for his desire to take away her pain. Clasping his jaw, she whispered against his lips, "Distract me and make me *want* every painful twinge, my sexy mate."

Caine stared at the waning moonlight shining through the window, highlighting Emma's arresting eyes and sparkling hair. All he wanted to do was drown in this amazing woman. He loved her for her dedication to those she loved and felt responsible for, respected her steadfast resolve and admired her ability to keep him mentally on his toes, not to mention their amazing physical connection. He wanted to make her scream with sexual fulfillment, to make her his. Forever.

Running his hand through her hair, he spoke in a low voice. "I never thought I'd find someone who would make me question my path in life as you have. You excite me on many levels and challenge me on others. As far as I'm concerned, I'll never get enough alone time with you."

Emma kissed his palm and tears glistened in her eyes. "We'll have to make sure we take the time. Our pride will just have to understand."

Caine's chest ached with his deep love for this woman. She shared every part of herself and her race with him. Openly. Willingly and lovingly. Cupping the back of her head, he pulled her close and kissed her neck, sliding his lips along the soft skin. "I will take it slow and you tell me if something hurts. Okay?"

Emma wrapped her arms around his shoulders and buried her nose against his neck, nodding.

Sliding his hands up her sides, Caine lifted her off him and laid her back on the bed. Emma sighed and tried to pull him close when he leaned over her. "Not yet," he teased as he traced his fingers along the curve of her breast and down to her waist. When he bent and kissed her belly button, sparks zinged between them, making his lips tingle. Emma mewled, arching, pressing closer to his mouth.

Caine smiled against her skin. He reveled in the fact she couldn't get close enough. He understood the reaction. Their connection was so strong, it knocked him off-kilter while at the same time jacking him up.

He slid a finger deep in her sweet body and groaned when she clenched her muscles around him. He wanted nothing more than to sink deep into her heat, to make her scream and lose herself in her lustful urges, but he held back and nipped her skin where her leg met her body.

Emma's fingers tangled in his hair and she wrapped her leg around his neck. "Taste me again!" she begged, but he didn't need any encouragement. Her musky smell was driving him nuts.

Her flavor exploded on his tongue.

Emma thrashed and bucked, crying out. She was close. When he started to guide his finger inside her once more, she dug her nails into his shoulders and shook her head, panting as she pulled him up her body.

"Now!" she begged, locking her legs around his waist.

Caine leaned up on his elbows and guided himself into her. It took all his willpower not to ram deep, like he wanted. Emma wasn't helping his honorable goals. She was rocking her hips and making sexy moaning sounds. Driving him freakin' insane.

Take her, his inner wolf snarled.

Not yet. He tensed, holding himself back as he eased farther inside her, stretching her muscles. Withdrawing, he set his jaw and pushed deeper as ecstasy rippled through him. Emma's claws ripped at his skin. The bite of pain along with the smell of his own blood ratcheted up his desire.

A flood of heat shot through Caine's body, moving straight to his erection. Tiny pinpricks of molten pleasure-pain skittered across the thin sensitive skin along his shaft. His wolf was mating. If he didn't get this part over, she'd be in even more pain.

Caine spoke in her mind, right before he thrust all the way inside her. *You've taken my wolf to the edge. I have to now or I'll hurt you more.*

Emma tensed and gasped simultaneously. Preparing to mate, Caine forced himself to remain still. He kissed her jaw and whispered in a raw, ragged voice, "Are you all right?"

Undulating her hips underneath him, she panted. "I feel you stretching me and getting hotter." She keened, then kissed his jaw. "You are my other half. Make me scream again."

Caine swallowed the heavy emotions slamming through

him that she'd apparently gotten past any pain he may have caused. Running his lips along her temple, he stayed buried deep and slowly began to rock his hips. Each time her muscles tightened around his erection, a shudder of sheer pleasure rushed through him. *Mine!* he grated in her mind.

She let out an excited cry and met each of his thrusts with aggressive movements of her hips. "Yours. Always."

He ran his canines along the soft skin between her shoulder and her neck, needing to stake his claim, but he wanted Emma to ask for it. To know she understood and accepted everything that being his mate entailed.

Withdrawing from her, he pistoned deep once more and felt the beginnings of her body vibrating. She was so close. Tremors rocked his entire frame from his groin to his head. "I love you, Em. You are everything to me."

Tears slid down her temples and she fisted her fingers in his hair. "I love you so much it hurts to breathe sometimes. I want your mating mark. Bite me and make me yours," she sobbed, near frantic.

Caine pushed her hips deep into the mattress with his last thrust. At the same time Emma's gasp of pleasure and orgasm slammed through her, he sank his canines into her sweet skin and took the deepest level of possession for a Lupreda.

Her slick muscles fluttering around his erection, clasping even tighter, along with her heightened scream of passion, sent Caine spiraling into his own, explosive orgasm. With each pulse of his body sharing with hers, he experienced an intense bond and an even deeper emotional link to his mate. *Emma, mine.*

An hour later, Emma lay on her side, running her fingers along Caine's hard chest. Propping up on his elbow, he traced his knuckles gently over his bite wound on her shoulder. "Amazing!"

"What?" Emma lifted her head slightly and tried to see what he saw but couldn't. She'd need a mirror. "What is it?" she asked, glancing his way.

He smiled and tiny lines crinkled around his eyes. "You're already healed. All that's left behind are faded red marks."

Her brow furrowed. "Isn't that the way it works?"

Caine's eyebrows rose. "If my saliva could heal you, then yes, I would've licked your wound to close it and you'd already be healed. But we both know my saliva doesn't heal a panther, so this means your wound closed and healed on its own."

Emma adopted the same position, propping up herself. "I thought panthers didn't heal as fast as a wolves."

Sweeping her hair over her shoulder, Caine leaned close and kissed her forehead, then slid his lips to her temple. "Maybe that was my mating bite's gift to you—giving you the ability to heal quickly."

She smiled mischievously. "Do you think I can shift to a wolf now?"

Caine snorted and ran his fingers across her hip. "Was I able to shift to a panther?"

Laughing, Emma shook her head. "It'll be interesting to see what other changes, if any, develop within me."

"Indeed." Caine's finger made tiny swirls around her belly button.

The contemplative tone of his voice drew her attention. She looked at him, but Caine's gaze was fixated on her stomach.

He was thinking about children. Grabbing his wrist, Emma kissed his palm then flattened his hand against her belly.

"We're truly going to be merging our races one day and then our differences won't matter."

Caine gripped her rear and scooped her under him with a deep growl. "They never did, my little panther. Not to me." Sliding his gaze down her body, his feral smile held all kinds of naughty promises. "I can see all the ways we're the same, but learning all the ways we're different…now that's something I look forward to exploring with you in intimate and excruciating detail for the rest of our lives."

* * * * *

INTRIGUE

Coming next month

2-IN-1 ANTHOLOGY

THE SHERIFF'S AMNESIAC BRIDE by Linda Conrad

When a woman on the run shows up in his life, Sheriff Jericho Yates takes her in. Even if she can't remember who she is or why she is a hitman's target…

SOLDIER'S SECRET CHILD by Caridad Piñeiro

They'd shared one night of passion eighteen years ago, but Macy Ward had never told sexy military man Fisher about the consequences!

2-IN-1 ANTHOLOGY

QUESTIONING THE HEIRESS by Delores Fossen

Texas Ranger Egan is the one man socialite Caroline can turn to, yet now he's spearheading an investigation that may uncover the dark past they share…

DAREDEVIL'S RUN by Kathleen Creighton

After a tragic accident rugged Matt shunned his fiancée and business partner, Alex. But can he find a way to let her back into his heart?

SINGLE TITLE

UNBOUND by Lori Devoti
Nocturne

Risk is a hell-hound, doomed to shapeshift between human and canine form, until he meets witch Kara, the one woman who can break his curse.

On sale 21st August 2009

⊚™ INTRIGUE

Coming next month

2-IN-1 ANTHOLOGY

HER BEST FRIEND'S HUSBAND by Justine Davis

Gabriel's wife disappeared eight years ago. Now he's falling for her best friend – yet could his newfound feelings for Cara help him uncover a dark, dramatic truth?

THE BEAST WITHIN by Lisa Renee Jones

Jag was torn from his wife, Caren – and the mortal realm – by the soulless Darkland Beasts. Resurrected, he will stop at nothing to recover the love he lost!

SINGLE TITLE

THE MYSTERY MAN OF WHITEHORSE by BJ Daniels

Laci can't keep her eyes off her new boss, mysterious and brooding Bridger. Yet his timely arrival also provides a clue in the murders that haunt the town of Whitehorse.

SINGLE TITLE

PRIVATE S.W.A.T TAKEOVER by Julie Miller

When Liza witnessed the murder of KCPD's deputy commissioner, top cop Holden was appointed her official protector – but falling for her wasn't part of the bargain!

On sale 4ᵗʰ September 2009

From No. 1 *New York Times* bestselling author Nora Roberts

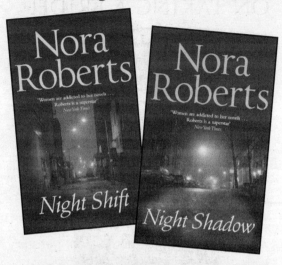

Night Shift **available 7th August 2009**

When her stalker's threats start to escalate, late-night DJ Cilla O'Roarke and Detective Boyd Fletcher are led into a terrifying situation that they might not both walk away from…

Night Shadow **available 4th September 2009**

Faced with a choice between her own life and the law, can prosecutor Deborah O'Roarke make the right decision – before someone else dies?

Passion. Power. Suspense.
It's time to fall under the spell of Nora Roberts.

2 FREE BOOKS
AND A SURPRISE GIFT

We would like to take this opportunity to thank you for reading this Mills & Boon® book by offering you the chance to take TWO more specially selected titles from the Intrigue series absolutely FREE! We're also making this offer to introduce you to the benefits of the Mills & Boon® Book Club™—

- **FREE home delivery**
- **FREE gifts and competitions**
- **FREE monthly Newsletter**
- **Exclusive Mills & Boon Book Club offers**
- **Books available before they're in the shops**

Accepting these FREE books and gift places you under no obligation to buy, you may cancel at any time, even after receiving your free books. Simply complete your details below and return the entire page to the address below. You don't even need a stamp!

YES Please send me 2 free Intrigue books and a surprise gift. I understand that unless you hear from me, I will receive 5 superb new titles every month, including two 2-in-1 titles priced at £4.99 each and a single title priced at £3.19, postage and packing free. I am under no obligation to purchase any books and may cancel my subscription at any time. The free books and gift will be mine to keep in any case.

Ms/Mrs/Miss/Mr _____ initials _____

Surname _____

address _____

_____

_____ postcode _____

Send this whole page to: Mills & Boon Book Club, Free Book Offer, FREEPOST NAT 10298, Richmond, TW9 1BR